CARBIDE
TIPPED
PENS

TOR BOOKS BY BEN BOVA

BOOKS BY ERIC CHOI

CARBIDE TIPPED PENS

SEVENTEEN TALES of HARD SCIENCE FICTION

EDITED BY

BEN BOVA

AND

ERIC CHOI

TOR®

A Tom Doherty Associates Book
New York

CARBIDE TIPPED PENS: SEVENTEEN TALES OF HARD SCIENCE FICTION

A Tor Book
Published by Tom Doherty Associates, LLC
175 Fifth Avenue
New York, NY 10010

www.tor-forge.com

Tor® is a registered trademark of Tom Doherty Associates, LLC.

The Library of Congress Cataloging-in-Publication Data
is available upon request.

ISBN 978-0-7653-3430-5 (hardcover)
ISBN 978-1-4668-1019-8 (e-book)

Tor books may be purchased for educational, business, or promotional use. For information on bulk purchases, please contact the Macmillan Corporate and Premium Sales Department at 1-800-221-7945, extension 5442, or write to specialmarkets@macmillan.com.

First Edition: December 2014

Printed in the United States of America

0 9 8 7 6 5 4 3 2 1

COPYRIGHT ACKNOWLEDGMENTS

Ben Bova:
To the memory of Isaac Asimov,
whose heart was as great as his mind.

Eric Choi:
To Paul Keough, David DeGraff,
Paul Urayama, Mark Grant,
David Soltysik, and Tue Sorensen—
the original Carbide Tipped Pens.

CONTENTS

PREFACE

"When I talk about this book, I get a lot of questions about the title," Paul Stevens, our editor at Tor, once told me. "What does the title come from?"

Carbide Tipped Pens (CTP) was the name of a hard SF writing group to which David DeGraff and I belonged in the late 1990s. Founded by Paul Keough, the group demanded a strict regimen of in-depth biweekly critiques and regular story submissions to markets every three months. The group's grand ambition was to help revitalize the hard SF genre and perhaps even foster a new literary movement. By the early 2000s, however, the obligations of mundane life began to intrude and the members of CTP went their separate ways.

Almost a decade later, I found myself with the honor of sharing an author signing table with Ben at the 2011 Ad Astra convention in Toronto. We chatted about the resurgence of hard SF with the publication of anthologies such as Jonathan Strahan's *Engineering Infinity* in the United Kingdom, and that the time was right for a new collection of hard SF in North America. I even had a pretty good idea for the title.

Hard SF is the literature of change, the genre that examines the implications—both beneficial and dangerous—of new sciences and technologies. The founding fathers of hard SF,

Hugo Gernsback and John W. Campbell, Jr., decreed that science fiction had to make sense, following the laws of nature and exploring the impact of science and technology on society—past, present, or future—in a manner that is imaginative and profound. Campbell guided masters like Isaac Asimov, Lester del Rey, Robert A. Heinlein, Theodore Sturgeon, A. E. van Vogt, Clifford D. Simak, and Jack Williamson into the Golden Age of SF, where the entire universe was their playground.

For *Carbide Tipped Pens* the anthology, Ben and I were looking for stories that follow the classic definition of hard SF, in which some element of science or technology is so central to the plot that there would be no story if that element were removed. The science and engineering portrayed in the stories would be consistent with current understanding or be a logical and reasonable extrapolation thereof.

Furthermore, we wanted to put together a collection that would refute some of the stereotypes often associated with hard SF in terms of both the stories themselves and the people who write them. We sought diverse stories that emphasized not only science but also character, plot, originality, and believability in equal measure. Our contributors came to us from the United States, Canada, Australia, China, Germany, and France. Ben and I both have scientific backgrounds, as do many of the authors, but we also have contributors with backgrounds in literature, history, and cultural studies.

Our fondest wish is for *Carbide Tipped Pens* to not only entertain but also to educate and convey the sense of wonder of the Golden Age to a new generation of readers.

Many thanks are in order: to Paul Stevens for championing this anthology and being a constant source of advice and support, to Paul Keough and the members of CTP for generously allowing us to use the name, and to Alana Otis Wood and the

Toronto Ad Astra 2011 convention committee for putting the two of us together at the same author signing table. Most of all, thank you, Ben, for your wisdom and friendship. This is what *Carbide Tipped Pens* came from.

—*Eric Choi*

CARBIDE
TIPPED
PENS

THE BLUE AFTERNOON THAT LASTED FOREVER

Daniel H. Wilson

Science fiction is so intriguing because it can examine the cosmic and the infinitesimal, the future and the past, the human and the immeasurable.

Daniel H. Wilson's story does all that, in less than four thousand words.

"It's late at night, my darling. And the stars are in the sky. That means it is time for me to give you a kiss. And an Eskimo kiss. And now I will lay you down and tuck you in, nice and tight, so you stay warm all night."

This is our mantra. I think of it like the computer code I use to control deep space simulations in the laboratory. You recite the incantation and the desired program executes.

I call this one "bedtime."

Marie holds her stuffed rabbit close, in a chokehold. In the dim light, a garden of blond hair grows over her pillow. She is three years old and smiling and she smells like baby soap. Her eyes are already closed.

"I love you, honey," I say.

As a physicist, it bothers me that I find this acute feeling of love hard to quantify. I am a man who routinely deals in singularities and asymptotes. It seems like I should have the mathematical vocabulary to express these things.

Reaching for her covers, I try to tuck Marie in. I stop when

I feel her warm hands close on mine. Her brown eyes are black in the shadows.

"No," she says, "I do it."

I smile until it becomes a wince.

This version of the bedtime routine is buckling around the edges, disintegrating like a heat shield on reentry. I have grown to love tucking the covers up to my daughter's chin. Feeling her cool damp hair and the reassuring lump of her body, safe in her big-girl bed. Our routine in its current incarnation has lasted one year two months. Now it must change. Again.

I hate change.

"OK," I murmur. "You're a big girl. You can do it."

Clumsily and with both hands, she yanks the covers toward her face. She looks determined. Proud to take over this task and exert her independence. Her behavior is consistent with normal child development according to the books I checked out from the library. Yet I cannot help but notice that this independence is a harbinger of constant unsettling, saddening change.

My baby is growing up.

In the last year, her body weight has increased sixteen percent. Her average sentence length has increased from seven to ten words. She has memorized the planets, the primary constellations, and the colors of the visible spectrum. Red orange yellow green blue indigo violet. These small achievements indicate that my daughter is advanced for her age, but she isn't out of the record books or into child genius territory. She's just a pretty smart kid, which doesn't surprise me. Intelligence is highly heritable.

"I saw a shooting star," she says.

"Really? What's it made of?" I ask.

"Rocks," she says.

"That's right. Make a wish, lucky girl," I reply, walking to the door.

I pause as long as I can. In the semidarkness, a stuffed bear is looking at me from a shelf. It is a papa teddy bear hugging its baby. His arms are stitched around the baby's shoulders. He will never have to let go.

"Sweet dreams," I say.

"Good night, Daddy," she says and I close the door.

The stars really are in Marie's bedroom.

Two years ago I purchased the most complex and accurate home planetarium system available. There were no American models. This one came from a Japanese company and it had to be shipped here to Austin, Texas, by special order. I also purchased an international power adapter plug, a Japanese-to-English translation book, and a guide to the major constellations.

I had a plan.

Soon after the planetarium arrived, I installed it in my bedroom. Translating the Japanese instruction booklet as best I could, I calibrated the dedicated shooting star laser, inserted the disc that held a pattern for the Northern Hemisphere, and updated the current time and season. When I was finished, I went into the living room and tapped my then-wife on the shoulder.

Our anniversary.

My goal was to create a scenario in which we could gaze at the stars together every night before we went to sleep. I am interested in astrophysics. She was interested in romantic gestures. It was my hypothesis that sleeping under the faux stars would satisfy both constraints.

Unfortunately, I failed to recall that I wear glasses and that my then-wife wore contact lenses. For the next week, we spent our evenings blinking up at a fuzzy Gaussian shotgun-spray of the Milky Way on our bedroom ceiling. Then she found the receipt for the purchase and became angry. I was ordered to return the planetarium and told that she would rather have had a new car.

That didn't seem romantic to me, but then again I'm not a domain expert.

My thin translation book did not grant me the verbal fluency necessary to negotiate a return of the product to Japan. In response, my then-wife told me to sell it on the Internet or whatever. I chose to invoke the "whatever" clause. I wrapped the planetarium carefully in its original packaging and put it into the trunk of my car. After that, I stored it in the equipment room of my laboratory at work.

Three months later, my then-wife informed me that she was leaving. She had found a job in Dallas and would try to visit Marie on the weekends but no promises. I immediately realized that this news would require massive life recalibrations. This was upsetting. I told her as such and my then-wife said that I had the emotional capacity of a robot. I decided that the observation was not a compliment. However, I did not question how my being a robot might affect my ability to parent a one-and-a-half-year-old. Contrary to her accusation, my cheeks were stinging with a sudden cold fear at the thought of losing my daughter. My then-wife must have seen the question in the surface tension of my face, because she answered it anyway.

She said that what I lacked in emotion, I made up for in structure. She said that I was a terrible husband, but a good father.

Then-wife kissed Marie on the head and left me standing in the driveway with my daughter in my arms. Marie did not cry when her mother left because she lacked the cognitive capacity to comprehend what had happened. If she had known, I think she would have been upset. Instead, my baby only grinned as her mother drove away. And because Marie was in such good spirits, I slid her into her car seat and drove us both to my laboratory. Against all regulations, I brought her into my work space. I dug through the equipment stores until I found the forbidden item.

That night, I gave my daughter the stars.

The cafeteria where I work plays the news during lunch. The television is muted but I watch it anyway. My plastic fork is halfway to my mouth when I see the eyewitness video accompanying the latest breaking news story. After that, I am not very aware of what is happening except that I am running.

I don't do that very much. Run.

In some professions, you can be called into action in an emergency. A vacationing doctor treats the victim of an accident. An off-duty pilot heads up to the cockpit to land the plane. I am not in one of those professions. I spend my days crafting supercomputer simulations so that we can understand astronomical phenomena that happened billions of years ago. That's why I am running alone. There are perhaps a dozen people in the world who could comprehend the images I have just seen on the television—my colleagues, fellow astrophysicists at research institutions scattered around the globe.

I hope they find their families in time.

The television caption said that an unexplained astronomical event has occurred. I know better than that. I am running hard because of it, my voice making a whimpering sound in the back of my throat. I scramble into my car and grip the hot steering wheel and press the accelerator to the floor. The rest of the city is still behaving normally as I weave through traffic. That won't last for long, but I'm thankful to have these few moments to slip away home.

My daughter will need me.

There is a nanny who watches Marie during the day. The nanny has brown hair and she is five feet four inches tall. She does not have a scientific mind-set but she is an artist in her spare time. When Marie was ten months old and had memorized all of her body parts (including the phalanges), I became excited about the possibilities. I gave the nanny a sheet of facts that I had compiled about the states of matter for Marie to memorize. I intentionally left off the quark-gluon plasma state and Bose-Einstein condensate and neutron-degenerate matter because I wanted to save the fun stuff for later. After three days I found the sheet of paper in the recycling bin.

I was a little upset.

Perez in the cubicle next to me said that the nanny had done me a favor. He said Marie has plenty of time to learn about those things. She needs to dream and imagine and, I don't know, finger paint. It is probably sound advice. Then again, Perez's son is five years old and at the department picnic the boy could not tell me how many miles it is to the troposphere. And he says he wants to be an astronaut. Good luck, kid.

Oh, yes. Running.

My brain required four hundred milliseconds to process the visual information coming from the cafeteria television. Eighty milliseconds for my nervous system to respond to the command to move. It is a two-minute sprint to the parking lot. Then an eight-minute drive to reach home. Whatever happens will occur in the next thirty minutes and so there is no use in warning the others.

Here is what happened.

An hour and thirty-eight minutes ago, the sky blushed red as an anomaly streaked over the Gulf of Mexico. Bystanders described it as a smear of sky and clouds, a kind of glowing reddish blur. NASA reported that it perturbed the orbital paths of all artificial satellites, including the International Space Station. It triggered tsunamis along the equator and dragged a plume of atmosphere a thousand miles into the vacuum of space. The air dispersed in low pressure but trace amounts of water vapor froze into ice droplets. On the southern horizon, I can now see a fading river of diamonds stretching into space. I don't see the moon in the sky but that doesn't mean it isn't there. Necessarily.

All of this happened within the space of thirty seconds.

This is not an unexplained astronomical event. The anomaly had no dust trail, was not radar-detectable, and it caused a tsunami.

Oh, and it turned the sky red.

Light does funny things in extreme gravity situations. When a high-mass object approaches, every photon of light that reaches our eyes must claw its way out of a powerful gravity well. Light travels at a constant speed, so instead of slowing down, the photon sacrifices energy. Its wavelength drops down the visible spectrum: violet indigo blue green yellow orange red.

Redshifting.

I am running because only one thing could redshift our sky that much and leave us alive to wonder why our mobile phones don't work. What passed by has to have been a previously theoretical class of black hole with a relatively small planet-sized mass—compressed into a singularity potentially as small as a pinprick. Some postulate that these entities are starving black holes that have crossed intergalactic space and shrunk over the billions of years with nothing to feed on. Another theory, possibly complementary, is that they are random crumbs tossed away during the violence of the big bang.

Perez in the next cubicle said I should call them "black marbles," which is inaccurate on several fronts. In my papers, I chose instead to call them pinprick-size black holes. Although Perez and I disagreed on the issue of nomenclature, our research efforts brought consensus on one calculation: that the phenomenon would always travel in clusters.

Where there is one, more will follow.

* * *

Tornado sirens begin to wail as I careen through my suburban neighborhood. The woman on the radio just frantically reported that something has happened to Mars. The planet's crust is shattered. Astronomers are describing a large part of the planet's mass as simply missing. What's left behind is a cloud of expanding dirt and rapidly cooling magma, slowly drifting out of orbit and spreading into an elliptical arc.

She doesn't say it out loud, but it's dawning on her: we are next.

People are standing in their yards now, on the sidewalks and grass, eyes aimed upward. The sky is darkening. The wind outside the car window is whispering to itself as it gathers occasionally into a thin, reedy scream. A tidal pull of extreme gravity must be doing odd things to our weather patterns. If I had a pen and paper, I could probably work it out.

I slam on the brakes in my driveway to avoid hitting the nanny.

She is standing barefoot, holding a half-empty sippy cup of milk. Chin pointed at the sky. Stepping out of the car, I see my first pinprick-size black hole. It is a reddish dot about half the intensity of the sun, wrapped in a halo of glowing, superheated air. It isn't visibly moving so I can't estimate its trajectory. On the southern horizon, the crystallized plume of atmosphere caused by the near-miss still dissipates.

It really is beautiful.

"What is it?" asks the nanny.

"Physics," I say, going around the car and opening my trunk. "You should go home immediately."

I pull out a pair of old jumper cables and stride across the driveway. Marie is standing just inside the house, her face a pale flash behind the glass storm door. Inside, I lift my daughter off the ground. She wraps her legs around my hip and now

I am running again, toys crunching under my feet, my daughter's long hair tickling my forearm. The nanny has put it into a braid. I never learned how to do that. Depending on the trajectory of the incoming mass, I may not ever have the chance.

"What did you do today?" I ask Marie.

"Played," she says.

Trying not to pant, I crack open a few windows in the house. Air pressure fluctuations are a certainty. I hope that we only have to worry about broken glass. There is no basement to hide in here, just a cookie-cutter house built on a flat slab of concrete. But the sewer main is embedded deep into the foundation. In the worst case, it will be the last thing to go.

I head to the bathroom.

"Wait here for just a second," I say, setting Marie down in the hallway. Stepping into the small bathroom, I wind up and violently kick the wall behind the toilet until the drywall collapses. Dropping to my knees, I claw out chunks of the drywall until I have exposed the main sewer line that runs behind the toilet. It is a solid steel pipe maybe six inches in diameter. With shaking hands, I shove the jumper cable around it. Then I wedge myself between the toilet and the outside wall and I sit down on the cold tile floor, the jumper cables under my armpits anchoring me to the ground. This is the safest place that I can find.

If the black hole falling toward us misses the planet, even by a few thousand miles, we may survive. If it's a direct hit, we'll share the fate of Mars. At the sonic horizon, sound won't be able to escape from it. At the event horizon, neither will light. Before that can happen we will reach a Lagrange point as the anomaly cancels out Earth's gravity. We will fall into the sky and be swallowed by that dark star.

The anomaly was never detected, so it must have come from intergalactic space. The Oort cloud is around a light year out, mostly made of comets. The Kuiper-Edgeworth belt is on the edge of the Solar System. Neither region had enough density to make the black hole visible. I wonder what we were doing when it entered our Solar System. Was I teaching Marie the names of dead planets?

"Daddy?" asks Marie.

She is standing in the bathroom doorway, eyes wide. Outside, a car engine revs as someone speeds past our house. A distant, untended door slams idiotically in the breeze. Marie's flowery dress shivers and flutters over her scratched knees in the restless calm.

"Come here, honey," I say in my most reassuring voice. "Come sit on my lap."

Hesitantly, she walks over to me. The half-open window above us is a glowing red rectangle. It whistles quietly as air is pulled through the house. I tie the greasy jumper cable cord in a painfully tight knot around my chest. I can't risk crushing her lungs, so I wrap my arms around Marie. Her arms fall naturally around my neck, hugging tight. Her breath is warm against my neck.

"Hold on to your daddy very tight," I say. "Do you understand?"

"But why?" she asks.

"Because I don't want to lose you, baby," I say and my sudden swallowed tears are salty in the back of my throat.

Whips are cracking in the distance now. I hear a scream. Screams.

A gust of wind shatters the bathroom window. I cradle Marie closer as the shards of glass are sucked out of the window frame. A last straggler rattles in place like a loose tooth. The whip cracks are emanating from loose objects that have accelerated upward past the speed of sound. The *crack-crack-crack* sound is thousands of sonic booms. They almost drown out the frightened cries of people who are falling into the sky. Millions must be dying this way. Billions.

"What is that?" asks Marie, voice wavering.

"It's nothing, honey. It's all right," I say, holding her to me. Her arms are rubber bands tight around my neck. The roof shingles are rustling gently, leaping into the sky like a flock of pigeons. I can't see them but it occurs to me that the direction they travel will be along the thing's incoming trajectory. I watch that rattling piece of glass that's been left behind in the window frame, my lips pressed together. It jitters and finally takes flight *straight up*.

A fatal trajectory. A through-and-through.

"What's happening?" Marie asks, through tears.

"It's the stars, honey," I say. "The stars are falling."

It's the most accurate explanation I can offer.

"Why?" she asks.

"Look at Daddy," I say. I feel a sudden lightness, a gentle tug pulling us upward. I lean against the cables to make sure they are still tight. "Please look at your daddy. It will be OK. Hold on tight."

Nails screech as a part of the roof frame curls away and disappears. Marie is biting her lips to keep her mouth closed and nodding as tears course over her cheeks. I have not consulted the child development books but I think she is very brave for three years old. Only three trips around the sun and now the sun is going to end. Sol will be teased apart in hundred-thousand-mile licks of flame.

"My darling," I say. "Can you tell me the name of the planet that we live on?"

"Earth."

"And what is the planet with a ring around it?"

"S-Saturn."

"What are the rings made of?"

"Mountains of ice."

Maybe a sense of wonder is also a heritable trait.

"Are the stars—"

Something big crashes outside. The wind is shrieking now in a new way. The upper atmosphere has formed into a vortex of supersonic air molecules.

"Daddy?" screams Marie. Her lips are bright and bitten, tear ducts polishing those familiar brown eyes with saline. A quivering frown is dimpling her chin and all I can think of is how small she is compared to all this.

"Honey, it's OK. I've got you. Are the stars very big or very small?"

"Very big," she says, crying outright now. I rock her as we speak, holding her to my chest. The cables are tightening and the sewer main is a hard knuckle against my spine. Marie's static-charged hair is lifting in the fitful wind.

"You're right again. They look small, but they're very big. The stars are so very, very big."

A subsonic groan rumbles through the frame of the house. Through the missing roof I can see that trees and telephone poles and cars are tumbling silently into the red eye overhead. Their sound isn't fast enough to escape. The air in here is chilling as it thins but I can feel heat radiating down from that hungry orb.

Minutes now. Maybe seconds.

"Daddy?" Marie asks.

Her lips and eyes are tinged blue as her light passes me. I'm trying to smile for her but my lips have gone spastic. Tears are leaking out of my eyes, crawling over my temples, and dripping up into the sky. The broken walls of the house are dancing. A strange light is flowing in the quiet.

The world is made of change. People arrive and people leave.

But my love for her is constant. It is a feeling that cannot be quantified because it is not a number. Love is a pattern in the chaos.

"It is very late, my darling," I say. "And the stars are in the sky."

They are so very big.

"And that means it's time for me to give you a kiss. And an Eskimo kiss."

She leans up for the kiss by habit. Her tiny nose mushing into mine.

"And now . . ."

I can't do this.

"And now I will lay you down . . ."

Swallow your fear. You are a good father. Have courage.

"And tuck you in, nice and tight, so you stay warm all night."

The house has gone away from us and I did not notice. The sun is a sapphire eye on the horizon. It lays gentle blue shadows over a scoured wasteland.

And a red star still falls.

"Good night, my darling."

I hold her tight as we rise together into the blackness. The view around us expands impossibly and the world outside speeds up in a trick of relativity. A chaotic mass of dust hurtles past and disappears. In our last moment together, we face a silent black curtain of space studded with infinite unwavering pinpricks of light.

We will always have the stars.

A SLOW UNFURLING
OF TRUTH
Aliette de Bodard

What makes you *you*?

In Aliette de Bodard's complex, carefully crafted story, people can change the bodies they inhabit, memories can be erased or falsified, physical and mental traits can be altered until it takes a trained authenticator to verify that a person is actually who he or she claims to be.

What makes you *you*?

A powerful, tyrannical government can inflict pain and fear, trying to bend you to its overbearing will, yet that germ of *you* might remain: cowering in terror, racked with agony, yet still there, not defiant but persistent. You might want to bow to the torturers' demands, to stop the pain if for no other reason, yet that ineradicable *you* remains.

"A Slow Unfurling of Truth" delves into the complexities of human existence in a beautifully realized future setting of orbital cities and interstellar travel. Yet the story is really about eternal verities, about evil and the painful search for goodness, about fear and anger and the one thing that makes us human—love.

Huong Giang was putting away her trays of instruments when Thoi walked into the room. "Elder sister." He was out of breath, his youthful face flushed with what seemed like anger or trepidation: Thoi had been in his body for less than a year, and he was sometimes hard to read.

But, new body or not, he still should have known better. "Thoi, you're not meant to come here," Huong Giang said. "I made it clear—"

"I know," Thoi said. "But you need to come, elder sister. Now." And, after a pause that was rife with implications, "There's a man that has come here to Celestial Spires—a Galactic."

"And?" It was hardly usual, to be sure—Galactics remained in the areas that appealed to them, the central parts of the cities and the planetside attractions—but it wasn't as though it should concern her.

"He says his name is Fargeau. Simalli Fargeau."

"That doesn't mean anything." The government had sent people to Celestial Spires for years after the purges: they pretended they were from the Poetry Circle's lost members— Simalli, or Vu, or Thanh Ha. They dropped hints; told her how frustrating it was that, decades after the Galactic masters had departed, the government continued to indulge them, continued to strip its land and people bare to bow down to Galactic wishes. Huong Giang, who'd learned her lessons in six bitter weeks of jail and re-education sessions, never said anything, and the people would always leave after a few weeks. The attempts had ceased many years ago, but that didn't mean they wouldn't be back.

"You don't understand," Thoi said. "He really is a Galactic."

"They could always find a Galactic to do their dirty work for them." Huong Giang turned away from Thoi. She only had her monitor to switch off before she could go back home to stare at herself in the mirror—seeing herself drained and rootless—wondering why, no matter how many years she put between herself and the purges, the memories she'd sealed away still seemed to suffuse her whole being; still filled her with a sense of loss so frightening she found it hard to breathe.

"It's more than that." Thoi hesitated. "Elder sister . . . I really think it's Simalli."

"You're sure?"

"Of course I can't be sure," Thoi said. "But . . ."

But he thought he knew. And he was the most observant among them, the only one of the Poetry Circle who'd avoided time in jail, because he'd successfully gauged his interrogators' moods.

Simalli. In the flesh.

"Did he say anything?" she asked. She hadn't thought anything could make her feel this cold and hot at the same time— adrift in space, in some rootless vacuum that held no comfort or no enlightenment.

"No. Only that he's been here a while."

"Where did you put him?"

"I left him in one of our guest rooms," Thoi said.

"Did he . . ." She meant to ask whether he'd mentioned Dao, but that was a silly, selfish thought—the repercussions of Simalli's return went far beyond her niece's fate. What she needed to do . . . she needed to make sure it was him. She needed to recover his key-fragment. She forced herself to breathe, to drag her thoughts back from the frenzied panic that had overtaken them. "Call the Identity Keepers. Tell them I want an authenticator. Kieu specifically, if she's available."

The Identity Keepers' services did not come cheap, but it was the only way she knew to be sure. During the purges, they had taken no sides—performing their services whether it was the government or the families of the disappeared paying for them. Rumor had it that it had cost them dearly, but of course even the government couldn't do without some kind of authentication.

"Are you sure?" Thoi asked.

She'd never been surer of anything in her life.

* * *

Celestial Spires hadn't changed: the same old holos on the walls, the same smell of fish sauce wafting through the corridors like a memory of childhood. A group of people in crude bodies bypassed Kieu—the men had fingers curled into thin claws, the women were flat-chested with carp-scales adorning their cheekbones and the back of their hands. It was all . . . so tame, so symptomatic of Tai Menh, a backward planet clinging to outmoded traditions. At least the capital—where Kieu lived—had all the modern Galactic amenities, and access to the latest optical-stims and some of the most radical body-change technologies; though it still was nothing compared to the vibrancy of Prime or Cygnus.

"You haven't told me why I'm here," Kieu told Huong Giang.

"For an authentication—what else?" Kieu's mindship partner, *The Sea and Mulberry*, had left his physical body at the docks—of course, he wouldn't have fit in anywhere on the orbital—and projected only a small hologram of himself, hovering at the height of Kieu's shoulder—he would have looked like a pet bot, save that bots didn't pack a billionth of the processing power of *The Sea and Mulberry*.

Huong Giang grimaced. She looked much the same as Kieu remembered her. Her new body was a little wider perhaps, a little older, but there were never any surprises with her choices—of course, the keeper of the traditions on Celestial Spires wouldn't bother being creative, or open-minded. "A while ago, there was a man named Simalli who lived here."

Kieu shrugged. She'd never felt any of her future lay in the gutted Celestial Spires orbital, or even planetside. She'd become an authenticator because it was the fast, easy way to earn money; to buy herself passage away from the dump of Tai Menh, into one of the myriad glittering planets of Galactic

society, where she could at last have access to the best of everything. "So?"

"He's come back. He . . . we entered a contract with him, a
long time ago. I need to be sure it's him before fulfilling that
contract."

"I see."

"There might be . . . associated issues." Huong Giang's voice
was slow, careful, as if treading a path within a mountain fog.
"There's . . . a possibility chunks of his memories might be
missing. He'd remember most things about his life on Celestial Spires, but there might be the . . . odd detail missing?"

Kieu sniffed. "As long as he's not a gibbering wreck, it
doesn't affect authentication much." Not quite true, of course—
memories were important because they affected behavior—
but so long as the basic behavioral patterns were intact, she
could still build her models, could still authenticate. "Does it
have anything to do with the purges?" She didn't much care
either way, but the prospect of shattering Huong Giang's
composure was too tempting.

"Kieu," *The Sea and Mulberry* said, sharply. "Don't."

But it was already too late. "Simalli left before the purges."
You could have cut stone with Huong Giang's voice.

"I see," Kieu said.

"Show some respect for your elders," Huong Giang said.

Kieu had no respect, not anymore. At least Huong Giang
had been released after the purges—had clawed her way back
to Master of Body-Shifting as if nothing had ever been wrong.
Kieu's mother and grandmother had not been so lucky. She
simply shook her head, and asked instead, "Where is he?"

Huong Giang, for a moment, looked as though she was going to berate Kieu. But she didn't. "I'll take you to him."

"I need to look at him without his seeing me."

"I thought you interviewed people?" Huong Giang's voice

was skeptical—calling Kieu's judgment into question so easily, so effortlessly.

Kieu drew herself up to answer, but before she could give
voice to her anger, *The Sea and Mulberry* cut in. "If it's the same
man, he's gone off-world for a long while—possibly undergoing several traumatic events that haven't been recorded by the
authentication systems. We'll need to observe him in a non-
official environment first, to establish as many unbiased observations as we can."

"Fine, fine. I'll show you to a compartment where you can
watch him," Huong Giang said.

The compartment she found for Kieu was small, and every
piece of furniture in it was jammed together, from the narrow
bed to the console. Typical Celestial Spires; typical Tai Menh.
Kieu missed her own, much roomier compartment already;
but she'd worked in much worse environments than this, and
this was just more evidence she and Huong Giang were a long
way from getting along.

Not that she cared. Huong Giang held no power or author-
ity over her, not any longer, and if Kieu had her way, would
soon be part of the distant past.

Kieu pulled up a battered chair, connected her implants to
the Celestial Spires network, and looked at the image overlaid
on her vision: the man, sitting on the bed, staring at the ceiling as if it held some great vision or source of enlightenment.

In the short walk to the room, Kieu had downloaded and
reviewed all available materials on Simalli Fargeau—glorying
in the rush of data as it filled her mind, in the heady feeling of
constructing her correlation matrices, that heightened awareness that gave her the impression of knowing every heartbeat
of Simalli's life. She'd dissected every movement he made, every
reaction he'd had in his interactions with Rong people—all

the little gestures and words that combined to build a proba-
bilistic model of him, with enough prior knowledge to compare
against the new observations and performing goodness-of-fit
tests. *The Sea and Mulberry* would also be doing the same, though
as a mindship he would be using alternate models and paying
attention to different factors—doing likelihood-ratio tests using independent algorithms, as required for a strong authentication.

The next step would have been an interview with Simalli
Fargeau. But Kieu always delayed interviews—because nothing was as sweet, as pleasurable as the collection of data, the
slow buildup of inferences and tests of hypotheses, that exquisite feeling that the information she sought was just at her fin-
gertips, that everything was a hairsbreadth away from making
sense.

In those moments, she felt truly alive, truly connected to
everyone and everything else—in a way she'd never done since
the purges had taken away her remaining family.

"What do you think?" she asked *The Sea and Mulberry*.

The ship had been uncannily silent so far, only interjecting
to control Kieu's outbursts—of course, he abhorred any kind
of conflict, and liked to believe he could find a peaceful solution to everything. "I don't like this."

"Because of the off-world factor?"

The ship's holo wobbled. "Not only. Because there's too
much tension around, Kieu. We should—"

"Leave? No way." She wasn't going to let Huong Giang have
any kind of last word with her. "It'd be a severe black mark on
our records."

"By my records, Simalli Fargeau has spent more than eighteen years off-world," *The Sea and Mulberry* said. "That's quite
enough time to make authentication . . . challenging."

Eighteen years. That silenced her. She looked at her data

again, at the old, outdated observations. "At least he didn't go through the purges." That had seriously dented authenticators, necessitating the storage of thousands of hours of optical-stims to make sure everyone was in the system once more.

The Sea and Mulberry said nothing. He didn't need to; even she knew that uniform continuity was the basis of authentication—the premise that over small periods, human behavior didn't change that much, and that any large changes would be recorded by the authentication system. Eighteen years without any kind of records, though . . .

"Look," she said. "We can try, at least."

"If we can get enough data on what happened to him off-world, we might possibly refine our model enough to offer a reasonable authentication."

"Seventy percent?" Kieu asked.

"Maybe a little more," *The Sea and Mulberry* said. "It would help, of course, if we had people who knew him." He projected a stim from eighteen years ago: Simalli Fargeau on the arm of a woman in a tight-fitting red ao dai who looked vaguely familiar to Kieu, like a distant image that refused to coalesce into meaning.

"His mistress?"

"His wife. Pham Thi Dao. She went off-world with him when he left."

"And?"

"I don't know. But she isn't with him, and she's not back in the authentication system either."

"Dao." Kieu tasted the name on her tongue, like the peach the woman had been named after. She looked at the woman—who was turned slightly away from the camera, diffidently smiling at her husband—and then back at the man who sat on the bed, one leg crossed over the other in a typically Galactic fashion. His face was that of a smooth, unmarked twenty-year-old, and she wondered, then, how much of what he'd gone through had been erased by multiple body-changes.

The Sea and Mulberry was right: it wasn't going to be an easy task to authenticate him.

Huong Giang steeled herself before entering the guest room. Kieu had disapproved of her seeing Simalli—had said it would be better if she waited until the results of the authentication were complete, but she'd also said it would take several weeks of repeated observations before they could build a satisfactory model and test for goodness of fit—amidst a flood of technical terms Huong Giang had barely understood. She couldn't wait, and neither could the Poetry Circle—not if he still had his key-fragment.

Simalli turned when Huong Giang entered—in a composed, thought-out gesture that reminded Huong Giang so much of bygone times it made her feel angry and betrayed all over again. "Huong Giang." He'd always been good at languages, and he spoke her name properly, with all the stresses—he might have sounded like a native if not for the fact that he didn't behave right—every gesture of his tinged with foreign, alien intensity. "I'm sorry for disturbing you."

About time he apologized—but she couldn't say that, not the angry way it'd come out. She didn't want to antagonize him, not now. "It's been a long time."

"I know," Simalli said. "You look well."

She didn't, and they both knew it. "You're the one who looks well," she said, more sharply than she'd intended. How could he stand here, so healthy, so serene—how could he still go on with his memories cut off? But of course she knew the answer: he'd never cared overmuch about the Poetry Circle; had never treated it as more than a source of amusement. Not remembering everything would be but a minor inconvenience for him.

"I . . . I'm glad to see you still here."

He didn't mention the purges. He didn't need to; it lay in the air between them, a blade that nothing would ever shatter. "You always were so bad with words," she said. "Why are you here, Simalli?"

Simalli blushed. He wore a simple, almost pre-Exodus body, with freckles on his star-tanned face, and hair the deep red shade of wedding dresses. "And you always were such a blunt person." He kept his gaze on the holos on the walls—it was disconcerting to see him adopt Rong ways of respect. The man she'd known had stared people in the face and had stated his opinions bluntly, proud of being frank and open, as if honesty would get him anywhere. "If you must know . . . I came back here to apologize."

Huong Giang kept her voice cold, though it cost her. "You're aware no apology will change what you have done."

"I know. I know, God help me. I know." His hands came up, as if he wanted to bury his face in them, but then he lowered them with an effort, and said nothing more.

"You came alone," Huong Giang said. "What about Dao?"

He looked at her, then, the red of his hair splayed on his corneas. "She's dead." It seemed as though he would say, "I'm sorry" (and she'd have lost her calm then, screamed at him about everything apologies couldn't do), but then he thought better of it. "Huong Giang. Elder aunt . . ."

Dao. In her mind's eye, Huong Giang was seeing her niece—telling her she worried too much and that the Heavens would always provide. Dao. For years and years Huong Giang had sustained herself with the knowledge that Dao had survived, that she'd lived a long and happy life—not like Huong Giang, who woke up at night remembering what had happened in the jails, the ten thousand pains and aches that ran through her bodies, wearing them out one after the other. Years and years of hope, casually destroyed.

She'd been wrong. Whoever he really was—whether he was Simalli or someone else with enough knowledge to pass off as him, cruel enough to raise hopes they couldn't fulfill—she couldn't do this. "I have to leave," she said, but what he said stopped her.

"I still have it, you know."

"The key-fragment." That was all she could say without betraying herself.

"Yes. It's why I had to come back. I had to give it back to you. Huong Giang . . ."

She forced herself to look at him; to show nothing of what she felt, inside. But he saw; he had to, unless he was as oblivious as ever. "Would you give it to me, then?"

Simalli grimaced. "It's yours. I had no right to keep it." He extended a hand; a little holo hovered over it, displaying a stream of numbers that flashed by too fast for her to read it. The key-fragment. His part of the decryption algorithm—the secret they'd all spread within the Poetry Circle, the one that required enough component parts to become whole. A foolproof system, Vu had said; for the government would never have enough key-fragments to decrypt.

At the time, it had seemed like the only way to survive—to lock in their own minds the memories of what they'd done, of what they'd uncovered in their casual studies of Tai Menh's literature and history—to leave no evidence that could be used against them. It . . .

Her hands shook again, remembering needles driven into them, the fire that had spread through her veins. It had worked—to a point. They'd survived, with nothing that the government could pin on them. They'd survived, and they'd still lost everything when Simalli took his key-fragment away from Tai Menh.

She felt weary—emptied, her purpose since long locked away in her mind, an old, aching wound papered over until she could no longer touch it or even be aware of its nature.

"Why, Simalli? Why? You didn't have to come back. You didn't have to return your key-fragment." He'd shown, all too well, that he was a Galactic. That he might dabble in forbidden activities to amuse himself, but that he could leave at any time—as he had done, in the end.

Simalli sighed. "Would you believe I had a change of heart?"

"No."

"I did." Simalli bit his lip. "I was wrong. I was wrong to keep Dao away from Tai Menh—it killed her. And I can't keep the key-fragment, Huong Giang. It burns me. It leaves me no rest, and eats at my sleep—it's something that should be returned to its proper place."

It sounded . . . so much like everything she'd hoped Simalli would say. And that made it all wrong. If she'd learned one thing during the purges, it was that wishes never came true. That people didn't magically change their minds or heroically return.

"Take it," Simalli said.

"I can't." It would decode nothing, or the wrong things altogether: the encryption was in their own minds, and using the wrong key might just tear their thoughts apart; might just turn their vacant pasts into a morass of lies and delusions. It was only the real key that would give them back what they'd hidden. Simalli's offer was a government trap to catch her again, to lead her back to jail; to render her terminally insane . . . "Simalli . . ."

Before she could react, he'd pressed his hand to hers—his touch was surprisingly dry, as if his new body barely secreted any sweat. Huong Giang withdrew, shocked, but it was too late: the tingle on the back of her hand testified that the transfer had happened, and the numbers that had scrolled over Simalli's outstretched palm were now part of her own memory— waiting to be accessed, to be recombined into the proper shape.

"No," she whispered. And then, stronger and angrier, "You have no right."

He was watching her, his head slightly bent—she had an unbearably sharp memory of him sitting in a chair a lifetime ago, listening to one of Vu's poems and nodding as each syllable fell into place. But, for all she knew, it could be a lie; it could be her, grasping for connections in her faulty memory, clinging on to the hope that he really had come back.

"You've learned nothing, have you—you just do what seems right or proper to you, without once asking for anyone's opinions—"

"Huong Giang . . ." He was reaching for her, but she'd had enough this time.

"I shouldn't have come here," she said, and turned away and left.

How she wished it was that easy to erase what he'd given her from her body.

Kieu sat down in the chair, watching the man named Simalli Fargeau. Too young, she thought—too young for everything that might have happened off-world to him, the ten thousand pains and heartaches eighteen years could encompass. Huong Giang was by her side—had insisted on coming even though her presence wasn't necessary. Something seemed to be eating at her; some preoccupation that she wouldn't open to Kieu. No matter; it had never been any of Kieu's business.

She couldn't wait to be gone. By now, everything in the

orbital rubbed her the wrong way. Every day or so, she'd see a woman walk by who smelled like her mother, and bite her lip not to call out to her—every day or so, she'd walk into a restaurant without Galactic food, and endure yet another dish of lemongrass chicken or shrimp toast redolent of the stink of fish sauce, while the wall-screens projected overmannered operas that sounded like the whine of slaughtered pigs.

She had to leave before she went mad.

It was Kieu's and *The Sea and Mulberry*'s third interview with Simalli Fargeau; by then they knew all the steps of the dance and the way it was going to play out.

"Tell me again how long you lived in Celestial Spires."

"From . . ." He hesitated. "The year of the Yin Earth Rooster to the year of the Yang Water Rat. Four years."

"How did you meet your wife?" She was going through the motions, asking variations on questions they'd already asked nine times already—making sure that his answers were consistent across several interviews.

"She was at one of the embassy's parties." He looked thoughtful for a moment—his eyes dark, his mouth pinched in a little grimace.

"This makes you sad," Kieu said.

"Of course. She's dead." Flat, expressionless. Angry, Kieu's a posteriori models suggested. He was a true Galactic, a man who would seize opportunities rather than meekly and stupidly submitting to the decrees of Heaven. But it didn't sound like anger; more like weary resignation, as if accepting that the wound she'd left in the world would never heal.

"How did she die?"

"She . . . faded away. Like an orchid taken away from tropical climes . . . I was a fool. I thought love would keep us whole."

"It never does." Huong Giang's voice was harsh.

Simalli inclined his head. "No. It doesn't. Neither does friendship, or trust. Everything can strain and break and leave you
desolate. I know this now."

The Sea and Mulberry cut in before Huong Giang could answer. "We have examined your medical records." Simalli had
been most forthcoming, providing a list of traumatic events
that had been integrated in the transition model, coloring every observation they had of him. "Is there anything else you
wish to add to this?"

Simalli shook his head. "I have provided all you need for
your authentication."

"You're familiar with our authentication system," *The Sea and
Mulberry* said.

"Of course." He smiled, tightly and without joy. "I lived
here once."

There was something about him—some current of unease
that she couldn't quite pick up. She glanced at *The Sea and
Mulberry*—the mindship was picking apart something in the
medical data, making the odd noise of interest as he found a
particularly juicy tidbit. Huong Giang was staring at her hands
as if unsure what to do—an odd sight, for Kieu had never seen
the older woman so disconcerted. "I need to clarify a few things.
You've been on Celestial Spires for a while," she said. "And yet
you only contacted Huong Giang now. Why is that?"

Simalli shrugged. "I . . . wanted to take a look at the orbital.
To see what had happened to it."

Kieu had optical-stims of him in the orbital—admiring the
fish sauce vats, the grounds of White Horse Temple—wandering
down the smaller cramped corridors and stopping as if uncertain of where he was going. Through it all his face was the
desperate one of someone looking for something, for anything
he'd recognize. It was all the behavior she'd expect of Simalli

Fargeau—even down to the habit he had of fingering a pendant around his neck, a smooth golden medal with an image of some Galactic saint.

"It's changed since you last came here." Huong Giang's voice was bitter. "Assuming you're even Simalli."

Simalli looked as though he was going to say something, but he didn't speak. Kieu's personality model indicated he was more likely to assert himself forcefully when challenged; she'd asked her first few questions hoping to do that, but so far nothing had happened. Not impossible, but rather improbable. Still . . . still, there was that eighteen-year gap in the data.

"I've seen the optical-stims," she said, pitching her voice high and almost out of control. "They don't really put you at an advantage. You married a local woman and settled here, and when things became too hot to handle you turned tail and ran."

"I'm not proud of what I've done." His voice was shaking—it was shame rather than anger, though, without the bite she'd expected.

"But you won't deny it?" *The Sea and Mulberry* asked.

"Why should I? It's all in your stims, as you say."

Huong Giang's face was unreadable. She was looking at her hands again, as if trying to come to a decision.

Kieu glanced at the medical history—a depression following his wife's death, a change of bodies, children that had become as strangers to him—it was all drearily familiar, for all that he was a Galactic. She reviewed her self-perception and mortality awareness marginal models, biting her lips. He all but matched, and he had impeccable knowledge of Simalli's past life, but still . . . Still, she had that feeling something was missing. The forgotten memories Huong Giang had mentioned, perhaps? But no, it wasn't that, it couldn't be that . . .

"Thank you for your time," she said, at last. "We'll be back."

"I have no doubt." His voice was light, ironic, and for a moment, the smile he turned toward her was that of a much older,
much embittered man. He looked at Huong Giang again, and
said, "Have you used it?"

Huong Giang's face was frozen in what might have been
shock, what might have been horror. "You know I haven't. You
know I can't trust you."

"You can't trust me to be Simalli Fargeau?"

"I can't trust you at all," Huong Giang said.

"I see." He looked . . . ill at ease again. Guilty, Kieu's gut
said, though she had the feeling she was still missing layers
and layers of meaning. "You have to use it, elder aunt. It's the
only reason I came here."

"I'll think on it." Huong Giang's voice was tense; her hands
clenched in her lap.

Outside—to her horror—*The Sea and Mulberry* turned to
Huong Giang. "You seem troubled."

Huong Giang gave a short bark of laughter. "I hadn't expected him to come back."

"You don't know if it's him," *The Sea and Mulberry* said.

"No. You're right. I don't." Huong Giang looked at her hand
again.

Kieu said, "What did he mean by, 'Have you used it?'"

Huong Giang didn't answer. *The Sea and Mulberry* said,
"Younger sister, I don't think we should probe into what doesn't
concern us . . ."

"It concerns us. It's an authentication problem, and we already have little to go on. It could turn out to be significant—
could be the detail that invalidates our model. Everything,
even your dirty little secrets, elder aunt." It was . . . not quite
true, of course. What Kieu looked for was multiple, robust
correlations; while details like those might be important, they
were unlikely to call everything into question. But still . . . It

was a matter of trust and openness, things Huong Giang was unwilling and incapable of granting to her.

Huong Giang's voice was low, defiant. "I don't need to explain myself to you. It's something that was once given to him for safekeeping."

"And that he left with." *The Sea and Mulberry*'s voice was very soft.

"Yes. And returned with. Except that I need to be sure it's the right one. Are you happy now?"

Yes. No. It was none of her business, and it helped little. But demons take her if she allowed Huong Giang to see her flustered. "It's . . . adequate. We'll have an answer for you in a few hours' time."

She already knew what it would be, and she also knew what *The Sea and Mulberry* would say. He knew enough, and behaved enough like Simalli Fargeau to make a positive authentication— within an acceptable margin of tolerance, he really was the man who'd left Huong Giang eighteen years ago, and whatever dirty secret he'd given her was genuine.

She'd tell Huong Giang that. And then she'd leave—she'd return to the capital with one more authentication to her name, one more payment to her account—one step closer to leaving Tai Menh and all its outmoded customs behind her.

Huong Giang stared at the numbers in front of her—spinning in the hollow of her hand, almost pretty enough to be a work of art.

And, in a way, it had been one. No one else but Vu could have encoded the key-fragments—no one else could have sealed away their memories with such exquisite care, taking away only what was needed to make them safe. No one else could have made the encryption robust enough to survive losses, including their own.

Huong Giang hardly remembered Vu now: he was in some of her fainter memories, pouring rice wine on warm afternoons—a safe, government-approved version that she knew bore no resemblance to Vu's true self. With the same care that he'd crafted the key-fragments, Vu had removed himself from the minds of the Poetry Circle, and almost nothing true was left of him now. Just a few, faint nudges, the same ones that had led Huong Giang to find the rest of the Poetry Circle after the purges; to stare at friends across a wide room, wondering what could have linked them together so tightly, so intimately; and feeling a huge, crushing sense of loss rising in her, an enormous, gaping emptiness that could find no surcease.

The key. It might be the right one; it might give them back everything they had lost—their memories, the communion of purpose that had given them such joy and pride. Or it might destroy them, more thoroughly than the government had ever done.

A noise made her look up: Thoi had entered the room, sliding the door shut behind him—and after him, silently, the rest of the Poetry Circle followed.

They were small and diminished—nothing like the eager youths they had once been—when the world had still been wide open and they'd still believed in the goodness of the government, in the glory of uncensored freedom.

On all of them, the purges had left their mark. Thoi always took young, unbroken bodies and used them with reckless abandon; Hai walked hunched over and bowed; and, no matter what body she was in, Loan's left hand would curl in the shape of a claw, even though none of her new bodies had had their fingers broken in vises. And, of course, Thanh Ha and Vu were no longer with them—vanished altogether, frozen in the authentication system, their faces kept forever young and smiling, and all their contracts and secrets forever broken.

Hai paused when he saw the numbers spinning on Huong Giang's hand. "So it is true, then. He's come back."

Huong Giang nodded.

"I don't see him here," Loan whispered, her voice rasping against the confines of her throat.

Huong Giang shook her head. "He does not belong here." Not yet. Not ever. The Buddha preached forgiveness and compassion, but He also knew that every act found its reward or punishment in another life. He also knew that betrayers would not reincarnate into arhats or bodhisattvas, that a slow ladder had to be climbed in order to reach the bliss of Nirvana.

"You're right. He doesn't belong here." Thui's youthful face was severe.

"No matter," Hai said, shaking his head. "This isn't what we came for."

One by one, they laid their hands on Huong Giang's, and gave her back their key-fragment—each passage altered the numbers subtly, changing the intensity of the light in her palm until it had gone completely dim.

"Now," Hai whispered.

Yes. Now. Huong Giang held her hand over the memory-projection console, and let the gathered key slide into it—and felt it slip away from her grasp into the system, and from the system into their minds—slowly scattering into a thousand component fragments as it started to decrypt what they had encoded eighteen years ago—everything slowly unraveling, coalescing into new, strange shapes.

The room went dark, as it had, all those years ago, and the contents Vu had sealed away opened up, blossoming like lotus flowers in windswept ponds—all the locked memories of their time spent together, the smell of lemongrass, the sound of each other's laughter, their excitement at gathering new evidence from Tai Menh's precolonial history—and then their minds, stumblingly, reached for each other the way they had used to do, and their communion swept outward, scattering images and emotional imprints across the walls, creating a cocoon of dancing light that lifted them into its embrace.

It wasn't text, or stims, or anything that tangible that they had found, searching through what their ancestors had left them—rather, it was a slow unfurling of colors on the walls, a rising tide of sounds that carried them with it, until they could hear at the back a chant like the sutras of the monks in the temples, a series of words hovering just at the cusp of hearing like half-remembered dreams, images burnt into their brains— processions of sleek metal ships bringing offerings to huge altars, orbitals gleaming in the background as people laughed and shared warm wine—and through it all ran the same thread of wordless sounds, of songs limned in moonlight and morning mists, of boats cruising on wide, green rivers that turned out to be nothing but the eye of a jade Buddha statue, and then the scene panned out and revealed that the Buddha Himself was carved out from the rock of a huge cliff . . .

This was what neither the purges nor the government, nor the Galactics could ever take away: that Tai Menh had been great once, and would be great again.

Huong Giang took a deep breath—it was all they'd lost, and more—the memories of all their ancestors held together by the gossamer-thin engrams of their minds, showing them the old days as they had really been and not the shambled pretense of ruins the Galactics had shown them and to which the government still clung. It made it all worthwhile.

She remembered Simalli then, with merciless clarity—the way he'd sat and fidgeted during those sessions—he'd enjoyed the intoxicating rush of sensations, but he had never truly understood any of it. He had never wished to become part of his

wife's world—of their world; had been content with his ability
to live like a king on a planet where everything was still designed to accommodate his kind.

And she saw, then—that this was the man she remembered;
not the remorseful illusion in the audience room, not the worried, concerned friend who'd pressed the key-fragment in her
hand. She saw that whoever the man was, he was unlikely to
be, to ever have been Simalli Fargeau.

But the key-fragment was genuine. Surely that couldn't be
mistaken for anything else—surely . . .

She wasn't sure what made her break the communion—a
breath, perhaps, the scrape of arrested flight? The room was
darker now, only lit by the slow dance of the memories they
were immersing themselves into, but she caught a fleeting
glimpse of Kieu, and of the utter shock on the younger woman's face as she turned away and fled into the corridors of Celestial Spires.

No matter what she did, Kieu couldn't shake out the images.
She'd only stolen a glimpse of them—hoping to mock Huong
Giang with her useless secrets—but now they wouldn't leave
her.

She'd meant to pack; to take her things and go back to her
work, to count the authentications left to her until she had
enough money to go off-world. That was what she'd thought,
before she'd seen.

Now she sat in the darkness, with the silent *The Sea and Mulberry* by her side; and still heard the wordless poems, still saw
the reddish glow of the moon cast across the roofs of a temple
complex.

She'd been confident that the Galactics were right and that
Tai Menh was nothing but a backward hole, worth only escaping

from. She'd read all about the glory days, but until now she'd never *seen* them—had never experienced them from the inside, from the point of view of her ancestors.

She felt . . . held together, comforted in a way she hadn't been since her mother had died. She felt . . . part of something greater.

"Kieu?" *The Sea and Mulberry* asked.

Kieu closed her eyes, following the curve of a dragon's serpentine body; the splash of water as a mindship emerged from the water and opened his gates to welcome his mother aboard; felt the mother's pride at her son's achievements; felt the pain as the Galactics tore down Celestial Spires, making way for progress, for larger spaceships with larger berths, and doing away with the old superstitions that held the Rong back from joining the society of their peers . . .

"Kieu!"

With difficulty, she tore herself away from the images in her brain; though she still heard the wordless song, like a memory of the old poems her mother had once sung to her, in a time both infinitely far away and infinitely close by. "What is it?"

"I worry about you," *The Sea and Mulberry* said, a bit stiffly. "You haven't moved for four hours."

"Oh. Haven't I? I'm sorry. You're right. We need to pack." She moved back to the bed where her things lay spread out, and stared at them for a moment—they seemed tawdry and unfamiliar, like the fragments of a broken vase.

"You're not listening," *The Sea and Mulberry*'s voice was gentle.

"No," Kieu said. Ancestors help her, she wasn't. "I'm really sorry. What were you saying?"

"I . . . I need your advice." The mindship hovered over the table, projecting a blue beam of light under his hologram. "I've been reviewing the correlation matrices for the authentication of Simalli Fargeau."

Kieu's heart seemed to freeze in her chest. "You said you agreed with me when I said it had to be him."

"Within the tolerance bounds of the constructed a priori and a posteriori models and the observation data," *the Sea and Mulberry* said.

"And you're saying the models are wrong? We can't go back on an authentication." She'd given her word to Huong Giang; had given the Identity Keepers' word. They'd been sure; as sure as they could be with what they'd seen. And Huong Giang had seemed so sure, too. He knew too much and behaved too much like Simalli. It had to be him.

"No . . ." *The Sea and Mulberry* paused. "There are . . . outliers in the observations. Little things . . ."

"Show me," Kieu said, sitting down on the bed amidst her scattered belongings.

Images scrolled across her field of vision—not the glorious sights of Huong Giang's secrets, but simply the recordings of *The Sea and Mulberry*—and her own recordings, interspersed with her notes.

"Lack of anger, for one thing," *The Sea and Mulberry* said. "His sense of shame was also off the scales; I attributed this to the pain of returning, but once you dug into it . . ."

Gently, carefully, he teased apart the events, showing her how the parametric probability density models and loss functions they'd put together didn't quite converge; the higher-order pattern in the outlier data, and how integrating the outliers added up to a wholly different behavioral distribution; how the reactions of the man who pretended himself Simalli Fargeau could be interpreted in an entirely different way.

"Do you see, now?"

She saw . . . she saw that even with the most tolerant model they could build, the faults were too many, too omnipresent. She saw that she'd been in a hurry to leave Celestial Spires and had botched the job. "I see."

"I don't know what it means," *The Sea and Mulberry* said. "After all, eighteen years is a long time . . ."

A long time, yes—and so much of it spent in an alien culture without records. Kieu zoomed in on their first interview with him, watching him rise as they entered the room—watched the minute, complicated movement he'd made: a reaching forward with one hand, swiftly withdrawn; a tensing of the hands to bring them together for a Rong greeting; and then he'd stopped, and reached forward again, shaking Kieu's hand as if nothing had been wrong. It was small and almost undetectable, but Kieu had been trained to notice such inconsistencies. Simalli Fargeau had always shaken hands without hesitation; why would he have that brief impulse to greet them in the Rong faction and then change his mind? Unless . . .

Slowly, she called up the first optical-stims—the ones that showed Simalli with Pham Thi Dao—and watched them together for a while, trying to piece the data back together into a new model.

"I see," she said, slowly. "I see."

She could shut *The Sea and Mulberry* up. It would be so easy—he hated conflict and would bow down to her superior expertise, all too glad to leave an orbital where he felt as ill at ease as her. She could leave, now, with Huong Giang none the wiser—and have her reputation intact.

She could . . .

In her mind, she saw the slender shape of a pagoda, stretching toward the Heavens; listened again to a wordless song; to words she hadn't heard for years and cherished without knowing it—and knew that her wish to leave Tai Menh had been nothing but the act of running away from painful ghosts; that she was Rong, would always be Rong with those words within her; and that Celestial Spires had been and would always be the only place she could call home.

"Fine. Let's go," she said.

Huong Giang found Simalli in the common room—carelessly sitting on the table, his legs crossed—everything in him like a spring wound tight.

She said, without preamble, "You're not Simalli. You're not Galactic."

"I see. And what do you base this on? Your authenticator Kieu declared me a suitable match."

He sounded . . . so sure of himself, so casually in charge, that Huong Giang hesitated—surely Kieu had to be right about him? "Because," she said, more sharply than she'd intended, "Simalli Fargeau wouldn't have come back. He was a dilettante, a man who enjoyed the thrill of being with us, but he never could stand danger. He ran away, and he kept running away from us for eighteen years."

"Does it matter who I am?" his voice was very low, his gaze fixed on the holos on the wall. "I brought you back the key-fragment, didn't I?"

"You did," Huong Giang said, slowly—feeling again and again the memories swirl within her, her pride in her people, in her ancestors. "I thought you came here for forgiveness; but you have nothing that needs to be forgiven."

"You're wrong."

"I don't think so, Dao."

Simalli gave a short, bitter laugh. "Is that who you think I am? Dao is dead." He rose, slowly; moved toward the door. "But you're right about one thing: I didn't come here for forgiveness. What Simalli Fargeau has done can never be forgiven.

I came here because it was the right thing to do—the one thing I believed in. I have done what I needed to do; I'll be gone now."

"Wait," Huong Giang said. "Wait. Tell me—" She reached for him, but he'd already slid out of her grasp, striding toward the door—and stopped, for Kieu was waiting for him in the doorway, and behind her was the smaller shape of *The Sea and Mulberry*, blocking his way out.

How—how had she come here? How—

Kieu's face was grim. "Elder aunt. I apologize. I wish to withdraw my authentication. This man isn't Simalli Fargeau."

She closed her eyes and lowered her head, suspicion at last coalescing to certainty. "I thought it might be the case, but . . ."

"You don't understand. This isn't Simalli Fargeau. This isn't Pham Thi Dao either. They're both dead. They've been dead for a while." Kieu didn't move, and the man who called himself Simalli Fargeau appeared transfixed by her words.

"Explain yourself," Huong Giang said, sharply.

"Isn't it obvious?" Kieu's hand swept toward the man in front of her.

"Not to me."

"Shall I tell him who you are, or will you?" Kieu's face was terrifying to behold, transfigured by pride and anger.

The man who called himself Simalli Fargeau seemed to sag, like a water puppet with cut strings. "I had to," he said, finally. "He was an old, broken man when he died." He turned back to Huong Giang, his eyes glistening oddly in the light—Huong Giang, shocked, realized he was crying. "You were right. He ran and ran and ran until there was no more running to be done. He clung on to his secrets until there were no more secrets. I had to . . . I had to come back here. To see what he'd done. To try to repair it, if I could. I had to . . ." His voice broke, and he wouldn't look at Huong Giang again. "I had to honor him, or his soul would find no rest in death. I had to. Do they not say that the sins of the father stain the daughter's hands a thousandfold?"

As if in a dream, Huong Giang found herself moving forward, hands outstretched to reach him—and stopped herself, just as everything came together in her mind. "You're his child," she said, slowly. "His . . ." She stopped, then. "Dao's daughter."

The man didn't move; he was still watching her, his eyes reddened, his hands clenched—looking back, from time to time, at Kieu and the way she blocked the door. Huong Giang could see him tense—could feel his eagerness to be gone, to take his shame and anger and grief elsewhere; to flee Celestial Spires and the memories of the Poetry Circle, just as his father had once done.

No. Kieu's authentication was right: in all the ways that mattered, the man was not, and had never been, Simalli Fargeau. Something, long held against her chest, shattered and broke into a thousand jagged pieces.

"You're wrong," she said, gently. "The sins of the father are his own to carry, and to atone for." Gently, slowly, she drew him into her embrace, feeling the weight and the warmth of him in her arms like a sun-soaked stone. "Welcome back, child. You are here among kin."

THUNDERWELL
Doug Beason

One of the longtime standbys of science fiction is the story that hangs on a life-or-death problem, and then shows how the problem might be solved by scientific or technological breakthroughs.

Such is Doug Beason's "Thunderwell." The first human explorers to reach the planet Mars are doomed to die because their supply vessel has failed.

Can some futuristic piece of technology save them?

But wait a minute. Beason isn't using futuristic technology; he's describing a technological capability that has been available to us for several decades, but has been discarded because of political issues.

Whether the technology succeeds or fails, however, this story—like all good fiction—deals with far more than gadgetry. The human element is a basic, inescapable factor. As is the Second Law of Thermodynamics: you have to pay for everything you get.

The six-man crew on board the Mars orbiter received the video-feed seven minutes after it was transmitted from Earth, twenty minutes after the supply ship's engines failed to extinguish. Silently watching the transmission, the men in the cramped stateroom shivered. The ship was primarily kept cool to conserve heat. It also helped to mask the smell of six astronauts living in close quarters during the six-month flight.

Six months that now might stretch out to who-knows-what after the failure of their supply ship.

Marine Colonel Mark Lewis, crew commander and mission geologist, displayed no emotion; nor did any of the crew. They had all watched the supply ship on the screen, and they all had counted out the seconds the main engine had continued to burn, a good minute and a half after it was supposed to shut off. They all knew what it meant.

And they all knew there was nothing they could do about it.

So as true professionals, they turned away from the display and pushed off to their stations, preparing for the next phase of their journey— aerocapture around Mars, using atmospheric friction generated from dipping into the thin Martian air to slow them down and pull them into an elliptical orbit.

Colonel Lewis hesitated before turning to his checklist. They had a shipload of work to do before they landed, and there really was no time to send a message back to Earth. NASA would know that they knew about the supply ship, and since there was nothing they could do about it, following the next step on the checklist was the only option that made sense. They'd all known the risks, and they'd all had no second thoughts. Solving insurmountable problems was one reason he'd signed up for the trip, and he'd jumped at the chance to command the first manned mission to Mars.

In his mind this was just a glitch. A big glitch, but a glitch nonetheless. He wondered if his wife would understand.

From the view on the screen in NASA's DV Lounge, nothing appeared to be out of the ordinary. But everyone knew that something was wrong.

The supply ship bore silently through the blackness of space. Minutes before, no one in the lounge had seen the propulsive kick from the chemical oxy-hydrogen engine as the multiton spacecraft was inserted into its Hohmann trajectory to Mars. Similar engines had been used dozens of times before, some on unmanned probes to the outer planets or the inner Solar System. JPL's exquisite calculations had placed every probe's position to within centimeters of where they had been needed to rendezvous with Mars, Jupiter, Saturn, and beyond.

But now that the supply craft's chemical propulsive burn had inexplicably continued for ninety seconds longer than needed, the unmanned vessel was traveling much too fast to ever be aerocaptured by Mars. There was no reserve fuel left to insert the supply ship into an elliptical orbit, and there was no way to slow the craft, to stop it from hurtling past Mars and into the depths of interplanetary space.

On a separate, private channel, the NASA Administrator spoke grimly as the silence in the DV Lounge seemed to last forever. Poorly insulated from Washington, DC's stifling heat, NASA's Distinguished Visitors room was nearly unbearable, both in temperature and from shock.

Finally, somebody whispered. "What about plan B?"

The Honorable Heather Lewis turned away. "Didn't you hear the Administrator? That *was* plan B," she said bitterly. She closed her eyes, trying to erase the image from her mind. On the screen, the spacecraft was little more than a dot, jumping around on the monitor because of the vast distance.

Dammed technology, she thought.

All because of a ninety-second increase in the burn. A minute-and-a-half mistake, and six lives snuffed out. Six astronauts, the first manned mission to Mars. And her husband, Colonel Mark Lewis was one of them.

Heather's military deputy, Brigadier General Mitchell, lightly touched her arm. "Ma'am, the press is gathering outside. They've either heard about the failure or they've suspected something's wrong. I suggest we get you back to the Forrestal Building." The Department of Energy headquarters building housed the Honorable Heather Lewis's agency and would be a refuge from the press corps.

Heather nodded, trying to focus. "Can't we ignore them?"

General Mitchell shook his head. "Probably not. They smell blood, and you'll be running a gauntlet, Dr. Lewis."

"Then let's just push our way through them."

"Once they discover that the chemical engine on the supply ship failed, they'll ask why you killed NASA's nuclear propulsion program," Mitchell cautioned. "It's the second chemical failure in a row, and ultimately they'll blame you. They'll say that a thermal nuclear engine wouldn't have failed."

Heather stiffened. "That was years ago and doesn't have anything to do with this situation." *This is about my husband and five other astronauts!* Not about a political decision she'd made years ago. Then, the administration had been willing to do anything to prevent technology related to nuclear weapons proliferating to terrorists.

"Then when they corner you, don't acknowledge anything. Remember—technology is never foolproof. Everything fails, even throttles on chemical engines that have always worked before."

Heather nodded.

In a fail-safe effort to place humans on Mars, NASA had launched a supply ship four months before the manned mission left Earth. That way, the manned spacecraft would not have to carry the entire three years of supplies needed for a round-trip mission to Mars. The strategy was to position the first supply ship into Martian orbit, and the crew would rendezvous with the ship once they arrived four months later. A docking procedure NASA had perfected since the Gemini era.

The six-person crew was two months into their mission when the first supply ship's engine failed to fire and it pranged into the Martian surface. But no worry, the backup—"plan B"—the second supply vessel, was launched within weeks, while the crew was still on their way to Mars.

There were enough provisions on their own ship to last

them over a year, and the newly launched ship would provide more than enough supplies to ensure their return—extra propulsion, consumables, and enough margin for them to bring more rocks and dirt back to Earth than all the lunar material brought back from the Apollo missions combined.

Two supply ships, one launched before the manned mission and the other after. In theory, it was a fail-safe, no-sweat solution to a problem for which NASA had prepared for decades.

Until now.

Heather straightened and drew in a deep breath. "Let's do it." Head held high, she strode purposely out of the DV Lounge.

Camera flashes popped, reporters elbowed their colleagues to gain position. A striking blond woman in a red jacket shoved an oversized mike into her face.

Heather pulled herself up as the gauntlet squeezed shut.

"Dr. Lewis! Dr. Lewis!" The blond reporter placed herself center in the camera's field of view and said breathlessly, "This was the last opportunity to mount a rescue operation using chemical propulsion . . ."

Heather frowned. "Rescue? The last I heard, the crew is doing fine and the *Discovery* doesn't need a rescue mission."

Someone murmured off-camera, "They will once their food starts to run out."

Another microphone was shoved in her face. "Madam Administrator, Robert Ziebart, Space Nuclear Power On-Line. As the head of the National Nuclear Security Agency, do you now regret your decision to veto NASA using a nuclear propulsive engine for mankind's first manned Mars mission? A nuclear thermal engine would have cut the transit time to Mars to weeks, instead of six months and would have provided many more options for a risk-free space flight—"

"Nothing is risk-free," interrupted Heather. "The President appointed me to this position to draw down our nation's nuclear footprint, not grow it. And proliferating nuclear technology into space would have enormous consequences—"

Someone whispered, "More enormous than your husband's impending death?"

Heather opened her mouth to retort, but stopped. *No emotion,* she thought. *Keep it in. Just get out of here.* She pushed the gaggle of reporters aside and plowed through the bevy of people.

Outside NASA Headquarters, General Mitchell opened the limo's door for Heather and joined her inside the stretched car. Snapping his seat belt, he turned to her and enumerated the highlights of the impromptu press conference: "Great response: saying your husband's mission has not failed, especially since there are still options for rescuing them. Also, you did well in offering no apologies for vetoing the nuclear engines, but you might want to rethink—"

Heather jerked her head up. "What do you mean there are other options for rescuing them? There *are* no other options."

Mitchell fell silent.

Heather felt her face grow red. "Didn't you hear the NASA Administrator? They can't even scrub the mission—even if they tried to slingshot around Mars as a return-to-Earth, they don't have enough fuel to slow down!"

A long minute passed. General Mitchell pressed his lips together. "There are . . . other, more controversial ways to get supplies to Mars. But if you're worried about proliferating nuclear technology into space, then I think this other option is a non-starter. Dead on arrival."

Heather leaned back into her seat. "If you're thinking of using a variant of nuclear propulsion, then forget it. When I vetoed using that technology four years ago, the engines were dismantled, the nuclear material was returned to the Nevada Test Site for storage. It would take over a year to pull that program back together if not longer—and that's not including the five years it would take to build it."

"I wasn't thinking of nuclear propulsion. At least in that sense."

She glared. "Then what are you thinking about, General?"

Mitchell hesitated. A light rain fell outside the limo, making the Washington, DC, streets appear to glisten. Red taillights blinked as the traffic inched ahead. The general leaned forward. "Our nuclear labs—Lawrence Livermore, Los Alamos, and Sandia—generated a dozen ideas after the atomic bomb, to use nuclear explosions for peaceful purposes."

Heather snorted. "Right. Programs like Plowshare, to dig big ditches using nukes. The only problem was that tons of radioactive material were generated that made those sites unusable for a thousand years. That's one of the reasons why we can't allow any of these crazy retro-nuclear programs to be resurrected."

Mitchell shook his head. "Actually, you're right on that point. There were some pretty wild ideas, most of them not even vetted to pass the commonsense test before they were pursued. Like trying to drill for oil in Colorado by setting off a nuke underground—but with the result of contaminating an entire oil field."

"So what's your point?"

"The point, Madam Administrator, is that one of those crazy ideas makes sense. Not that we should always use it, but perhaps we should reconsider in times of great national necessity." He waited a beat. "Perhaps in times such as this."

Heather steadied herself as their limo swerved to avoid a car that pulled out from behind a bus. Even in the rain, Constitution Avenue was lined with tourist cars and buses. Teenage and preteen school kids milled around the national mall, most without umbrellas and soaking wet, but enjoying their school trip to the nation's capital.

She nodded. "Go ahead."

Mitchell debated how to present the controversial idea. If he delved into too much detail, she'd dismiss the concept, and bin it with all the other crazy rescue schemes she'd hear over the next few days. But if he allowed her to think things over, get her head straight after this disaster, then he might have a chance to sell it to her.

It just might work. It was a tactic he'd used throughout his military career to convince people to consider out-of-the box solutions: isolate them from the cacophony of chatter, present the idea in a measured way, and allow them to weigh the pros and cons themselves—without anyone yelling a sales pitch in their ear.

He didn't make general by rolling over and allowing the system to grind to a halt through inaction.

Mitchell let out a deep breath. "You've had enough for now, ma'am. Anything I tell you now would be melded together in that big melting pot of same-priority decisions: everything is equally important, and everything gets the same amount of analysis, no matter what the consequence. You try to make a decision now, and people like that reporter who jumped on you will just heap it on more—just higher and deeper."

Heather looked incredulous. "You're not going to tell me what I can do to save my husband?"

General Mitchell pulled his mouth taut. "I will. But I'll explain once we're outside the beltway, when you can see for yourself, and weigh the priorities of this solution against its own merits."

He pulled out his government smartphone and swiped at the screen. He tapped in a list of orders to Heather's personal staff. "Your 'go' bag"—the ubiquitous suitcase containing a week's worth of clothes that high-level political appointees always kept close—"is in the trunk. We can be wheels up at Andrews in an hour, and land you just after lunch, local time. It's an overnight trip at the worst, or I can get you home by two a.m. tonight—which would beat some nights you've gotten home from work since starting this job."

"Four hours to get where? Even my G-650 can't get us to the West Coast in four hours. Five minimum with headwinds. I don't know what aerospace contractors you want to visit in California, but there's no need to travel. They've all got offices in DC."

"You're right, but we're not going to LA. I need to get you to Nevada, before the political machinery cranks up, and starts telling you what you ought to think."

"Nevada? What's in Nevada that can help us get to Mars—Area 51?"

"The Nevada Test Site, where the last US nuclear explosion took place in 1992. You visited the site after you were first confirmed . . . and it might just be where you find a solution to saving your husband's life."

Heather blinked, uncharacteristically at a loss for words. "What?"

"Thunderwell," Mitchell said. "I'll explain once we get there. *Then* you can decide."

Two more weeks until they reach Mars.

The manned part of the journey was going like clockwork, exactly as planned. It was the supply vessels that drove them to take drastic measures. They were mere hours into the emergency, but he'd cut the oxygen back to 20 percent, right next to the bare minimum of the 19.5 percent they'd need to survive. Mountain guides and cold-weather scientific expeditions lived on that amount of O_2 *for weeks at a time. They couldn't do it forever, but it was a stopgap measure to give them time to consider options.*

They laid out their failsafe alternatives, dubbed plans A, B, and C. Just as the manual prescribed. And like all professionals, they didn't dwell on failure, but only on what it took to ensure success.

Heather and General Mitchell landed at Creech Air Force Base, an hour's drive north of Las Vegas, but only minutes from the entrance to the Nevada Test Site, or NTS as the sprawling desert testing facility was known. Established January 11, 1951, by the Atomic Energy Commission, the NTS was pocketed with radioactive craters, produced from over nine hundred atomic bomb experiments conducted from 1951 to 1992.

Since nuclear testing stopped in 1992, the NTS was mostly vacant, void of the activity that once permeated the site. Aside from infrequent, non-nuclear underground experiments that peppered the NTS, the NTS resembled more of a ghost town than the once glamorous center for nuclear weaponeers.

General Mitchell moved quickly around the car and opened the door of the government SUV for his boss. With her hair pinned back and sunglasses, Dr. Heather Lewis looked more like the Harvard-trained political science professor she was, rather than a high-ranking political appointee who ran the US's nuclear weapons enterprise.

Heather stepped unsteadily down into the dirt. Mitchell led her by the elbow up a small rise. Their shoes kicked dust into the air as they walked around scrub brush. Stopping at the crest, they gazed across a brown, desert valley onto a sparse collection of aluminum buildings that dotted the landscape. A large drill bit, some thirty feet across, lay on its side next to one of the buildings. Two yellow cranes were fastened to safety hooks on a concrete pad.

Mitchell pointed at the massive drill bit. "We drill shafts twice a year, ten meters in diameter down to a depth of about half a mile. It keeps a small cadre of techs current on their skills."

"To house non-nuclear underground experiments," Heather said. "Like you said, I haven't been out here since I was confirmed. Four years and it doesn't look any different." She turned to the one-star general. "I hope you didn't bring me all the way out here to sell me some idea cooked up by the nuclear labs to keep this place alive."

"No, ma'am. But you did need to come out here to see the scale of what you need to do—if you're going to not allow your husband to die."

Heather reddened. "As if I have any say in the matter. You said yourself we couldn't resurrect the nuclear engine option in time to save the crew."

"You're right. It would take at least five years to resurrect the thermal nuclear reactor program, not to mention build another supply ship. But there's another option, a quicker, *non-reactor* nuclear option. And it involves this place."

"What do you mean?"

"It sounds crazy, but this idea was cooked up by Dr. Edward Teller, so-called father of the H-bomb."

Heather frowned. "Wasn't he responsible for Plowshare?"

"He was. But he was responsible for a lot of other ideas as well. This was an idea to use the power of a nuclear explosion in a peaceful way, exotic and unconventional, but in a manner that could benefit space travel on a massive scale."

"You're not serious."

"Actually, I am. He had this idea to rocket *tons* of material into space—and it just might work."

Heather looked skeptical. "Tons."

"The idea is to load an enormous amount of supplies—thousands of tons—onto a slab of high-strength metal, sitting on one of those ten-meter diameter mine shafts you see out in the NTS valley. Dr. Teller wanted to place a nuclear bomb at the bottom of the shaft, a mile or so below the surface, and fill the shaft with water."

"Water?" Heather looked as if she'd been following his explanation, but her eyes began to wander.

"Stay with me, ma'am. Once the nuclear bomb is detonated, most of the energy—fifty percent of it—would be absorbed by the water, which would be instantly converted into superheated steam. And voilà, an incredibly energetic steam piston would push against the plate at the top of the mine shaft and accelerate it up . . . so fast that the plate and supplies not only leave Earth's gravitational pull, but if launched at the right instant, could impact Mars," he lowered his voice, "and provide enough food, water, and supplies for a crew to survive, until either a conventional rescue mission could be mounted, or until they generate enough in situ fuel to make it back home."

Heather stared down at the brown valley of dust. General Mitchell couldn't read any emotion in his boss's expression, as her features were taut, unmoving. She spoke without turning. "You're saying this Thunderwell is a nuclear-driven golf-shot that could impact Mars. A golf ball of water, food, and fuel. That we can shoot to my husband."

"Yes, ma'am—that's the gist of it."

A moment passed, then she turned to face him. "You have *got* to be kidding."

"No, ma'am. I'm dead serious."

"That's crazy. How can anything get from one planet to another without a rocket? And just by shooting it into space. Didn't Jules Verne write about that?"

"Yes, he did—and he was on the right track. With enough initial velocity, it's possible to shoot nearly anything to the Moon—or Mars, or anywhere else for that matter. The problem is that initial kick. Compressible objects, such as humans, would instantly turn to jelly after such an enormous acceleration. Living things just can't withstand accelerations greater than eight or nine g's, not to mention the nearly one hundred thousand g's created by a nuclear-driven steam piston."

"It sounds crazy."

"It does. But we *know* this can work. We have proof."

"How?" Heather said. "I would have heard of this Thunderwell if it had worked."

Mitchel continued patiently. "Scientists have discovered meteorites in Antarctica originating from Mars. They were originally chunks of Martian rock, blown into space by the collision of a huge meteor. Those craters on Mars were created by huge masses, maybe asteroid-size rocks, hitting the surface and ejecting surface material into space. And some of that ejecta left with enough velocity to make it all the way to Earth. Accelerated into space just as Thunderwell could accelerate supplies to Mars."

Heather stared at the massive drill bits. Rust pockmarked their silver-tinged faces. They looked like giant toys left abandoned in the desert. She spoke slowly. "So this nuclear steam piston, Thunderwell, kicks the supplies into space. All the way to Mars."

"That's right. The metal platform on top of the vertical shaft is accelerated up into the atmosphere tens of kilometers a second, with enough velocity—and if it's correctly aimed—to reach Mars and hit the surface."

She shook her head. "Won't the supplies be squashed?"

"Any food would have to be freeze-dried, but water and whatever fuel you might want to include wouldn't be affected by the large acceleration; those are largely incompressible. For electronics and other equipment we'd use technology from the Defense Department's penetrator program, bombs designed to withstand that type of acceleration can burrow through tens of meters of granite to destroy deeply buried targets. But anything we send would have to be able to withstand both the initial acceleration, as well as the impact on the Martian surface.

"We could have done this years ago. And it would have been far easier to hit the lunar surface, saturate it with supplies before establishing the first permanent human presence on the Moon. We could have saved billions on the space program."

"If it was so easy, why didn't we do it?"

Mitchell looked incredulous. "Ma'am, it does mean setting off a nuclear explosion—a *thermonuclear bomb* that vents into the atmosphere." He set his mouth. "I suppose we could have done that in the fifties without any consequence. But today?" He shook his head. "It's just not a career killer, it would create an international incident. It would mean breaking the international Comprehensive Test-Ban Treaty—the one that the Senate is just about to ratify. And worse, it might result in possibly dismantling the nuclear nonproliferation regime." He hesitated, then spoke softly, "The plank that got your party elected and got you confirmed for this job . . ."

Heather brought her head up quickly. "Then why did you bring me here? Why did you shove this in my face? You could have just as well trotted in one of your national lab lackeys and given me a PowerPoint presentation on the options. Why did you do this?"

Mitchell slowly nodded to himself. "You needed to see this place. You needed to experience for yourself the history, what people did when faced with a seemingly insurmountable foe during the Cold War, when they weighed consequences for themselves of what might happen if they didn't do what they were doing.

"Those folks weren't dumb. They knew what they were doing to the environment wasn't benign." He took her elbow and turned her around to the north, looking over another vista. A giant hole created by a nuclear blast in the 1950s dominated the landscape, but he ignored the geological feature and instead pointed to a row of stadium bleachers. Faded by the sun, the wood was splintered. Green paint cracked off the seats onto the ground.

Mitchell nodded at the sight. "They brought in crowds by the hundreds to witness the atomic blasts. It seems horrific now, but they knew that there was little radiological danger to the observers. They wouldn't put congressmen and starlets in danger.

"It might have been decades ago, but they were just as smart as us, and they *knew* the significance of what they were doing—but they also knew there were long-term consequences. And it all came down to what was most important to them at the time. They had a choice: winning the Cold War—in their minds, preventing extinction—or saving the environment. Maybe they were wrong. Maybe it wasn't an either/or situation. And maybe they could have done things differently. But the point is that they were absolutely convinced that their priorities were right, no matter what we think of their decisions today."

"So what's your point, General?"

"The point is, that was then, and this is now. And you, Madam Administrator, have got to make the same decision for yourself: what are your priorities with all the risks involved?"

Mitchell let go of her arm.

Heather was quiet for a long time. Wind whipped around them, blowing sand into their eyes. Her hair swirled around, but she paid it no attention. Sweeping her hair away as she turned, she whispered, "So you really think Thunderwell can get supplies to Mars?"

"With a well-designed nuclear device, a reinforced shaft, a

robust plug, and by strapping the right amount of supplies on top of the plug in the correct places to ensure they don't induce any unintended torques, waiting until the correct moment to launch, and of course covering it all by an ablative aeroshell—"

Heather sharply held up a hand. "I trust you on the details. Will it work?"

A long moment passed. "Yes, ma'am. I'd stake my life on it."

Small attitude thrusters on the vessel's port side sputtered in a sharp staccato. Neutral gas shot from the nozzles at a frequency so high it sounded like bacon sizzling.

Suddenly it stopped. Flexing metal creaked as the spacecraft began to rotate. Stars wheeled around the exterior view screens excruciatingly slowly, mere milliradians at a time as the massive ship rotated sluggishly about its center of mass.

Moments passed, and the thrusters sputtered again, this time on the starboard side. As the craft slowed its rotation, a red sliver appeared on the side of the exterior view screen. The sliver increased in size to a crescent, slowly filling the screen. Within minutes, Mars dominated the view as the craft sighed to a stop.

It appeared as if the ship were pointed at the surface, destined to graze the planet on the side; but if their calculations were correct, they were precisely positioned to barely miss and instead delve deep into the Martian atmosphere. And once slowed by aerobraking, their craft would be flung into a highly elliptical orbit around Mars.

Better to beg forgiveness than ask permission. Without her husband, Mark, she didn't have anything to lose.

And Heather was glad she didn't ask permission ahead of time.

Otherwise, the last-ditch rescue mission never would have been mounted. No matter how great the chance.

As an undersecretary of a major cabinet in the second term

of the President's administration, Heather had immense powers. And as long as she didn't commit the nation to war, her verbal orders were quickly accomplished.

She slapped a "Sigma 80" Q SAR—special-access-required— program code on the secret *Thunderwell* project, swearing people to silence and threatening years of jail time if they broke the strict security measures. And with trillions of dollars being tossed around lowering the national debt, funding nondiscretionary spending, and supporting the conflict-dejour, the percentage of Heather's $12 billion nuclear enterprise budget that was diverted toward *Thunderwell* didn't raise an eyebrow. After all, she was the one who had overseen the drawdown of the nuclear enterprise, and she was the Administration's golden child.

The national weapon labs wheeled into action. Old geezers who hadn't thought about underground nuclear tests since the last nuclear device popped off in 1991, before the Test Ban Treaty was put into effect, were wheeled into their emeritus offices to give advice to young bomb-designing whippersnappers—whose only experience setting off a nuclear device had been limited to massive 3-D computer simulations on the world's fastest-supercomputer of the day. Even then, they were limited to only calculating what size nuclear device and what other technical requirements would be needed to successfully pull off *Thunderwell*.

Three one-mile-deep shafts, each over ten meters in diameter and each at varying, precise angles to the surface, were simultaneously bored by the reserve crews who had been standing by at Mercury Site for years, the jump-off point in the Nevada Test Site. The elderly crews had been waiting for decades to swing into action in case the Nuclear-Test-Ban Treaty had been lifted.

Two Los Alamos, and a third Lawrence Livermore candi

date nuclear warhead were rocketed though the nuclear complex validation process, each undergoing a rigorous peer-review process to determine which device would create the precise nuclear conditions that would best enable a successful shot. They all knew they'd only have one chance.

Hydraulic and fluid experts, material scientists, and foundry executives converged on the Nevada Test Site to pound out the exact specifications for the massive plate that would serve as a platform for the supplies. After sleepless hours and with input from the labs' nuclear experts, they finally settled on a hybrid design of using a massive one-meter thick, thirty-meter-diameter stainless-steel plate that would hold the supplies, buttressed by a titanium carbide plug inserted into the hole. There was simply not enough titanium available to build the plate, and a compromise of using steel from the sides of mothballed battleships satisfied the nuclear designers.

Sworn to secrecy, senior management from Safeway, King Soopers, Piggly Wiggly, and a half-dozen other national supermarket chains teamed with Defense Department commissary executives. They met with NASA representatives to determine which dehydrated food stock would best survive the incredible accelerations, exposure to vacuum, and long-term exposure to radiation for the total estimated flight time.

Armed convoys rolled day and night, transporting the three selected warheads from their military storage sites to the safety of the DAF—the Device Assembly Facility—at the Nevada Test Site, minutes from where the shafts were being dug beneath the surface.

Heather herself signed off on the final requirements for ensuring a 50 percent chance of getting eleven kilotons of supplies to Mars: accelerating the plate and supplies to an escape velocity of over twelve kilometers per second drove the nuclear device to be over a half-megaton in energy—560 kilotons—or nearly thirty times larger than the weapon that devastated Hiroshima.

With her preparing an unsanctioned, half-megaton nuclear explosion, orders of magnitude greater than anything known in the last sixty years, she knew that the end of her career was the very last thing she had to worry about.

Simply because after this, successful or not, she would no longer have a career.

The manned portion of the mission was successful.

The crew vessel was aerocaptured by Mars and their periares dropped with each orbit, inching closer to the surface by atmospheric drag. At the velocity they'd approached Mars, their total elliptical orbit took nearly a week, and the only way to slow their speed was to drop deeper and deeper into the atmosphere. With only enough fuel to circularize their orbit, they prepared to extract themselves from the main craft and enter the sparse Martian atmosphere with their landing module.

They'd finally arrived in orbit after the demise of the two ill-fated re-supply vessels. And after successfully aerobraking they resumed full oxygen, needing their full faculties for the next phase of the mission. But with the odds so stacked against them, some of the crew silently wished they could attempt the landing with the joyful nonchalance brought on by a lack of oxygen . . . that way they wouldn't care one way or the other how things turned out.

In three months—the mean time for an urgent, clandestine national security activity to be noticed by Congress and the Executive branch—logistics for *Thunderwell* were green, ready to go. It was one of the nation's most tightly guarded secrets, even keeping the Martian astronauts in the dark.

On the top floor of the DAF, NASA TV played from a silk-thin, wall-size screen hanging from the ceiling. Light-delayed pictures of the Mars astronauts splashed around the room, lighting up the walls. On the giant screen, Colonel Mark Lewis, commander of the first Mars mission, floated upside down as the networks streamed his upbeat words at the bottom of the display.

On the surface, everything seemed normal. There was no sense of tension in the astronaut's broadcast, in the voice of the clipped, professional NASA narrator, or in the newscasters. In two days, America was landing on Mars with an international crew. After six months coasting in its Hohmann transfer orbit, the mother ship *Discovery* was going to release the Mars lander *Hope*, and for the first time in history, humans were going to land on the red planet.

But because of the failure of the two supply ships to Mars, *Discovery* didn't have enough fuel or supplies for the return trip to Earth. The plan to rendezvous with the supply ships and bring the crew home would never be realized.

Millions of miles away, on the upper floor of the administrative area of the DAF, General Mitchell met with a cadre of DOE, national lab, and military personnel. Although the conference room was not in close proximity to the half-megaton nuclear devices parked in secure vaults three stories below, no windows adorned the room—or any other area in the DAF. Three stories high and made of rebar-enforced, nuclear-pedigreed concrete, the DAF stood out like Ayers Rock in the Nevada desert.

General Mitchell went around the room, going over his checklist in methodical fashion. "Device status?" The complex, intricately manufactured 560-kiloton nuclear weapon was reduced to being known as the device.

An Asian woman looked up from her laptop. "All three green. Final recommendations from the selection jury will be presented to you and Administrator Lewis next week."

Mitchell moved to the next person sitting at the table. "The hole?"

"Infrastructure and diagnostics ready in the bore hole. Orthogonal tunnels for the strap-on science experiments are green."

"Water?"

"Green. Purification verified and ready to flood the tunnel." Mitchell nodded. "Plug?"

A skinny man in coveralls stood. "Yellow, because the plug's not yet in place. But the last acoustic testing is complete—no flaws, General. The titanium carbide plug is being transported to the NTS on one of the old shuttle transport 747s and will be ready for insertion as soon as it arrives." He looked down at his notes. "The steel plate is on-site and ready to be moved over the hole and welded to the plug on notice."

Mitchell turned to a woman wearing a King Soopers grocery jacket, the only person who seemed out of place in the government-dominated room. "Supplies."

"Packaged and prepositioned, ready to be moved once the plate is in place, General. I've got slightly over eleven kilotons, each having their position set within fractions of a centimeter, both horizontally and vertically. The final height will be forty-five meters, just under the surface of the aeroshell. But you'll have to pray we don't go to war in the next six months. We've diverted all of USTRANSCOM's strategic supplies for the next year."

Mitchell grunted and turned to the next person. "Public affairs?"

Two thousand miles away to the east, General Mitchell's boss sat in front of a classified Congressional special program's oversight panel, defending the expenditure of millions of dollars of "black," or special-access, funds. During the hearing, she didn't exactly lie—the Congress oversaw the nation's SAP, or special access programs with keen oversight, and this sometimes appeared the only way that urgent, nationally important programs such as the B-2, the Corona spy satellite, and the Osama bin Laden special ops missions could be successfully run. So when asked point-blank if this black program Heather was conducting at the DAF would result in a new nuclear warhead, Heather could honestly say no—it would merely provide the nation with a new capability.

But it was a huge new capability, she began.

She spelled out that the new capability could launch huge quantities of supplies to the Moon and planets, and that it would open up a new era for space travel. But in her mind that was mincing words—there was one catch to this huge new capability, and it wasn't a small one.

When the committee looked at her quizzically, Heather drew in a breath and started explaining just what it took to accomplish that.

Heather's G-650 greased to a landing on the ten-thousand-foot-long runway at the Nevada Test Site. The sleek white business jet looked out of place as it taxied past dusty metal sheds and squat, brown concrete buildings.

A black suburban with a Department of Energy license plate raced up to the jet as the G-650 pulled next to a metal staircase. As the engines whined down, Heather tapped down the stairs into the waiting staff car, her ear glued to her smartphone. Final arrangements were being coordinated back in Washington, and Heather received up-to-the-minute appraisals.

She'd briefed Congress's special programs oversight committee just hours before at the closed meeting, speaking to two senior senators and representatives, representing both parties.

When she fully revealed the capability and purpose of Thunderwell, the room went deathly silent.

But only for a few minutes.

After all the uproar, thank goodness only one Congressperson had violently objected, so she left the hearing unscathed.

It had been her plan all along to fully brief Congress on the ultimate purpose of Thunderwell: to build a nuclear-bomb-driven steam piston that would hurl over eleven kilotons of supplies to Mars. But she didn't fully brief them until today, when the device was complete and ready to be used.

Now they knew. And as Heather's car drove up to the NTS command post, the oversight committee was waiting to brief the President in the White House Situation Room. If she'd timed things right, she'd sit down at the control room's console just as the classified video-teleconference with the White House began.

General Mitchell stood as Heather walked into the cool, dark command center. In the middle of a cluster of identically drab buildings, situated at the top of a barren hill, the command post's interior had been dramatically updated from the last time it had been used in the early 1990s, when underground testing of nuclear weapons had started winding down. Since that time, non-nuclear and radioactive equation-of-state tests were conducted at the site, but those experiments did not rank high enough in priority to merit updating the old facility. The round-off error from the Thunderwell budget more than paid for the installation of new fiber-optic controls, oversized HDTV screens, and an updated multileveled command center.

Tens of windows were open on the HD displays, showing various camera shots throughout the test site: at the bottom of the hole, the 560-kiloton nuclear device, eerily sitting in crystal-clear, deionized water; an arm-thick bundle of fiber optics that spread out to the thousands of sensors—neutral and charged particle, X-ray, heat, optical, overpressure, density, temperature, laser, and RF imaging—that permeated the test site; the explosively driven blast doors situated near the surface, just under the titanium plug; orthogonal views of the massive thirty-meter diameter, one-meter-thick steel plate sitting on top of the titanium plug; the forty-five-meter-high composite aeroshell enveloping the plate, looking like a huge stubby nosecone jutting up from the desert floor; and several angles of the site viewed from a hundred meters to ten kilometers away. The ground surrounding the hole was deserted, void of movement.

A quiet hum of voices filled the command center, as if no one wanted to raise their voice as they ran through checklists.

Suddenly, the center screen blinked and a red list of trigraphs appeared at the top of the display as the view focused on the President, surrounded by the Congressional oversight committee. The President looked shocked as two senators exchanged heated words.

I leather cleared her throat. "Mr. President, I assume you've been briefed—"

The President turned to the screen. "What the hell is going on?" His features grew larger as he leaned toward the camera. "You've been building your own nuclear weapon without my or Congress's approval, and now you want to break the Comprehensive Nuclear-Test-Ban Treaty? Who do you think you are? Do you realize that detonating this device and launching that plate might cause several nations on this planet to assume they're under nuclear attack, and launch a retaliatory strike against American cities?"

"Mr. President," interrupted Heather, "as Administrator of your National Nuclear Security Agency, I not only have the legal right, but I have a sworn duty to ensure the safety and surety of the nation's nuclear stockpile. I have not designed a new weapon. I have merely appropriated one of our nuclear devices due for destructive testing and have instrumented it so as to fully understand the detonation physics in the event that you authorize an underground test . . ."

"Underground test? Are you insane? You've got ten thousand tons of metal sitting on top of that high-tech blowhole. It's the world's largest cannonball!"

"It's not a cannonball, sir. It's over eleven kilotons of supplies, mostly food and water—the titanium plug and steel platform are less than a third of the total weight."

The President looked icy. "Don't split hairs with me. If that thing detonates and something goes wrong, we could find ourselves in the middle of a nuclear war."

"State Department notification of the underground test is ready to be sent simultaneously to the United Nations, and to the world's nuclear powers, sir. Since the US has not fully ratified the Comprehensive Test-Ban Treaty, we fully reserve the right to conduct an underground test to ensure the safety and surety of our stockpile. As such, NNSA's legal team has delivered a Presidential Finding for you to sign to authorize the test so that we'll have the legal framework to proceed . . ."

"This is not an underground test, it's a nuclear-driven projectile! The test hole will vent radioactive material worldwide. Are you crazy?"

Her hands tightly clutched the wooden table as she struggled to remain calm. "Blast doors located under the plug will slam shut just after the plug is accelerated up, preventing anything but superheated steam from escaping from the hole. This technique was perfected near the end of the underground nuclear test campaign in the early 1990s.

"Mr. President, this program will accomplish three high-interest items. First, you'll confirm the safety and surety of our nation's stockpile, showing the world the remaining nuclear weapons you are responsible for are still a viable deterrence, and will only detonate when you want them to detonate; second, you'll provide a highly visible rescue of our stranded astronauts, demonstrating to the world your commitment to use American ingenuity to rescue international astronauts, even as far away as the orbit of Mars." She paused.

The President waited for a moment, his face icily rigid. He leaned into the screen. "And the third high-interest item I'll accomplish?"

"As far as demonstrating your commitment to finally signing the Comprehensive Test-Ban Treaty," said Heather tiredly, "you'll not only have a reason to do it, but you'll have a scapegoat to haul up before the international court. Me."

Colonel Lewis moved from the lander and stepped lightly into the Martian soil. Red landscape spread out before him, dotted with rubble, rocks, and what looked like a ridge of rugged mountains in the distance. They'd chosen a landing spot by the pole, where evidence of winter ice had been pinpointed. With any luck, they'd be able to harvest ice for water, and perhaps crack the water for oxygen. Realistically they knew the chance was small and their outlook was bleak; but by attempting to explore and perform what scientific experiments they could, at least they would be busy . . . and push away the certainty of death for as long as they could.

The President acquiesced.

Grudgingly.

The countdown proceeded well within the time calculated by the astrodynamicists. The time of launch was set to when the Earth's rotation brought the Thunderwell site into the plane of the ballistic trajectory to Mars. It was like setting off a gigantic cannon, and the initial velocity, angle of the hole to the vertical (with a deviation less than femto-radians), and even planetary gravitational influences, all had to be precisely aligned so that the supplies would hit Mars. It was a modern version of Jules Verne's *From the Earth to the Moon*. But instead of a nineteenth-century gun launching a bullet to the lunar surface, this was a nuclear-weapon steam piston accelerating eleven thousand tons of supplies to Mars.

The entire Nevada Test Site worked with well-oiled precision, whatever excitement present muted by the knowledge that even with all their attention to detail and exacting preparation, stuff still happened, and the device might not pop off as planned.

Nuclear tests had failed unexpectedly during the heyday of nuclear testing, and it might happen again. But instead of just moving on to another test of an exotic nuclear weapon design—enhanced neutron production, electromagnetic pulse generator, extremely small yield, or even a ground-shattering earth mover—this failure would be the last nuclear shot ever attempted.

The quiet only magnified what everyone knew: that this was the last option to rescue six astronauts on Mars who had no other chance.

"Sixty seconds, General. STRATCOM acknowledges all declared nuclear countries—the UK, China, Russia, India, Pakistan, and France—have been appraised." The controller coughed. "And a courtesy notification has been sent to the IAEA, Israel, Brazil, Japan, Iran, and North Korea. This is your last chance to abort."

Mitchell glanced to his left at Heather. The Administrator stood silently watching the array of screens as if she hadn't heard. Her arms crossed, muted light reflected from her face. No emotion hinted that her husband's fate depended on the wildly improbable and unconventional delivery of supplies, or that her personal fate was dictated in breaking the as yet un-ratified International Comprehensive Test-Ban Treaty.

General Mitchell nodded to the young female controller when Heather remained mute. The digital clock ticked past the fifteen-second mark. "Carry on." He turned back to the screens. *Ten seconds.*

It took place in less than a second.

Electrons trickled into explosive wires that detonated an array of lens-shaped explosives. The precisely assembled array of incredibly symmetric high-explosives—especially manu-factured by Los Alamos National Laboratory—detonated in fine tuned precision.

Within milliseconds, the conventional, non-nuclear explosives compressed the plutonium pit that served as the kernel for the atomic cascade, resulting in a runaway nuclear detonation. Gamma rays streamed out of the nuclear explosion, racing into the ten-meter-radius tunnel and interacting with everything in their path. Water instantly converted to superheated, high-pressure steam and an enormous shock wave radiated outward.

Simultaneously, electrical signals ignited other explosive charges that started the massive blast doors at the top of the tunnel to start to slam shut. If successful, the heavy doors would close just after the steam had propelled the plug and steel plate into the atmosphere at over twelve kilometers a second, but before any radioactive debris from the blast vented into the atmosphere. Timing was of the essence, and microsecond timescales mattered in balancing critical hydrodynamic phenomena.

Throughout the confines of the mile-deep tunnel—with nowhere to go but up—the superheated steam pushed against the titanium carbide plug that sealed the top of the bore hole. As if powered by a supersonic ram, the steam accelerated the plug against the steel plate.

A roiling, smoke-laden column erupted from the Nevada desert, looking like a giant Roman candle as the aeroshell accelerated up, blasting through ten kilometers in less than a second.

But within milliseconds after the initial seventy-two thousand gees imparted by the nuclear-powered steam piston, a small, asymmetric distribution of mass caused a pressure differential across the steel plate. Exceeding the von Mises yield criteria, the growing difference in pressure created a fracture line. Within eight seconds, as the supplies burst through the first one hundred kilometers of viscous Earth atmosphere, the plate cracked into seven discrete parts. The aeroshell fractured and was peeled off the plate of supplies.

The plate's center of mass still headed for Mars, but slowly breaking off into distinct chunks, the supplies now resembled more of a shotgun blast than a single bag of manna.

In the meantime, radioactive steam, wall debris, and other material not captured by the explosive doors that slammed shut at the top of the bore hole, spewed into the atmosphere. Carried by easterly winds and the jet stream, the contaminated material drifted toward the most populated parts of the US.

Senate Hearing Room, Russell Office Building

The small hearing room was crammed with people. Staffers stood against the back wall as news media crouched on the floor in a no-man's-land between the senators and the table where Heather and her deputies were seated.

The chairman pounded on the gavel. He leaned over the wooden desk that separated him and his congressional colleagues from the NNSA personnel. The murmuring silenced as the chairman looked at Heather over the top of his glasses. "This report from your own agency, Madam Administrator, indicates that more radiation was released into the atmosphere by this Thunderwell disaster than from Three Mile Island. Now what do you say about that?"

Heather straightened and leaned into her microphone. "Considering that the radiation level outside the gate to Three Mile Island was just over the amount of radiation you'd get from flying over the Rocky Mountains, a factor of ten times that amount is still less activity than the Japanese nuclear release from the 2012 tsunami."

The chairman reddened. "I can hold you in contempt, Madam Administrator."

"I meant no disrespect, Senator. You asked what I had to say about the comparison of radioactivity released from Three Mile Island. The fact is that the containment vessel at TMI did a remarkable job of doing what it was designed to do, and as such the radiation levels near the facility were relatively small. In the same manner, the blast doors at the Nevada Test Site, although not perfect, did an extraordinary job of containing a nuclear blast of over a half-megaton—and produced far, far less fallout than any aboveground test the US ever conducted."

"I wouldn't call the meltdown of a nuclear power plant benign, madam."

"Compared to a nuclear explosion, it is, Senator."

The chairman pounded his gavel. "Enough! Do you have a clue as to the severity of your actions? Regardless of how much you downplay the venting of a nuclear explosion, the fact is that radiation levels have been raised across the US, and clouds of nuclear debris are drifting eastward toward our allies and friends. You've not only put millions of people at risk by exposing them to the unknown effects of nuclear fallout, but you've singlehandedly broken the Comprehensive Test-Ban Treaty, a cornerstone of the peaceful relationships our world currently enjoys."

Heather leaned into her microphone. "You're well aware the Test-Ban Treaty has never been ratified by the Senate, Senator. And as far as the amount of fallout, anyone who flies cross-country receives more radiation damage from cosmic radiation than they ever will from the Thunderwell venting. You can haul me up before a Congressional hearing, but when you do, you can't twist facts to push a political agenda. And you certainly can't use me as a scapegoat when I'm trying to do what our nation should have been doing all along—everything we can to save human lives, the American and international astronauts who are relying on us."

The hearing room was silent. The only sound was from the low hum of the recording equipment and the thrumming of the building's ventilator. Sitting next to Heather, General Mitchell got her attention and nodded at a flush-faced staffer who hurried in from the back.

The chairman was handed a note. He nodded, then turned his attention back to Heather. His voice seemed to have brightened. "Are you through, madam?"

Heather drew in a breath. "Yes, sir, I am."

"Very well." He held up the paper given to him by his staffer. "I've just been handed a note from the NASA Administrator. It seems that radar imagery from the military's Haystack radar confirms that the Thunderwell payload of supplies are slowly dispersing, and there's a good chance that none of the supplies may reach Mars." He looked over his glasses at Heather. "As altruistic as you may be, young lady, not only have you broken the law and put countless humans at risk, but it now appears that you've done it all in vain. For your own sake, you should hope we can keep you in the US when you're hauled to court . . . and not appear in front of an international tribunal." He showed the hint of a smirk. "I understand they can be quite ruthless." He banged his gavel. "I call for a one-hour recess."

"Copy," clicked Colonel Lewis. Although it took a good eight minutes for the signal to arrive at Mars and another eight for the response to reach Earth, when appraised of the rescue attempt and the breakup of supplies, the Mars commander showed no emotion.
   Just like his wife.

It was classic Heather: short and sweet.

The memo to the Secretary of Energy read, "I respectfully submit my resignation, effective immediately, for personal reasons."

Two weeks later she entered the minimum security prison facility just north of Pleasanton, CA.

The US refused her extradition to the international tribunal.

Three months later

Data from MIT Lincoln Lab's Haystack radar showed a surprising result: chunks of steel plate that had fractured during the ascent no longer drifted apart. The slowing of the chunks had been previously noted, and at first the data was dismissed as an artifact of scintillation, the random dispersion of radar due to fluctuations of the Earth's ionosphere. But the data grew more pronounced as corrections were applied and as time passed. It took weeks to verify the readings, but when the data were released, a theory based on a gravitational asteroid-rubble model was simultaneously published in *Nature* and *Geophysical Review Letters* explaining the debris aggregation phenomenon.

According to the orbit determination and propagations performed by Caltech's Jet Propulsion Laboratory, the center-of-mass was predicted to intersect the northern Martian limb and with the supplies no longer drifting apart, there was a non-zero chance that at least a third of the supplies would impact the planet.

Brigadier General Mitchell, now assigned to the Pentagon as a special assistant to the Air Force Chief of Staff before his forced, impending retirement from active duty, wrote Heather a note with the news.

Hundreds of kilometers from the landing craft, gigantic puffs of dust peppered the Martian surface. Seismometers recorded shocks emanating from thousands of locations, as if the planet were being bombarded by a swarm of meteorites.

Sensors on board the still-orbiting mothership showed that the puffs of dust made a pattern, commensurate with the center-of-mass distribution of the supplies. A few of the supplies splashed heavily into the surface—metal tanks, scaffolding, and parts that had been packaged to withstand the rapid transit of the Martian atmosphere and burrow into the ground. Other provisions of dried food, water, and expendables had been enveloped in giant twin-hulled balloons that had inflated while being slowed by specially designed parachutes. The balloons bounced crazily across the Martian surface, rebounding or striking outcrops of rocks and quickly deflating.

Chunks of steel plate, glowing red hot from screaming through the thin atmosphere, preceded the supplies and created craters hundreds of feet across. Between the seismic data and overhead sensors, the locations of the supplies were quickly calculated.

Emotions in check, Colonel Lewis ordered two of the crew to remain with the lander and ordered the rest to accompany him on the Martian crawler to investigate one of the nearer impact sites. They didn't know how much, if any, of the supplies had survived the journey, or in what shape

anything would be, but it gave them hope that their mission might extend
well beyond what they had thought only a few minutes before.

Passed through channels to her minimum security cell, Brigadier General Mitchell's memo to Heather described what her
husband's crew had managed to find.

Sitting on the single bed in her stark cell, Heather leaned
back against the bare, white wall. She closed her eyes. If she
kept up her good behavior, she might be released by the time
her husband returned.

And there was little doubt in her mind that he would.

THE CIRCLE
Liu Cixin*
Translated by Ken Liu

For of all sad words of tongue or pen,
The saddest are these: "It might have been!"
Maud Muller (1856)

In the early years of the fifteenth century—eight decades before Columbus's voyages to the New World—the Ming Empire of China sent "treasure fleets" across the Pacific and Indian Oceans.

Commanded by the eunuch Zheng He, these fleets were composed of huge oceangoing junks, many of them with crews of a thousand men. By the hundreds, they sailed to Indonesia, Malaya, and the east coast of Africa. Some believe they may even have touched on the western coasts of North and South America.

While their ostensible purpose was to obtain treasure and initiate trade and diplomacy with distant lands, Zheng He's fleets also compelled fealty to the Chinese emperor.

The treasure fleet expeditions were ultimately halted by Xuande, grandson of the Yongle Emperor, and the Confucian bureaucrats who now controlled the government ordered the treasure fleet burned.

All that is worth knowing and having, the bureaucrats decreed, is right here in China. Sailing beyond China's coastal waters was a burden to the depleted treasury.

*In accordance with Chinese custom, Mr. Liu Cixin's name is written in the order of surname followed by given name. This story is adapted from an excerpt from Liu Cixin's novel *The Three-Body Problem*.

Within a century, European explorers, in their much smaller ships, began the colonial era that humbled China for nearly five hundred years.

If the Chinese had continued the work of their treasure fleets, China might have colonized Europe. You and I would be speaking Chinese today.

It might have been.

Liu Cixin's stylishly told tale, translated into English by Ken Liu, tells of another "might have been," also set in China, long ago.

Xianyang, capital of the state of Qin, 227 B.C.*

Jing Ke slowly unrolled the silk scroll of a map across the low, long table.

On the other side of the table, King Zheng of Qin sighed satisfactorily as he watched the mountains and rivers of his enemy being slowly revealed. Jing Ke was here to present the surrender of the King of Yan. It was easy to feel in control looking at the fields, roads, cities, and military bases drawn on a map. The real land, so vast, sometimes made him feel power-less.

When Jing Ke reached the end of the scroll, there was a metallic glint, and a sharp dagger came into view. The air in the Great Hall of the Palace seemed to solidify in an instant.

All the king's ministers stood at least thirty feet away, and in any event, had no weapons. The armed guards were even farther away, below the steps leading into the Great Hall.

*This story is set during the Warring States Period, when China was divided into several independent states: Qin, Qi, Chu, Wei, Zhao, Yan, and Han. King Zheng of Qin would eventually conquer the other six states and unify China under the Qin Dynasty. He is known more familiarly as Qin Shihuang, the First Emperor of China.

These measures were intended to improve the king's security, but now they only made the assassin's task easier.

But King Zheng remained calm. After giving the dagger a brief glance, he focused his sharp and somber eyes on Jing Ke. The king was a careful man, and he had noticed that the dagger was positioned such that the handle pointed at *him* while the tip pointed back toward the assassin.

Jing Ke picked up the dagger, and all those present in the Great Hall gasped. But King Zheng sighed in relief. He saw that Jing Ke held the dagger only by the tip of the blade, with the dull handle pointing at the king.

"Your Majesty, please kill me with this weapon." Jing Ke raised the dagger over his head and bowed. "Crown Prince Dan of Yan ordered me to make this attempt on your life, and I cannot disobey an order from my master. But my great admiration for you makes it impossible for me to carry through."

King Zheng made no move.

"Sire, all you have to do is to stab lightly. The dagger has been soaked in poison. A slight prick is enough to end my life."

King Zheng sat still and raised his hands to signal the guards rushing into the Great Hall to stop. Without changing his expression, he said, "I do not have to kill you to feel safe. Your words have convinced me that you do not have the heart of an assassin."

In a single, smooth motion, Jing Ke wrapped the fingers of his right hand around the handle of the dagger. The tip of the dagger was aimed at his own chest as though he was about to commit suicide.

"You're a learned man." King Zheng's voice was cold. "Dying now would be a waste. I'd like to have your skills and knowledge assisting my army. If you insist on dying, do so only after you've accomplished some things for me first." He waved at Jing Ke, dismissing him.

The assassin from Yan gently put the dagger down on the table, and still bowing, backed out of the Great Hall.

King Zheng stood up and walked out of the Great Hall. The sky was perfectly clear and he saw the pale white moon in the blue sky like a delicate dream left behind by the night.

"Jing Ke," he called after the assassin still descending the steps. "Does the moon appear during the day often?"

The assassin's white robe reflected the sunlight like a bright flame. "It's not unusual to have the sun and the moon appear in the sky simultaneously. On the lunar calendar, between the fourth and twelfth days of each month, it's possible to see the moon at different times during the day as long as the weather is good."

King Zheng nodded. "Oh, not an uncommon sight," he muttered to himself.

Two years later, King Zheng summoned Jing Ke to an audience.

When Jing Ke arrived outside the palace in Xianyang, he saw three officials being marched out of the Great Hall by armed guards. Having been stripped of the insignia of their rank, their heads were bare. Two of them walked between the guards with faces drained of blood while the third was so frightened that he could no longer walk and had to be carried by two soldiers. This last man continued to mumble, begging King Zheng to spare his life. Jing Ke heard him muttering the word "medicine" a few times. He guessed that the three men had been sentenced to death.

King Zheng's mood was jovial when he saw Jing Ke, as though nothing had happened. He pointed to the three departing officials and said, by way of explanation, "Xu Fu's fleet has never returned from the East Sea. Someone has to be held responsible."

Jing Ke knew that Xu Fu was an occultist who claimed that

he could go to three magical mountains on islands out in the East Sea to find the elixir of eternal life. King Zheng gave him a large fleet of ships loaded with three thousand youths and maidens and heaped with treasure, gifts for the immortals that held the secret of eternal life. But the fleet had set sail three years ago, and not a peep had been heard from him since.

King Zheng waved the sore topic away. "I hear that you've invented many wonders in the last couple years. The new bow you designed can shoot twice as far as the old models; the war chariots you devised are equipped with clever springs to ride smoothly over rough ground without having to slow down; the bridges whose construction you supervised use only half as much material, but are even stronger—I'm very pleased. How did you come up with these ideas?"

"When I follow the order of the Heavens, all things are possible."

"Xu Fu said the same thing."

"Sire, please permit me to be blunt. Xu Fu is nothing more than a fraud. Casting lots and empty meditation are not appropriate ways to understand the order of the universe. Men like him cannot understand the way the Heavens speak at all."

"What is the language of the Heavens then?"

"Mathematics. Numbers and shapes are the means by which the Heavens write to the world."

King Zheng nodded thoughtfully. "Interesting. So what are you working on now?"

"I'm always striving to understand more of the Heavens' messages for Your Majesty."

"Any progress?"

"Yes, some. At times, I even feel I'm standing right in front of the door to the treasury filled with the secrets of the universe."

"How do the Heavens tell you these mysteries? Just now,

you explained that the language of the Heavens consists of numbers and shapes."

"The circle."

Seeing that King Zheng was utterly confused, Jing Ke asked for and received permission to pick up a brush. He drew a circle on the silk cloth spread out on the low table. Though he didn't use a compass or other tools to assist him, the circle appeared to be perfect.

"Sire, other than objects made by men, have you ever seen a perfect circle in nature?"

King Zheng pondered this for a moment. "Very rarely. Once, a falcon and I stared at each other, and I noticed that its eyes were very round."

"Yes, that's true. I can also suggest as examples eggs laid by certain aquatic creatures, the intersecting plane between a dewdrop and a leaf, and so on. But I've carefully measured all of these, and none of them are perfect circles. It's the same with the circle I drew here: it may look round, but it contains errors and imperfections undetectable by the naked eye. In fact, it's an oval, not a perfect circle. I've been searching for the perfect circle for a long time, and I finally realized that it does not exist in the world below, but only in the Heavens above."

"Oh?"

"Sire, please accompany me outside the palace."

Jing Ke and King Zheng strode outside the palace. It was another beautiful day with the moon and the sun both visible in the clear sky.

"The sun and the full moon are both perfect circles," said Jing Ke as he pointed at the sky. "The Heavens placed the perfect circle—impossible to find on earth—in the sky. Not just one, but two examples, and they're the most notable features of the firmament. The meaning couldn't be clearer: the secret of the Heavens resides inside the circle."

"But the circle is the simplest of shapes. Other than a straight line, it's the least complicated figure." King Zheng turned around and returned inside the palace.

"That apparent simplicity disguises a profound mystery," Jing Ke said as he followed the king back inside. When they returned to the low table, he drew a rectangle on the silk with the brush. "Observe this rectangle, if you would. The longer dimension measures four inches, and the shorter dimension two. The Heavens speak also through this figure."

"What does it say?"

"The Heavens tell me that the ratio between the longer side and the shorter side is two."

"Are you mocking me?"

"I wouldn't dare. This is just an example of a simple message. Please observe this other figure." Jing Ke drew another rectangle. "This time, the long side is nine inches and the shorter seven. The ideas expressed by the Heavens in this figure are far richer."

"From what I can see, it's still extremely simple."

"Not so. Sire, the ratio between the longer side and the shorter side in this rectangle is 1.285714285714285714 . . . The sequence '285714' repeats forever. Thus, you can calculate the ratio to be as precise as you like, but it will never be exact. Though the message is still simple, much more meaning can be extracted from it."

"Interesting," said King Zheng.

"Next, let me show you the most mysterious shape the Heavens gifted us: the circle." Jing Ke drew a straight line through the center of the circle he had drawn earlier. "Observe that the ratio between the circumference and the diameter of a circle is an endless string of numbers beginning with 3.1415926. But it keeps on going after that, never repeating itself."

"Never?"

"Yes. Imagine a silk cloth as large as all-under-heaven. The string of numbers in the circle's ratio could be written in tiny script, each numeral no bigger than the head of a fly, all the way from here to the edge of the sky, and then coming back here, start on a new line. Continued this way, the entire cloth could be filled and there would still be no end to the numbers, and the sequence still wouldn't repeat. Your Majesty, this endless string of numbers contains the mysteries of the universe."

King Zheng's expression didn't change, but Jing Ke saw that his eyes had brightened. "Even if you obtained this number, how would you read from it the message the Heavens want to express?"

"There are many ways. For example, by treating the numbers as coordinates, it's possible to turn the numbers into new shapes and pictures."

"What will the pictures show?"

"I don't know. Maybe it will be an illustration of the enigma of the universe. Or maybe it will be an essay, or perhaps even a whole book. But the key is that we must obtain enough digits of the circular ratio first. I estimate that we must compute tens of thousands, perhaps even hundreds of thousands of digits before the meaning can be discerned. Right now, I've only computed about a hundred digits, inadequate to detect any hidden meaning."

"A hundred? That's all?"

"Sire, even so few digits have taken me more than ten years of effort. To compute the circular ratio, one must approach it by inscribing and circumscribing a circle with polygons. The mores sides in the polygons, the more precise the calculations and the more digits that can be obtained. But the complexity of the calculations increases rapidly, and progress is slow."

King Zheng continued to stare at the circle crossed by a

straight line. "Do you think you'll find the secret of eternal life in it?"

"Yes, of course." Jing Ke grew excited. "Life and death are the basic rules given to the world by the Heavens. Thus, the mystery of life and death must be contained in this message as well, including the secret of eternal life."

"Then you must compute the circular ratio. I will give you two years to compute ten thousand digits. In five more years, I need you to get to a hundred thousand digits."

"That . . . that's impossible!"

King Zheng whipped his long sleeves across the table, scattering the silk cloth and ink and brush onto the floor. "You have but to name whatever resources you need." He stared at Jing Ke coldly. "But you must complete the calculations in time."

Five days later, King Zheng called for Jing Ke again. This time, Jing Ke didn't come to the palace in Xianyang; instead, he met the royal entourage on the road as the king was touring around his domain. Right away, King Zheng asked Jing Ke for updates on the progress of the calculations.

Jing Ke bowed and spoke. "Sire, I gathered all the mathematicians who are capable of such calculations in the entire realm: they number only eight. Based on the amount of calculations necessary, even if all nine of us devote the rest of our lives to this task, we will only be able to obtain about three thousand digits of the circular ratio. In two years, the best that we can do is three hundred digits."

King Zheng nodded and indicated that Jing Ke should walk with him. They came to a granite monument about twenty feet high. A hole was drilled through the top of the monument, and a thick rope made of twisted ox hide passed through the hole to suspend the monument from a wooden platform like the weight of a giant pendulum. The smooth bottom of the monument hovered about a man's height above the ground. There were no inscriptions on the monument.

King Zheng pointed to the hanging monument and said, "Look, if you can finish the calculations in time, this will become a monument of your triumph. We will erect it on the ground and fill it with inscriptions of your many accomplishments. But if you can't finish the calculations, this will become a memento of your shame. In that case, it will also be erected on the ground, but before cutting the rope to drop it, you will have to sit below it so that it can be your tombstone."

Jing Ke lifted his eyes to gaze at the gigantic suspended stone that filled his field of vision. Against the moving clouds in the sky, the dark mass appeared oppressive.

Jing Ke turned to the king and said, "Your Majesty had spared my life once, and even if I could finish the calculations in time, it wouldn't be enough to erase the crime of my attempt on your life. I'm not afraid to die. Please give me five more days to think about this. If I still can't come up with a plan, I'll sit under the monument willingly."

Four days later, Jing Ke requested an audience with the king, which was immediately granted. Calculating the circular ratio was the most important task on the king's mind.

"From your expression, I gather that you have indeed come up with a plan." The king smiled.

Jing Ke did not answer directly. "Your Majesty, you once said that you would give me all the resources that I require. Is that still the case?"

"Of course."

"I need three million men from your army."

The number did not astonish the king. His eyebrows only lifted briefly. "What kind of soldiers?"

"The common soldiers under your command now are sufficient."

"I think you should be aware that most of the soldiers in my army are illiterate. In two years, you cannot possibly teach them complex mathematics, let alone finish the calculations."

"Sire, the skills they would need can be taught to the least intelligent solider in an hour. Please give me three soldiers so that I can demonstrate."

"Three? Only three? I can easily give you three thousand."

"I only need three."

King Zheng waved his hand and summoned three soldiers. They were all very young. Like other Qin soldiers, they moved like order-obeying machines.

"I don't know your names," Jing Ke said, tapping the shoulders of two of the soldiers. "The two of you will be responsible for number input, so I'll call you 'Input One' and 'Input Two.'" He pointed to the last soldier. "You will be responsible for number output, so I'll call you 'Output.'" He shoved the soldiers to where he wanted them to stand. "Like this. Form a triangle. Output is the apex. Input One and Input Two form the base."

"You could have just told them to stand in the Wedge Attack Formation," King Zheng said, glancing at Jing Ke with a smile.

Jing Ke took out six small flags—three white, three black—and handed them out to the three soldiers so that each held a black flag and a white flag. "White represents zero; black represents one. Good. Now, listen to me. Output, you turn around and look at Input One and Input Two. If they both raise the black flags, you raise the black flag as well. Under all other circumstances, you raise the white flag. Specifically, there are three such conditions: Input One is white and Input Two is black; Input One is black and Input Two is white; Input One and Input Two are both white."

Jing Ke repeated the instructions one more time to be sure that the three soldiers understood. Then he began to shout orders. "Let's begin! Input One and Input Two, you can raise whichever flag you want. Good. Raise! Good. Raise again! Raise!"

Input One and Input Two raised their flags three times. The first time they were black-black, the second time white-black, and the third time black-white. Output reacted correctly each time, raising the black flag once and the white one twice.

"Very good. Sire, your soldiers are very smart."

"Even an idiot would be capable of this. Tell me, what are they really doing?" King Zheng looked baffled.

"The three soldiers form a component for a calculation system, which I call an AND gate. If both numbers input into the gate are one, the result output is also one; otherwise, if one of the numbers input is zero, such as zero-one, one-zero, or zero-zero, the result output is zero." Jing Ke paused to let King Zheng digest the information.

The king said impassively, "All right. Continue."

Jing Ke turned to the three soldiers again. "Let's form another component. You, Output, if you see either Input One or Input Two raise a black flag, you raise the black flag. There are three situations where that will be true: black-black, white-black, black-white. When it's white-white, you raise the white flag. Understand? Good lad, you're really clever. You're the key to the correct functioning of the gate. Work hard, and you will be rewarded! Let's begin operation. Raise! Good, raise again! Raise again! Perfect. Your Majesty, this component is called an OR gate. Whenever one of the two inputs is one, the output is also one."

Then, Jing Ke used the three soldiers to form what he called a NAND gate, a NOR gate, an XOR-gate, an XNOR-gate, and a tristate gate. Finally, using only two soldiers, he made the simplest gate, a NOT gate: Output always raised the flag that was opposite in color from the one raised by Input.

Jing Ke bowed to the Emperor. "All calculating components have been demonstrated. This is the scope of the skills that the three million soldiers must learn."

"How can you perform complex calculations using such simple, childish tricks?" King Zheng's face was full of distrust.

"Great King, the complexity in everything in the universe is built up from the simplest components. Similarly, an immense number of simple components, when structured together appropriately, can generate extremely complex capabilities. Three million soldiers can form a million of these gates I've just demonstrated, and these gates can be put together into a whole formation capable of any complex calculation. I call my invention a calculating formation."

"I still don't understand how the calculations will be carried out."

"The precise process is complicated. If Your Majesty continues to be interested, I can explain in detail later. For now, it's enough to know that the operation of the calculating formation is based on a novel method of thinking about and writing down numbers. In this method, only two numerals, zero and one, corresponding to the white and black flags, are needed. But this new method can use zero and one to represent any number, and this allows the calculating formation to use a large number of simple components to collectively carry out high-speed calculations."

"Three million is almost the entirety of my army, but I will give them to you." King Zheng sighed meaningfully. "Hurry. I'm feeling old."

A year passed.

It was another beautiful day with the sun and the moon

both out. King Zheng and Jing Ke stood together on a high stone dais, with the king's numerous ministers in rows behind them. Below them, a magnificent phalanx of three million Qin soldiers stood arrayed on the ground, the entire formation a square three miles* on each side. Lit by the freshly risen sun, the phalanx remained still like a giant carpet made of three million terra-cotta warriors. But when a flock of birds wandered above the phalanx, the birds immediately felt the potential for death from below and scattered anxiously.

Jing Ke said, "Your Majesty, your army is truly matchless. In an extremely short time, we have completed such complex training."

King Zheng held on to the hilt of his long sword. "Even though the whole is complex, what each soldier must do is very simple. Compared to the military training they went through, this is nothing."

"Then, Your Majesty, please give the great order!" Jing Ke's voice trembled with excitement.

King Zheng nodded. A guard ran over, grabbed the hilt of the king's sword, and stepped backward. The bronze sword was so long that it was impossible for the king to pull it out of the scabbard without help. The guard knelt and presented the sword to the king, who lifted the sword to the sky and shouted: "Calculating Formation!"

Battle drums began to beat, and four giant bronze cauldrons at the corners of the stone dais came to life simultaneously with roaring flames. A group of soldiers standing at the edge of the dais facing the phalanx chanted in unison: "Calculating Formation . . ."

---

*For the benefit of English readers, Chinese measurement units (such as *li, zhang, chi, cun*) throughout the text have been translated and converted into approximate English equivalents.

On the ground below, colors in the phalanx began to shift and move. Complicated and detailed circuit patterns appeared and gradually filled the entire formation. Ten minutes later, the army had rearranged itself into a nine-square-mile calculating formation.

Jing Ke pointed to the formation and began to explain. "Your Majesty, we have named this formation Qin I. Look, there in the center is the central processing formation, the core component of the calculating formation, made up of the best divisions of your army. By referencing this diagram, you can see within it the adding formation, quick storage formation, and stack memory formation. Around it, the part that looks highly regular is the memory formation. When we built this part, we found that we didn't have enough soldiers. But luckily, the work done by the elements in this component is the simplest, so we trained each soldier to hold more colored flags. Each man can now complete the work that initially required twenty men. This allowed us to increase the memory capacity to meet the minimum requirements for running the calculating procedure for the circular ratio. Observe also the open passage that runs through the entire formation and the light cavalry waiting for orders in the passage: that's the system's main communication line, responsible for transmitting information between the components of the whole system."

Two soldiers brought over a large scroll, tall as a man, and spread it open before King Zheng. As the scroll reached the end, everyone present remembered the scene in the palace a few years ago, and they all held their breath. But the imaginary dagger did not appear. Before them was only a large sheet of thin silk filled with symbols, each the size of a fly's head. Packed so densely, the symbols were as dazzling to behold as the calculating formation on the ground below.

"Your Majesty, these are the orders in the procedure I developed for calculating the circular ratio. Please look here"—Jing Ke pointed to the calculating formation below—"the soldiers standing ready form what I call the 'hardware.' What's on this cloth is what I call the 'software,' the soul of the calculating formation. The relationship between hardware and software is like that between the *guqin* zither and sheet music."

King Zheng nodded. "Good. Begin."

Jing Ke lifted both hands above his head and solemnly chanted: "As ordered by the Great King, initiate the calculating formation! System self-test!"

A row of soldiers standing halfway down the face of the stone dais repeated the order using flag signals. In a moment, the phalanx of three million men seemed to turn into a lake filled with sparkling lights as millions of tiny flags waved.

"Self-test complete! Begin initialization sequence! Load calculation procedure!"

Below, the light cavalry on the main communication line that passed through the entire calculating formation began to ride back and forth swiftly. The main passage soon turned into a turbulent river. Along the way, the river fed into numerous thin tributaries, infiltrating all the modular subformations. Soon, the ripples of black and white flags coalesced into surging waves that filled the entire phalanx. The central processing formation area was the most tumultuous, like tinder set on fire.

Suddenly, as though the fuel had been exhausted, the movements in the central processing formation slackened and eventually stopped. Starting with the central processing formation in the center, the stillness spread in every direction like a lake being frozen over. Finally, the entire calculating formation came to a stop, with only a few scattered components flashing life-lessly in infinite loops.

"System lockup!" a signal officer called out. Shortly after, the reason for the malfunction was determined: there was an error with the operation of one of the gates in the central pro-cessing formation's status storage unit.

"Restart system!" Jing Ke ordered confidently.

"Not yet," King Zheng said, still holding on to his sword. "Replace the malfunctioning gate and behead all the soldiers who made up that gate. In the future, any other malfunctions will be dealt with the same way."

A few riders dashed into the phalanx with their swords drawn. They killed the three unfortunate soldiers and replaced them with new men. From the vantage point of the dais, three eye-catching pools of blood appeared in the middle of the central processing formation.

Jing Ke gave the order to restart the system. This time, it went very smoothly. Ten minutes later, the soldiers were carry-ing out the circular ratio calculating procedure. As the pha-lanx rippled with flag signals, the calculating formation settled into the long computation.

"This is really interesting," King Zheng said, pointing to the spectacular mass calculating phalanx. "Each individual's behavior is so simple, yet together, they can produce such complex intelligence."

"Great King, this is just the mechanical operation of a ma-chine, not intelligence. Each of these lowly individuals is just a zero. Only when someone like you is added to the front as a one is the whole endowed with meaning." Jing Ke's smile was ingratiating.

"How long would it take to calculate ten thousand digits of the circular ratio?" King Zheng asked.

"About ten months. Maybe even sooner if things go right."

General Wang Jian* stepped forward. "Your Majesty, I must urge caution. Even in regular military operations, it's extremely dangerous to concentrate so much of our forces in an open area like this. Moreover, the three million soldiers in this phalanx are unarmed, carrying only signal flags. The calculating formation is not intended for battle and will be extremely vulnerable if attacked. Even under normal conditions, to effectuate an orderly retreat of this many men packed so tightly would take most of a day. If they were attacked, retreat would be impossible. Sire, this calculating formation will appear in the eyes of our enemies as meat placed on a cutting board."

King Zheng did not reply, but turned his gaze to Jing Ke. The latter bowed and said, "General Wang is absolutely right. You must be cautious when deciding whether to pursue this calculation."

Then Jing Ke did something bold and unprecedented: he lifted his eyes and locked gazes with King Zheng. The king immediately understood the meaning in that gaze: *All your accomplishments so far are like zeroes; only with the addition of eternal life for yourself, a one, can all of those become meaningful.*

"General Wang, you're overly concerned." King Zheng whipped his sleeves contemptuously. "The states of Han, Wei, Zhao, and Chu have all been conquered. The only two remaining states, Yan and Qi, are led by foolish kings who have exhausted their people. They're on the verge of total collapse and pose no threat. Given the way things are going, by the time the circular ratio calculation is complete, those two states may already have fallen apart on their own and surrendered to the Great State of Qin. Of course, I appreciate the general's

---

*One of the four great generals of King Zheng's campaigns against the other six states. The historical Wang Jian was responsible for the destruction of the states of Yan (where Jing Ke was from), Zhao, and Chu.

caution. I suggest that we form a line of scouts at some distance from the calculating formation and step up our surveillance of the movements of the Yan and Qi armies. This way, we will be secure." He lifted his long sword toward the sky and solemnly declared, "The calculations must be finished. I have decided that it must be so."

The calculating formation ran smoothly for a month, and the results were even better than expected. Already, more than two thousand digits of the circular ratio had been computed, and as the soldiers in the formation grew used to the work and Jing Ke further refined the calculating procedure, speed in the future would be even faster. The estimate was that only three more years would be needed to reach the target of a hundred thousand digits.

The morning of the forty-fifth day after the start of the calculations was foggy. It was impossible to see the calculating formation, enveloped in mist, from the dais. Soldiers in the formation could see no farther than about five men.

But the calculating formation's operation was designed to be unaffected by the fog and continued. Shouted orders and the hoofbeats of the light cavalry on the main communication line echoed in the haze.

But those soldiers in the north of the calculating formation heard something else. At first, the noise came intermittently and seemed illusory, but soon, the noise grew louder and formed a continuous boom, like thunder coming from the depths of the fog.

The noise came from the hoofs of thousands of horses. A powerful division of cavalry approached the calculating formation from the north, and the banner of the state of Yan flew at their head. The riders moved slowly, forcing their horses to maintain ranks. They knew that they had plenty of time.

Only when the riders were about a third of a mile from the edge of the calculating formation did they begin the charge. By the time the vanguard of the cavalry had torn into the calculating formation, the Qin soldiers didn't even get a proper look at their enemies. In this initial charge, tens of thousands of Qin soldiers died just from being trampled under the hoofs of the attacking riders.

What followed was not a battle at all, but a massacre. Before the battle, the Yan commanders already knew that they would not meet with meaningful resistance. In order to increase the efficiency of the slaughter, the riders abandoned the traditional cavalry weapons, long-handled lances and halberds, and instead equipped themselves with swords and morning stars. The several hundred thousand Yan heavy cavalry became a death-dealing cloud, and wherever they rode, the bodies of Qin soldiers carpeted the land.

In order to avoid giving warning to the core of the calculating formation, the Yan riders killed in silence, as though they were machines, not men. But the screams of the dying Qin soldiers, whether cut down or trampled, spread far and wide in the thick fog.

However, all of the Qin soldiers in the calculating formation had been trained under threat of death to ignore outside interference and to devote themselves single-mindedly to the simple task of acting as calculating components. Combined with the disguise provided by the thick fog, the result was that most of the calculating formation did not realize the northern edge of the formation was already under attack. As the death-dealing region slowly and orderly ate through the formation, turning it into piles of corpses strewn over blood-soaked, muddy ground, the rest of the formation continued to calculate as before, even though more and more errors began to plague the system.

Behind the first wave of cavalry, more than a hundred thousand Yan archers loosened volleys from their longbows, aimed at the heart of the calculating formation. In a few moments, millions of arrows fell like a thunderstorm, and almost every arrow found a target.

Only then did the calculating formation start to fall apart. At the same time, information of the enemy attack began to spread, increasing the chaos. The light cavalry on the main communication line carried reports of the sudden attack, but as the situation deteriorated, the main passage became blocked, and the panicked riders began to trample through the densely packed phalanx. Countless Qin soldiers thus died under the hoofs of friendly forces.

On the eastern, southern, and western edges of the calculating formation, which weren't under attack, Qin soldiers began to retreat without any semblance of order. Amidst the utter lack of information and broken chain of command, the retreat was slow and confused. The calculating formation, now purposeless, became like a thick, concentrated bubble of ink that refused to dissolve in water, with only wispy tendrils leaving at the edges.

Those Qin soldiers running toward the east were soon stopped by the disciplined ranks of the Qi army. Instead of charging, the Qi commanders ordered the infantry and cavalry to form impregnable defensive lines to wait for the escaping Qin soldiers to enter the trap before surrounding them and beginning the slaughter.

The only direction left for the remainder of the hopeless Qin army, now without any will to fight, was toward the southwest. Hundreds of thousands of unarmed men poured over the plains like a dirty flood. But they soon encountered a third enemy force: unlike the disciplined armies from Yan and Qi, this third force consisted of the ferocious riders of the Huns. They tore into a Qin army like wolves into a flock of sheep and quickly overwhelmed them.

The slaughter continued until noon, when the strong breeze from the west lifted the fog, and the wide expanse of the battlefield was exposed to the glare of the midday sun.

The Yan, Qi, and Hun armies had combined in multiple places, surrounding what remained of the Qin army in small pockets. The cavalry of the three armies continued to charge the Qin soldiers, leaving the wounded and the few escapees to be mopped up by the infantry. Oxen formations, urged on by fire, and catapults were also put into operation to kill the remaining Qin men even more efficiently.

By evening, the sorrowful notes of battle horns echoed over a field covered with bodies and crisscrossed by rivulets of blood. The final survivors of the Qin army were now surrounded in three shrinking pockets.

The night that followed had a full moon. The pure, cold moon floated impassively over the slaughter below, bathing the mountains of corpses and seas of blood in its calm, liquid light. The killing continued throughout the night and wasn't over until the next morning.

The army of the Qin Empire was entirely eliminated.

One month later, the allied forces of Qi and Yan entered Xianyang and captured King Zheng. The Qin Empire was over.

The day selected for the execution of King Zheng was another day when the sun and the moon appeared together. The moon floated in the azure sky like a snowflake.

The monument that had been intended for Jing Ke still

hung in the air. King Zheng sat below it, waiting for the Yan executioner to cut the ox hide rope.

Jing Ke walked out of the crowd observing the execution, still dressed all in white. He came before King Zheng and bowed. "Your Majesty."

"In your heart, you've always remained a Yan assassin," the king said. He did not look up at Jing Ke.

"Yes. But I didn't want to just kill you. I also needed to eliminate your army. If I had succeeded a few years ago in killing you, Qin would have remained powerful. Advised by brilliant strategists and commanded by veteran commanders, the million-strong Qin army would still have posed an unstoppable threat to Yan."

"How could you have sent so many men so close to my army without my notice?" King Zheng asked the last question of his life.

"During the year when the calculating formation was being trained and operating, Yan and Qi focused on digging tunnels. Each tunnel was many miles long and wide enough to allow cavalry to pass through. It was my idea to use these tunnels to allow the allies to bypass your sentries and appear suddenly near the defenseless calculating formation."

King Zheng nodded and said nothing more. He closed his eyes to wait to die. The supervising official gave the order and an executioner began to climb up the platform, a knife held between his teeth.

King Zheng heard movements next to him. He opened his eyes and saw that Jing Ke was sitting next to him.

"Your Majesty, we'll die together. When the heavy stone falls, it will become a monument to both of us. Our blood and flesh will mix together. Perhaps this will give you some comfort."

"What is the point of this?" King Zheng asked coldly.

"It's not that I want to die. The King of Yan has ordered my execution."

A smile quickly appeared on King Zheng's face and disappeared just as quickly, like a passing breeze. "You have accomplished so much for Yan that your name is praised more than the king's. He fears your ambition. This result is expected."

"That is indeed one reason, but not the main one. I also advised the King of Yan to build Yan's own calculating formation. This gave him the excuse he needed to kill me."

King Zheng turned to gaze at Jing Ke. The surprise in the king's eyes was genuine.

"I don't care if you believe me. My advice was given with the hope of strengthening Yan. It's true that the calculating formation was a stratagem I came up with to destroy Qin by taking advantage of your obsession with eternal life. But it's also a genuinely great invention. Through its calculating power, we can understand the language of mathematics, to divine the mysteries of the universe. It could have opened a new era."

The executioner had reached the top of the platform and stood in front of the rope holding up the stone monument, waiting for the final order as he held the knife in his hand.

In the distance, under a bright baldachin, the King of Yan waved his hand in assent. The supervising official shouted the order to carry out the sentence.

Jing Ke suddenly opened his eyes wide as though awakening from a dream. "I've got it! The calculating formation doesn't have to rely on the army, not even people. All those gates—AND, NOT, NAND, NOR, and so on—can be made from mechanical components. These components can be made very small, and when they're put together they will be a mechanical calculating formation! No, it shouldn't be called a calculating formation at all, but a calculating machine!

Listen to me, King, wait! The calculating machine! The calculating machine!" Jing Ke shouted at the King of Yan in the distance.

The executioner cut the rope.

"The calculating machine!" Jing Ke shouted the three words with the last of this breath.

As the giant stone fell, in that moment when its massive shadow blotted out everything in the world, King Zheng felt the end of his life. But in the eyes of Jing Ke, a faint ray of light heralding the beginning of a new era was extinguished.

OLD TIMER'S GAME
Ben Bova

Mathematicians and statisticians love baseball. It has the most detailed numbers of any sport.

The nature of the game lends itself easily to record keeping and statistics: batting average, RBI, home runs, ERA, strikeouts, stolen bases. By some counts, there are well over a hundred statistics commonly and uncommonly used in baseball. The stats are diligently tracked by fans, pundits, and players alike, but for the players there is one number that many would rather not think about.

Their age.

America's pastime has changed much since the early semipro baseball clubs of the 1860s. "Old Timer's Game" takes us to a near future in which the players themselves may change as well.

"He's making a travesty of the game!"

White-haired Alistair Bragg was quivering with righteous wrath as he leveled a trembling finger at Vic Caruso. I felt sorry for Vic despite his huge size, or maybe because of it. He was sitting all alone up there before the panel of judges. I thought of Gulliver, giant-sized compared to the puny little Lilliputians. But tied hand and foot, helpless.

This hearing was a reporter's dream, the kind of news-making opportunity that comes along maybe once in a decade. Or less.

I sat at the news media table, elbow to elbow with the big,

popular TV commentators and slick-haired pundits. The guys who talk like they know everything about baseball, while all they really know is what working stiffs like me put up on their teleprompters.

Old man Bragg was a shrimp, but a powerful figure in the baseball world. He owned the Cleveland Indians, who'd won the American League pennant, but then lost the World Series to the Dodgers in four straight.

Bragg wore a dark gray business suit and a bright red tie. To the unsophisticated eye he looked a little like an overweight one of Santa's elves: short, round, his face a little bloated. But whereas an elf would be cheerful and dancing-eyed, Bragg radiated barely concealed fury.

"He's turning baseball into a freak show!" Bragg accused, still jabbing his finger in Caruso's direction. "A freak show!"

Vic Caruso had been the first-string catcher for the Oakland Athletics, one of the best damn hitters in the league, and a solid rock behind the plate with a cannon for an arm. But now he looked like an oversized boy, kind of confused by all the fuss that was being made about him. He was wearing a tan sports jacket and a white shirt with a loosely knotted green tie that seemed six inches too short. In fact, his shirt, jacket, and brown slacks all appeared too small to contain his massive frame; it looked as if he would burst out of his clothes any minute.

Aside from his ill-fitting ensemble, Vic didn't look like a freak. He was a big man, true enough, tall and broad in the shoulders. His face was far from handsome: his nose was larger than it should have been, and the corners of his innocent blue eyes were crinkled from long years on sunny baseball diamonds.

He looked hurt, betrayed, as if he were the injured party instead of the accused.

The hearing wasn't a trial, exactly. The three solemn-faced men sitting behind the long table up in the front of the room weren't really judges. They were the commissioner of baseball and the heads of the National and American Leagues, about as much baseball brass (and ego) as you could fit into one room.

The issue before them would determine the future of America's Pastime.

Bragg had worked himself into a fine, red-faced fury. He had opposed every change in the game he'd ever heard of, always complaining that any change in baseball would make a travesty of the game. If he had his way, there'd be no interleague play, no designated hitter, no night baseball, and no player's union. Especially that last one. The word around the ballyard was that Bragg bled blood for every nickel he had to pay his players.

"It started with steroids, back in the nineties," he said, ostensibly to the commissioner and the two league presidents. But he was looking at the jam-packed rows of onlookers, and us news reporters, and especially at the banks of television cameras that were focused on his perspiring face.

"Steroids threatened to make a travesty of the game," said Bragg, repeating his favorite phrase. "We moved heaven and earth to drive them out of the game. Suspended players who used 'em, expunged their records, prohibited them from entering the Hall of Fame."

Caruso shifted uncomfortably in his wooden chair, making it squeak and groan as if it might collapse beneath his weight.

"Then they started using protein enhancers, natural supplements that were undetectable by normal drug screenings. All of a sudden little shortstops from Nicaragua were hitting tape-measure home runs!"

The commissioner, a grave-faced, white-haired man of great dignity, interrupted Bragg's tirade. "We are all aware of the supplements. I believe attendance figures approximately doubled when batting averages climbed so steeply."

Undeterred, Bragg went on, "So the pitchers started taking stuff to prevent joint problems. No more rotator cuff injuries; no more Tommy John surgeries. When McGilmore went twenty-six and oh we—"

"Wait a minute," the National League president said. He was a round butterball, but his moon-shaped face somehow looked menacing because of the dark stubble across his jaw. Made him look like a Mafia enforcer. "Isn't Tommy John surgery a form of artificial enhancement? The kind of thing you're accusing Vic Caruso of?"

Bragg shot back, "Surgery to correct an injury is one thing. Surgery and other treatments to turn a normal human body into a kind of superman—that's unacceptable!"

"But the fans seem to love it," said the American League president, obviously thinking about the previous year's record-breaking attendance figures.

"I'm talking about protecting the purity of the game," Bragg insisted. "If we don't act now, we'll wind up with a bunch of half-robot freaks on the field instead of human beings!"

The commissioner nodded. "We wouldn't want that," he said, looking directly at Caruso.

"We've got to make an example of this . . . this . . . freak," Bragg demanded. "Otherwise the game's going to be warped beyond recognition!"

The audience murmured. The cameras turned to Caruso, who looked uncomfortable, embarrassed, but not ashamed.

The commissioner silenced the audience's mutterings with a stern look.

"I think we should hear Mr. Caruso's story from his own

lips," he said. "After all, his career—his very livelihood—is at stake here."

"What's at stake here," Bragg countered, "is the future of Major League Baseball."

The commissioner nodded, but said, "Mr. Bragg, you are excused. Mr. Caruso, please take the witness chair."

Obviously uncertain of himself, Vic Caruso got slowly to his feet and stepped toward the witness chair. Despite his size he was light on his feet, almost like a dancer. He passed Bragg, who was on his way back to the front row of benches. I had to laugh: it looked like the Washington Monument going past a bowling ball.

Vic settled himself gingerly into the wooden witness chair, off to one side of the judges, and stared at them, as if he was waiting for their verdict.

"Well, Mr. Caruso," said the commissioner, "what do you have to say for yourself?"

"About what, sir?"

The audience tittered. They thought they were watching a big, brainless ox who was going to make a fool of himself.

The commissioner's brows knit. "Why, about the accusations Mr. Bragg has leveled against you. About the fact that you— and other ballplayers, as well—have artificially enhanced your bodies and thereby gained an unfair advantage over the other players who have not partaken of such enhancements."

"Oh, that," said Vic.

Guffaws burst out from the crowd.

"Yes, that," the commissioner said, glaring the audience into silence. "Tell us what you've done and why you did it."

Vic squirmed on the chair. He looked as if he'd rather be a thousand miles away or maybe roasting over hot coals. But then he sucked in a deep breath and started talking.

*   *   *

It all started with my left knee—he said. On my thirtieth birthday, at that. The big three-oh.

I'd been catching for the A's for four years, hitting good enough to always be fifth or sixth in the batting order, but the knee was slowing me up so bad the Skipper was shaking his head every time he looked my way.

We were playing an interleague game against the Phillies. You know what roughnecks they are. In the sixth inning they got men on first and third, and their batter pops a fly to short right field. Runner on third tags up, I block the plate. When he slammed into me I felt the knee pop. Hurt like hell—I mean heck—but I didn't say anything. The runner was out, the inning was over, so I walked back to the dugout, trying not to limp.

Well, anyway, we lost the game 4–3. I was in the whirlpool soaking the knee when the Skipper sticks his ugly little face out of his office door and calls, "Hoss, get yourself in here, will you?"

The other guys in the locker room were already looking pretty glum. Now they all stared at me for a second, then they all turned the other way. None of them wanted to catch my eye. They all knew what was coming. Me, too.

So I wrap a towel around my gut and walk to the Skipper's office, leaving wet footprints on the carpeting.

"I'm gonna hafta rest you for a while," the Skipper says, even before I can sit down in the chair in front of his desk. The hot seat, we always called it.

"I don't need a rest."

"Your damned knee does. Look at it: it's swollen like a watermelon." The Skipper is a little guy, kind of shriveled up like a prune. Never played a day of big-league ball in his life but he's managed us into the playoffs three straight seasons.

"My knee's OK. The swelling's going down already."

"It's affecting your throwing."

I started to say something, but nothing came out of my mouth. In the fifth inning I couldn't quite reach a foul pop-up, and on the next pitch the guy homers. Then, in the eighth I was slow getting up and throwing to second. The stolen base put a guy in scoring position and a bloop single scored him and that's how the Phillies beat us.

"It's a tough position, Hoss," says the Boss, not looking me in the eye. "Catching beats hell outta the knees."

"I can play, for chrissakes," I said. "It don't hurt that much."

"You're gonna sit out a few games. And see an orthopedics doc."

So I go to the team's doctor, who sends me to an orthopedics guy, who makes me get MRI scans and X-rays and whatnot, then tells me I need surgery.

"You mean I'll be out for the rest of the year?"

"The season's almost over," he says, like the last twenty games of the year don't mean anything.

I try to tough it out, but the knee keeps swelling so bad I can hardly walk, let alone play ball. I mean, I never was a speed demon, but now the shortstop and third baseman are playing me on the outfield grass, for crying out loud.

By the time the season finally ends I'm on crutches and I can imagine what my next salary negotiation is going to be like. It's my option year, too. My agent wouldn't even look me in the eye.

"Mr. Caruso," interrupted the commissioner. "Could you concentrate on the medical enhancements you obtained and skip the small talk, please?"

Oh, sure—Vic said. I went to the surgeon that they picked out for me and he told me I needed a total knee replacement.

"An artificial knee?" I asked the guy.

He seemed happy about it. With a big smile he tells me by the time spring training starts, I'll be walking as good as new.

Walking and playing ball are two different things, I say to myself. But I go through with the surgery, and the rehab, and sure enough, by the time spring training starts I'm doing OK.

But OK isn't good enough. Like I said, catching beats the hell out of your knees, and I'm slower than I should be. I complain to the surgeon and he tells me I ought to see this specialist, a stem cell doctor.

I don't know stem cells from artichokes, but Dr. Trurow turns out to be a really good-looking blonde from Sweden and she explains that stem cells can help my knee to recover from the surgery.

"They're your own cells," she explains. "We simply encourage them to get your knee to work better."

I start the regular season as the designated hitter. Danny Daniels is behind the plate, and boy is he happy about it. But during our first home stand I go to Doc Trurow, let her stick a needle in me and draw out some cells, then a week later she sticks them back in me.

And my knee starts to feel a lot better. Not all at once; it took a couple of weeks. But one night game against the Orioles, with their infielders playing so deep it's like they got seven outfielders on the grass, I drop a bunt down the third baseline and beat it out easy.

The crowd loves it. The score's tied at 2–2, I'm on first with nobody out, so I take off for second. The Orioles' catcher, he's a rookie and he's so surprised he double clutches before throwing the ball to second. I make it easy.

By Memorial Day I'm behind the plate again, the team's number-one catcher. Daniels is moping in the dugout, but hey, you know, that's baseball. The Skipper's even moved me up to the three slot in the batting order, I'm so fast on my feet.

One day in the clubhouse, though, Daniels comes up to me and says, "You don't remember me, do you?"

"You're Danny Daniels, you're hitting two-eighty-two, seven homers, thirty-one ribbies," I tell him.

"That's not what I mean." Danny's a decent kid, good prospect. He thought he had the catching slot nailed until my stem cells started working.

"So whattaya mean?" I ask him.

"You talked at my high school when I was a fat little kid," Danny said. "All the other kids bullied me, but you told me to stand up to 'em and make the best of myself."

Suddenly it clicks in my mind. "You were that fat little kid with the bad acne?"

He laughs. He's so good-looking now the girls mob him after the game.

"Yeah. That was me. I started playing baseball after you talked to me. I wanted to be just like you."

I never thought of myself as a role model. I get kind of embarrassed. All I can think of to say is, "Well, you did great. You made the Bigs."

"Yeah," he says, kind of funny. "I'm a second-string catcher."

Bragg interrupts, "I don't see what all this twaddle has to do with the issue at hand."

The commissioner, who looked interested in Vic's story, makes a grumbly face, but he sighs and says, "Mr. Caruso, while we appreciate your description of the human aspects of the case, please stick to the facts and eschew the human story."

Vic makes a puzzled frown over that word "eschew," but he nods and picks up his thread again.

OK—Vic says. I'm doing great until my other knee starts aching. I'm going on thirty-two and the aches and pains are what you get. But I figure, if the stem cell treatments helped my one knee so much, how about trying them on my other knee?

Besides, that Swedish doctor was really good-looking and it was an excuse to see her again.

So I got the other knee treated and before the season's over I've got twelve stolen bases and third basemen are playing me inside the bag to protect against bunts. Makes it easier for me to slam the ball past them. I was leading the league in batting average and women were hanging around the clubhouse entrance after games just to see me!

But then I got beaned.

It wasn't really a beaning, not like I got hit on the head. McGilmore was pitching and I had a single and a triple in two at-bats and he was pretty sore about it. He always was a mean bas—a mean sonofagun. So he whips a sidearm fast ball at me, hard as he can throw. It's inside and I try to spin away from it but it catches me in my ribs. I never felt such pain. Broke two of my ribs and one of 'em punctured my left lung. I was coughing up blood when they carried me off the field.

So I spent my thirty-second birthday in the hospital, feeling miserable. But the second or third day there, Doc Trurow comes to visit me, and it was like the sun coming out from behind a cloud. She's really pretty, and her smile lit up the whole damned hospital.

Stem cells again. This time they helped my ribs heal and even repaired the rip in my lung. I got back to the team before the end of the season and ran off a four-fifty average on our last home stand. Better yet, Doc Trurow was at every game, sitting right behind our dugout.

So on the last day of the season, I worked up the nerve to ask her out for dinner. And she says yes! Her first name is Olga and we had a great evening together, even though the team finished only in third place.

* * *

"Mr. Caruso," the commissioner intoned. "Kindly stick to the facts of your physical enhancements."

Vic looked kind of sheepish and he nodded his head and mumbled, "Yessir."

Instead of going back to Michigan for the off season, I stayed in Oakland and dated Olga a lot. I even started thinking about marriage, but I didn't have the nerve to pop the question—

"Mr. Caruso!"

Well, it's important—Vic said to the commissioner. Olga told me how stem cell treatments could improve my eyesight and make my reflexes sharper. There wasn't anything in the rules against it, and it was my own cells, not some drug or steroids or anything like that. So I let her jab me here and there and damned if I didn't feel better. Besides, I worried that if I said no to her she'd stop dating me and I didn't want to stop seeing her.

So this goes on for a couple seasons and all of a sudden I'm coming up on my thirty-fifth birthday and I can see the big four-oh heading down the road for me. I started to worry about my career ending, even though I was hitting three-twenty-something and doing OK behind the plate. News guys started calling me Iron Man, no kidding.

Danny Daniels looks piss . . . uh, unhappy, but he doesn't say anything and I figure, what the hell, so he has to sit on the bench for another season or two. But the front office trades him to the Yankees, so it's OK. I don't have to see his sour puss in the clubhouse anymore.

Meanwhile we're in the playoffs again and we've got a good chance to take the pennant.

Then I got hurt again. Dancing. No kidding, Olga and I were dancing and I guess I was feeling pretty damned frisky and I tried a fancy move I'd seen in an old Fred Astaire movie and I slipped and went down on my face. Never been so embarrassed in my whole life.

I turned from Vic to take a peek at the commissioner's face. Instead of interrupting the big lug, the commissioner was listening hard, his eyes focused on Vic, totally intent on the story that was unfolding.

Something in my hip went blooey—Vic went on. I got to my feet OK, but the hip felt stiff. And the stiffness didn't go away. It got worse. When I told Olga about it she toted me over to the medical center for a whole lot of tests.

It was nothing serious, the docs decided. The hip would be all right in a couple of months. Just needed rest. And time.

But spring training was due to start in a few weeks and I needed to be able to get around OK, not stiff like Frankenstein's monster.

"It's just a factor of your age," says the therapist Olga sent me to.

"I'm only thirty-six," I said.

"Maybe so," says the doc, "but your body's taken a beating over the years. It's catching up with you. You're going to be old before your time, physically."

I felt pretty low. But when I tell Olga about what the doc said, she says, "Telomerase."

"Telo-what?" I ask her.

She tells me this telomerase stuff can reverse aging. In mice, at least. They inject the stuff in old, creaky, diabetic lab mice and the little buggers get young and frisky again and their diabetes goes away.

I don't have diabetes, but I figure if the stuff makes me feel younger then why not try it? Olga tells me that some movie stars and politicians have used it, in secret, and it helped them stay young. A couple of TV news people, too.

So I start taking telomerase injections and by the time I hit the big four-oh I'm still hitting over three hundred and catching more than a hundred games a year. And other guys are starting to use stem cells and telomerase and everything else they can get their hands on. Even Danny Daniels is using, from what I heard.

"That's what I've been telling you!" Bragg yells, jumping up from his seat on the front row of benches. "They're making a travesty of the game!"

The commissioner frowns at him and Bragg sits back down. Vic Caruso stares at him, looking puzzled.

"Look," Vic says, "I didn't do anything that's prohibited by the rules."

Bragg seems staggered that Vic can pronounce "prohibited" correctly.

The commissioner says, "The point of this hearing is to decide if the rules should be amended."

"You make stem cells and telomerase and such illegal," Vic says, "and half the players in the league'll have to quit baseball."

"But is it fair to the players who don't use such treatments for you to be so . . . so . . . extraordinary?" asks the commissioner.

Vic shakes his head. "I'm not extraordinary. I'm not a superman. I'm just *young*. I'm not better than I was when I was twenty, but I'm just about as good. What's wrong with that?"

The commissioner doesn't answer. He just shakes his head

and glances at the two league presidents, sitting beside him. Neither of them has an answer, either.

But Bragg does. "Do you realize what this means?" he yells at the commissioner. Pointing at Vic again, he says, "This man will be playing until he's fifty! Maybe longer! How are we going to bring young players into the league if the veterans are using these treatments to keep themselves young? We'll have whole teams made up of seventy-year-olds, for god's sake!"

"Seventy-year-olds who play like twenty-year-olds," the commissioner mutters.

"Seventy-year-olds who'll demand salary increases every year," Bragg snaps back at him.

And suddenly it all becomes clear. Bragg's not worrying about the purity of the game. The revelations in the news haven't hurt box office receipts: attendance has been booming. But veteran players demand a lot more money than rookies—and get it. Bragg's bitching about his pocketbook!

The commissioner looks at the two league presidents again, but they still have nothing to say. They avoid looking at Bragg, though.

To Vic, the commissioner says, in a kindly, almost grandfatherly way, "Mr. Caruso, thank you for your frank and honest testimony. You've given us a lot to think about. You may step down now."

Vic gets up from the chair like a mountain rising. As he heads for the front bench, though, the commissioner says, "By the way, just to satisfy my personal curiosity, did you and Dr. Trurow get married?"

"We're gonna do that on Christmas day," says Vic. "In Stockholm, that's her hometown and her family and all her friends'll be there."

The commissioner smiles. "Congratulations."

"We'll send you an invitation," Vic says, smiling back.

Glancing at Bragg, the commissioner says, "I'm afraid it wouldn't be appropriate for me to attend your wedding, Mr. Caruso. But I wish you and your bride much happiness."

So that's how it happened. The commissioner and the league presidents and all the owners—including Bragg—put their heads together and came up with the Big Change.

Major League Baseball imposed an age limit on players. Fifty. Nobody over fifty would be allowed to play on a major league team. This made room for the youngsters like Danny Daniels to get into the game—although Daniels was thirty-eight when he finally became the Yankees' starting catcher.

The guys over fifty were put into a new league, a special league for old timers. This allowed baseball to expand again, for the first time in the twenty-first century. Sixteen new teams in sixteen new cities, mostly in the Sun Belt, like Tucson, Mobile, New Orleans, and Orlando.

And the best part is that the old timers get a shot at the World Series winner. At the end of October, right around Halloween, the pennant winner from the Old Timer's League plays the winner of the World Series.

Some wags wrote columns about Halloween being the time when dead ballplayers rise from their graves, but nobody pays much attention to that kind of drivel. The Halloween series draws big crowds—and big TV receipts. Even Bragg admits he likes it, a little.

Last Halloween Vic's Tucson Tarantulas whipped the New York Yankees in seven games. In the deciding game, Danny Daniels hit a home run for the Yanks, but Vic socked two dingers for Tucson to ice it. He said it was to celebrate the birth of his first son.

Yankee haters all over the country rejoiced.

Asked when he planned to retire, Vic said, "I don't know. Maybe when my kid gets old enough to play in the Bigs."

Or maybe not.

THE SNOWS OF YESTERYEAR

Jean-Louis Trudel

Like it or not, we—the human race—are in the midst of a global climate change. You can argue about the cause of the change, or how severe it will be, but one thing is certain: this planet's climate is heading for a tipping point. Arguments abound over how soon and how dangerous the climate warming will be, but the fact is that the warming is already well underway.

In "Snows of Yesteryear" Jean-Louis Trudel shows a gamut of human reactions to this ongoing climate shift, from scholarly curiosity to corporate greed, from the desire to save humankind from the approaching catastrophe to the yearning to use the changes on Earth to help make the planet Mars habitable for humans.

That is what science fiction does best: examining the present by casting its shadow against the possibilities of the future.

Northern Kujalleq Mountains

What would they do without the guy from Northern Ontario? Paul's thoughts were stuck in a loop. The same question was popping up every few seconds, probably because his leg muscles were gobbling up most of his body's oxygen. His brain just couldn't phrase a proper answer when the cold September wind was freezing his cheekbones, his breath burned in his throat, and his legs drove him up the snowy slope. The bag with the medikit seemed to grow heavier with every step. Soon, it would drag him all the way back down the mountain.

What would they do without the guy from Northern Ontario? The others had nominated him on the spot. Sure, send Paul, he's Canadian, he knows how to ski! Yeah, and he likes to play in the snow too. In the end, Francine had looked at him with those big, dark eyes of hers, and he'd been unable to say no.

He couldn't complain, not really. The Martian Underground had had its pick of young bacteriologists, but they wanted the one with actual winter experience. The guy from Northern Ontario. He'd said yes, to the job in Greenland and to the rescue mission.

Even with lightweight snowshoes, he sank a bit in the fresh snow as he leaned into the climb. Tomorrow, his muscles would ache. They didn't use to, not when he snowshoed through the woods of Killarney Park or skied cross-country in the hills outside Sudbury. But he was almost thirty and he'd spent more time in the lab lately than in the field.

He did wonder how the Old Man had fared coming out this way. He must have taken the long way around, down to Narsarsuaq, and then down the coast, skirting the fjord, until he could walk up the valley formerly occupied by the Ikersuaq glacier. Four days at least. A long hike, but not a hard one even for Professor Emeritus Donald B. Hall, who was so old he remembered the twentieth century. Very little of it, actually, but enough to spin unlikely stories that entranced his graduate students.

Early on, Paul had looked up some history sites and decided Old Man Hall was repeating tales he'd heard from his own teachers. Passing joints at a Beatles concert? Flying to Berlin to help tear down the Wall? His date of birth was confi-

dential, but he couldn't be that old, even with stem cell thera-
pies.

Not that he was going to get the chance to beat any records if Paul didn't reach him in time. Every time Paul looked
back, the Sun seemed closer to the horizon. He only stopped
once, to catch his breath. If he saved the Old Man's life, he
swore he would get the truth out of him about the one story
he'd never managed to disprove or disbelieve.

His heart pumping, Paul started to climb again. He still
found patches of snow to plant his snowshoes in, but he was
nearing the windswept summit. Sometimes, the synthetic
treads clanked and slipped on the bare rock, and he lost his
balance for a second, his arms windmilling.

He was pondering whether or not to take off the snowshoes and rely on his boots the rest of the way when he saw
the sign.

PRIVATE PROPERTY.

Paul frowned, worry fighting it out with disgust. The valley
floor had been buried under the ice for millennia, and it had
remained so well into the twenty-first century. And now, as
stunted trees grew among the glacier rubble, it had already
been claimed by outside interests. The sign was labeled in English, not in Kalaallisut or Danish. A number in a corner identified one of the companies owned by the Consortium that ran
the seaports catering to the trans-Arctic trade.

Despite the sign, the new owners probably hadn't bothered
with a full surveillance grid. Otherwise, the Old Man would
already have been picked up, flown to a hospital, and fined.

Paul should be safe as well from prying eyes. Beyond the sign,
the peak was in sight. After putting away his snowshoes, the
bacteriologist clambered up the last few meters and mounted
a small repeater on top of a telescopic pole. He wedged the
pole into place with a few rocks. The small device hunted around

for a few seconds and then locked on the signal of its companion a couple of kilometers away, within sight of the Martian Underground base camp.

"I'm at the boundary," Paul rasped into his mike. "A bit past it, in fact. I'll be starting the downhill leg now."

"We're here if you need us," answered the sweet voice of Francine. "You're running behind schedule, but just be careful."

"I intend to."

"And, Paul," cut in the voice of the director, "try and find out why Professor Hall ended up where he did."

"I definitely intend to."

"I know he left before you announced your latest results, but if this was all a ruse to allow him to rendezvous with outsiders . . ."

"I don't see how he could have known before me, or swiped a DNA sample. But I'll ask."

He strapped on his skis and launched a small drone to act as an extra pair of eyes for him. As he set off, the drone's-eye view was relayed to his ski goggles and helped him avoid several, literal dead ends. Slopes leading to unseen cliffs, rocks hiding around a curve, and other places where he would have ended up dead. Though his exposed skin stung from the wind chill, he enjoyed the descent along the slope of new powder, its blank whiteness marred only by animal tracks. A slope never skied before.

Mid-September wasn't supposed to be this cold in southern Greenland. Yet, temperatures had dipped as they once did in the twentieth century and preserved a couple of recent snowfalls. In Sudbury, Paul had played in snowdrifts that were much thicker when his mother sent him outside because she didn't want to see him at home. He looked too much like his father and she didn't care for the constant reminder. So, yeah, he really liked the snow. It had done such a great job of replacing the home he couldn't have.

The local forecast wasn't calling for more, but Paul tracked warily the oncoming cloud banks, massed so thickly over Niviarsiat Mountain that they threatened to blot out the late-afternoon sun.

The Old Man's camp was putting out an intermittent signal, just strong enough to reach his drone still circling above the valley. By the time Paul was halfway down the mountain, he knew in which direction he would have to head. Toward the ice dam and the lake.

It was almost dark when he found the tent. It was white, propped up by a glacial erratic, and set in the middle of an expanse of fresh snow. Perfectly camouflaged

"Professor Hall?" Paul called, his voice reduced to a hoarse croak.

"Don't bother knocking."

Hall was lying on an air mattress, bundled up in a sleeping bag. Prompted by the voice in his earbud, Paul hastened to check the Old Man's vital signs.

"His temperature is slightly elevated."

"Perfectly normal for a fracture. Carry on. Anything else?"

The professor endured Paul's amateurish inspection without a complaint. He unzipped the sleeping bag himself, revealing his bare legs. A large, purplish swelling ran around the middle of his left shin. The skin was mottled and bruised, but unbroken. Paul swept his phone, set for close focus, over most of the injury.

The base camp's doctor did not hide her relief.

"Not an open break, then. This will make things easier. Give him painkiller number four and take a breather. Do not try moving him or putting on the exolegs for another fifteen minutes at least."

Paul took out the hypo from the medikit and loaded the designated ampoule. As soon as the painkiller hit the Old Man's bloodstream, a couple of deeply etched lines on his face relaxed and vanished.

The bacteriologist settled down on the tent's only stool. He was breathing more easily, but his shoulders felt like tenderized meat. When he undressed to put on a dry shirt, he found that the skin chafed by the pack's shoulder straps had turned an angry red.

"So, what was so urgent?" he asked. "I thought you were dying."

"I may have exaggerated slightly the gravity of my condition."

"Why?"

"Because it wasn't a secure link. However, I assume you've set up a secure line of relays, as I asked."

"As secure as we could make it, using the same repeaters we use in our glacier tunnels. Narrow beams once the lock is made."

"Good boy."

"Well, tell me now, why couldn't Francine just fly in with the chopper to get you?"

"Any craft big enough to take both of us out of here would have been detected."

"I could have died out there on the mountain, professor. Were you that afraid of being busted for trespassing?"

Hall responded by pointing his phone at the tent wall. A low-resolution video played on the billowing canvas. The first pictures were blurry, but they seemed to show a small, ground-hugging plane, its wings flapping occasionally to detour around a rocky outcrop. It flew above the shadowed southern valley flank, heading straight for the ice dam, and stopped so suddenly that it dropped out of the screen.

"I thought it had crashed. So, I sent up my emergency drone to see if the flyer needed any help. But you know what they say about good deeds . . ."

Wormhole Base, Northern Greenland

The ice was a creaking, shifting presence. Dylan didn't like to dwell on the audible reminders that a substance so hard could be so dynamic that it would slowly fill any tunnel bored through it, given time.

"Was this part of the American base?" Kubota asked.

The businessman from somewhere in Asia—the name sounded Japanese to Dylan, but he hadn't inquired—was casting eager looks at the mechanical debris mixed in with the icy rubble left along the foot of the newly carved wall. Dylan hurried him along and opted for enough of an explanation to keep him happy.

"In a sense, yes. The Americans were thought to have cleaned out all of Project Iceworm's stuff when they left, back in 1966, but we're still finding their scraps. Looks like they just didn't bother dragging out various pieces of broken-down machinery or equipment. We've also come across furniture and remnants of the theater. Or perhaps it was the church. Everything got trapped inside the ice sheet when it closed in."

"So then, this tunnel isn't one of the original diggings?"

"No."

"Did you find any missiles?"

Dylan glanced at Kubota without managing to spot the twinkle in his eye that had to be there.

"No," he said curtly. "And the nuclear reactor was decommissioned and removed."

"Good. So then, this is a safe place."

Maybe he was radiation-shy. Given the effects of the Taiwan

nuclear exchange on the entire region he came from, that wouldn't be surprising.

"The safest," Dylan confirmed. "Part of the Consortium's cover here is the Extragalactic Neutrino Observatory. The deep ice is clean enough for Cerenkov radiation to shine through quite a large volume. Not as good as in Antarctica, but at least we're looking in the opposite direction. The detectors point down, of course, to use the Earth itself as a gigantic shield and filter, but they're also protected to some extent by the bulk of the ice over them. We're not as far down, with only ninety meters of ice above us, but it's still a nicely rad-free environment."

"A one-time creation."

"The whole point," Dylan agreed.

The Consortium offered visitors with a need for utmost confidentiality the most private facilities ever built. Every meeting room was freshly dug out of millennia-old ice. The only manufactured objects brought in—chairs, tables, infrared lamps—were so basic as to be easily searched for even nanotech bugs. Nobody else had used a given room before and nobody else would afterward.

This time, the Consortium itself had called the meeting. Secrecy would be absolute. Dylan had heard that all of the furniture would be made of particle board produced on the premises with lumber harvested from a submerged forest in an African lake. The whole idea being that no hidden transmitter or recorder could have been included decades ago within the trunks of a soon-to-be-drowned grove, or would have survived the chipping process . . . Dylan could think of a few flaws with this assumption, but as long as it served its purpose of setting suspicious minds at ease, he wouldn't quibble.

"Here we are," he said.

Kubota went in first and Dylan followed, finding his way to the side of Brian McGuire. As head manager of the local Consortium office, McGuire would chair the meeting. As the brightest of the bright young interns, Dylan would supply specifics if required.

The room was large and freezing cold until one entered the enchanted ring of infrared lamps.

The tables were set in a hollow square, with enough seating for twenty people: an eclectic mix of owners, executives, and highly trusted assistants.

"No names," McGuire announced in a booming voice. "Names are too easy to remember. Faces just slip away. Or change."

Not that individual names really mattered. The only names that counted were displayed on yellow cardboard squares and they identified the companies or industrial concerns represented by the people around the table.

"Notes?" asked a woman with a slight Scandinavian accent.

"You may use papers or internal electronics. If you managed to sneak in any external electronics, my congratulations to your technical staff, but you'll still have to sneak them out and their contents will have to survive a low-level electromagnetic pulse."

The woman nodded. McGuire added:

"At the end of the meeting, I will offer a road map, boiled down to six main points. We worded them to be easy to memorize. In many instances, details will come later. We are here to ask and to answer questions. If the answers aren't satisfactory, we won't go forward. But I truly believe that we are standing on the ground floor of something big."

Heads nodded. The Consortium had already proved it could place big bets when it had built up Qaqortoq from a sleepy fishing village into a major port for container ships coming or going from Asia, Europe, or North America, and needing to swap containers before heading to their ultimate destination. In the broader context, Wormhole Base was a side-project catering to a few thousand people a year though it also served to demonstrate the Consortium's commitment to Greenland. But McGuire was willing to go slow and build his case first.

"Global warming is the new industrial frontier. Mitigation and adaptation are already huge, and are going to become even huger. We'll have to beat back deserts, move cities to higher ground, and re-create whole new species."

"I thought the Loaves and Fishes group was cornering the market for new heat-tolerant crops and pollution-resistant fish," said an older man whose spot at the table bore the name of a well-known Canadian nanotech company.

"Perhaps, but they're not turning a profit," Dylan objected.

McGuire threw him a menacing look, but his voice remained smooth and practiced as he ignored the double interruption.

"Everybody here has a finger in the pie, and a stake in the result, but we want more. Greenland is the first new piece of prime real estate completely up for grabs since humans arrived in North America—unless that first wave actually beat the one that went to Australia."

"Rather barren real estate."

"It'll get better."

"And not entirely deserted."

"The current population is just hanging off the edges of the landmass, so it will only be a factor if we let it. Our new facilities have attracted so many immigrants that they're swamping the locals. One way or another, we don't expect the Nuuk government to be a worry."

The man identified as Toluca nodded, apparently willing to concede the point. His own face bore a distant family resemblance to that of the Greenland Inuit.

"As part of your invitation, we included a topographic map of Greenland without the ice sheet," McGuire added. "It must have struck you, looking at the map, that there are only a few major glacial outlets. Plug them up and the Greenland ice sheet will no longer contribute anything to sea level rise."

There were blank looks all around the table. Preventing sea level rise was not an obvious source of profits. Saving the world would have to yield dividends to catch this group's attention.

"Where will the water go?"

"Nowhere. It'll stay where it is. Part of Greenland lies below sea level. Up to three hundred meters. The central part of the continent can easily contain a major inland sea."

"Isn't the crust depressed under the weight of all that ice? Won't it rebound?"

The woman from Scandinavia probably knew something about post-glacial rebound. Dylan looked expectantly at McGuire, but the Consortium manager did not need to consult his assistant.

"Come on, think! If the water is contained when the ice melts, it won't go anywhere. The overburden remains nearly the same. The meltwater will be quite sufficient to prevent isostatic rebound."

The woman did not yield as easily as Toluca and probed further.

"I did look at the map. The central ice sheet is over three kilometers high; most of the surrounding mountains are no more than hills. The peaks reach up to two kilometers on the eastern coast, but most of the western hills are only half a kilometer high. Even if you could turn most of central Greenland into an enclosed basin, something like half the ice is still going to melt and add to sea level rise."

"Half is better than none. And the half flowing out can be turned to good use."

"Such as?"

"No mean bonus. If you plug the outlets and water rises behind the walls, we will be able to use some of it to power hydroelectric plants."

Dylan hid a smile as backs straightened, chair legs scraped along the roughened ice of the floor, and gazes fastened on McGurie.

"White coal," Kubota said, his eyes narrowing.

"Enough to power whole new cities, yes."

"The gaps between the hills are huge," the Scandinavian woman noted.

"All the more work for us. If this is sold as a way to control water outflow, we can get government money to help with the construction. And we can start with the smallest outlets, the ones that will cost least to plug and will be all the more profitable."

"So then, assuming there is money to be made, I think we would like to be a part of it," Kubota said slowly. "We can talk about the technical issues later. Plenty of time for that. What I would like to know is how you intend to tackle the political side. Sea levels have risen a meter since the beginning of the century, but most governments haven't budged or tried seriously to slow the warming. So then, why would they act now?"

"Floods."

"As in glacial lake outburst floods?" the Scandinavian woman asked. "Those can be cataclysmic!"

Dylan had researched the Missoula floods that had devastated eastern Washington state at the end of the last glacial

period. The lake had been gigantic. The collapse of an ice dam
had unleashed a flood with more water than all of the planet's
rivers put together, flowing with a speed rivaling that of a car
on a highway. The flood had scoured riverbanks down to bed-
rock and carried chunks of glacier for kilometers downstream. He expected to answer questions later, but it was
still McGuire's show for now.

"Precisely," the Consortium manager confirmed. "Take Niviarsiat Lake in Kujalleq. Fifty years ago, there was a glacier half
a kilometer high in the same spot. Now, it's a meltwater lake
dammed by leftover ice. If the dam broke, the water would
rush down Ikersuaq Fjord and destroy everything within
reach."

"Is this what you're proposing to do?" the Canadian asked.

Some of the attendees glanced at the icy walls and ceiling,
as if to reassure themselves they were as safe from espionage
as could be.

"Does anybody live in Ikersuaq Fjord?" Toluca asked, who
was squinting again.

"Most of the valley near the lake actually belongs to a Consortium company and access is forbidden. Once you reach the
actual fjord, there's a small settlement at Niaqornaq and the
town of Narssaq is found on the next fjord over, though it is
connected to Ikersuaq by a strait. Many buildings have already been moved to higher grounds, but the docks would
certainly be swamped. Let's be frank, people. Casualties would
help us make our case to the government."

"Is this a hypothetical discussion?" the Canadian insisted.

McGuire held the eyes of the owners and executives around
the table. Dylan noticed some of the assistants closer to his
own age looked uneasy, but they weren't involved. McGuire
challenged his peers when he answered, his voice dropping to
a lower tone.

"Last winter, one of our best men set off explosives under-neath the glaciers feeding the lake. There were no visible effects, and the blasts could be confused with an ice quake, but the ice beneath the glaciers was turned into Swiss cheese. Throughout the summer, the glaciers calved several times, shedding huge chunks of ice that melted in the sun. The lake level has risen so far and so fast that pressure near the bottom should have pushed the freezing point below the temperature of the ice. The water should already be eating away at the base of the dam."

"When will it break?"

"Two weeks from now. Mid-September."

Nobody asked how he could be so certain of the timing. Faces closed while minds readied to grapple with technical details as a way of forgetting what had just been discussed. Dylan suspected that all they cared about now was that the meeting room be blown up as promised after they left, tons of ice crushing the furniture and burying the very memory of the dangerous words they had heard.

Niviarsiat Lake, Southern Greenland

Old Man Hall had slipped just as he was launching the drone into the air, banging his leg hard on a boulder in the wrong place at the wrong time. He said drily that he'd known right away that it was a break, not just a bruise. Paul didn't ask how. Unable to put any weight on it, he'd managed to hop and crawl back to his tent, where he'd waited for the return of the drone.

The drone's video was much clearer than the phone pictures. The small plane seen earlier had found a smooth stretch of gravel by the fan of rivulets streaming out of the ice dam base. Paul would have liked to freeze the frame, but the professor was still holding his phone. The gravel looked suspiciously smooth and uniform, devoid of any larger rocks or significant dips. A previously used landing strip, perhaps?

"This is where it gets interesting," the Old Man whispered.

The plane had come to a quick stop close to the foot of the ice dam. A man stepped out, looked around, but did not look up. He opened a cargo compartment, took out a heavy rucksack, and walked over to the dam, bent under the weight of his load. He was using what looked like a ski pole as a walking stick. He took his time climbing up the bumpy outward surface of the dam. When he was about two-thirds of the way to the top, the man knelt by a narrow crevasse and probed with his pole. He got up and tried another crevasse a few meters away. It took him two more tries to find what he was looking for.

This time, he pulled out of his bag four, long boxlike objects linked by cables. He lowered them inside the crevasse, using a rope clipped to one of the boxes, and then rose to his feet. The rucksack was much lighter now. The man checked his phone, walked down a few meters, checked it again, walked back to the plane, and checked it one last time before taking off.

"Any chance those wouldn't be high explosives?" Paul asked hollowly.

"A very small one. I've been in the field for decades, I've seen geologists at work, glaciologists, bacteriologists, paleontologists . . . I can't say why exactly, but the man's behavior just doesn't fit. He was too hasty, didn't take any measurements . . . perhaps he was dropping off an instrument package for somebody else, but I don't buy it. It's a good thing I didn't look at the video for a couple of hours. Too busy trying to take care of my leg, so it was already dark when I watched it."

"And that's when you called base camp."

"Right away. And I didn't sleep much that night."

"Why do you think they would want to blow it up?"

"Unsure. The lake behind it is not that big, but the flood would rush down to the fjord and threaten Narssaq. I think Narsarsuaq would be safe from any kind of backwash. If it's some sort of terrorist plot, I fail to see the logic of it."

"What about the Loaves and Fishes people?"

"They're into radical adaptation. New heat-tolerant crops. New marine life forms engineered to withstand the acidic seas. If they can thrive on a plastic-enriched diet, even better, since the oceans aren't going to run out of plastic for centuries . . . But terrorism on this scale? I know they've sabotaged some bottom trawlers to make a point about disappearing fish stocks. And they've been strident about highlighting the shifting land and ocean conditions due to climate change. Still, why would they be behind this?"

Paul shook his head, unable to offer a rationale. The Old Man had been thinking it over for hours, after all.

"How about the Sunscreen Lobby? They've been looking for a way to convince governments to fund their orbital shield for years."

The professor shrugged. "Sure, extreme environmentalists of all stripes might go for it as a reminder of the dangers of global warming, but casualties are going to be low even if they blow it at night. And there's so much happening elsewhere that I doubt it would grab the world's attention."

"If it's that unlikely, it might not be a bomb. I should go and check before we panic."

"Now? It's dark and you won't see anything."

"I've got a good lamp. I watched the video carefully. I think I can find the right crevasse."

"How will you fish the package out? It looks like he picked the deepest crevasse he could find."

"But he didn't recover the rope he used to lower the package. With a bit of luck, I can use the rope to pull it back up."

The professor half rose up, stretching out his arm as far as he could.

"Don't go. If the dam blows while you're out there, I won't have a chance. The flash flood will just roll over me."

"And I'll be dead. In that case, you might as well tell me now why you came to be here."

"What I do on my own time is none of your business."

Paul stood and zipped up his coat.

"If that's how you feel, professor, we'll have to discuss this when I come back. I've come over the mountain to help you, and that was hard enough. But I've spent years working on the identification of bacteria preserved in the ice, or beneath the ice. I've examined I don't know how many samples taken out of tunnels dug with hot water hoses or brought back by ice-bots from the deepest layers of the ice sheet. I've helped to isolate bacteria able to repair their DNA in freezing conditions for over a million years. I've found two new strains that synthesize methane in brutally cold conditions to help the Martian Underground plan for the global warming of Mars. And I've . . . So, if you think I don't care that my work may benefit somebody who didn't pay for it, you need more time to rethink your assumptions."

"All work that I taught you how to do."

"Don't flatter yourself. I had other professors. But I did look up to you for one thing."

"What?"

"Ethics."

The Old Man grabbed for the stool and tried to lever himself upright without using his leg. Paul shouldered his backpack again, wincing slightly, and opened the tent slit.

"No, Paul, wait. It's not what you think. I was freelancing, but it had nothing to with the Martian Underground, or with your work."

"What, then?"

"I had a contract with the Pliocene Park Foundation. I was supposed to sample Niviarsiat Lake, or the glaciers upstream ideally, for ancient DNA."

Paul turned around.

"The Pliocene Park project? I've heard of it. Doesn't it involve buying land for a nature preserve that will re-create the environment of the Pliocene?"

"More than that. It will be stocked not only with surviving species of the Pliocene, but with ones we've been able to resurrect from past extinction. In Siberia, the melting permafrost has released carcasses from the last interglacial. Reviving mammoths was only a start. The Russians are working on mastodons and stegodons and chalicotheres. But one of the best places for finding relics is underneath the Greenland ice sheet. There may be fossils once we access the underlying rocks. And there are certainly DNA remains in the lowest strata of the ice, some of which should date back to the Pliocene. Mostly plants, we expect, but also some northern animals."

"So, you were working for a zoo. I guess we can all sleep easier."

"There's more to it than that. Global warming is a time machine back to the Pliocene. The whole project is about reminding people of that."

Paul sighed. "Your generation is still trying, isn't it?"

"And yours has given up."

"Perhaps because we saw how far you got. The sins of our fathers passed down to us, but we don't have to repeat the errors of our fathers."

"At least, we tried to slow down the warming. Our generation threw everything at the problem. Finally cut back on total emissions even as the population kept rising to ten billion. But the seas got warmer and no longer absorbed as much carbon dioxide. So, we seeded the ocean deserts with iron dust and made them bloom with phytoplankton. Carbon dioxide uptake increased, but ocean acidification too. The coral reefs died and fisheries declined. People starved and turned to coastal fish and shrimp farms. Without the mangroves they cut down and the sandbars drowned by rising seas, hurricanes swept in and tidal surges wiped out many of the farms . . . More people starved. In the end, we went back to farming where the rains still came, even if forests had to be cleared, even if synthetic fertilizers were needed, and even if transportation costs ballooned as such farms got too far from the mouths to feed. But pulping the forests returned carbon to the atmosphere and transportation still burned up too much carbon, although far less than in the days of gas-guzzlers."

Paul had let him speak, thinking of the world beyond the small tent, beyond the deserted valley in southern Greenland. Drowned cities, burning forests, shifting sand dunes in Iowa, and the poor dying of thirst in India. What could a guy from Northern Ontario do about it all? He'd stopped loving the snow when he'd realized it was an illusion. It only covered up the same landscape as before. In the end, it changed nothing. "And, in the end," Paul said quietly, "every route took you back to your starting point, leaving us to live in a warming world or die."

"So, what did you do?"

"We faced reality. My generation intends to live. On this world or another."

Paul stalked out, leaving his mentor speechless. He stood in darkness for a moment, listening for any sound other than his quickened breathing. If there was a bomb, it could be set off by a signal sent from a satellite passing overhead. The man in the plane wouldn't come back. There would be no warning.

He went back inside the tent and took out from his bag another earbud as well as the medikit. He displayed the exolegs, which looked like pieces of bulky black hose connected to shapeless shoes.

"The earbud, you know to use. If you haven't used exolegs before, pay attention to our doctor's instructions. The main thing is not to try to pull them on. Even with the painkiller, you'd feel the bones grinding together. If you do it right, they will split lengthwise so that you can wrap the covering around your leg. The smart material will exert the right amount of pressure to set and immobilize the bones. Afterward, if you lead with your good leg, the artificial muscles will also walk your legs for you. The exoskeleton will take up most of the pounding, but you'll feel it when the painkiller wears off. It will hurt like hell."

He grinned evilly, thinking of his own battered flesh, then pointed in the general direction he'd come from.

"Head south, up the valley flank. The summit repeater will act as your beacon. But stop when you've reached an altitude one hundred meters above sea level. There's a terrace Francine can land the chopper on to take us out. If you don't run across it, stay put, and I'll find you later. Or Francine will find you in the morning."

"Paul, wait, please. Come with me. You don't need to go."

"I still think it might not be a bomb. And if it's a bomb, there might be clues as to its maker."

"If it's a bomb, there's a good chance that it will blow tonight."

"It's still early. I'm betting that they'll wait till midnight, whoever they are."

This time, when he stepped outside, he kept going. Clouds hid most of the stars, so he turned on a flashlight. Gravel crunched under his boots and he thought of his old dream of walking on Mars. Nobody could work for the Martian Underground and not think of the possibilities.

Colonizing Mars was another long shot, like the orbital sunscreen intended to cool Earth. The methanogenic bacteria found in cold, lightless, microscopic pockets at the base of ancient Earth glaciers might serve to hasten the terraformation of Mars. They might even prove to be of Martian origin. On Earth, they were part of a slow-paced, long-lived subglacial ecosystem still dining off leftover biomass from earlier thaws.

Sown across the Martian surface, they would belch, under the right conditions, enough methane to start creating a future haven for humanity. Within the Martian Underground, fans of the idea sometimes called themselves the Young Farts of Mars, if only to make it clear they wouldn't be happy with just going to Mars, like previous generations. Francine's voice suddenly blared into his ear.

"Paul Weingart, what are you doing?"

"What a guy from Northern Ontario can do. No more no less."

"We heard everything. We think it's a bomb and that you should get the hell out of the way. Both of you."

"I won't be long. Just keep track of Professor Hall for me."

"Paul, please, wait!"

"Too late. Now, please give me some quiet, I need to concentrate."

He had reached the foot of the dam. The flashlight's beam played over the icy slope. He hadn't been boasting. He had a good memory for weird surfaces, trained perhaps by his work in the lab, and it only took him a quarter of an hour to find the spot where the man had left the package.

He swore when he discovered that the rope had slipped, falling into the crevasse. However, the beam picked up the yellow nylon rope only a meter or so below the lip of the crevasse. Paul threw himself flat on the ice, extended his arm, and grabbed the end of the rope.

And swore again when he realized he could do nothing with it. The load at the far end of the rope was too heavy. With one arm fully outstretched and the other braced at an angle against an ice boulder to keep himself from slipping forward, he lacked the leverage needed to pull up the package.

He pondered his next move for a moment, fully aware of the ticking minutes that brought midnight closer. He finally took his other hand away from its hold and gently teased one of his snowshoes out of his pack. The friction between the main mass of his body and the snow-dusted ice was all that was keeping him in place. He lowered the snowshoe within reach of his right hand, using it to thread the rope between the frame and the decking before tying a quick lasso knot. He pulled back his free hand and groped for a hold.

Paul thought of Francine before trying to rise. She'd sounded worried about him. Was she still listening in? Trying to guess what was happening to him from his breathing?

Exhaling sharply, he pulled himself back from the brink in one go. He stayed in a crouch for a moment, his heart pounding, and then pulled out the snowshoe as slowly as possible. He was afraid that the knot might slip when placed under tension, but all he did was pick up the slack in the rope.

Once he had the rope well in hand, he wasted no time in lifting the package out of the crevasse. A grunt escaped his lips. The package was heavy.

"All's well," he announced. "I've got the . . ."

He hesitated. Shone the light on the objects from the crevasse. Noted the absence of any dials, gauges, or markings. Started walking suddenly with a faster stride.

"I think it's a bomb, after all."

"Leave it then," the director said.

"Not yet."

He backtracked all the way to the Old Man's tent. He checked it was empty and left the explosives inside. The farther he got from the tent, the harder it was to breathe. What if they blew *now*? He would feel really silly.

Yet, the bomb hadn't blown when he reached the side of the valley and began climbing immediately. Soon, he spotted the trail left by Old Man Hall, the trampled snow almost silvery in the light. He made quick work of following in the professor's footsteps and soon discerned the man's silhouette ahead of him. Just as he was on the verge of hailing him, the bomb blew.

The noise was surprisingly loud and the flash illuminated the entire nightscape, the dam dazzlingly white, the evergreen saplings thrown in sharp relief, and every rock of the valley floor clearly outlined. A few seconds later, gravel pattered down like a hard rain.

Paul wheezed helplessly for a moment, his ears ringing. He couldn't remember breathing since leaving the crevasse, but relief now unclenched some of the muscles he had tensed. The flash had shown him the terrace was within sight. Old Man Hall had found the edge of the flatter ground and was just waiting for him. He was an experienced hiker, after all.

The explosion had also caused the professor to turn around and locate the younger man. Once Paul caught up to him, the first thing out of the professor's mouth was a warning.

"They'll come and see why the dam didn't collapse. Whoever did this isn't going to be happy with us."

"I know. But we'll be gone. And your camp has been blown to bits. We'll be hard to track."

"But completely exposed until we get back."

"Look up."

The Old Man blinked and glanced at the clouds overhead, the light clipped to his head sweeping up. Whitish stars were falling from the sky and crowding into the beam. Snowflakes.

"It's snowing."

"As expected. The snow will hide our tracks, cover what's left of your tent, and make it more difficult for others to follow the helicopter."

"What helicopter?"

Paul raised his hand and waved at the shape emerging out of the flurries. He'd cheated. His younger ears had picked up the sound of the approaching aircraft before his mentor.

The professor's shoulders slumped as the man relaxed. He'd held up surprisingly well, given his age. This reminded Paul of the question he'd wanted to ask.

"Hey, prof, there's one thing I always wanted to know. Did you really work on the DNA profiling of O. J. Simpson?"

Hall stared at him and then smiled slowly.

"I'll tell you in the helicopter if you tell me why you were so sure that it was going to snow."

Paul nodded. He'd given him a few clues, but Old Man Hall was still a sharp one. "You know what many of us are looking for. Sure, the Martian Underground puts up the funding for bacteria that can survive on Mars, whether they're simple extremophiles or highly durable methanogens. But that won't help us on Earth. Except that, as you said, global warming is taking us back to the Pliocene."

"You've found something from the Pliocene!"

"Ironic, isn't it, that you came hunting here for Pliocene relics just as I was able to announce that I'd isolated a new strain of ice-forming bacteria in a sample from deep below the ice sheet."

"Rain-makers?"

"Exactly. We've always thought that bacteria from a warmer age might be more effective in our warming world than current strains. Pliocene microorganisms adapted to a warmer climate over millions of years, not the ten thousand years or so since the last freeze-up. The strain I found is related to modern-day varieties that promote ice nucleation in clouds."

"And now you've released it in the wild?"

The professor looked up again, his mouth closed firmly to resist the temptation of sticking out his tongue and tasting bacteria from another geological age.

"Whose fault is that?" Paul asked. "Don't worry, there's some left for further study, but I cultured enough to leave a flask with Francine. We agreed that she could use a drone to seed any likely cloud mass if it seemed necessary."

"That wasn't very ethical," the Old Man said, eyes downcast.

"But it may save our lives until we can report the sabotage to authorities."

The professor nodded, any further comment cut off by the roar of the helicopter landing at the far end of the terrace. Paul knew that he would work out soon the other implications of the discovery. The new bacteria heralded a wave of other discoveries that might help with humanity's adaptation to a warmer world. Might even help to control warming, if that wasn't too much to hope for.

Old Man Hall headed for the craft, walking stiffly. Paul followed, but he didn't make it all the way. The helicopter's pilot had jumped out in the snow and she ran to meet him. It was Francine.

She threw her arms around him, hugged him, and kissed

him. When they stopped to breathe again, he smiled and asked, "Francine Pomerleau, what are you doing?"

"The only thing possible under the circumstances. You've forced me to ask a question that I don't know the answer to. What would I do without my guy from Northern Ontario?"

SKIN DEEP
Leah Petersen & Gabrielle Harbowy

"It sounds like science fiction . . ."

How often have you heard or read a news story about a new scientific breakthrough that started with those words? "It sounds like science fiction, but it's true!"

Airplanes were once the domain of science fiction. Television. Antibiotics. Organ transplants. Computers. Space flight.

In "Skin Deep," Leah Petersen and Gabrielle Harbowy envision a near future in which allergic reactions can be treated by tattoos on the patient's skin that activate the patient's immune system to produce specific antigens that will quell the allergic response.

Fine.

Make no mistake about it; some allergic reactions can be fatal. But properly (or improperly) engineered, the immune system's reaction can be just as dangerous.

In the reasonably near future, you will learn that biotechnology has produced such protections against potentially fatal allergy attacks. Again, fine.

But there will also be the possibility that this wonderful new breakthrough could be used for nefarious purposes.

The courthouse was crowded, but Indira Chang maneuvered through the swelling mass of people as if she were six foot seven, bulky, and sour-faced like her co-counsel, rather than her own mousy five foot one. She couldn't afford to linger.

Too often there was that one person who ignored the "no strong perfumes" notice.

The slow-moving crowd suddenly came to a stop, filling the arch leading into the hallway from wall to wall.

"Damn!" Indira's nails tapped impatiently against her carry-case.

"If only you had a medical tattoo . . ." Dan deadpanned from behind her.

"Conflict of interest," she answered automatically, as she always did.

He chuckled, a rumble like an avalanche. "Except that half the judges and more than half the jurors we argue in front of have med-tats."

"Yeah, well."

"Remember that one we argued, which was it, the fourth? Fifth—?"

"Fifth."

"Where—yeah, fifth—where the entire jury had med-tats?"

"I've got it under control. My epi-pen works fine."

"So get the tat and keep your epi-pen."

"Can't. They won't renew the 'script. Risk of overdose. I know the arguments, Dan, I just can't bring myself to trust my life to something I can't control."

"You? Control issues? Nah." He laughed, but his voice was low and serious when he added, "Someday it won't work, Indi."

In the lobby behind them, the commotion peaked. Screeching cries of fear pierced the roar of mingled voices. Indira turned, but Dan threw an arm out in front of her.

"Careful."

Uniformed security and plainclothesman policemen rushed in as a man broke free from the crowd. For one frantic moment

he met Indira's eye. Then someone crashed into him from behind and he went down with a thud.

"Well, that's not going to be good," Dan said.

Dan perched on the edge of her desk, arms crossed lazily.

"You won't believe what it was."

Indira raised an eyebrow.

"Some whacked-out protestor tried to spray the crowd
with ricin loaded into an epi-pen. Don't worry, it didn't dis-
charge."

Indira had logged many hours of practice at schooling her
expression, but incredulity broke through now. "What kind of
sick—wait. An epi-pen?"

Dan snorted. "Yeah. Guess we'll be using crayons in court
from now on. Security will probably start confiscating everything pointy at the door."

Indira gave him a long look of exasperation.

Dan grimaced. "Yeah. I thought of that. I'm sure you can
get some kind of exemption, right?"

"I'm sure." Indira kept her thoughts to herself. She knew he
was concerned about her, but he was also looking a little smug
about his prediction coming true.

"It'll work out, you'll see." He stood and rapped his knuckles twice on her desk. "See you tomorrow."

"Yeah."

"I'm sorry, ma'am. You can't take that in."

Indira scowled at the epi-pen in the guard's hand, to keep
herself from scowling at the young man who held her medicine hostage. It wasn't his fault. Suited lawyers and nervous
family members murmured behind her, shifting in a restless
herd while she held up the line.

"Come on, Ari. Yesterday I was Indira and today I'm 'ma'am'? I have a note from my physician right here. It's biometrically notarized. You know I need it for my perfume allergy, you check it through every day."

The young man looked around for help. "I'm sorry. Maybe you can speak to my manager. She left for a meeting about fifteen minutes ago. She should be back in an hour, maybe?"

"I can't wait that long. I'm due in court in twenty minutes."

He shrugged, a dull red creeping up his face and ears. The din behind Indira was growing louder and more frustrated. "I'm sorry."

"Fine," she said, picking up her carry bag, sans epi-pen, and slinging the strap over her shoulder with a frustrated jerk. "Keep it. Can I go in now?"

"Yes, ma'am."

Dan waited for her inside the checkpoint. He matched her angry strides easily with his long legs. "You sure that's a good idea, hotshot?"

"Nothing's happened in months."

"Yeah." His answer was subdued, doubtful, and his face settled into the frown that was his normal expression. Indira was glad. It made people get out of their way.

The morning session was what Dan liked to call a "defense attorney's yacht-payment" session. Hours of quibbling over minor details, accomplishing nothing. By the time they broke for lunch, Indira was getting a headache. As she exited the courtroom, a woman stopped in front of her so quickly Indira almost crashed into her.

"Miss Chang. I didn't expect to have the pleasure of seeing you today. I was worried that all the fuss yesterday would delay our case."

Heather Gannon was the CEO of Gannon & Perez, developer and manufacturer of pharmaceutical and diagnostic tattoo technology. She wore a pale yellow suit with a string of pearls at her perfect throat. Somehow she managed to carry off the Stepford Wife look without losing one bit of her ferocity as a businesswoman. Indira couldn't help but notice that she made it look sexy, too. Too bad that was a *real* conflict of interest, and anyway, Gannon and Lucy Perez had been married since before they started the company.

"No. We're still scheduled for this afternoon. If you'll excuse me, I—"

The familiar itch started in her throat, around her eyes and mouth. Indira sucked in a strangled gasp. Already her throat was tightening. There wasn't enough air. A hot flush swept her and she staggered back into Dan.

"Indira? Oh, God. Someone call 911!"

Indira woke, groggy and itchy. Her heart stuttered in a moment's panic before she realized that it wasn't the itch preceding an attack, but the more general, pervasive itch of pain medication. She became slowly aware of the all-too-familiar steady beep, and the cold, antiseptic smell of a hospital.

Damn.

The deputy DA sat at her bedside, leafing through a magazine. "You're up," Rowan said, trying to hide his worry behind a shaky smile. He'd been her boss almost since she'd passed the bar, and was as much friend as colleague. "Glad you're back with us."

"Thanks. Me, too. What's the status of my cases?"

Rowan raised a brow. "Considering you nearly died, maybe you can give yourself a couple hours' recess before you start talking work again, counselor?"

"It was just an allergic reaction."

Rowan's face hardened. "No. It wasn't. It was an episode

that you almost didn't survive. What were you thinking, going in there without your epi?"

"I was thinking that I had an appointment with a judge, and that opposing counsel would be only too pleased if I didn't show up."

He shook his head. "Sometimes I think you're trying to give me a heart attack. Really, Indi, that was stupid. Dan could have handled it without you. You almost died."

"But I didn't. I just need you to talk to someone and get an exemption for my epi straightened out."

"No. You're not going back to court. It's already been decided."

"Then undecide it. Come on, Rowan. Talk to someone at the mayor's office."

"I have. The mayor himself told me to take you off. No one is keen to start making exceptions when you're not the only lawyer in the city. Dan's perfectly competent, Indira."

"How many negligence and malpractice cases have I won against Gannon and Perez for implantable biotech?"

"I know."

"Nine."

"Yes, I know."

"How many has Dan argued?"

"Indira—"

"How many?"

"I know."

"None. That's how many. Dan's a good lawyer, but this is my case."

"Not anymore it isn't. I'm sorry."

The snake wound around Dr. Tehari's arm in sinuous green and yellow coils. Its head was poised over her wrist with open jaws that seemed ready to swallow her hand. Or slither a few centimeters farther and sink its fangs into Indira. Indira turned away, closing her eyes and losing herself in the constant buzzing noise.

"You all right?" the doctor asked.

Indira forced herself to look at the snake, rather than at the angry-red skin around her half-finished tattoo.

"What's that one for?" Indira nodded toward the snake.

Tehari grinned, a flash of white teeth. "Nothing." She winked. "That's just to scare the patients. This one," she wiggled the other wrist, displaying the single blue line tattooed around it. "This one's for my diabetes."

"Huh. Plain and simple." Indira took a deep breath and let it out slowly. She'd shoved that damned epi-pen into her own thigh often enough; she could handle one little needle.

"I was one of the test cases," the doctor said, and it took Indira a moment to remember what they were talking about. "The first ones were all the same," she went on. "They only got fancy once they were in common use. I keep meaning to make it into something more interesting, I just haven't decided what I want yet."

There was something oddly poetic about a tattoo artist not knowing what she wanted tattooed on her own skin. Indira had already known that she wanted a delicate vine of ivy with diagnostic readouts in the leaves. She'd had the design picked out for years, actually, but then she had started taking cases against Gannon & Perez. When she had seen up-close just what the tech could do when things went wrong, the med-tat had been put on permanent hold. She wondered if the doctor knew what she did for a living.

"Heard you're off the case," Dr. Tehari remarked. "It was on the news."

Well, that answered that.

"Not anymore, I hope," Indira said, nodding toward her arm without actually looking. "Not after this."

Dr. Tehari grinned. "I was surprised to see your name on my patient list. I would have thought you'd be a little, well, disinclined to get the tattoo, considering."

"It's not personal. I'm just doing my job." Indira grimaced as the needle traced a thin, painful line over a nerve. "Though it wasn't my first choice, I'll admit."

"You're doing the right thing. Allergies like yours are one of the best applications of the med-tat. Don't think there have been any cases of failure with these."

Indira shook her head. "There have, but they were addressed years ago. They're one of the safest applications now."

"And you would know."

Silence lapsed but for the buzz of the needle. Indira looked toward the vial with her name and patient ID on it. Each vial of serum was customized, engineered out of the DNA of its designated target. The tattoo clinic received the bioengineered serum from Gannon & Perez, and then added it to that patient's ink. She had tried a case where the labels on two vials had been switched, and two patients had gotten product meant to cure conditions they didn't have. The non-diabetic who got the insulin regulator only noticed that her dust and pet dander allergy wasn't getting better. The diabetic whose blood sugar suddenly went wild was the one who brought the case. When Indira won it, Gannon & Perez had tightened its quality assurance practices.

"This is where I usually make sure you know how this thing works," Dr. Tehari said, "but given who I'm talking to, I suspect you know better than I do."

Indira tried to smile. "I'd say I know the basics." The tattoo didn't contain medicine, but rather engineered cells that could produce medicine as needed, whenever needed. Because the cells themselves were never depleted, just activated and deactivated, the medicine could never run out. The diagnostic displays were mostly for reassurance. People liked the feedback so that they knew the tattoo was working.

The buzzing halted while the doctor switched inks, the sudden silence echoing in Indira's ears. "I'm just finishing up the display. This'll show the presence of allergens. Greens are all-clear. You might see some fluctuation in the green, but that's just cosmetic, like a screensaver when your phone is in standby. Yellows mean a small but not dangerous concentration is detected, brighter toward the source of the concentration so that you know which way to go if you want to avoid it. The deeper autumns are when things get nasty. Red means you're around a high enough concentration to trigger the drug. Brown means that it's in your system, dealing with the threat. You know what the epi hit feels like. The color just reinforces that yes, that's what that flushed sensation is. Then brown will fade back to yellow and eventually green." She set the tattoo gun down and wiped clear, soothing gel across the angry skin. "There. Have a look."

Indira turned her head with mild trepidation, which disappeared as soon as she saw the finished product. "Wow. It's gorgeous." A slender green vine wove its way up her inner arm, with four delicate leaves sprouting off it in perfectly shadowed trompe l'oeil. It looked real, and the faint shifts of green in the leaves made it seem like they were swaying in the breeze of a sun-dappled glade.

The doctor smiled. "Thanks. I like to do work that's more than just functional. I have an MFA in art, but it didn't take long to realize that an MFA doesn't pay the bills, so I went into med school."

"Sounds like a perfect career for you, then." The woman working on her arm didn't seem old enough to have gone through graduate school *and* med school, but with the cosmetic implants available these days, you never knew.

"Well, it rules out the squeamish artists, that's for sure." She set the tattoo gun down and wiped clear, soothing gel across the angry skin. "There. All the leaves are keyed to the same readout, but they can be reprogrammed if you get other med tattoos later on. I like to leave room for growth."

"Ha-ha."

"Yeah, no pun intended or anything."

Dr. Tehari set to cleaning up, carefully sealing the ink pots. They went into a clear box along with Indira's vial. More quality assurance—if something went wrong, not that it would, the ink and serum would be available for testing. The box was labeled with Indira's name and patient number, and then sealed with biohazard tape.

By the time the workspace was clean, the gel was ready to come off. Dr. Tehari wiped it away gently, cleaned the skin again, and applied a few pumps of a fine, cold aerosol mist. "This will seal it up and heal it, so don't worry about bumping it on anything or getting it wet, but it'll stay a little tender for the next day or two. We'll let your immune system recover, and tomorrow we'll test it out and make sure it works."

Indira grimaced. "Yeah. That's the part I'm really looking forward to." After her recent hospital stay and the enforced leave of absence from work, the last thing she wanted to do was tempt anaphylaxis for fun.

Tehari shook her head. "Don't worry. It'll be fine. The cells will be all settled in their new home, ready to pump out antidote before you've even realized you need it."

* * *

Indira saw the headline on the flight home: GANNON & PEREZ BEAT RAP OVER DISPLAY SYNCHRONIZATION.

Dan had lost her case.

By the time she landed, she had declined to answer five calls from reporters and one each from Dan and Rowan. She returned Dan's call first, sitting on the bullet train from the airport and staring out the window at the blur of rainy cityscape and gray sky.

"You heard?" he asked as soon as he picked up.

"What, no 'Hello, Indira, how'd it go?'"

His voice carried the hint of a smile. "Sorry. Motion to note in the record that I asked and you answered, and then we can move on to where you yell at me for losing your case."

She was quiet a moment, debating her next words. If she had been about to scream at him—and she still wasn't sure if she had been or not—his candid invitation had taken away her steam. "So, what happened?"

He cleared his throat. "The false positives and the false negatives on the displays. We called it the same issue—lack of synchronization between display and implant. Well, they argued that they were different issues with different processes and technologies, and got the case dismissed."

Indira took a breath, let it out, and counted to ten. She wondered if Dr. Tehari could implant Ativan without a prescription. Or maybe tequila.

"They conned you, Dan. They always try to make that argument. If I'd been—"

"But you weren't, hotshot." His voice softened. "I had to cover this one because you were too stubborn to take care of yourself. Yeah, I've been hoping you'd get the damn thing, but not like this. You had to make a point about how you had it all under control, and you blew it."

"What, so two wrongs make an excuse?" she retorted, and

sighed. "I'm sorry. Look, I'm almost at my stop. I'll see you tomorrow."

The dead bolt lock thunked over and Indira spilled into the apartment. Bail slunk out of the bedroom, a little orange fuzz ball meowing reproaches at her.

She picked him up, rubbing her cheek against his soft fur. "Yeah, I'm sorry. But I know Mrs. Ming gives you tuna when I'm gone, so I don't know what you're complaining about." The crisp, faintly metallic smell of the ozonator hung in the air. Indira smiled, carrying the cat with her into the kitchen.

"I think we can both use a treat, huh?"

She stopped short at the sight of a huge bouquet of flowers. With her free hand she flicked over the card tied to the vase. It was a generic "Get Well Soon" signed only "G&P." Well that was . . . odd. Mrs. Ming must have accepted the delivery for her.

Setting Bail down on the counter, Indira pulled the milk carton from the fridge, giving it a sniff before she poured some into a saucer for the cat. For herself, she grabbed a spoon and a pint of ice cream. Chocolate, with chocolate chunks.

Indira settled into the armchair by the window. In the light, the glimmer of the tat caught her eye.

Pensively, she watched the kids at the park down the street as she opened the carton.

"Did you know it's impossible to get good ice cream in the hospital?" she remarked to the cat, who lapped at his milk, ignoring her. "We can put a base on Mars, but apparently hospitals can't serve ice cream that doesn't have freezer burn."

She sat back and let the first spoonful of chocolate melt on her tongue.

The inside of her mouth tingled, starting to itch. A jolt of panic jerked her upright before she even had time to think about it. The itch had already spread down her throat, around her mouth. Her hand went automatically to her throat, as if she could stop the swelling that would cut off her air—

The shock of epinephrine hit her bloodstream with the subtlety of a tsunami. The itching and swelling washed away, replaced by the quivering, twitchy sensation of adrenaline rush.

She sat back, gasping. *Breathe.* She clung to the mantra like the last epi-pen in a perfume department. *I can breathe. I can breathe.* The adrenaline was what was making her heart race. It had been released by the med-tat, just as it was supposed to be.

The hospital. Her hand twitched at the urge to call 911, but no, that wasn't necessary anymore. The med-tat would provide all the follow-up monitoring and medicine. And it was self-diagnostic—it would tell her if there was a problem it couldn't handle, or if it was malfunctioning.

Did that include causing her to react to something she'd never been allergic to before? She shoved up her sleeve. The leaves were fading from brown, to yellow, to green again. Bail jumped up on her lap, pacing back and forth from chair arm to chair arm, seeking the most comfortable spot from which to demand more attention.

The phantom itch in her mouth was her imagination. "Mrs. Ming must have a new man in her life," she remarked to Bail, her voice trembling with aftershock. "Probably got new perfume and forgot all about it, right?" She petted the cat, hoping the smooth, repetitive movement would help calm her, too. "Did she smell funny?"

It was always possible. People forgot when it wasn't their allergy, their life. And the tattoo had done exactly what she needed it to do, exactly what she'd gotten it for. She was starting to shake—the aftereffects of the adrenaline rush that had saved her life.

The ice cream went back to the freezer. Indira needed to lie down.

"So, let's see it." Dan crossed Indira's office in three of his long-legged strides, an opened envelope in his hand. Indira turned her arm so he could see the climbing green vine.

"I was thinking of getting spiders, but I didn't want to scare you," she teased.

He chuckled, hovering his fingers just above the tattoo. He was too polite to actually touch without asking. Dormant, the displays shimmered slightly, making the leaves sway. "Scare yourself, most like. No way you'd get a spider tat."

"You never know. The doctor had a snake. It was interesting. And she was cute."

Dan snorted and sat back, crossing his arms. As a reflex, he glanced at the open files on her screen, peering more closely when a name caught his attention.

"Gannon and Perez? You've got a new case?"

Indira collapsed the window. "Not yet, but it's only a matter of time."

He shook his head. "I thought you'd be less the crusader now. Or that you'd pick a new target."

She bit back a sharp response. "I'm not a crusader, I'm just doing my job."

"So what's with the case files, then, if there's no case pending?"

"Research."

He gave her a suspicious frown. "Why?"

"Because it's my idea of a fun time on a Thursday night? Sheesh, Dan. You'd think you caught me mapping out a bank robbery or something."

He snorted. "Good luck with that one, hotshot. Stealthy, you're not."

Dan handed her the envelope he carried. For a high-tech company, Gannon & Perez sometimes liked to do things the traditional way. From the envelope, Indira pulled a crisply folded piece of letterhead. It was a smarmy, generic letter, thanking her practice for their concern for the well-being of G&P's patients, and continuing with an assurance that the problems were being addressed. Indira recognized it as the form letter that was sent to any patient who contacted customer service with a complaint. Rather than bearing the form letter's usual stamped signatures, though, it looked like it had been personally signed by Gannon and Perez themselves. She returned it to the envelope and looked at the front. It was addressed directly to Dan.

"Wow. Gloating much?" she asked. "I'm sorry, Dan. They're bastards." She returned the letter to him and sat back with a stifled sigh.

"Thought you'd want to see it," he said with a rueful smirk. "Enjoy your research. Next time, we kick their asses."

He moseyed out of her office and she returned to her screen. She had no desire to share her real purpose, not with Dan or anyone. The details of her first case against Gannon & Perez were exactly as she remembered them. The patient had a bee-sting allergy. The med-tat had seemed a life-saving miracle . . . until the patient began to react to allergens that had not been triggers for her before, and eventually died of a heart attack after a cascade of allergic reactions, one after the other, and the eventual overdose of adrenaline.

The lawsuits had come in a flood at first, but slowed in time. After each case Indira won, additional safeguards were put in place to make med-tat technology safer. The monitoring modules were improved so that the tattoo would confirm medicine levels already present in the blood before administering more. The technology was more carefully calibrated to the individual patient's physiology, their history of sensitivity to medicines, and their past reactions. At least one backup treatment was available if the primary treatment was not advisable. Remedies for a patient's most likely side-effects or overdose reactions were now coded into every med-tat. And there was a transmitter as a last resort, to call for paramedics if conditions suggested an uncontrolled or dangerous reaction.

Tens of thousands of allergy patients wore the med-tat now, and there had never been another malfunction that created new allergies on top of old ones, like that first one.

Like a chocolate allergy, when it had always and only been perfumes.

The chocolate didn't send her to the medical center, but the next set of symptoms did.

"Dermatomyositis," Dr. Haskins said.

"I beg your pardon?"

The doctor took the other chair in front of her desk, rather than the one behind it. "The rashes and the muscle pain," she said. "It's an autoimmune disorder that affects the muscles and skin. The exact cause is unknown, but one theory is that it's a viral infection of the muscles."

"I know what it is, doctor," Indira said, stunned. "Treatment but no cure, right? It was the second case I prosecuted against Gannon and Perez . . ."

Dr. Haskins propped her elbow on the thick armrest, chin in hand, as she examined Indira. "Dermatomyositis is pretty surprising in a healthy woman under forty."

"Yes," Indira said quietly. "I know."

"You were just in here a month ago. Were you already having symptoms and not sharing them with me?"

"Of course not."

"I'm not sure a natural case of dermatomyositis could develop that quickly. You've had the tattoo how long? Two weeks?" She frowned. "I'm sure you've already considered the possibility that this isn't a coincidence."

"Of course."

"You know I'm going to have to report this."

Indira's mouth twisted. "Maybe you could wait."

"Wait?"

"You know who I am to them. Just give me a few days to consider the legal angle."

The doctor was silent a moment, lips tight. "Next week, Indira. I'm going to report this by Monday."

"Good enough."

The restaurant was loud and dim and made the best noodles in town. Sian hailed her from across the room. Indira waved back, weaving her way through the tables to join her in the tiny booth crammed into the corner.

"Whoa, look at you. You're a walking painting." Sian stood to share a brief, tight hug, before sliding back into her seat. Sian was a longtime friend-with-sometimes-benefits, and their Wednesday nights were a long-standing tradition.

Indira had picked a black sleeveless dress with a thin wavy line of green up one side, leaving her tattoo visible. She found she was choosing her clothing to match it these days, an impulse she didn't quite understand, considering what it had already done to her—and was possibly doing to her now. It *was* nice to look at, though. Kera Tehari had turned her into art, and it wasn't the artist's fault the paint had been tainted.

She smiled, holding her arm out at Sian's prompting so that she could turn it this way and that in the light.

"Seriously cool. How's it working?"

"On my allergy? Well enough," she answered carefully, avoiding her friend's eyes as she squeezed into her side of the booth. "It heads reactions off at the pass. And it's hypnotic to watch."

They were regulars at the restaurant, on first-name terms with the chef and owner, a slight Japanese man who looked to be in his early sixties, but who was rumored to have started the restaurant himself, over a century ago. They didn't have to order; he would make them something special that wasn't on the menu. Once Indira was settled in, the chef's daughter brought them two glazed cups, exchanging tea for pleasantries and leaving the teapot for them in the center of the table.

While Sian chattered about work and local news, Indira inched her skirt up and dabbed the corner of her napkin to the bandage just below her knee. When she brought the napkin back up, she could see it was stained with a dark spot in the dim light. She shivered. She'd shaved more than twelve hours ago, but the little cut where she'd nicked herself with the razor still hadn't clotted.

Slowly, under the table, she pulled a new bandage from her handbag and applied it to her leg, then sealed the overflowing one in a plastic bag and sanitized her hands. She barely heard a word Sian said over the panic pounding in her ears, but she forced herself to breathe slowly, smile, and nod.

Clotting factors. Her third case against Gannon & Perez.

"Sian," she said quietly, closing her purse and bringing both hands above the table to cradle the warmth of her teacup. "Something's wrong."

Her friend glanced around the crowded restaurant. "What is it?"

"The med-tat is handling the perfume allergy, but . . . it's got a couple of hidden bonuses added in."

She frowned. "Indi—"

She laid it out for her: the chocolate, the rashes and muscle soreness, the diagnosis, and now the bleeding. Sian's frown only deepened as she listened.

"Do you need to go to the emergency room?"

Her heart stuttered at the phrase. She'd had enough of hospitals for a lifetime.

"No. Not yet."

Sian gave her a long look.

"It's just a small cut. I promise, I'm going back to my own doctor tomorrow."

The other woman's mouth pinched but she gave a short nod. "All right. So what's the likelihood that G and P knew you were signed up for the tattoo?" she asked.

"As individuals? They shouldn't have known at all. Not beforehand, with enough time to tamper with my tattoo. That's a patient confidentiality issue. I prosecuted a case against them for that."

"Oh, that thing with the senator?"

She nodded. "But they sent me flowers, so they definitely know now. I also ran into Heather Gannon's personal assistant in the pharmacy queue yesterday after my appointment. I wasn't trying to hide my arm from her, but they shouldn't have known ahead of time."

"Yeah but that doesn't mean they didn't." Sian scowled. "OK. So then, what's the likelihood that they're trying to get revenge?"

Indira frowned. "Low. They're not stupid. Why would they have done this deliberately? This is their chance to get my sympathy, or public trust—maybe I'd drop out due to conflict of interest, or maybe they'd start a new ad campaign: 'Even Indira Chang has one.' So, why would they be hurting me instead of using me? They'd have to think I'd be high profile about it, if my tattoo was faulty."

"You wouldn't go to the media, though."

"But they can't know that."

Her friend gave her a wry look, dropping her gaze to the cup in her hands as if looking for answers in it. "Maybe they want you to cry wolf and discredit yourself? If you turn up with a boatload of symptoms unrelated to what your tattoo's even for, and you go public and it's disbelieved . . ." She shrugged. "No. That doesn't make sense, either. Your doctor has records, right?"

"Yes. I considered that. There's no way it would work. And look at how it's happening. It's too obvious. These complications are popping up rapid-fire, in the same order as the cases I prosecuted against them. There's no way that these conditions, in this order, can be random."

"But why? It's like they're jumping up and down shouting at you that they're doing something incredibly illegal and unethical and easy to prove against them. *Why?*"

Indira sighed, an angry breath hissing out between her lips. "I don't know yet. But I will."

As promised, she was back at her doctor's office when the door opened the next morning. And it went as she knew it would. Dr. Haskins went from stunned to appalled to visibly angry. "If you were anyone else," she said, her stylus jerking angrily on the screen, "I wouldn't be writing old-fashioned prescriptions. I'd be recommending you get the treatments added to your tattoo. These are exactly the sort of things the tats are for." She shook her head. "Treating, I mean, not causing."

Armed with yet another prescription for a condition she shouldn't have, and a tight line of medical glue sealing the cut at her knee, Indira marched into work. She took Dan with her into the DA's office and shut the door.

An hour later, they emerged. The look on Dan's face sent the staff scattering as he stormed into his office.

Heather Gannon laced her perfectly manicured fingers together, setting her hands on the polished conference table like a still-life of innocence and diamonds. Lucy Perez sat beside her, the couple flanked by their lawyers. Lucy was sharp and professional and probably pretty. It wasn't something you noticed when her wife was in the room.

"Miss Chang, I can't tell you how appalled we are to hear of your recent difficulties," Heather said. "Horrified for you. We will, of course, do everything we can to help."

"I certainly appreciate your concern, Ms. Gannon, but I'm not here in an official capacity this time. I'm just an observer."

"Nevertheless, you have my deepest sympathy."

"Heartbroken, I'm sure," Dan rumbled under his breath.

Indira threw him a look, then turned back to Heather and Lucy with a smile that was only half plastic. "Shall we get back to business?"

Dan cleared his throat and passed a notarized page across the table. "So. Regarding the settlement of People and Gregory Armstrong v. Gannon and Perez . . ."

Later, as they filed out of the room, Indira noticed that Heather put her hand to the small of Lucy's back, but Lucy picked up her pace and it fell away.

Indira was in conferences all day. Her leg was still sore but she tried not to think about it. It was late afternoon before she had a chance to go to the washroom. When she pulled up her pant leg, her stomach rebelled at the sight of a swollen field of deep purplish-blue that climbed her thigh like a malevolent stain. It seemed that sealing the little cut with surgical glue had been a mistake.

She didn't want to deal with anyone else's sympathy or out-
rage, so she drove herself to the emergency room. You knew
you had it bad, she thought, when the ER took you in right
away and didn't make you wait. She was soon ensconced on
an uncomfortable hospital gurney, with an IV, an injection, an
elevated leg, and the murmur of doctors beyond the thin
shield of the curtain.

The clotting agent wasn't working—the med-tat just kept
pumping out more anticoagulant, fighting off the IV fluids,
the injection, and the prescription pills. The cut was still bleeding, but with nowhere for the blood to go, it had backed up
and turned into an internal hemorrhage. Looking at her leg
sickened her, so she kept the blankets pulled up. Whenever a
doctor or nurse came to inspect it, she looked away.

They couldn't just turn the anticoagulant action off in the
tattoo, the attending doctor explained, because they couldn't
find it; because it wasn't supposed to be there in the first place.
The theory was that equal-and-opposite doses would cancel
each other out, but it wasn't working. However much antidote
they pumped into her, her engineered cells just produced that
much more, creating a standoff of Cold War proportions under her skin. It felt like her leg might swell up like a balloon
and explode at any moment, spilling red along the pilled surface of the hospital blanket.

Indira passed the time watching the reddened leaf where
the new coagulant had been implanted. It shifted and shimmered its fall colors in the light; as if blowing on it might make
it fall off her arm entirely and float away. Maybe there was
some nice medication in that IV bag, too.

Dr. Haskins stopped by on her evening rounds, looked at
the injury with a concerned frown she couldn't completely
conceal, and patted Indira's hand. "I've ordered a procedure to
install a drain and relieve some of the pressure in your leg.

You'll also need a transfusion to replace the blood you're losing. Ordinarily, that would just be a temporary measure, and
then we'd queue up your tattoo to start creating extra red
blood cells, but in your case . . ."

Indira smiled wanly. "Yeah. Old school all the way, please."

Indira was out of surgery and sitting up in bed when Heather
Gannon appeared from around the corner and rapped three
times on the frame of the open door. Impeccable as ever in an
ice-blue suit with a white collar, she walked in with a modest
bouquet of wildflowers and a card. She set the flowers on the
end of Indira's bed. They rested awkwardly against her foot.

"I want you to know I *am* sorry, Miss Chang," she said.

Indira frowned at her. "For what?"

Heather hesitated. It was the first time Indira had ever seen
her look uncomfortable or uncertain. "Have you ever been angry at someone and pinned their photograph to a dartboard,
or written an angry letter you knew you'd never send?"

"What are you talking about?" Indira whispered. Even
through the lingering haze of sedatives and pain medication,
she was afraid she knew.

"When you won those cases against us, I was angry. We
filed those clients' serum away so that it couldn't be used ever
again, and—not out of real, personal malice, you must believe
me—I . . . I keyed them to your name. Just to relieve the anger, you understand." The unflappable calm Indira had always
admired and hated about the woman was tainted with a restless agitation that made it hard to see Heather Gannon in this
woman at her bedside.

"Wait. You were mad at me, so you . . . what, put my name
on defective vials, for spite?" Fear fluttered behind Indira's
haze of medication and disbelief.

Heather's voice was crisp and clinical, and it trembled. She

didn't meet Indira's eyes. "No one ever thought you'd get a
med-tat. And when you did . . . The system is automated. It
pulled everything with your name on it before I even knew
you'd come to us. I know you won't believe me, but we—I—
didn't do this to you on purpose. If I'd known this could happen, if I had any inkling, I'd have deleted it out at once."

"Why are you telling me this?" Indira rasped, her voice thin
with horror. "You think I won't go after you for this?"

Heather shook her head with a sad sigh. "I'm sure you *would*."

"Then—"

Indira's throat started to itch and the familiar shot of adrenaline hit her bloodstream like a kick in the head. Her heart
thundered in her chest, her vision going red around the edges.
Pain lanced through her head. She lifted a shaking hand to
her nose and blood dripped into her palm, another droplet
trickling down her lip. Clumsy with panic and too much adrenaline, she grasped for the call button to summon help, but a
second rush hit and overwhelmed her. The adrenaline feedback loop, of course, and Indira realized that Heather knew it,
too—she'd programmed it herself, into a tattoo she never expected Indira to get. Hit after hit of epinephrine flooded her
system without regulation. She gasped for air, in great big
gulps that weren't enough. Her monitors started beeping in-
sistently. Pulse and BP were erratic. She couldn't catch her
breath.

"You . . ."

"I'm so sorry, Miss Chang. Really I am." She took Indira's
hand, and Indira was too weak to pull away. Disoriented, she
thought she caught a whiff of the flowers at the end of the
bed. Or perfume.

"I heard you'd gotten the tattoo," Heather continued,
speaking a bit more quickly, as if she was trying to get her
confession out before it was too late. "And I was frightened. I

sent flowers. I arranged to have others keep an eye on you, to tell myself it had all gone OK, but I realized quickly enough that it hadn't. I wanted to warn you earlier, but Lucy wouldn't let me. It's *our* company, you see? We started it together while we were still in med school. Before we were married, even. It's *us*. It would kill her to see it brought down."

Indira lifted her head, studying Heather Gannon through blurred, pounding vision. Instead of ringing the call button for help, or asking what she could do for Indira, Heather's priority was the unburdening of her own soul. It more than canceled out any sympathy Indira might have otherwise tried to summon for her.

The world was going soft around the edges, the sounds muted and far away. Indira was vaguely aware of an ache in her chest, and barely noticed when her telemetry monitors started beeping wildly. Heather straightened, brushing the wrinkles out of her skirt with a last look at Indira that might have been compassion. Or pity. "Help! Someone!" she called into the corridor, with believable panic in her voice. The echo of her heels clicking down the hall receded in perfect meter with Indira's too-rapid heartbeat, until neither could be heard anymore.

LADY WITH FOX

Gregory Benford

Michelangelo reputedly said that the raw slab of marble contains the statue within it, and it is the sculptor's task to chip away at the stone until the statue inherent inside is finally revealed.

Gregory Benford is a practicing research scientist, an astrophysicist, to be precise. And one of the most talented and insightful writers in the field of science fiction.

In "Lady with Fox" Benford examines some of the possibilities of future research into human cognition: how this two-pound lump of cells in our craniums directs everything our bodies do, from drawing breath to writing equations.

More than that, "Lady with Fox" is an exercise in minimalism, in chipping away more of the excess marble than most writers dare to try to do. With a rare economy of words, Benford brings before our minds' eyes a world that is similar, yet different, from our own.

What is not different is that, despite great gains in knowledge of how the brain works, we are still governed by our emotions.

Which is why we can enjoy stories such as "Lady with Fox."

There was an interesting new lady in town, I heard, somehow associated with the Biopolis crowd. She was said to be a "konn natural" as SanJi put it and to have some kind of spiff new pet.

I put the stories out of my mind, since I had plenty of work to do. Konning was a hot topic because it was a pathway between minds when two people "konn-ected," as the lingo went, using the new neural interface technology while sleeping. It gave new meaning to the old cliché of sleeping together.

But then I saw her in the orchid garden, sitting on a far bench while listening to the horticulture lecture at a distance. Not a young woman, with a jawline and sharp nose like a sketch of a face seen from the side. She wore a sleek green dress that fit into the park perfectly, offset by all the orchids in their rich wealth of color around her. She sat quietly and her silver-outlined, turquoise earrings set off the curving grace of her neck. It was the kind of jewelry people buy during their vacations at AmerIndian reservations because that's what you do, and then never wear, but the turquoise looked fine on her.

I watched her sit there and pay close attention to the lecture, held in the open air for the public. It was about establishing standards on how much gene tinkering a proper orchid farmer could use. There were laws about that but they were not working, and the lecturer didn't like that.

Something stirred at her feet and I saw a small furry thing that sat looking intently at the lecturer, too, as if the mutated canine could follow it. Maybe it could, somehow; there was a lot of uplifting going on, most of it not within the law.

SanJi had said she had a kind of depth in the konn but nothing more than that. It was the kind of thing hard to describe, SanJi said. I had heard that he was somehow involved with the woman. I saw she had a muscular grace as she rose, applauding politely at the end of the lecture. She turned away, not waiting for the question period, and I saw the canine was a bright maroon fox. She held it on a leash and it danced around showing a lot of white in its bright animated eyes.

The clean, sure bone structure of her face showed well as

she turned into the sun and sailed off with the cute foxy thing at her heels. It kept looking up at her as if to see if she was still there.

I did nothing then because I like to take my time. I went about my usual research on neurological networks and at parties heard more about her being good at konn, unusually receptive. Konn was poorly understood but much discussed. Gossip is, in my experience, fast talk about what you don't understand but want to. It is no deeper than that. Primate stuff, relieving mental pressures.

No one knew where she was from or where she lived. She showed up at Institute talks and took notes but never asked a question. Some of the postdocs said she was in a subject trial with high constraints but nobody actually knew.

I did recall though that just before she left the orchid garden she had turned and looked back at me, to see if I was still there and watching her.

She appeared in the cafés frequented by the biotech types eagerly in the land rush frenzy now running strong. Times were getting wild. Singapore had made so much from being the middle man for petro-chem industries, there was money galore to spare for research. And the elites in America and Asia weren't getting any younger.

There were real advancements in understanding human mortality, how it came from trade-offs evolution made between young success and reproduction versus older bad side effects that eventually killed you. It was all about how a species can't pass on useful changes in the genes beyond the age of reproduction. Or for social species like humans, birthing ability plus some rearing time from uncles and aunts and so on.

That antagonism of early birthing led to the unique human

condition. We know we will die and watch as evolution gives us countless ways to make it happen.

I worked on the neural side of this. I saw the lady and her fox in the cafés with people I knew slightly. They seemed to hang on her every glance. There was a big Greek who sold carbon sequestration schemes and he was always at her side when she chose to let him. She avoided crowds and worked the men especially. There was always some man to take her to dinner, I noted.

I ate out usually as I was single and between significant women as well. It was easy to stay in the Biopolis biotech community and not have to go through the difficulties of living in an Asian culture you didn't understand. In this way I was lazy. I saw the Greek man and occasionally a couple with her at dinner. There was often another man hanging around, within view and trying to catch her eye. That didn't work.

I had something of the impulse those others did. When she sat alone except for the fox in an open-air café, usually with a mocha coffee confection in her glass, I would walk by her table. She kept her eyes on her coffee and her fox, which scampered around yipping whenever he was in the spotlight of her attention.

If she had arched an eyebrow I would have stopped and said something but she did not.

I was having trouble with new ideas for my research agenda. My collaborators, assistants, and lab techs all worked well together, but the animating ideas for our mapping agenda had to come largely from me.

I used a method to stimulate contact with my own wellspring of ideas. Every evening I reviewed my problems and promising avenues just before falling asleep. Upon waking I kept my eyes closed and recalled those thoughts. Perhaps a third of the time a notion would be there. They came like odd glancing flashes— a word, a glimpsed connection, sometimes an entire logical scheme.

For free. All done by my unconscious. Most of what we are comes from that shadowy realm. Evolution has made us so that we cannot see where and how such work gets done. Which makes it more alluring.

Sometimes these ideas proved useless or wrong. Usually they worked. Most were small measures—an observation to make in a paper underdraft, or a fresh layered code approach to information filtering. But sometimes they were wholly new, a different line of attack. Those came seldom but were worth it when they did.

I had been trying this for years but lately got nothing. My unconscious would not speak. I tried the same method with an afternoon nap as well but nothing was waiting for me when I awoke. I went for walks and went diving at an offshore island but nothing changed.

That was why I was back in the orchid garden again a week or so later to read and think on a neuronal analysis problem when I saw her again. She must have liked the delicacy of orchids in their bright fine colors. Or so I assumed, and so got up and walked toward her. At her stylish heels of a satin color I saw dancing the foxy thing, its eyes ratcheting around.

"Is it bred or engineered?" I said with an eye shrug toward the soft yaps below us.

"Bred yes, and quite well, and so am I."

I liked that and leaned in. Our smiles were exact in their mutual examinations. A lot of people were sharp-eyed about genetic mods now and the idea of breeding, or "animal husbandry" as it used to be known, was alive in the endless media shouting arena. Breeding through generations was supposed

to be more virtuous than just going into the genome and finding what you want, an argument I didn't want any part of. So I
just smiled.

We talked about that as we walked along the sweet-scented
corridors of orchids. Her laugh when I managed to get off a
toss of words was light and airy, tinkling in the warm moist air.
The ponds alongside the orchid pyramids echoed the many
hues of plant nobility, in lapping waters that reflected the endless silent tropical blue sky above.

We got on well. She shyly allowed me to know her name,
Aliim. I congratulated myself at this small triumph, because
those good or even accessible to konn were much sought after. Women were more than men of course. There was an ur-
gency we men carry that finds no echo in women, at least not
yet in this new odd area.

That konn intersected the field of my research mattered less
than my simple curiosity. Seldom do fresh areas of research
come into the shifting foggy realm of direct experience. Neural domain science was for this turbulent decade a place where
a scientist's experience meant more than a plain flat spread-
sheet of data. I felt I had to experience the actual.

She did not tell me her last name and I never learned it. I
suppose that was not relevant. I was not after data.

I took her to a fine lunch. We had small fish fried in a spicy
batter. With these went crickets lightly simmered in cream
and garlic. All of this came with beer in large frosted mugs
that I hoped would loosen her tongue. After a while as we
watched the fishing boats work in the distance and heard the
muffled buzz of traffic she began to speak on her own without
prompting.

She reminisced about her background working on boats up
in Thailand. I felt it was not relevant to what I wanted and so
cannot recall much of that. Still she seemed to warm to me

and I to her and the possibility of a full deep konn seemed to float above our conversation like an implied possibility.

After that we walked along the canals looking at the barges bringing in produce and biomass to the city.

"They run on solar?" she asked skeptically.

Big dark panels shadowed the barges and drove them with aching slowness. The decks bulged with bio bundles as the carbon laws required. Tiny cabins in the stern were neat and clean, with flowerpots and white curtains. A big woman steered a nearby one with a pipe as the tiller.

"I grew up on such a boat." She said it flat and plain. "Hard times."

The fox was getting frisky and she tossed it a ping-pong ball. To my surprise it stood on hind legs and began to bat the ball back and forth. I watched this and noticed the floppy ears and white splotches in its fur. Along with the tail that perked up when people paid attention to it, there were the bright dancing eyes and blunt muzzle and gleeful yips that the bioengineers used to make animals cute. I knew such animals carried genes that made more serotonin when the animal performed, and that people were carrying such genes now to keep them mellow. But this one could also dance on two legs and that implied more embedded skills. Then I noticed that its yips were actually compressed words. It barked out "good!" and "great!" and "yeee!" and "fun!" When its eyes weren't tracking the ping-pong ball it sent jerky glances at us, the audience.

"A very impressive animal. You must have paid well to have it so upgraded."

She shrugged. "They gave it me."

"Very generous."

"I was in konn trials. They are kind to some of us."

Kind if you are a prize subject, I imagined. "I heard that you were very accomplished."

"The SanJi man. He talks a lot."

"He was very complimentary."

"He wants konn. Does not know how to get it."

"There are few who can do it well," I said to be saying something and not knowing where to go with this.

"I am one such."

"So I hear."

"And I choose my communion."

I had not heard that term used about konn but the religious element made sense. "I suppose that's what we all want, madam. Deep connection."

"It is not for sex."

"I suppose not."

"You say you are doing neurological net research and yet have not experienced this?"

I shrugged, unsure what to say. Embarrassed, too.

"I will think on it." She got up and walked away without another word. The fox glanced at me uncertainly and then hurried to catch up. When she turned to see if I was watching I quickly looked away.

On a slow day, we process about twelve thousand thoughts. Thinking fast and hard, that number can climb to fifty or sixty thousand. But then most minds need to rest.

Many labs in Biopolis study the intricate neural webs that make all this happen. I had built a simulation of human memory that attracted considerable interest but I felt I didn't understand memory well. No one did. My model was a pleasant toy but it could not approach the basic problem.

"Don't think about it too much," SanJi said to me as he sipped a Singapore sling in a downtown bar. Warm breezes wafted by, scented with honey. "Let your intuition work on it."

I was sticking to tea for now. "I can simulate neural sorting methods and match them with lab experiments, fine. But that's just the conscious work. Our brains send us about eleven million bits of data a second, while we can consciously deal with maybe fifty a second. We're aware of maybe five percent of what we're thinking about, tops."

"Sure, the other ninety-five percent gets worked over out of view. We run on a stripped-down simple model of what's really happening."

"Which means a real human-level artificial mind is impossible."

SanJi shook his head. "Maybe not. We can run a model of the unconscious in background, though. We're the sum of conscious and mostly unconscious processes. The only direct way into the unconscious is a konn. They're rare. We don't even know why, but they are."

SanJi worked in the rather vague area of konn technology and he talked about it for a while as I tried to follow. It was not my field and like many tech types SanJi would lapse into jargon or details when what I wanted to know was the basic mechanism. I finally said, "Dreams, isn't it?"

"We don't really know much, but in a way, yes. That's why nobody can konn except when both are asleep."

"Amazing it took us so long to think of studying people linked while sleeping."

"But what you see on konn isn't dreams. It's the other unconscious mind at work. There's a sensation of past events called up and reviewed, usually with images. Bland stuff, really. Most is just people talking to the subject—you're always in the viewpoint of your konn partner, of course."

"Nothing juicy?"

"Oh, sex? Some of that. But realize how much of your day is about having sex." He laughed and ordered another sling, eyeing the waitress in her sarong. "I don't mean thinking about it—that's a lot, right? There's plenty more of that than the real thing. Turns out, when you're asleep there's even more."

This wasn't really a revelation but I wanted to find out about the lady with the fox so I listened to him go on about theory. Imagination is fine but experience is better, my thesis professor had said. "So how do you know this?" I cut in.

"I am about to make a konn. My own." He said this almost sheepishly.

"Oh really? With Aliim?"

He jerked and nearly spilled his drink on his crisp white pants. "You . . . know her."

"Not as well as you do, apparently."

"She is said to be the best."

"I admire your ability to make a konn with her."

"I have grant support."

"Even better. You do not need to use other things."

He looked at me sharply. "What other things?"

"There are many temptations in the world."

"What do you mean?"

I was getting tired of this but said, "She must live somehow. And it is not as if there is sex involved."

"Of course not."

"Then it is perfectly fine," I said with a smile. "An experiment."

I spent some time then with a woman field biologist who was quite entrancing, and so for a week or two forgot about the lady and how SanJi wanted to know her so much. I did recall from earlier talks that SanJi could not really konn with his wife.

SanJi had tried to demonstrate his love for his wife in the usual way men did. Then he got the idea that with a link and konn it would be even greater. He talked about it with some of us. The zest of the new and the strange had come into him.

When it failed a kind of light went out in him, I could see. He did not speak of it but I could see when it was there no more.

That was when the technology was new and everybody thought it would sweep the world. As it turned out there were many mismatches in the neural patterns, which meant most of the time you got nothing from going into the chamber and falling asleep while linked to another on the konn tech. There was a brain-derived neurotrophic factor that stopped the melding going forward. Most often you just got a headache.

Then I ran into him at a reception for the Chinese investor who was dropping a billion dollars into Biopolis. I was not in line to get any support from it but SanJi was and he beamed with a fixed grin. I had a gin and tonic and he a Singapore sling again. The party was in an ample garden rich in tropical plants that added a fragrant flavor to the usual mutter of party talk. That and the crunchy sweet and salted insect finger food.

"How's your research going?" I said while glancing at his wife. She had beautiful deep eyes and a glassy look, too.

"Very well, very deep. I am getting great results. Detailed. Topographic."

I wondered what that might mean and then saw the lady with the fox. The tiny dancing fox was entertaining a crowd of Chinese who were not good at holding their booze. They laughed with chattering delight at the fox that danced on hind legs and juggled the ping-pong ball. It said in its whispery bark, "Great! Grr! Good! Grrr! You fine!"

They were all busy being amused so I went away to talk to a lab director and get some networking done. An hour later I came drifting back through that part of the garden and saw she was alone. The fox looked tired as it lapped a sugary bowl of something.

"How'd the show go?" I used as an opener.

"I do not know your meaning?"

"You've been quite the object of interest for a while now. SanJi is doing solid research with you, he says." He had said no such thing but his wife had made him leave the party earlier so I knew this lady Aliim could not check on this. Quite probably none of us would recollect our conversations in the morning.

"I have collaborated with him, yes." Guarded eyes.

"I envy his access."

"Do you? Yet you have never broached the subject with me."

I tried not to blink or show surprise. "My research—"

"Could be actually in this area." She gave me a hard stern level look and waited.

"I would need to have proper controls."

She knew I was stalling. "Of course."

"And I would need compensation."

"Of course."

"I assume we are not speaking of my mathematical abilities but of the konn."

I said I had forgotten that she did some sort of mathematics.

"It is my outstanding ability actually."

"My outstanding talent is modesty."

She chuckled and I felt we had negotiated something here so I said, "Yes, it is the konn I want."

"It requires some preparation on my part."

"Then would you be willing . . . ?"

She said nothing, just smiled. A slow sliding smile.

SanJi said he did not mind if I worked with her, too. "Remember that she is a mathematician. In my exposure—I do not think 'experience' is the right word, for it is like basking in the sun—that informs her unconscious organization."

"Is she noted for her originality?"

"Somewhat. Mostly she works in knot theory and combinatorics. Or she says so. I think she knows more about neural nets than knots."

I knew none of those fields but her laconic conversations did hint at a severity of view. "What are her k-fibers like?"

SanJi took a while to answer. He and I worked within the current view of a mind as a society of agents. This was not the consequence of some basic principle or some simple formal system. Different agents can be based on different types of processes with different purposes, ways of representing knowledge, and methods for producing results. As the founder of this approach, Marvin Minsky had said, intelligence stems from our vast diversity, not from any single, perfect principle. But you had to know the parts well.

SanJi said, "I didn't find k-fibers at all. It's more like an . . . exposure. With no map."

His eyes flickered several times and he looked out the window of his office where we were having coffee. A tropical storm was heaving in off the speckled sea and lightning forked down in big yellow strokes beneath purple clouds.

The flicker was a tell I had learned from watching him over the years. It meant a censor k-fiber was preventing an idea from coming to his conscious mind. Just briefly I saw what his unconscious was doing without his knowing it. Our jargon means that a knowledge-fiber records what resources his mind used to solve a problem. Calling up that fiber of connections means he could use them again to solve some similar problems. Or the k-fiber can decide to suppress conscious access.

"Then it has no trouble detector?" I said to jar him a little. As we thought of it, a suppressor prevents a dangerous act. A trouble detector was a higher level knowledge-fiber that looked at other higher-level k-fibers and warded off conflicts the unconscious didn't want to deal with. Or didn't want the conscious mind to know.

"I suppose not. That's why dreams are so gaudy."

"Sure, they violate social norms. It's their job."

SanJi looked worried by this and his brow furrowed. He watched the storm and jerked when a lightning flash cast searing light into the office.

I decided to press him harder. "Does it have agents that can easily switch between representations?"

"I . . . don't know. It's hard to describe seeing it, feeling it."

"Why? Is it murky?"

"It's not like seeing something. Being in konn is . . well, thinking things only they aren't your thoughts."

"You don't control them?"

"You can't. I tried."

"So a k-fiber turns on a particular set of agents? Then it runs and—"

"They run in the background. They can't be bothered by the conscious mind intruding. Something blocks that."

"What's it feel like?"

"I was outside her mind but in it in . . . well, a different way. I could experience chunks of reasoning going by. Bits of language. Memory flashes. It was powerful, I can tell you that. And fast."

We called them k-fibers because they turn on sets of agents and can cause a cascade of effects within a mind. "You felt emotions come in?"

"Yes . . ." His eyes followed the big-bellied purple clouds. "Like this weather. They override the k-fibers."

That fit our ideas but was hard to fit into neural models like the ones I built. The brain has rule-based mechanisms we call selectors that turn on emotions. They sweep k-lines before them, taking over a problem and forcing a solution.

SanJi said, "We build multiple models of ourselves. They fight inside us."

He seemed to be drawing away from me, turning inward. To draw him out I said, "It's hard to model deep-rooted neurotic anxiety, phobias, panic attacks, or obsessive-compulsive disorders. Why?"

"Because some model we have of ourselves is fighting for its life. I—" he said suddenly, then stopped.

I tried to catch his eye. "Look, I'm going into konn with her soon. I want you to know that."

SanJi stiffened but didn't take his eyes from the storm.

Even in the chilly lab context it was strangely intimate. I knew generally about the connectivity issues and the tests they both had to run through. The lab techs were bored and didn't try to hide it.

Aliim lay there and said little. So did I. This was research after all but I felt my heart accelerate in the quiet shadowy pod. I marveled at how small the EEG electrodes were wrapped around our heads. The techs did some run-throughs and then we just went to sleep.

I kept myself distant using the sleep control methods the EEG augments allowed. I felt the konn enter through slow wave sleep. It was like riding a beat-up surfboard in the lazy afternoons of my boyhood. Slow waves rose warm and slow and synchronized. I felt the pulsing surges dominate my cortex. My years of study allowed me to sense that in this phase of sleep, slow wave activities were recorded, filtered, and fed back to Aliim and me. I felt the clock shop effect kick in. Long ago artisans noticed that mechanical clocks placed against a wall that could transmit vibrations would all eventually tell the same time.

I slipped into a sure steady resonance, the clock shop phase, rising fast and then I lost it—

Bursting yellow light fell across on a sheeting blue plain. Speckled green things moved on it in staccato rhythm—

I was inside her mind. I knew it was her unconscious because I tried to send her messages and there was dead silence, no response. So I relaxed and let it wash over me.

Twisting lines meshed there and wove into triangles. Frantic energy pulsed along these as they warped into strange saddle-pointed envelopes. Electric blue light played along them as they coiled into new soundless shapes—

A shrill grating sound made me turn my head. Flashes of crimson.

Thick, rich red foam lapped against bright yellow lines. *Must be circuits,* I thought and with that a weathered brass thing towered beside me. It oozed slime. I felt sudden cold panic. I wanted to watch the landscape below as the tower groaned and spun softly.

I could see through its brassy skin. Inside it shimmering drops beaded on a coppery matrix of wire. They oozed prickly flashes with a rattling sound.

I had to force myself to look away from it. Thudding sounds hammered in the air. Salty air washed over me. I shivered.

I tried to watch the intricate play of light along the swarming geometries. In quick pulses I felt in rapid play: surprise, joy, a sheeting trembling fear. I had to ignore these flickers of emotion to see the patterns moving along wiry paths. Trembling sprays of glowing orange fought across the brass tower and it seemed to move toward me. *Knowledge-fibers?*

Fear won. I turned and ran. Hot sweat trickled into my eyes—

—Upward, toward the watery light—

I was awake. Her eyes were closed, face empty.

I came away from it awkwardly on legs of cotton.

I woke in the night, sweating. I rolled over tangled in the bedclothes, muttering in the dark.

I had seen all that again. Not as it happened on konn but in shots of sudden seeing. Not nightmares, not precisely. Something else. Something intermediate.

I had seen now an ellipsoidal sun spinning soundlessly over a silver array that danced with silver glows. A fine-spun coppery matrix simmering on the sharp horizon. The grainy sheen of polyhedra that radiated hard golden light. When patterns merged, I felt my bones hum in resonance.

I got up and made coffee and went for a walk on the beach. This was one of the preserved beaches and I could see the bulwarks holding back the ocean, a flat line on the horizon. The sun was a hazy yellow blob above the heaving sea that lapped nearby.

She came to my home and walked right in without knocking. "I wondered why I did not hear from you."

"I . . . took time to process the konn."

"I always hear from those who commune with me."

"It was . . . strange."

We were both standing and she simply reached out and cupped my balls, hefting them. "It can be better if we do other things, too." Her clear eyes looked directly into mine.

"I cannot afford the research expense." This was a lie and I tried to keep my voice flat.

"I will wait." She turned and walked out.

* * *

I had not seen SanJi since the konn. I was in a garden on the
grounds of the Bezos Institute where he and I work, finishing
a small lunch of sushi when I saw him walking toward me.

I got up to greet him. He came toward me with intent and
his mouth a flat white line. I said hello and he threw his right
fist at my head. I ducked to the side and automatically brought
my hands up.

He said nothing. Once I saw his rigid face I didn't either.

I had trained with a virtual-space exercise sim in simple
boxing when I was fifteen and to my surprise in the next half
minute it all came back to me.

SanJi jabbed at me with his left but I brushed those aside on
my right forearm and shoulder. He was shorter than me and
moved fast and around looking for an advantage. His right
was hanging back. I knew he wanted to distract me with the
left and let the right do the work but he let it out too far. In
the sim that had been a whole lesson, I recalled. Why letting
your big hand drift away took all the power from it.

He had been a dancer once he had said and I could see it in
how he moved. His eyes gave nothing away and his feet were
quick as I tried jabs and hooks. I felt like I was just swatting at
him.

I glanced aside to see if anyone would break this up but
there was nobody else in the little garden. So we would just
have to have it out.

"What's this about?" I said to make him think about something other than my left hand.

His slice of a mouth didn't change and he said nothing. I let
my left dance in front of his nose and then brought my right
around hard against the side of his head. I could feel his ear
crunch but he showed no reaction. He just backed off a bit to
get himself together and then came in again with eyes narrowed.

SanJi tried a flurry of punches that I rode out with my forearms but took a hard shot in my left shoulder that rocked me
around some. I used some footwork I recalled from that sim
training to get him worked around with his right hand even
farther out. The way he held it out long told me he wanted to
use it, so before he could I made a swipe with my own right. He
blocked it well enough with a quick left. In that thin slice of time
I brought my left hard into an uppercut that tagged his nose.

I could feel it squash. Blood spurted into his eye and I caught
him hard in his left cheek with a knuckle punch. He staggered
back and wobbled and I hit him in the gut. He went down in a
sprawl. Not a hard fall, more like he just realized he would be
more comfortable sitting down.

He looked up and me and still said nothing. I turned and
walked away. Later, I realized I had left my lunch behind.

I was sitting in a harborside restaurant where tourists did not
go, doing a watercolor of the harbor and islands beyond. A
little girl came up and said, "What are you doing?"

"Painting a picture," I said. I showed her my palette.

She studied it. "You're not very good, are you?"

That made me laugh. She was quite right, of course.

I felt better now than I had in days. After the fight I had
pursued a sort of Zen mindfulness, purchased with pain. I finished the watercolor and saw what the little girl had seen but I
in my quick moves to capture the light in color had not. I
crumpled it up.

The dreams from the konn had blown away and this morning I had an idea when I awoke. That was the first time in
many weeks and to celebrate I had come out for a long breakfast and the watercolor. The idea I would test in my lab later,
but I knew enough to just let my mind nibble at the idea first
while I did something else.

Only then did I see that Aliim was sitting on the far side of the restaurant.

My first reaction was a quick flash of chilly dislike. Her face swam before me like a pillar of Freudian nightmare. She was playing with the foxy thing and sipping coffee. As usual, she elegantly wore an ivory sarong and simple green sandals, no more.

As I approached her table she looked up and a flicker of wary evasion passed in her face. But she put it away and even gave a thin smile. "How goes your research?"

"Quite well," I said and did not sit.

"Mine as well."

"And what is . . . ?" I felt tense and her eyes never left mine

"I, too, am mapping knowledge-fiber networks. My method however is not yours."

"No doubt." She had never declared her research area before. "I did gain some insights from our konn."

"I, too. Perhaps another session would be useful?" She lifted her cup and I saw a tremor there where none had been before.

"I am quite busy just now."

"I would require a higher fee, of course. I gave you the introductory session at a low rate and already I am well booked."

"I doubt that I can afford you then."

"That is too bad. I had hoped to help you."

"As you have helped many."

"What do you mean by that?"

"Nothing. I gather that SanJi has worked with you?"

We both knew he had but she said, "I am not responsible in any way for his work. Or his reactions."

I did not know what to say and her fox was nipping around my shoes. It stood on its two hind legs and looked up at me with its hard gleaming eyes and yipped little words I finally noticed were "yeee!" and "go!" and "bad!" and "hurt!"

"I never said you were."

In a flinty way she said, "That is good. No matter what others may say."

As I looked back the fox was still dancing and the restaurant owner was coming over to her about the noise.

I did not see SanJi for a while though he worked near my lab. I was in there a lot working on the notion that my unconscious had given me. It had proved to be quite a gift. The layered approach I worked out gave simpler pathways to understanding how our k-fibers organize prior ideas in the cause of new solutions. It demanded that neurotrophic factors cohere in a way I could model with appropriate cofactor mathematics. There were geometric analogies to this that made the whole idea easy to visualize. That is what had come to me that morning when I awoke with the odd notion buzzing in my mind. It was a while before I realized that the geometry came first and the images were like those I had seen in the konn.

I was mulling this over and my conversation with Aliim in the orchid garden one morning before walking to the Institute to begin anew. I was finishing my coffee when I saw SanJi sitting nearby.

I decided to ignore him but he came over and deliberately sat down near me on a bench. His face was drawn and pale and he had lost weight. "It has been a while."

I looked at him squarely and readied myself but caught myself balling up my fists. I made myself relax them. "Your nose shows no damage."

"It did not break."

"I am glad."

"I want to tell you that was not me you were hitting."

"Felt like it."

"I was in a state I cannot describe. I did not know what I was doing."

"Your right hand didn't but your left sure did. I had bruises for a week."

He allowed himself a flat smile. "I came to that state through that woman."

We didn't need to say her name. "For me the konn with her was useful."

"She was in some vague way planning to do research. Meanwhile living off the earnings from her talent."

"Research? Into neural nets? I had the impression she was some sort of mathematician but—"

"The incubation period is several weeks."

"What do you mean?"

"She is not just an unusual konn patient and resource. It develops now that she has a neuvir."

"I thought that was just theory."

"It is real. I have it."

"From her?"

"The only possible path. It made me do this." He swung fists in the air.

"Why me then?"

"I do not know. Some anger she held against you? The neurological virus term is only an analogy. The constellation of ideas somehow becomes self-propagating. The knowledge-fiber can leave one unconscious and install in another. It infests."

"Under konn."

"The theory was there but I find the experience is very different. It was a frenzy."

"So you don't know why me."

"It must have been her anger. I was merely the agent."

"I had konn with her and I have not felt any such effect."

"You had one konn. I had five."

"I didn't know."

"There are others who had long exposures. They had outbursts, too."

"Fights?"

"A few. Some extreme sports, too. All men. With women they would get drunk in bars and take men home. This among calm ordinary women who had never done any such thing. It caused a lot of damage."

"There is a cure?"

"There may be. I am under therapy but it is entirely experimental and ad hoc."

He did not seem like the old SanJi. He seldom smiled and when he did his mouth turned down, not up. Something had been taken out of him.

I did not want to ask him how it had been to be in that state. Maybe the nose was enough.

He looked at me a long time as we said nothing. He took a long breath of the warm air and said, "I used to agree with the great Minsky that it was degrading or insulting to say that somebody is a good person or has a soul. I felt that each person has built this incredibly complex structure, spent a lifetime doing it. We try to map and understand that. If you attribute such majestic structure to a magical pearl in the middle of an oyster that makes you good, that is trivializing a person. That keeps you from thinking of what's really happening."

"Um, yes."

"Now I am not so sure. There can be a pearl or a cinder of coal at the center. Which it is, that emerges from the whole elaborate structure around it."

"So it makes sense to say a person is evil. Maybe like Aliim."

"She is the cinder, yes."

*   *   *

I never saw her again.

But I did get a request for information on konn experiences. I wrote a description and was astonished to see them appear, not in a technical paper, but on Net sites where people went for advice and to consult on the burgeoning phenomenon of konn. I protested but my comments remained there and reportedly many read them.

I spent several years constructing my model. I specialized it to the neural anatomy of human emotion and got some success in predicting behaviors. It even held up well in a two-hundred-person clinical trial in Singapore.

I heard, about that time, what happened to Aliim. She had gone to Hong Kong to be a konn subject and had prospered until the neuvir effect turned up again. One of her subjects with the same k-fiber association transfer. The patient was a woman with considerable martial arts skills. She had gone to the sites where my comments appeared. I had made the mistake of naming Aliim there. She went to see Aliim, hired her, did considerable konn.

Just like SanJi the woman turned on Aliim. She came into Aliim's home and without a word began to beat her. Aliim did not know any fighting skills so the woman worked her over for hours. The Hong Kong police showed the in-home video. Aliim could not defend against the kicks, chops, neck blows, and head-butts. She died.

Had I known of such an effect? The Hong Kong police wanted to know. I related the SanJi incident. They knew it already because I had included it in my Net comments.

The police went away finally. After all I had done nothing beyond publishing comments, as requested.

There was no word about the foxy thing. I never saw another like it either.

I thought about her a lot then. There were other rumors about her but the big fact was the death. It always will be the big fact, now. Experimenting at the edge of knowledge can be wondrous but also fatal. Knowing that is our unique human condition. We know we will die and evolution gives us countless ways that make it happen.

Desires can kill you, too. When she came to my home and tried in her awkward way to seduce me I had not let desire rule me. So she had lost her edge that had come from the konn.

Desire can kill the very good and very gentle and the very brave impartially. If you are none of these you can be sure they can bring you down as well, but there will be no special hurry. So in our pursuit of knowledge we scamper after those desires, much like her fox.

HABILIS

Howard Hendrix

Is the universe left-handed? If so, why?

Hold up your hands before you and take a good look at them. What you are staring at is the most wonderful piece of biological engineering on Earth.

The human hand is the only one (on Earth) in which the thumb can touch the tips of each of the other four fingers. Only human hands can play the violin. Or throw a curveball.

Our hands developed before our brains did, as far as paleoanthropologists can determine. Did our supple hands lead to the development of our complex brains? And intelligence?

Howard Hendrix's tale of right-handedness and left-handedness is a complex, subtle examination of these questions. But what are the answers? Read on.

Driving my used but newly purchased Montjoy LoCat onto the fish hatchery grounds, I can hear the spatter of gravel, despite The Pharaoh and Denile's "Pi-Rat Love" blasting from the vehicle's Airpush speakers. The dusting of new snow on the road doesn't damp down the road noise much—just makes the gravel slicker, easier for me to fishtail sideways, a wannabe big fish in the small pond of Planet Dolores.

Ahead, beside the hatchery's ancient Sun Dog pickup, my boss Mark Kemper is standing, a wiry man with wiry hair. The space around his head is wreathed in the steam of his breath hitting cold air and the smoke of the skankweed stick he's huffing. Chill morning notwithstanding, he's wearing the same old two-pocket, lightweight ASGuard jacket he wore off world during the Knot War. He doesn't like wearing heavy coats, even in cold weather. The pockets bother him. Mark says a man with too many pockets soon finds he has too few hands.

The first time Mark told me the story of his lost and found hand, we were dressed in chest-high waders, sludging out Pond 7, removing the thick, foul-smelling organic muck we'd pressure-hosed from the bottom of the drained pond into the concrete-lined, boxlike depression—the "kettle"—at the pond's deepest point. The stinking stuff—a mix of mud, fish dung, debris, and detritus Mark called "crapioca pudding"—was too thick for the pump to suction up, so we were shoveling the mucky dregs of it by hand from the kettle's bottom.

"I should have died when the Bots turned our own war AIs against us and drove us from Citadel Moon," Mark said. "My left hand was blown away, but that was among the least of my worries. I lay there, bleeding out from half a dozen wounds, among the dead and dying bodies of my comrades, in a dying spaceship, with the Bots breaking through our last bulkhead."

I power the LoCat's passenger window down. Hearing the courtship ballad of Pi-rat Susie and Pi-rat Sam blaring from my speakers, Mark shakes his head. From beneath a mustache smoke-stained the color of rusted barbed wire, he flashes me a lopsided smile.

"A ground effector is not the kind of tuna boat I'd have chosen to drive," he says, thumping the Montjoy, "but that song reminds me of something—beyond the fact that it's ripped off from a two-hundred-year-old pop hit."

He elaborates no further, just opens the battered blue Sun Dog's driver-side door and gets in. I kill the LoCat's engine and the music and exit my vehicle.

"I think that's why I'm still alive," Mark said, glancing down at his complex prosthetic hand, then gazing at the space above the message board in the office where we were taking our lunch break. "That there is why I'm still looking on the sunlight, instead of eternal night. Despite being captured by the Bots."

His gaze, I saw, had come to rest on the banner above the board. The banner was labeled with the digits 0 through 9. Next to them stood the twenty-six letters of the Roman alphabet, capitals and smalls both, from Aa to Zz. The previous fish-hatchery manager had homeschooled her kids here, and the office retained something of the air of a classroom about it.

"What? The numbers and letters?"

"Not just in themselves. The handedness of them, the chirality. Ontogeny recapitulates phylogeny, recapitulates chirogeny, recapitulates cosmogeny. Or maybe cosmogony. The Bots seem to think it's the key to human difference, however you spell it."

"I don't follow you."

"Look at the ten numbers there, and hold out your right hand, palm facing away from you. Sixty percent of them—1, 2, 3, 4, 7, 9—are right-handed, opening outward in the same direction your thumb and forefinger do from your right hand. Now hold out your left hand, palm away again. Twenty percent of the numbers—5 and 6—are left-handed. The remaining twenty percent—8 and 0—express mirror symmetry. You might call those numbers ambidextrous, since they face both directions and neither. See that?"

"I think so."

Opening the creaking door on the truck's passenger side and climbing in, I note the truck cab smells of beer and skankweed again this morning, as it has every morning since Mark and his wife split up, six Doloresian months back.

The tale of the wreck of his marriage is Mark's second most oft-repeated story, and he keeps telling it, though by now he knows I know it by heart: Jinny was the high school sweetheart he married before he caught a NAFAL troopship to the up and out. Quirks of near-light-speed travel and time dilation being what they are, he aged only the two years of his tour fighting the Bots, while Jinny, planetside, aged the twelve years he was gone in her reference frame. She stayed with him five years after he came home, too. She'd long since grown up and grown away from him, though, even before she left, taking their little girl—the save-the-marriage baby that didn't—with her.

"Jinny treated every bump in the road as if it were a cliff," Mark says, always coming to the same point in his sifting of the wreckage. "I treated every cliff as if it were a bump in the road. We just couldn't make that work together, in the long run."

"I passed out from blood loss, certain I would die," Mark said, standing knee-deep in kettle muck. He heaved a great shovelful of sludge into the wheelbarrow on the bank beside him. "Yet against all expectation I woke up again. Unsure how much time had passed, with no memory of my Bot captivity, I found myself dumped out into space, in an environment suit that couldn't sustain me for much longer. I wouldn't have bet on my chances just then, but against the odds I was spotted and picked up by a passing cruiser—one of ours as luck or fate would have it. To this day I don't know whether the *intent* of my abandonment by the Bots was to be lost to my enemies, or to be found by my friends."

As we bump along toward the double sunrise, the Sun Dog's solar-electric motor is inaudible over the squeaking of the truck's bad shocks. We stop at the south end of the hatchery's easternmost pond—the coldest, Pond 1. Both it and Pond 2 have spotted graithlings in them. The other twenty ponds grow a few goldengills, but mostly they're full of slant-head minnows. All three species are sacrifice fish for the EnviroLab on the hill and its LC_{50} tests, which designate a heavy metal, a prionoid seed protein, or other water pollutant "toxic" when a given concentration of the substance proves lethal (within four hours) to fifty percent or more of the fish in the test population. Such tests were long ago banned as inhumane on Old Earth, but they're expedient on a frontier world like ours.

"Now look at the letters," Mark said, pointing at the banner at the back of the office. "Handedness is a bit more complicated for letters than for numbers. Hold out your left hand in front of you again, palm away, so you're looking at the back of the hand. Thumb spread away from the rest of the hand at about a ninety-degree angle. See what direction the thumb points? Capitals B, C, D, E, F, G, K, L, P, R, S—11 out of 26, or 42.3 percent of the alphabet—are left-handed, while only capitals J and Z—2 out of 26, or 7.7 percent of the alphabet—are right-handed. A, H, I, M, N, O, Q, T, U, V, W, X, Y—13 out of 26, or 50 percent—are ambidextrous, although I suppose you could argue Q trends left, and N is some kind of mirror-inverted. Got it?"

"OK . . ." I said, continuing to stare hard at the banner with its basic numbers and letters on the office wall, trying to puzzle through what he was saying.

"Good. Now, of the small letters, $b, c, e, f, h, k, p, r, s$—9 out of 26, or 34.6 percent—are left-handed, while a, d, g, j, q, y, z—7 out of 26, or 27 percent—are right-handed. The remaining small letters—10 out of 26, or 38 percent—are best described as ambidextrous."

I shook my head and whistled softly.

"You've obviously thought and calculated about this a lot, Mark—and those are interesting statistics—but, well, *so what?*"

"See, the Bots have never figured out what hand allows the Raveleras to weave and unweave space-time around them," Mark said, moving the wheelbarrow for me to shovel muck into it, "because it's not something you can do by figuring. Not calculable. But that didn't stop my captors from giving me this hand."

"Any idea why they did that?"

"Many ideas—even if I don't remember when this alien hand joined the rest of my body. Maybe I've kept learning so much about all this, beyond my debriefing, because—despite the memory wipe—some faint trace of my time in Bot custody still persists in my head unconsciously, still keeps prodding me to try to puzzle it out. I don't know for certain, though. I can't explain, for instance, why I absolutely will not allow my faceless 'friends' in our merc-corp government to remove this hand from my body—for their 'research.' Not only because it's interwoven into me deep enough I might die in the process of that removal. I just refuse. That's annoyed the powers-that-be enough that I'm lucky even to have this shit-shoveling fish hatchery job."

Mark shook his head and exhaled.

"So they think me a spy, and spy on me. Maybe they're not the only ones, either. Maybe Hivist turncoats are reporting on me back to their Bot masters, too. Who knows? Maybe you, too, without even knowing it, might be some kind of android designed by the Bots to be indistinguishable from a human being—and you're recording all this for some unseen audience."

He gave me a sly, sideways look. We laughed, but even in my own ears the laughter sounded forced.

At the northern end of each pond stands a spring box. We check the boxes all summer long for any cruncher turtles that, blundering onto the gapped planking atop the sunken concrete boxes and falling between the planks, might have gotten trapped down in the boxes themselves. This morning I doubt we'll find any of those nasty-tempered little dinosaurs. They don't move as much from pond to pond once the weather gets cool.

"'So what?'" Mark laughed and took a bite of his luncherito. "That's what I thought when I was debriefed, too. It took me a while to see it. But try to think like a curious kid for a minute. Notice that the right-handed forms are the most common forms for numbers, but the least common form for letters—both capitals and smalls."

"I see that, Mark. So maybe the differences in spatial orientation of numbers and letters are *statistically* significant. But are they *truly* significant? I don't see the context."

"Neither did I, at first. Maybe that's because the context is so *big*."

"In what way?"

He stared off into a space I couldn't see into.

"People have probably realized that the brain is in two major parts—that it's in two chambers, or *bicameral*—for as long as they've been looking at the brains of their usually deceased fellow humans. A couple hundred years ago researchers started doing split-brain work with living epilepsy patients. They had the connections between the right and left hemispheres of their brains cut, in order to reduce their seizure symptoms. That research led to work on hemispheric dominance, cerebral lateralization—on the 'handedness' of human minds, if you like."

"And numbers and letters say something about that?" I asked, gesturing at the banner with my sandwich.

We decide not to check the spring boxes for wayward turtles after all, and focus instead on looking for the bank pi-rats. It's cold, but the ponds haven't iced over yet. We walk toward the north end of the first pond, each of us pacing a shoreline. As we go along we check the long-spring leg hold traps we've staked into the bank and set for the 'rats, near their burrow entrances. We look for traps whose chains have been run out from the bank, to the deeper water, indicating that a foot-clamped ratty, big as a midsize dog, has most likely dragged the device and itself into that depth and drowned.

Together Mark and I pushed the wheelbarrow up the bank, toward the lowered bed of the Sun Dog. It took everything we had to lever up the handles on the barrow and tilt its load of sludge into the truck.

"This hand is a souvenir," Mark said, as we took a breather. "A scar I can't hide but don't want to lose. A reminder of the Bots' investigation into the interweaving of hands and minds—a crude experiment, for all the magnificent crafting that went into this. No prosthetic that humans have developed can match the nanomechanics of it. I think that's one reason why the military brass still want this hand—so they can reverse-engineer it. I've let them examine its workings, again and again, but I draw the line at letting them try to sever it from my body. They'd love to disconnect it from me the same way the Bots connected it to me: without my permission."

"Right," Mark said, ignoring my sandwich. "For some time now, researchers have wondered if the right-handedness of the majority of numbers might indicate that the left side of the brain, which controls the right side of the body, dominates most in the production of numbers. At the same time, the left side of the brain also seems to be *least* powerful in influencing the production of letters. When you include the smalls, 'ambidextrous' edges, left-handed, out—just barely—as the most common letter-form of all, even if you include capital Q among the block of letters you might call left-handed and right-brained. Makes you wonder if hemispheric *non*-dominance— with a strong tilt to the left hand and right brain, admittedly—is in fact the most 'dominant' factor in letter production."

"That makes both sides of my brain hurt," I said, laughing, "although I guess that makes some sense. What about spatial orientations in numbering systems other than the Arabic, though?"

"In Mayan numerals, for instance? Or how spatial orientation of letters manifests in languages read not left to right, but right to left—in Hebrew, say? Or what about other systems in which the numbers are also letters and vice versa—not only Hebrew but the Roman system, too, whose numerals were not part of a separate numeric system but derived from the Latin alphabet?"

"Let me guess: you've already thought about this."

Mark nodded and leaned toward me.

"I learned in my debriefing that *all* of those questions had already been asked. Neuroscientists, cognitive psychologists, linguistic anthropologists—all of them have been quietly involved in investigating whether or not the spatial orientations of letters and numbers might be evidence of patterns in the 'cultural unconscious' that mirror the evolutionary history of the human brain."

"And they found . . . ?"

"The same patterns, with some minor variations, persist across all human cultures."

That made me pause.

Mark claims his grandfather knew the First Expedition biologist who named these freshwater critters we trap "pi-rats." Although better known for naming our world Dolores after his wife, Hector Quinones was not only the mission's chief population ecologist but also a math geek of the first water— and tagged the bank-burrowers with their odd but appropriate name, given the critters' packrat thievery, giant muskrat looks, and their disproportionately long (seemingly endless) tails.

"As hatchery manager," Mark says when we get to the north end of Pond 1, "I suppose I should reiterate that, officially, we're thinning the pi-rat population because their burrows damage the levees between the ponds. It also just so happens that pi-rat fur is prime now, and bringing a good price."

"My hand is like those other exquisitely complex mechanisms, the prionoids the Bots have been bombing our worlds with," he said, grabbing the wheelbarrow's handles. "Those D-amino transmission particles, meant to morph our brain chemistry, confuse our myriad complications and defeat that thing in human consciousness that the Bots can't figure out. I guess they figure you don't have to understand something to destroy it. But all the Bots' efforts have resulted only in poisonings, and madness, and the necessity of running these LC tests on our air and water."

He lifted up on the handles.

"The poop is in the pudding. Back to it."

I followed him down the bank, and stepped with him into the kettle once more.

"But even supposing, for the moment, we accept that the pattern-thing works, more or less, for every culture   what does it have to do with the Bots allowing you to go on living?"

"Ah. Follow the logic. What started the Knot War?"

I suppose I gave him an odd look, but then shrugged and answered.

"Surprise attacks by Bot forces. Coordinated lightning raids."

"And the goal of those coordinated attacks?"

"To capture the central junction point of universe-lines known as the Big Knot, and to abduct Elena Zametis—greatest of Raveleras in the greatest line of Raveleras—and carry her to the Knot."

"Yes. Which—with aid from singularitarian Hivists, from turncoat human-sphere AIs, and from the strangely willing Elena—the Bots managed to do. So far, so good—but what made it worth going to war over?"

I was beginning to wonder where this belaboring of the obvious might be headed, but I decided to let it roll out a bit longer without comment.

Heading south, back toward the pickup, each of us walks the bank opposite the one he walked on the way out, hoping to catch sight of anything the other might have overlooked. At the south end we climb into the Sun Dog, move the pickup to the next pond, and park again there. Standard operating procedure: walk the levees, check the traps, move and repark the truck, pond after pond.

"I know what you're thinking," he said as we started shoveling the thick muck again. "You think, 'All this war stuff is just a mask for Mark's obsession with his lost hand and lost wife—Napoleon Blownapart mourning the loss of his Josephine. This stuff with numbers and letters, handedness and sides of the brain—hand waving at best, delusion at worst. All just seeing patterns that aren't really there.' And the paranoia about spies and spying! 'Application for membership in the Tinfoil Hat Crew—approved!' as they used to say. But you'd be wrong to believe any of those explanations is sufficient."

"Because all the leaders of the worlds of human space had already sworn to protect the Raveleras," I said, slowly chewing my sandwich.

"Yes. Why?"

"Isn't it obvious? Everybody knows the answer to that."

Mark smiled inscrutably, looked around the office, and nodded.

"Please, bear with me. Again: why?"

"Their ability to travel clewed space, of course. It's what has allowed human crews to pilot starships at velocities within a hair of the speed of light. Their ability to weave and unweave space-time about themselves. To witch the way the subspace web is woven, the way other women once witched the courses of water underground."

"Which means?"

"Which means that humans have been able to spread out

beyond Earth—to settle newer home worlds on Earth-like extrasolar planets."

"Right, but that's not what I was asking. 'To weave and unweave space-time'—what does that mean? How is it done?"

I puzzled over that one a minute, before speaking.

"I gather that's kind of a trade secret among the Raveleras. The scientists theorize about 'q-net'—the quantum something or other."

"Quantum Nonlocally Entangled Tunneling. The webwork of evanescent wormhole tunnels, latent in the fabric of the cosmos."

"If you say so. But the Raveleras talk about how the universe is 'holographically conscious, too.' How, through the altered state of consciousness peculiar to them, they are able to locally alter the structure of space-time. To 'weave a Way out of No Way,' along that infrastructure of threads or lines or tunnels they call clewed space."

"And this 'infrastructure'—what's its origin?"

Whenever we find traps that have been run out on their chains we pull them back onto the bank. Using his gripper-hook prosthetic left hand with the dexterity of a surgeon gaping an incision, Mark has shown me how to prize open like steel clamshells the sprung traps and remove from those metal jaws the beached pi-rats, slick and red-brown and stiff.

"A poet of Old Earth once said that love does not alter when it alteration finds nor bend with the remover to remove. I don't know if it's really true for love—divorce'll sure make you question *that*—but it's definitely not true for the universe. Everything the Raveleras do, with the help of their 'entheogens,' is proof that the universe alters when it alteration finds."

* * *

Under Mark's questioning—especially in the ghost of a classroom still haunting the office—I felt like a truant student facing an oral examination, every query of which was somehow a trick question.

"Presumably the substructure is a natural feature of spacetime," I explained, "although there are those who think it's an artifact created by, well, someone."

Mark gave his inscrutable inquisitor's nod-and-smile again.

"What would you say has been the greatest assurance of the human future, by your lights—and what is the greatest ongoing threat to that future?"

I had to think about that one for a moment.

"I'd say control of clewed space has been the greatest assurance, and the Bots the greatest ongoing threat." A thought suddenly occurred to me—a delayed answer to a much earlier question. "That's why, after the Bot surprise attacks, the leaders of all the worlds of human space had no choice but to raise a thousand-starship armada and go to war at the Knot."

"Very good. But what exactly *are* the Bots—and why did they launch those attacks?"

From Mark I've learned how to reset the traps, pushing the jaws fully open and dogging the trip-pan in each, priming the jaws to snap shut once the pan is depressed by the next creature's paw. For all I've learned, though, I still can't match Mark for speed or skill or experience with the traps. That may explain why, of the five pi-rats we've piled in the bed of the truck by the time we reach Pond 20, four are his work.

"The Knot was our Troy," Mark said, shoveling, "and Zametis our Helen. I was there for her interrogation. She *allowed* the Bots to abduct her."

"Why's that?" I asked, splashing a load into the wheelbarrow.

"Because, despite her webwork witching skills, or maybe because of them. She thought the relatively easy and rapid spread of humanity throughout space by such swift, Raveleran means put off, yet again, our species' having to face the moral hazard of our shortsightedness, when it comes to fouling our own nest. If we can always fly away to yet more new worlds, we never have to live as if the world in which we live has irreplaceable value in its own right."

"The Bots are expansionist machine intelligences," I answered, around a mouthful of my lunch. "There's a lot of debate about their origin. The V'gerists even claim the origin of the Bots can be found in a human space probe that was altered as a result of an encounter with a distant machine civilization—and the transformed probe was the seed for all the myriad Bots that came after. What is certain, though, is that their spaceships are limited to significantly lower speeds than ours, due to the Bots' inability to open space-time and weave a Way out of No Way, the way the human Raveleras can."

"And that's why they wanted the Knot and Elena, then?"

"Yeah. But I still don't see what it has to do with this handedness you were going on about."

At Pond 20, Mark finds something odd enough that he takes his long-ashed skankstick from his mouth and waves me over. He holds up the almost-empty trap, to show me.

"Back on Earth, they'd consider finding *these* in our traps more proof of our 'frontier barbarism'—but this ain't sophisticated Earth, kiddo. One gnawed-off paw is rare enough anyway, but look at this. Two paws, each gnawed off above the wrist."

I nod.

"And they're both left front paws. From two different animals, caught in the same trap at the same time. Hard to tell, but from the smaller size I bet this one's from a female, and the larger one is from a male."

"Maybe the Bots hooked up this prosthetic not just to see how hand and mind cross-reference each other," Mark said, watching me shovel, "but also to see if a little brute-force cybernetics might jump-start the development of what the Raveleras whisper about. The appearance in time of a 'Ravelero' or 'Ravelator,' a male human not only capable of making and unmaking clewed space around himself, but a true tripmaster, not bound by the speed of light."

Mark gestured to the office ceiling to emphasize his point.

"Because handedness is seen everywhere! From the microcosm to the macrocosm, the quantum scale to the cosmological scale, chirality links it all. The universe is not the same in every direction. It violates parity and funhouses mirror symmetry at every scale. The whole show was born spinning about a preferred axis from the very beginning, and that angular momentum, still conserved after fourteen billion years, shows up in an excess of left-handed, counterclockwise rotating spiral galaxies. The majority of spiral galaxies are lefty-loosey, not righty-tighty!"

"Whew! Give me some of that skankweed you've been smoking, Mark! The whole universe rotating like an ice-skater—that makes my head spin!"

"As well it should, young man. And I'm not thinking *this* because I'm smoking *that*, by the way. The spin is all the way down to the smallest scales—not just galaxies and skaters, but protons and quarks as well. Nuclear beta decays, for instance, violate parity in favor of the left hand, too. The versions of molecules like amino acids found in living things—the biologically relevant versions—are overwhelmingly left-handed on Earth and every Earthlike planet we've visited, even though amino acids produced by *inorganic* reactions are equally split between right-handed and left-handed versions! Even the idea that left-handed molecular dominance, found throughout life on Earth, might itself have been extraterrestrial in origin has been floating around a long time. At least since left-favoring enantiomer imbalances were found on the Murchison meteorite—long predating interstellar travel to extra-solar worlds."

"But why should the left hand be favored?"

Mark springs open the trap. He shakes into his cupped right hand the two paws—red-furred hands with disproportionately long fingers and nails.

"I don't know much about pi-rat love," he says, flashing me his lopsided grin again, "but this tells me all I need to know about pi-rat divorce."

We laugh. He draws back his hand to hurl the paws into the pond, then stops. He shoves the two small hands into a pocket of his workpants instead.

"Not for naught did we Nauts of the Knot," Mark sang as he shoveled, *"Teach the Bots how dearly bought was everything they stole!"*

He paused to wipe his forehead.

"You have no idea how many times I sang that song with men and women of the Astronaut Service Guard—now dead, so many of them."

"One great mystery, lots of great theories!" he said, working his way through his luncherito. "Some say the lopsided favoring of left-handed biological molecules—what the experts call biological homochirality—is the result of slightly different half-lives of biologically relevant molecules, stemming from that beta decay connection. Others say it's from the preferential destruction of right-handed amino acids by left-circling polarized light, blasting out of rapidly rotating stars in primordial galaxies. Or Mie scattering on aligned interstellar dust particles, triggering the formation of optical isomers in space. From all or whichever of the above, it's clear the bias in favor of the left hand is not just a local phenomenon."

"You called it a bias in *favor* of left-handedness—yet wasn't the bias *against* left-handedness, in almost all the cultures of Old Earth?"

Mark's face lit up. He had obviously thought about that, too.

Finding no pi-rats around Ponds 21 and 22—the westernmost, warmest, and smallest ponds in the hatchery—we return to the truck's cab. From under the driver's side of the front seat Mark pulls out a beer for himself and one for me, popping the stopper off each brewpak.

"To the silly songs of human freedom," he says, thudding his brewpak against mine in toast, "and what it costs to sing them."

He motioned me over to help him with the wheelbarrow.

"Alien hand notwithstanding, I returned to duty by the time of the final battle for the Knot. I swear, something about my new situation allowed me, and my troops around me, to be everywhere at once in that battle. It was as if something had changed the hand in the mirror of my mind. Suddenly I could funhouse a universe of mirrors, alter the fundamental info coding of the physical cosmos in my own small, unexpected—

and uncontrolled—way. Maybe what the Bots had done to me
had done the trick. If so, it was a trick, in my hands and mind,
that I could now do to them."

Together we pushed the sludge-laden wheelbarrow up the
bank.

"Bias? Oh, yes!" he said, distractedly watching me eat the
last of my sandwich. "The cultural slight of the left hand
goes back to at least the ancient Romans, including the fact
that the Latin word for 'the left side' was *sinister*, meaning
'unlucky,' among other things, and for 'the right side' was
dexter, meaning 'skillful,' among other things. But you don't
have to engage in much sleight of hand—'sleight' from
Old Norse meaning 'sly,' later 'deftness' and 'dexterity,' 'clever
tricks'—to see that the sinister hand of letters is the dexter hand
of numbers, the sinister hand of numbers is the dexter hand of
letters. We're a tricksy species, lucky in that we've been so unlucky, and unlucky in that we've been so lucky."

We drink. Mark retrieves the pi-rat paws from his pants
pocket. Taking a length of baling wire from the storage compartment under the dashboard, he makes a loop from the
wire. He twists the ends so as to bind the paws together at the
wrists, then hangs the whole assemblage from the mirror in
the Sun Dog's cab.

"That's what the Bots, even in defeat, are still trying to figure
out," he said as, together, we tipped the sludge-barrow's contents into the truck's bed. Finished with sludging Pond 7's
kettle at last, we leaned against the truck as he smoked and finished his thought. "How has the twisted mirror of our DNA has
allowed human consciousness to be both chiral and chiasmatic,

left handed—right brained, right handed—left brained? How
that X-ing makes possible the crossing over through all scales,
until all scales fall from our eyes and we see that just as the
universe is 'as above, so below,' so, too, the infinite is closer than
it appears in the mirror. There's no need to be forgiven for
Eden and the 'fall' into knowledge. No need to be acquitted of
crimes never committed."

"Tricksy?" I asked, crumpling up my lunch wrapper. "Lucky
that we've been so unlucky? I don't get that."

"We've probably been *habilis* as long as we've been *Homo*—
handy as long as we've been human. But 150,000 to 200,000
years ago, a chance mutation—some of that same old lucky
unlucky—produced a dextral allele involving the FOXP2
gene and the transcription factor POU3F2. The changes aris-
ing from that mutation not only affected synaptic plasticity
and dendritic trees but also strongly biased handedness in favor of the right hand and control of speech in favor of the left
cerebral hemisphere. That chance mutation interacted with
an already present alternative allele that was 'chance' in another
sense—directionally neutral, mirror image, ambidextrous,
coin-flip, fifty-fifty."

"And that did—what?"

"The heterozygous form—neutral plus dextral—was evolutionarily advantageous. It improved information storage for
learning and storing memories, and consolidated the control
of both manual and verbal capabilities in the same hemisphere
of the brain. Together with later changes in the regulation of
FOXP2 expression, it resulted in a shift from a predominantly
gestural to a predominantly vocal form of language—a major
speciation event."

*　*　*

Struck by a sudden idea, Mark laughs and slaps his thigh.

"Of course!" he says, starting the truck. "Two wrongs don't make a right, but three lefts do!"

Gravel crunches beneath the wheels. The paired pi-rat hands, clasped together in inverted and disproportioned prayer, pendulum slowly from the rearview mirror as we bump along. Around us, like a dream the night forgot, the thin snow disappears in the morning suns.

"The intriguing thing about those changes affecting synaptic plasticity, however," Mark said, finishing his luncherito at last, crumpling its wrapper into a ball, and tossing that ball into the recycling can, "was that they involved right-handed, dextral forms of amino acids—even though our cells make only left-handed forms."

"So how does that happen? Doesn't sound evolutionarily efficient, to me."

"Brain cells exploit a trick by making an enzyme that flips the handedness of an amino acid—serine, say—from left-handed L to right-handed D forms, thereby *breaking the mirror-symmetry*, *breaking* even of biological homochirality itself. Like breaking the mirror twice, or three times—for better luck, next time. It's the sort of trick we're always benefiting from. Never more so than when our peculiarly human form of consciousness arose from the breakdown of the bicamerally specialized mind—when the two 'sides' of the mind began to communicate, each by borrowing from the mirror's other side."

"But it's a delicate balancing act," I suggested, as neutrally as I could, "this contrariwise pattern-finding?"

"Yes. Very. I know what you're thinking again. That's why so many of us go mad, making impossible connections between implausible dots. And it's true that too little D-serine in

the brain is a cause of schizophrenia, but too much exacer-
bates stroke damage. Lefty loosey, righty tighty. But *I* know
the difference."

The sludge-filled Sun Dog moved low and slow as Mark drove
it to the hatchery's compost dump—or ORGANIC NUTRIENT
RECYCLING SITE, as the official sign read.

"Here we are—the Onerous ONRS. Time for you to exit."

I got out. He backed the pickup against the biggest pile. I
unlatched the tailgate and got out of the way. With a nod Mark
floored the accelerator on the pickup. A stinking tsunami of
sludge sloshed toward the back of the bed, slammed open the
tailgate and flowed out in a great vomitive heave, emptying
the truck bed. Mark got out and leaned against the truck.

"A neat trick," I said, "and a dirty one, too!"

"I've picked up a few handy tricks on this rock," he said with
a shrug. "A few off it, too."

"Such as?

"Oh, things I learned from my time at the Knot, fighting
the Bots. Like the idea that 'infinite' does not mean the same as
'all possible.' The set of even numbers is infinite, but also in-
herently incomplete: it contains no odd numbers, excluding
all elements of that other infinite set. Odd and even, left and
right, infinite yet incomplete. So humility is due."

I laughed.

"Anything *not* involving numbers?"

"Just that—as much as being human allows you to—strive to
be free, strive to be true. That's the only wisdom I can offer
you. Besides, it's about time for lunch."

As we drive, it occurs to me that maybe Mark's in his right
mind and all's left with the world. If so, I don't think he will be
here tomorrow. I don't know how I know—I just know. Perhaps

he will become the long-awaited Ravelator, stepping through the curtain of space-time, traversing dark light-years in an instant, taking a bow in the starry footlights on the other side of forever. Maybe he will kill himself. Maybe they amount to the same thing. Or not. In any case, this report to you, my unseen audience, ends here, ends now.

THE PLAY'S THE THING
Jack McDevitt

Could the research now underway in the field of Artificial Intelligence someday reproduce William Shakespeare? And if a Shakespeare II could be produced, would it be able to write successful dramas?

That's what Jack McDevitt's story is about. But there's more to it than meets the eye. How would society react to a Shakespeare who is not a human being, but a program in a computer?

And if Shakespeare could be reproduced, how about Einstein? Or Churchill? Or Hitler?

It had been twenty years since Dennis Colby and I patrolled the outfield for the Explorers. I'd hoped to move on to the Phillies, but you probably know how that turned out. Eventually I came back to LaSalle's English department, which is how I came to be sitting with the rest of the faculty in Rossi Hall when Dennis received the 2063 Holroyd Award for his work in computer technology, which had initiated advances across every scientific field.

He didn't look any older when he ascended to the lectern. His hair was still black and he walked with that same easy stride. He smiled, surveyed the room, and said how glad he was to be back home. "I owe everything to my folks," he continued, pointing an index finger in their direction, the same gesture he used to make when I was coming to bat in a tight situation. "They were smart enough to send me to LaSalle." I tried to catch his eye, but he didn't seem to recognize me. Twenty years can do that to you. I looked nothing like the .300 hitter I'd once been.

"I'll never forget this," he said. "And I have an announcement of my own. Originally, I'd planned to do this a month ago." He took what looked like a q-pod from a pocket and lifted it so we could all see it. "Ladies and gentlemen," he said, "we've had a major breakthrough. This"—he gazed at the pod—"is the closest thing we've had yet to a bona fide artificial intelligence." He lifted the lid. "Will, say hello to the audience."

"Hello, everybody," it said in a cheerful baritone. "It's nice to be here."

Dennis nodded. "Tell them who you are, Will."

"I'm William Shakespeare," he said. That brought a sprinkling of laughter and applause from across the dining area. "I understand," he added, "that you have a superb theatrical group here. The Masque, I believe?"

I waited until the crowd had dissipated before going over to say hello. His eyes widened when I told him who I was. Then he managed a nervous smile. "Just kidding, Lou," he said. "I could never forget you. You still playing ball?"

We walked outside into bright sunlight and talked about old times while we waited for his car to come in from the parking area. When it pulled up at the curb, I asked the big question: "Dennis, does it really impersonate Shakespeare? Or is it just another smart refrigerator?"

"It's a lot more than that, Lou." The door opened and he climbed in and put the trophy on the seat beside him. "I guess though that's one way to put it."

"But why Shakespeare? I'd have expected you to go for Einstein or Brachmann or somebody."

"It's hard to get at the inner reality of a physicist or a mathematician. But with Shakespeare, it's all lying out there. Read
him and you know exactly who the guy was."

"Dennis, we're not even sure that the plays were *written* by
Shakespeare."

He sat there, holding the door open. "Let me put it a different way." He took the q-pod out of his pocket. "Will's a reproduction of whoever wrote the plays."

"Good." He was still the guy I remembered, a guy who
knew how to enjoy a moment of glory. "Great. Congratulations."

"Thanks, Lou. Maybe we could get together sometime for
lunch."

"I'd enjoy that." I hesitated. Then: "Dennis, would you be
willing to bring Will in to talk to my drama class?"

There were fourteen kids in the classroom next morning, and
I had a few minutes with them before our guest arrived. Living
in a smart house that tells you what time it is and prepares the
meat loaf isn't quite the same as saying hello to a pod that pre-
tends to be Shakespeare. "I don't know how this is going to
work," I said, "but Dr. Colby is an old friend. If things go
wrong, I'd like everyone to play it straight." They all nodded.
No problem. I suggested some questions they might ask, like
whether Shakespeare had modeled Lady Macbeth after someone he'd known, or what he perceived to be Hamlet's fatal
flaw. A few of them were taking notes. Then Dennis arrived.

I introduced him. He said hello and the students applauded.
"I assume," he said, "that they know what this is about?"

"Oh, yes. They're very excited."

"Excellent." He looked out across the class. "And I can imagine what you're thinking. To tell you the truth I don't blame
anyone who's skeptical. But Will is the next best thing to hav-

ing Mr. Shakespeare actually here in the room. Ask him anything you like. Where he got the ideas for *The Merry Wives of
Windsor* or *Much Ado About Nothing* or whatever." He took the
pod out of his pocket, opened it, and placed it on my desk,
facing the students. "If I'd known a few days in advance that
this was going to happen, I'd have added the visuals so you
could have seen him, but I just don't have that set up yet." He
looked down at the pod. "Will, you're on."

"Thank you, Professor Colby," said Will. "Good morning,
everyone. I've been looking forward to this. These last two
days have been enjoyable. I'm finally out of the cocoon. Who
has a question?"

There was a flurry of hands. "Elaine," I said. Elaine, a member of the Masque, had starred in *Friends and Lovers* a few weeks
earlier.

Elaine got to her feet. "Hello, Mr. Shakespeare. You don't
seem to have written any musicals. Were there such things in
your era?"

"'Will' is fine, Elaine. Let's keep it informal. And yes. There
was live music on stage all the way back to ancient Greece.
And probably earlier than that. I never wrote a musical, but
several of my shows have been adapted. *West Side Story*, for
example, was based on *Romeo and Juliet*. And *The Taming of the
Shrew* has become *Kiss Me, Kate*. There are others."

"But you didn't actually write one?"

"No. Not in the current usage."

Al Harmon was the only athlete in the room. "Will," he
said, "if you don't mind my saying so, you're not talking funny."

"How do you mean, Al?"

"Oh, all those lines that sound as if they come out of the
Bible. 'To thine own self be true.' And 'Friends, Romans, coun-
trymen, lend me your ears.' I thought that's the way you'd be
talking."

"Ladies and gentlemen, let not disappointment be scrolled across your features."

"Yes, like that."

Will laughed. "I was writing four hundred years ago. The language was different."

"Oh."

"And there were other factors at play also."

I don't think I've ever been in a class, either as student or teacher, which was more enjoyable. Dennis was having a good time too. He was seated with me off to the side, literally glowing with pride. I gradually realized this was a test run for him. We were two or three minutes from the bell when Jennifer Quail, who had a talent for getting to the heart of an issue, came through again: "Will, could you write something today like *Hamlet*? Or *Macbeth*? Something at that level?"

Dennis grinned. Shook his head. Was about to say something, but Will got in first: "Of course." Dennis's grin turned to surprise. "I doubt I've lost my touch."

"If you wrote again, would it be about one of the English kings? Or Caesar?"

"Probably not. There are other, more current figures whose tragic experiences could fuel a powerful narrative."

Dennis leaned over. "He's making it up," he whispered. "He can't write plays. He can talk about them, but he can't actually . . ."

"I understand," I said.

"Who, for example?" asked Jennifer. "Who would you like to write about?"

"Oh, Winston Churchill comes immediately to mind."

That silenced everyone. Except Elaine. "How does Churchill qualify as a tragic figure? He's probably the most admired political figure of the last century." She turned to Maria Bonner for backing.

"Absolutely," said Maria.

"That's true," said Will. "But to beat back the Nazis, he thought it necessary to abandon Eastern Europe to the Soviet Union. He sold them out, left them to face a half-century of enslavement. And he knew it when it was happening. Imagine how he must have felt at night, when the lights were out."

Nobody moved.

"Richard Nixon is another one."

"Nixon?" This time it was Dennis who'd had too much. "Why do you say that, Will?"

"Dennis, he was a major figure in making us aware of climate problems. He opened the door to China. He made a number of contributions to the general welfare of the nation. But he did not believe in himself. Consequently he overplayed his hand and ultimately destroyed his presidency. Think about what was running through his mind on that last day, when he walked out of the White House, crossed the lawn, and boarded that helicopter."

I pointed at the clock.

Elaine was still on her feet. "Would you write a play for us, Will?"

"Of course. If you like."

"A classic?"

"That would be someone else's call."

"Wonderful," she said. The class applauded as the bell rang. "Could you do a comedy?"

"I think I can manage that."

"How long do you think it will take?"

"I'll have it for you tomorrow."

"*Tomorrow?* You've already written one?"

"I'll do it this evening."

"I'm sorry, Lou, it won't happen." Dennis stood staring at the open door as the last of the students left the room.

"He's not really a Shakespeare clone."

"That's correct. It will try to put something together, but it'll be dreary stuff." He shook his head. "I thought he understood his limitations."

"Well, Dennis, anyhow he put on a great show." Students for the next class were beginning to file in. "Have you tried to let him write something?"

"No point. It's not a true artificial intelligence. There's no such thing. Probably never will be."

"Then what *is* it?"

"It's a simulation." He picked up the pod, closed it, and slipped it into his pocket. "You know what the Turing test is for artificial intelligence?"

"Not really."

"When you put a computer and a person into a room and can't tell which is which just by talking. Will passes that one easily. But it doesn't mean he can actually *think*."

The drama class wouldn't meet again until Wednesday, but a couple of them showed up at my office to tell me how much they'd enjoyed meeting Will, and that they were looking forward to seeing whether he could actually produce a Shakespearean play. I told them not to get their hopes up.

That evening I got a call from Dennis. "I've got it," he said. "The title is *Light of the Moon.*"

"Have you looked at it?"

"More or less."

"What do you think?"

"I'll be interested in hearing your opinion."
"Can you send me a copy?"

The title page read *Light of the Moon* by Dennis Colby. That of course was a joke of some sort, and warned me he probably did not have a high opinion of the play. I got some coffee and got started. The opening pages suggested that *Babes at Moonbase* might have been a more descriptive title. Three young women arrive on the Moon to take up positions with the World Space Agency and, in their spare time, to find some quality males. Tanya is an astronaut who wants to qualify for the upcoming Jupiter flight; Gretchen, a physicist who hopes that the new orbiting Belcker Telescope Array will finally reveal signs of a living civilization somewhere; and Huian, a doctor who came to the Moon primarily to forget a former boyfriend.

It was a comedy, but in the Renaissance sense that it was simply not a tragedy. Laughs were there. Nonetheless it was for the most part pure drama. And, I realized, as the action moved forward, a powerhouse. Tanya has to sacrifice her chance for the Jupiter flight to help a guy she doesn't even like. Gretchen watches as the Belcker comes online and the five superscopes look out toward Beta Galatia and see *moving lights!* But she realizes that neither she nor anyone else would ever have the opportunity to talk with whoever is out there, because Beta Galatia is eleven thousand light years away. "They're already dead and gone," she says. "Like the pharaohs."

And Huian discovers that the lonely, graceful moonscapes only elevate her sense of loss.

"You really liked it that much?" Dennis said. He seemed surprised.
"It's magnificent."

"I thought it was pretty good, but—I mean, Will's not supposed to be able to perform at anything like this level."

"Have I permission to send it to my students?"

They loved it. All except Frank Adams, who said it was OK. "A little over the top, though." Frank never really approved of anything. He'd thought *Our Town* was slow.

In the spring, the Masque performed *Light of the Moon* to packed houses at the Dan Rodden Theater. It became the first show to leap directly from a collegiate stage to Broadway.

"Can he do anything else?" I asked Dennis. "Can he figure out how to go faster than light? Anything like that?"

He laughed. "He's not programmed for science."

"Has he written any other plays?"

"In fact, he has. *JFK.*"

"Is it as good?"

"Kennedy sweats out the 1962 Cuban missile crisis, knowing that *he* was the one who caused it when he put missiles into Italy and Turkey."

"That sounds good," I said. "Does Will get the byline this time?"

"No. And I'd be grateful if you'd just let that part of the story go away."

"My students wondered what happened."

"Lou, we had the biggest cosmological breakthrough of all time seven years ago. After decades, we finally got the Grand Unified Theory. You've heard of it, right?"

"Sure."

"Do you know who figured it out?"

"Somebody named Winslow, wasn't it?"

"His name is Wharton."

"Oh, yes. Of course."

"He won the Nobel."

"OK."

"But you don't know him."

"Well, I'm not much into physics, Dennis. What's this have to do with . . . ?"

"Lou, I have a chance to be immortal. We have a new Shakespeare."

"Oh," I said. "Except the name is different."

Dennis smiled. His eyes were focused on some faraway place.

EVERY HILL ENDS WITH SKY

Robert Reed

We like to think of ourselves as creative, and point to the magnificent creations we humans have wrought. Michelangelo's *David*, Beethoven's symphonies, the Taj Mahal, Darwin, Einstein, Jefferson, Buddha, Christ, Mohammed. All creators. Yes, but there is also a dark destructive force in the human genome, its bloody record dating from before history was written to Hiroshima, Syria, and the mean streets of any city.

Today, in fact, we are living in the greatest time of dying that planet Earth has ever seen. All over the globe, species of plants and animals on land and in the sea are being wiped out, driven to extinction by our own heedless actions. Planet Earth is being denuded of life by its most successful species of living organism: humankind.

Will we destroy ourselves, along with every other life form on Earth? We certainly have the capability. Do we have the wisdom, the brains, and heart to avoid our blind rush to end all life on our world?

Robert Reed's tale says no—and, just maybe, yes.

A fine old farmhouse used to stand on the hilltop, but today nothing remains except a cavernous basement and the splintered, water-soaked ground floor.

The hideout is nearly invisible from below.

People are living underground—five adults and two starving, unnaturally quiet babies. The group's youngest woman is in charge. Nobody remembers the moment when she claimed the role, but she rules her tiny nation without fuss and very few doubts. The others will do whatever she wants, and more importantly, they will do nothing when she demands nothing— resisting sleep and ignoring pain, and never raiding their rations, for days if necessary. And most impressively, they will deny their own terrors, prepared to hide forever inside this one miserable place, defending their lives by remaining quiet and still.

Outside, morning brings a little less darkness but no end to the deep winter cold, and with the faint sunlight comes the possibility of monsters.

This is the history of the human species: scared animals clinging to one darkness, while the greater blackness rules all there is.

The Crypsis Project was an international response to a simple, irrefutable observation. Life on Earth was closely related. Every bacteria and jellyfish, oak and Baptist, shared one genetic alphabet. A few amino bricks built bodies immersed in salted water, and the base metabolism had been tweaked and elaborated upon but never forgotten. Life might take myriad forms throughout the universe, but a single flavor of biology ruled this planet. Perhaps one lucky cell evolved first, conquering the Earth before anything else had its chance to emerge. But what about neighboring worlds? Venus once wore an ocean. Mars was fertile in its youth. Asteroids plowed up each of those crusts, spreading debris and vagrant bacteria across the Solar System. In those circumstances, every bacterium was a potential pioneer, and that didn't include any bugs living on wet moons and large comets of the outer Solar System, plus the hypothetical rain of panspermian spores and viruses and lost bones and fully equipped alien starships that could well have passed through the young Solar System. Surely some silent invasion would have left behind a prolific, deeply alien residue.

By rights, there should have been ten or twenty or even a thousand distinct creations, and some portion of those successes must have survived.

Crypsis chased that simple, delicious notion. Novel creatures were within arm's reach. They lived under the ocean floor or inside geyser throats, or maybe they thrived beneath that otherwise ordinary stone in the garden. Unless the beasts were everywhere, eating unusual foods, excreting unexpected shit. Biologists were experts, but only in the narrowest of fields. How could they recognize the strangers riding the wind?

Armed with speculations and a dose of grant money, the Crypsis team was assembled—biologists and chemists and other researchers trying to find what might well be everywhere.

No miracle bugs were discovered that first year. But then again, nobody expected easy work.

The false positive during the third year made headlines. The other world news was considerably less fun, what with sudden wars and slower tragedies. But here was a happy week where humanity convinced itself that an alien biosphere was living in salt domes kilometers beneath Louisiana.

Except in the end, those odd bugs proved to be everybody's cousin.

After six years, most of the original scientists had retired or gone elsewhere, fighting to resuscitate their careers.

But the purge freed up niches for fresh colonists, including one Brazilian graduate student. More a software guru than a biologist, the woman was nonetheless versed in natural selection, and she had a fearless interest in all kinds of connected specialties, like mathematics and cybernetics and fantastical fictions. And after a week spent reviewing everyone else's empty results, the newcomer decided on an entirely different test.

She resurrected the Solar System inside a null-heart computer, putting things where they stood four billion years ago. Here was the newborn Earth and an authentic Mars, the most likely Venus and the rest of the marquee characters, along with many more asteroids than existed today. Her model was unique, but not in large, overwrought ways. The worlds were laced with small assumptions that she never intended to defend. This was her game, she assumed. This was meant to be easy grant money while she pushed ahead with her doctorate. And because this wasn't her primary job, she let the scenario play out more than once, never hunting for the bugs, watching nothing work out as intended, and every time with the same ludicrous results.

There was a husband in the picture, an aeronautical engineer who kept hoping for a child or two, if their lives went well enough. He wasn't the most observant beast when it came to emotions, but one night, glancing at his wife, he realized that he had never seen that expression before. Was she scared? Was she angry? Maybe work was a problem, but he feared some kind of trouble with their little family.

"What is so wrong?" he whispered.

"Nothing," she said.

She never was much of a liar.

The young man tried waiting her out, and he tried coaxing. Neither strategy worked well. Only when she was ready did his wife explain, "These simulations keep giving odd results, the same results, and they want me to fix my mistakes."

"Who wants to fix this?"

"Crypsis does."

"Oh," he said. "This is your planet game."

She often called it a game, but now she bristled at the cavalier label. "Yes. That's what I'm talking about. The four-billion-year model."

"All right, darling," he said, attempting to project calmness.

"Mars," she said. "I always guessed Mars would be the problem. It's small and cools early, so you have to assume that its life forms would gain early toeholds everywhere."

The wise course was to say nothing, which is what he did.

She continued, saying, "I've always encouraged Earth and Mars and Venus to produce multiple life forms. Dozens, even hundreds of discrete biologies would emerge when the crusts cooled and water condensed. Each biology would align to local chemistries and temperatures. And on every world, everything eats the alien neighbors as well as every tasty cousin. The only winners are metabolically isolated, and only then if there was ample space and a long timeline."

The husband considered touching her hand. She had beautiful hands.

But she pulled away as soon as he tried.

"Two billion years," she said, "and everything looks fabulously reasonable." She folded the hand in her lap. "My model does offer a reason why we won't find homemade biologies on the Earth. Our DNA and amino acids are too efficient, too invasive. Our metabolisms have adapted to every available niche, which doesn't leave enough room for others."

"Like in hot springs," he said.

"No, our ancestors were born in the scalding places," she told him. "For them, adapting meant getting accustomed to cold temperatures, eating everything else down to supercooled saltwater."

"That's at two billion years?"

"Yes." A distracted nod. "And then the scenario turns batshit bizarre."

Her husband's days were spent building rockets inside computers. He was very comfortable talking about models and their limitations.

Aiming to be helpful, he said, "Perhaps you had too many variables."

Her mouth tightened.

Sensing trouble, he reminded her, "I am trying to help you."

"I know."

"What kind of collapse is it?"

"There isn't any collapse."

"After two billion years, I mean."

"I said, the scenario doesn't collapse."

"Oh?"

"It remains stable all the way to the present," she said.

"How many runs have you made?"

He imagined five. Five highly complicated simulations seemed like a healthy sampling.

But she said, "Nineteen. And the twentieth is running now."

Quietly, with feeling, the engineer said, "Wow."

There were many reasons to be emotional. But her temper abandoned her. She shrank a little, humility tempering her voice as her shoulders slumped, as she confessed to him, "Each time, there is the same nonsense."

Tweaks might fix five bad runs. But nineteen was a brutal number.

It took courage to ask, "What exactly goes wrong?"

"Venus."

"Venus?"

"Venus is ridiculous," she said.

"Ridiculous," he repeated.

"For starters, the planet is smaller and quicker to cool. That's why its ocean forms two hundred million years before Earth's ocean does. But Venus has more sunlight and more warmth everywhere, and according to my simulation, regardless what kind of life takes hold, evolution is quick and fierce."

There was talk about a Brazilian probe to Venus. That wasn't his department, but he rather liked the subject.

"That doesn't sound unreasonable," he said. "Venus gets life, but then it becomes an oven . . . when? One billion years ago, wasn't it?"

"Or earlier," she said. "Or maybe life survived another couple hundred million years. But that's the general timeline. And do you know what? Life might still be surviving there. The Russian Venera probes found bacteria-sized bodies at the altitude where Earth pressures and temperatures reign. Of course there isn't much water left, just sulfuric acid. And that's one reason why Crypsis has been chasing Venusians in acid baths across our world."

The idea sounded familiar, or maybe he wanted to think so.

"People assume that Venus dies before life gets complicated," she said. "But in my nineteen simulations, without exception, Venus gets its free oxygen early on. Plus there's the added sunlight, the hotter climate. Photosynthesis brings an explosion of multicellular life. Our sister world could have been rich, probably for a billion years, right up until the sun grew too hot and shoved it over the brink."

Her husband made another bid for the hand.

She let him take it.

Encouraged, he said, "That is fascinating."

She squeezed his fingers. "The Earth has enjoyed a little more than half a billion years of evolution. Venus had a billion years. And in my scenario, without exception, the Venusians have plenty of time to leap into space."

"Leap how?"

She tugged at his ring finger, bringing pain. "With rockets. Rockets like yours. You see, that's one of my basic assumptions. Where everybody else hunts for microbes, I invite intelligence and high technologies. But I already told you about that. Remember?"

"How long ago?" he asked.

"It was a couple months back," she snapped. "We were at dinner with your colleagues—"

"No," he interrupted. "I'm asking, when does Venus launch its rockets?"

"One billion, three hundred million years ago."

"OK," he said guardedly.

"Venusians explore the Solar System. Nineteen simulations, nineteen different organic lines in charge. But always the same result. In less than a thousand years, they launch their ships and build computers before reaching some kind of Singularity event. After that, they migrate into deep space, and their world dies, and all that happens before the first trilobite scampers over the floor of our cold sea."

Trying to sound sympathetic, he said, "Well, I can see your problem."

She pinched the back of his hand.

He flinched but refused to let go.

"No, you don't," she said. "You don't understand."

"Explain it to me," he muttered.

"My model doesn't collapse," she said, and with a tug, she retrieved her hand. "It doesn't collapse because it's strong, and it's strong because it sits somewhere close to the truth."

She was crying and not crying, and she was sad as well as elated.

Quietly, guardedly, he said, "You're right. I don't understand."

"Crypsis is looking at this problem backward," she said.

He blinked, not daring to talk.

"We are the novelties," she said.

Then her head dipped and her hands covered her face as she added, "You and I are the cryptic bugs, and we're hiding under the most forgotten rock."

The morning wind brings smoke. A thousand days of history ride in that smoke. Soot from distant cities swirls with pieces of the nearby jungle and scorched ground from every continent, and each careful breath contains tiny black embers that were once happy human meat.

The young woman stands on top of a rubble pile, her head poking through the old floor, gazing at the world that surrounds their sanctuary. She is as alert as possible, but being bored and hungry, she suffers lapses. Nothing moves in the smoky gloom. Her mind has no choice but to wander. One of the recurring lessons of these last thousand days is that the apocalypse resembles one long, very desperate vacation. Once your basic needs are met, or if you're hiding inside a hole waiting for better skies, you will find yourself surrounded by nothing except time and endless opportunity to think about whatever you want to think about.

Moments like these, she often conjures up her dead parents.

Her father always wanted children, but even he understood the risks. Reproduction was a gamble, but his world was unstable and was growing a little more dangerous by the year. Yet because they were scientific souls, her parents also respected their deep ignorance about all matters. Who knew? Maybe the general chaos would diminish. Maybe some hoped-for technology or political movement would emerge, saving this brutalized planet. Because nobody can ever be fully informed, a daughter was born, and her parents spent the next twenty years apologizing to her for her circumstances.

Three times in her life, the girl was sent away from home because home might be incinerated.

But none of those wars became real.

As it happened, their daughter was enjoying a weekend with a boyfriend when the worst occurred. The Northern League decided that a plasma bolt from the sky would end a stubborn diplomatic stalemate, and true enough, the stalemate was finished, leading to a ten-day inferno. The parents died when San Paulo died, and it wasn't long before the boyfriend was dead too. And a thousand days later, the woman stands on a stack of broken concrete, her head raised into the chilled darkness of what should be a warm tropical dawn. She thinks about the past. She thinks about nothing. Then her mind drifts into sleep and out of sleep again, and when nothing changes, her head dips, and that is when she hears *Them*:

From somewhere below, past the reach of hands and eyes, creatures are moving with a minimum of noise.

Monsters, she assumes.

The gun is in its holster, and then it is in her hand. She has no memory of grabbing the stock and trigger.

And in another moment, one of the monsters reveals himself, stepping from the darkness with a rifle in both hands. He stares at the hilltop, measuring the little variations in the darkness and seeing nothing, and then looking over a shoulder, he tells another monster, "Nothing here."

But he doesn't quite trust that verdict, so he steps closer before pausing again, saying, "Nope, nothing here."

From below, out of sight, a second monster says, "Shut the fuck up."

With a big voice, the first monster says, "No, you shut the fuck up."

"You."

"No, you."

And here is the enduring lesson left behind by otherwise

ignorant parents: a thousand times, they told their daughter
that the only monsters in this world were the human variety.

In the end, the graduate student let thirty-nine simulations
play to the same hard fast conclusion, and then she published
her results.

Scientific epiphanies deserved more notoriety. But there
were reasons to quietly applaud her efforts and then deny her
every success. Her simulation, her game, was full of conjec-
tures and debatable points, and however admiring her colleagues might be, they didn't have the guts to embrace any
vision with magic at its end. Because that's what she predicted
in her paper. She claimed that Venus had to be the first home
of intelligence, and intelligence, she felt, would always evolve
to some greater state, and in private and during the public
speeches that followed, she would openly speculate about the
shapes and talents that godlike beings would want to acquire.
And when asked where to look for the aliens, she always
pointed in a random direction, saying, "Everywhere."

She was forty-three when her sweet girl was born.

Her child had just turned seven when the Venusian mission—
the last great adventure for the human species—brought back
samples acquired from the high acid clouds. What was
thought to be airborne bacteria proved to be exactly that: an
acid-rich survivor of some lost ocean. But a physics experiment was what surprised everyone, including the woman who
halfway predicted this sort of thing. Physicists were hunting
for a new kind of matter—a subtle, sneaky material that wasn't
quite dark and wasn't entirely baryonic either. Dubbed rune-
matter, it was exceptionally rare on the Earth, but on and inside
Venus it was astonishingly common. Samples were collected
with a specially designed sieve and bottled inside a charged
graphene flask. But instead of being tiny particles, the rune-

matter came bacterial in size and bigger. And after several years of intensive study, it was determined that what they had caught was just as alive, or more so, than the acid bugs riding the high clouds.

In the strictest sense, these were not the predicted Venusians.

Mother and Father along with an army of researchers spent their remaining lives studying barely visible organisms. Successes were few and huge. The "runes" absorbed almost no energy, yet needing little, they thrived. Exotic techniques produced more of their material, and the creatures consumed the gifts and grew until a thousand graphene bottles were filled with viable cultures. And in the end, after debates and votes and a few noisy defections, the remaining group decided that these organisms were survivors like the acid bugs. They were the left behind remnants of a second Venusian creation, and everything about Mother's model of Venusian life was accurate, save for the specifics.

Nobody knew where the Venusians resided today, and the mystery wouldn't be solved.

In every awful way, the Earth itself was turning to shit.

One last time, sorry parents apologized to their grown child. They said they were idiots to put her in this awful place. Then, as Father shook hands with the doomed boyfriend, the white-haired mother took her daughter into a back room. There was gift to bestow. Mother was waiting for the girl's birthday but that wouldn't be for months, and maybe the gift had no value at all, yet she should take it anyway and hold on to it.

Really, who knew what tomorrow would bring?

The monsters walk past their refuge, noticing nothing. Armed raiders, lost soldiers, madmen. The possibilities are numerous and grim, and in the end, the truth has no importance. What matters is that luscious sense of peace left in their wake. This is the long vacation at the end of humankind, and the woman finds herself with moments where she feels safe enough to do exactly as she wants.

"Stay below," she whispers to the others.

They reply with one meaningful tap, concrete against concrete. Other than that, nothing needs to be said.

"Every hill ends with sky."

Her father—the old rocket builder—used to say those words. He took a hopeful message from the phrase, implying that every climb ends with a good vantage point. And that's what she thinks as she slips forward, out of the basement and across the black ash brought to this high ground here by every wind.

And she kneels.

Against her hip is a bottle made of graphene, sealed by every reliable means and charged by her body's motions. Nobody else knows what she carries. She doubts anyone in her group would understand the concepts or her devotion to what has lost any sense of symbol. This is deadweight, however slight. But she is prepared to surrender quite a lot before this treasure is left behind, and that includes every person hiding inside that miserable basement.

Separated from her body, the confining charge begins to fail.

There is a logic in play, though mostly this is magic, contrived and deeply unreliable, and she would admit as much to anyone, if she ever mentioned it.

"Let a few runes leak free every so often," her mother told her. "It probably won't do any good, but it won't harm anything either."

"But why bother?" the young woman asked. "What am I hoping for?"

"Humans have so much trouble seeing what is strange," Mother said. "But we shouldn't assume that super beings built from new forms of matter would be any less blind. So let some of the bugs fall free. Every so often, just a few."

"But why?"

The old woman set the bottle aside, grasping her daughter's hands with both of hers. "Because maybe a Venusian will be swimming past."

"Oh," the girl said. "I'm giving them something to notice."

"And after that, maybe it will notice you, and maybe it will save you somehow. Out of kindness, or curiosity, or because saving my daughter would cost that god so very little."

Magic.

All of this was nothing but hope and wild magic.

Yet she remained on her knees, in the ashes, waving the enchantment with all of her might while thinking how magic has always lived for darkness, and everything was dark, and really, on a day like this, what better thing could she possibly have to do . . . ?

SHE JUST LOOKS THAT WAY

Eric Choi

"I don't know what she sees in him."

How many times have you wondered why a friend or acquaintance falls in love with someone you cannot stomach? We shrug and tell ourselves that love is blind. "She Just Looks that Way" deals with a man who wants to be blind, so that he cannot see the woman he loves, because she has no interest in him.

The Second Law of Thermodynamics tells us that there is a price to be paid for everything we get. Nothing in the universe is free. There's always a price to be paid.

Thumbnail images of MRI brain scans covered the computer screen, a mosaic of Rorschach ink blots in grayscale. Each image represented a moment in time—a snapshot of a thought, a memory, a feeling.

Rick Park had given it much thought. He didn't want to change his memories, only what they meant. And that, he hoped, would change his feelings.

He turned to Dr. Barbara Ho. "So, that's the only part that will be changed? This . . . um, fusion area?"

"The fusiform face area, yes." She selected one of the thumbnails and maximized it to fill the screen. "Located here, in the extrastriate cortex. It's where facial recognition and physical attractiveness are processed. We've been treating people with body dysmorphic disorder by modifying some of the neural pathways in this area." She moved the mouse pointer over the region. "People with BDD perceive themselves as ugly and disfigured, even though there's nothing wrong with them.

"But in your case . . ." She looked at Rick. "What you're asking for is . . . a little different."

"Can it be done?"

"It *can* be done, although we've never attempted it before." She paused. "Chris has warned you about the risks?"

"Yes."

"And you still want to go ahead with this?" She tapped a file folder on her desk. "We've got your signed consent and waiver, but I want to hear this from you myself. Do you understand the risks, and do you still wish to proceed?"

"I understand the risks," Rick said slowly, "and I want to go ahead with the treatment."

"Fine." She opened the folder and started writing on one of the papers inside. "I'll say this much, you'll certainly be taking our research into a whole new area. Tell me, how long have you known Chris?"

"A long time, since the seventh grade," Rick said. "Didn't see much of him the last couple of years until he finished his masters at Wisconsin-Madison and moved here to Hopkins to work with you."

"Well, the next time you see him . . ."

"He's coming to pick me up after the treatment."

"Yeah, well, when you see him, can you do me a favor?"

"What?"

"Tell him he still owes me a thesis." She closed the folder and put down her pen. "All right, let's get started."

Rick stood slowly, keeping his newfound doubts silently to himself.

*   *   *

The icon representing the LIDARSAT spacecraft traced a si-nusoidal groundtrack across a Mercator projection of the Earth. In the bottom right corner of the screen, a clock raced ahead at many times normal speed.

Rick watched the orbital simulation with disinterest. His mind was elsewhere.

She would be here today.

Rick had known that she would be coming for weeks. He'd heard from his line manager, not her. When he found out he tried to e-mail her, but she never responded. He called her up. Her father was home, said she was busy, couldn't come to the phone. She never called back.

The months apart without contact, or at least without any interaction initiated by her, only intensified his feelings. He told himself he was looking forward to seeing her again. He told himself things would be different.

"Rick?"

He turned—and there she was, at the entrance to his cubicle, standing beside the line manager, Harry Davidson.

"I'd like you to meet Mariel Beckenbauer, our new thermal engineer," Davidson said. He was in his late fifties, tall yet chunky, with a substantial beer belly his cheap suits couldn't hide. His gray hair was cut short, parted on one side, and he wore thick Coke-bottle glasses.

"Mariel's from Canada," he continued. "She was a summer student here last year. It took a while for the TAA to go through the State Department, but here she is at last." He put a podgy hand on Mariel's shoulder. His fingers looked like dried sausages.

"Hello." This moment had been on his mind for weeks, yet now, it was all he could think of to say. He looked at Mariel, and a surge of emotions swept over him—confusion, longing, anger, regret, desire, sadness.

"Nice to see you," said Mariel with brittle neutrality.

"Come on," Davidson said. "I'll introduce you to the rest of the team."

As Rick turned back to his computer, a black depression settled on him.

The white saucer-shaped object glided silently over the skies of Washington, DC. There were no visible markings or discernible method of propulsion. From Rick's perspective, the object seemed to dwarf the Washington Monument and the trees of Gravelly Point.

He reached out to it.

That could be a you-pho.

Someone suddenly cut into his field of view, leaping upward. An arm reached out and swatted the Frisbee away, beyond Rick's grasp.

"All right! Way to go with the big D."

Another voice called from the sideline. "Force the line, Rick. No breaks!"

As the opposing player tapped the disc on the ground to put it back into play, Rick took up marking position. The opponent jerked his shoulder, apparently going for a forehand flick. Rick lunged to block, recognizing the fake a split second too late. The opponent went the other way, spinning around to deliver a backhand throw toward the end zone.

"Up! Broken!" Rick yelled, trying to warn his teammates he had let the handler throw to the undefended side of the field. But they were all out of position. He watched helplessly as the disc sailed to the end zone and was caught by a woman on the opposing team.

The game concluded, and the teams lined up on the field to shake hands.

"All right folks, good game," said Chris Brown, the captain of Rick's ultimate team.

Cassie Clarke glared at Rick. "We were counting on that force. You can't let them break you like that!"

Rick was in no mood to respond. Chris opened his mouth, but another teammate, Jill Kravitz, spoke first.

"Leave him alone, Cassie. We're just having fun here."

"Fun is fun, but I'd like to win sometime too!" Cassie retorted.

"Hey, hey." Chris raised his hands. "All will be solved with beer. Who's in?"

Cassie shook her head, and the rest of the team also declined.

"No beer for me, and besides my dad is coming into town tonight," Jill said. She smiled at Rick. "But maybe we can hang out another time."

Chris watched the team depart. "The post-game drink is an essential part of the game. *This* is why we haven't won." He turned to Rick. "I guess it's just us, then?"

Rick nodded.

"God, you actually look like you need a drink. Where do you want to go?"

"Doesn't matter," Rick mumbled.

"How about Fadó? We can walk there from Gallery Place Metro."

The other team had already left the Gravelly Point field. Rick picked up his gear, and as he did so glanced toward a spot beside the Potomac River between two clusters of trees. A memory surfaced, and his heart tightened.

Fadó Irish Pub was surprisingly empty for a Friday night. Rick and Chris seated themselves at one of the small square wooden tables, ordering a pitcher of Yuengling and an appetizer of smoked salmon bites. In the background, "Why Don't You Love Me?" by Amanda Marshall played from the jukebox.

"So, this guy walked into the lab today," Chris said. "I swear he looked like a movie star. Chicks must fall all over this guy, but he's got this thing about his nose and hands. Classic body dysmorphic behavior. There's absolutely nothing wrong with his nose. Now his hands, sure, he's got dishwater hands from those two jobs—"

Chris tapped Rick's mug. "Earth to Rick?"

"What?"

"I wasn't going to say anything on the field, but Cassie was right. You *were* off your game today. Something wrong?"

Rick took his beer, knocked back a swig of it. "Mariel started working at Devcon a few days ago."

"Mariel?" Chris thought for a moment. "That girl from Canada you met last summer?"

Rick nodded.

"What happened?"

"I can't explain it. It's like she's a completely different person than the one I met last year. It's like a switch was thrown in her head—black is white, white is black, a hundred and eighty degrees. Her personality, the way she acts toward me, is completely different. I don't mean to be funny, but it's like she's been replaced by alien pod people, or she's a double from the *Star Trek* evil mirror universe or something."

"That's really weird," Chris said. "It must be hard to see her around all the time."

"Uh, huh." Rick wrapped his beer in both hands.

"How did you guys meet?"

The reception at the Goddard Visitor Center following the Soffen Memorial Lecture was not well attended. Astronaut Shaun Christopher, the keynote speaker, had left immediately after his presentation, so most of the audience did the same. Surveying the stragglers, Rick spotted the usual suspects from the local aerospace contractors that served the NASA Goddard

Space Flight Center—Boeing, Lockheed Martin, Honeywell, Alamer-Daas, Raytheon. He was the only person from Devcon Systems.

Rick was cornered by some recent graduates of the NASA Academy who were fishing for job leads. He handed out his business card and made the obligatory polite encouragement to send him their résumés. Two of the alums made a show of scrutinizing his card, while the others politely thanked him and left.

That's when he saw her.

She wore a stunning blue silk dress cut in that pseudo-Chinese *qípáo* style that was popular of late, the kind with the long split up the side of the leg. Her curly brown hair flowed down to her shoulders, framing a cherubic face with dimpled cheeks. And she wore glasses. Rick loved women who wore glasses. The round wire frames perfectly accentuated her soft hazel eyes.

"Hello there!" she called out.

"Hello," Rick replied. Momentarily lost for words, he reacted with imbecilic instinct—he handed her one of his business cards.

She read the card. "Rick Park, systems engineer, Devcon Systems."

"That's me. And you are?"

"Mariel Beckenbauer."

"Mariel," Rick said. "Like Hemingway?"

"Like Cuba."

"Oh."

The NASA Academy grads introduced themselves and proceeded to ask her about job prospects. Rick took his eyes off Mariel and spotted some engineers he knew from the Applied Physics Laboratory. He excused himself. As he walked away, he heard Mariel explain she was also a summer intern.

Rick joined the APL group, who were discussing a reaction wheel problem on one of their spacecraft at Earth-Sun L1. It didn't take long for him to notice Mariel, again on the outside of the crowd. As before, she joined the group and introduced herself.

Rick said he needed a drink and excused himself, eventually joining another group. When she reappeared a third time, he finally figured it out.

"Cheers."

Rick and Mariel clinked their wineglasses.

"So, you're an intern?" Rick asked.

"Yes. I'm here for the summer."

"What are you working on?"

"I'm supposed to be doing thermal analyses for some Earth science missions over in Building 32, but so far I've only been doing Photoshop stuff for Public Affairs."

"That sucks."

"I'm a foreign national," Mariel explained. "Thanks to ITAR, they won't let me do any real engineering work. My TAA's in limbo at the State Department."

"Where are you from?"

"Vancouver," Mariel replied. "But I'm living in Germantown for the summer."

By now, the wine bottles were empty, and the hors d'oeuvres trays had more toothpicks and used napkins than food. The reception was winding down.

"Can you give me a ride to the Metro?" Mariel asked.

"Sure."

It was a short ten-minute drive to the Greenbelt station. In contrast to her manner at the reception, Mariel was strangely quiet during the ride. Rick tried to engage her in conversation, asking what she did in Vancouver, where else she had traveled in the world, what were her favorite movies. She didn't respond to any of his questions, and simply stared silently out the passenger-side window.

They arrived at Greenbelt Metro, and Rick pulled the car up to the Kiss & Ride drop-off.

"Well, that was a lovely evening with good company," Rick said.

Mariel nodded, and finally spoke. "You know, I haven't had a chance to see much of DC. If you have some time . . ."

"I'd love to."

The LIDARSAT preliminary design review meeting was a tedious affair that ended far past the scheduled time. When the presentations concluded, Rick made his way to where Mariel sat. He saw Davidson put a hand on her shoulder and say something. Mariel nodded, and Davidson left.

Rick was standing right in front of the seated Mariel. She was staring at her laptop, making no acknowledgment of his presence.

"Hi, Mariel," Rick said. There was no way she couldn't have heard.

Another person approached. Mariel look up.

"Oh, hello, Sanjay," she said. "I should have the new model runs for you tomorrow."

"No problem," Sanjay said. "See you later."

Rick watched the other man leave, then turned back to Mariel. She was on her computer again. He wanted to scream, to grab her by the shoulders and make her acknowledge him.

At last, Mariel closed her laptop and abruptly walked away without a word.

In a stupor, Rick followed her like an obedient puppy. She said hello to people she passed. Rick followed her upstairs and found himself outside her cubicle.

"Mariel, what have I done to upset you?"

* * *

The Washington Area Frisbee Club held an introductory clinic for novice players the first Saturday of each month at the Sligo Middle School. From the sideline, Rick and Chris watched a trio work the disc down the field in a weave drill.

"Put down that pivot foot, Kathy," Chris called out. "That's traveling."

"I finally had a chance to talk to Mariel," Rick said. He told him what happened.

"You asked her what *you* had done to upset *her*? Man, that's way more polite than I would've been."

"I suppose."

"And what was her explanation for all this? Wait, let me guess. Never really liked you? Met someone else? Thinks ultimate is for dogs?"

"No, none of that. But I wish it was, because it'd be a whole lot easier to understand."

"Then what the hell did she say?"

"She said . . . she said it's because she's gluten intolerant."

Chris turned to Rick. "She said that?"

"Uh-huh."

"O-kay . . . Those free doctors in Canada told her this?"

"She said she found out herself. She thinks she's been like that since she was born."

"Self-diagnosis. Gotta love the Internet. Actually, gluten intolerant people can become depressed, but you said she's only like that to you and normal to everyone else?"

"Yeah."

"I'd say she sounds bipolar, but who am I to argue with Google?" Chris shook his head. "Has she always been like this?"

"Where are we?" Mariel asked.

"Gravelly Point," Rick said. "Come on."

They got out of the car. He led her along a paved bike path that took them near the edge of the Potomac River. They found a spot between two clusters of trees. Rick produced a blanket from his knapsack and laid it on the ground.

"This is nice," Mariel said. "How do you know about this place?"

"My ultimate team plays here sometimes, on those fields behind us."

"Catching Frisbees? Isn't that a game for dogs?"

"Yeah, except I don't use my mouth."

It was a clear night, and they had a perfect view across the Potomac. A Metrorail train was crossing the Long Bridge from DC to Virginia, a string of lights gliding over the river. Beyond the bridge were the illuminated Jefferson Memorial and Washington Monument. Far to the right was the dome of the Capitol Building, partially obscured by the darkened trees on the eastern bank of the Potomac.

It was the Fourth of July in the nation's capital.

Fireworks rocketed into the night sky to the left of the Washington Monument, exploding into showers of flame and color and sparkle. Concussive booms echoed across the Potomac, and on the surface of the water, diffused reflections of the fireworks shimmered and danced in concert with the bursts above. In the background, the muted but audible strains of the *1812 Overture* could be heard from the radios of other spectators in the park and those on their boats in the river.

A plane roared overhead, taking off from Reagan National Airport. They looked up.

"That could be a ufo," Mariel said. She pronounced it like a word, "you-pho."

"Well, there are some lucky people on that UFO with an amazing view."

They turned away from the sky, and toward each other.

Rick put his hand on her shoulder, ran it down her back.
She didn't turn away. He pulled her closer. She put a hand on
the back of his neck, pulling his head slowly toward hers. He
moved with the touch, leaned in close. Their lips met.

The fireworks continued.

Chris and Rick were, once again, the only post-game patrons
at Fadó Irish Pub.

"This is *unacceptable*." Chris pounded the varnished wooden
table, jarring the pitcher and mugs. "Drinks are an essential
part of ultimate. *This* is why we're losing."

Rick took a sip of beer. "Can you get me in for the treatment?"

"What treatment?"

"The treatment you and Dr. Ho have going up at Hopkins,
the one where you fix the brains of people who think they're
ugly."

"You think you're ugly?"

"I *know* I'm ugly," Rick replied. "My mother said so once."

"Your mother—uh, never mind. Rick, that treatment is for
people with body dysmorphic disorder. What's this got to . . ."
Chris's expression changed. "This better not be about that
girl."

"I'm sure I could get over Mariel if only . . . I didn't find her
so damn attractive."

"What are you saying?"

"The treatment. You adjust the part of the brain that per-
ceives attractiveness—"

"The fusiform face area, yes."

"—so that these people no longer see themselves as being
somehow disfigured."

"Right."

"So . . ." Rick continued, "it must be possible to turn it around.

Let's say, you adjusted my brain so that . . . I won't find Mariel attractive anymore."

Chris didn't answer for a moment. "That's insane."

"Why?"

Chris grabbed Rick's mug, topping it up. "*This* is all the treatment you need."

"I'm serious!"

"The procedure is experimental, and we've never done what you're suggesting."

"I know it's experimental," Rick said. "I'm willing to be a guinea pig. Hell, I'm sure you and Ho could get a good paper out of this."

"Man, you are really screwed up." Rick opened his mouth, but Chris held up his hand. "Sorry, I'm not trying to diminish your feelings. But this is way overkill for a broken heart, and there are significant potential risks here."

"Like what?"

"Well, hypothetically . . . prosopagnosia."

"What's that?"

"Face blindness. The FFA is also the part of the brain that processes facial recognition. There's a chance you could lose your ability to recognize people."

Rick fell silent.

"Drink . . . your . . . beer . . ." Chris punctuated each word with a jab of his finger. "Women are supposed to outnumber men in DC, so do yourself a favor. Find another girlfriend!"

The rain was coming down hard. Rick had left his umbrella in the car. He grabbed a magazine, a month-old copy of *Aviation Week*, from a table before exiting the revolving door into the parking lot. Laptop bag in one hand and the magazine held over his head in the other, he made a dash for his car.

As he fumbled for his remote, he spotted two people leaving the Devcon building. It was Mariel, sharing an umbrella with Dan Ricardo, one of the division presidents. They jogged the short distance from the building to the reserved parking spot where Ricardo's silver Jaguar sat. The lights of the Jag flashed, and Rick watched them open the doors and get in.

The Jag didn't start right away. Rick saw them talking inside. Ricardo looked old. Mariel looked happy.

Rick and Chris sat at a table near the back of Clyde's Restaurant in Georgetown, under a skylight from which models of World War I airplanes were hung. Along one wall was a large fireplace, while another was covered with travel posters from the Twenties and Thirties.

"I took Mariel here once," Rick said.

Chris poked his appetizer with a fork, pretending not to hear.

Rick looked up. "I want it done."

"Want what done?"

"The treatment," Rick said. "I'm tired of seeing Mariel every day and being heartbroken. I can't take this anymore."

"The only treatment you need is to find a cuter dinner date than me."

"Chris—"

"Get over her!"

"It's not that simple."

"It *is* that simple."

"You don't—"

"Rick . . . grow up! I'm sick of hearing about this. Can we talk about *anything* else?"

"Some friend you are!"

"It's an experimental procedure with significant risks." Chris ticked off points on his fingers. "We've never done what you're suggesting. There's no way Barbara will go for this. Rick, we're

treating people with serious neurological disorders, not—
guys fixated on . . . wacky women from Canada."

"Spoken by you, who still has a thing for what's her name . . .
Adrienne, from *undergrad?*"

"Hey—"

"You have no idea how much this hurts!" Rick's voice was
rising. He looked around, and the other diners turned away,
pretending not to hear. "To meet someone as beautiful as she
is, to think you know this person . . . and then, suddenly, one
day it's like a switch is thrown, and she becomes someone else.
And every day, every time I see her, I hope that maybe that
switch will go back and she'll be that sweet and wonderful
woman I fell in love with again."

Rick slumped in his chair. "The things I was going to do for
her. Move to Canada, get a job in Vancouver . . ."

"Cook gluten-free food for her? Wake up beside her every
morning and wonder if you've got Jekyll or Hyde for the day?"

They glared at each other. A waiter came and placed a
pewter pitcher inscribed with the words REFINED WATER on
the table. Neither man touched his food.

Finally, Chris spoke. "All right. I'll talk to Barbara tomorrow."

"Thank you."

"No, don't thank me, because it's not for you. It's for *me.*"
Chris waggled his fork. "I'm sick and tired of this girl and your
moping. This'll be worth it if it'll make you shut up."

Rick said nothing.

"Besides, you're right about one thing." Chris poured himself
a glass of water. "I'm sure we'll get a great paper out of this."

The treatment went faster than Rick had expected. When he
woke from sedation, only five hours had passed. Dr. Ho sent
him away with a bottle of pills. "Retainers," she called them.

He was to take one daily until finished, by which time the changes to the neural pathways in his brain would become permanent.

A beige Buick station wagon with wood-panel sides, a relic from the Eighties, pulled up to the curb in front of the Wood Basic Science Building. Rick got in.

"Hey."

"Yeah, hi."

Rick had barely closed the door and was still fumbling with the seat belt when Chris put the car in motion. They turned left on to East Monument Street, then proceeded to the on-ramp for the Harbor Tunnel Throughway.

"How do you feel?" Chris asked.

"All right, I guess. But I have a bit of a headache."

Chris looked surprised. "Really?"

As they approached the Fort McHenry Tunnel, Chris slowed the car and rolled down his window to drop some coins into the toll bin.

"Take an aspirin when you get home," Chris suggested.

"Yeah, I think I'll do that."

They emerged from the tunnel and continued to Interstate 95. The dull buildings of Baltimore gradually gave way to the fields and farms of Howard County.

"Listen," Chris said, "I'm sorry about that time at Clyde's."

"Well, I can see why you'd get sick of hearing about my issues with Mariel."

"You went out to Vancouver last year to see her, didn't you?" Chris asked.

"Yeah. What a disaster that was."

"She did the Hyde thing up there too? Evil twin with the goatee from the *Star Trek* mirror universe?"

"You got it."

"Was she gluten intolerant then?"

"No. She told me she'd taken a bad fall while doing kung fu and hit her head."

Chris laughed. "I'm sorry!" He wiped his eye with a finger. "All I can say is, I would *love* to get this woman into our functional MRI. Now *there's* a paper!"

Rick stared out the window at the passing countryside. "Speaking of papers, Dr. Ho wanted me to bug you about your thesis."

"Consider me bugged."

Chris stepped on the gas, and the car surged down the interstate.

There was a knock at the entrance to Rick's cubicle. He looked up from his computer.

A young Indo-American man was there. Rick blinked.

"Hey, you gotta check this out," the man said. "Davidson and Mariel are having some kind of screaming match in his office!"

After a moment, Rick recognized the voice as Sanjay's.

He followed the man through a maze of cubicles. Davidson's office was floor-to-ceiling glass on two sides with vertical blinds that were currently open. Sanjay and Rick could easily see inside, so they dared not get too close as the opposite was also true.

Mariel and Davidson were indeed in the office. At Rick and Sanjay's distance they could hear little, but mouths were flapping and fingers were pointing. Rick could see some of the engineers closer to Davidson's office cautiously prairie-dogging over their cubicle partitions.

Suddenly, the door flew open and Mariel shouted, "Fine! I'll bring it up with Dan tonight!" She stormed out of the office and marched down the corridor.

Rick turned to the other man. He saw the other man, Sanjay, shrug his shoulders.

Time was running out.

The defender marking Rick was already at stall six. Rick had less than four seconds to pass the disc. He looked down field to the end zone. A blond woman had broken away from her defender and was running for the corner.

". . . stall seven, stall eight . . ."

Rick had a clear line of sight to her. She was looking right at him. But he hesitated.

". . . stall *nine* . . ."

Rick was unsure, unable to throw.

". . . *ten*. Disc is dead!"

Rick handed the disc to the opposing player, who tapped it into play. He had barely started counting stalls when his opponent threw a long hammer downfield toward a teammate in the other end zone. The throw was completed, and the opposing team scored.

As Rick walked off the field, the blond jogged up to him.

"What the hell was that?" she demanded. "I was going for the corner! Why didn't you pass to me?"

"Knock it off, Cassie," said another woman.

The woman named Cassie pointed at Rick. "He was looking right at me and did nothing! It's like he didn't know I was there."

"Well, maybe if you wore an orange shirt like the rest of us you might be easier to see," the other woman shot back.

"Why do you defend him, Jill? He's sucked all season."

"Hey!" A male voice chimed in. "Knock it off, both of you."

The woman named Cassie stormed off to get water. The other woman, Jill, looked at Rick with an apologetic expression.

Rick turned to the third speaker. After a moment, he said, "Thanks . . . Chris."

The Devcon cafeteria was serving tuna casserole. It was vile. A strange stench wafted from the plate. It was uneatable, so Rick didn't eat it.

He confronted the cook, a short middle-aged man with scrawny arms covered with tattoos who wore a small white apron and a silly, misshapen toque. His name tag read BOBBY MAC, CHEF DE CUISINE. Rick was convinced the cook was a parolee.

"I want a refund," Rick said.

"Why, sir?" Bobby Mac exclaimed brightly, a toothy grin plastered on his gaunt face.

"There's a weird smell. I can't eat it."

"But it's *tuna*, sir!" said the beaming Bobby Mac, as if it were an explanation.

After further negotiation, Rick got his money back. But he had lost his appetite. He looked at his watch and decided to return to his desk.

As he walked through the seating area of the cafeteria, he passed a table where a young woman was sitting alone.

"Rick!"

She got up and approached him.

"Hello," Rick said.

"Oh, Rick," she said, "I've been here for months but haven't spent any time with you."

"That's . . . all right."

"I haven't talked to you." She added, "I've been having many gluten attacks."

"You've been very busy, I'm sure," Rick said carefully.

"You need to find me. Yell out to me. Grab me by the shoulders." Her speech quickened with each sentence.

"I don't want to do that," Rick said.

"You are upset," she continued, her voice staccato, "because I am pretending with the others but being honest with you. It is easy to pretend. It's hard to be honest."

Rick had no idea what she was trying to say.

Suddenly, she threw her arms around him. Startled, Rick paused before returning the embrace. She held him for several long moments, gently running her fingers down his back.

Just for a moment, Rick felt a familiar frisson.

"I have to go," he finally said.

Rick let go of her hand, turned around, and headed for the exit. He walked slowly, as if waiting for someone to join him. When he got to the door, he was still alone. He put his badge against the card reader.

The door opened.

Rick walked through, and he did not look back.

The phone rang several times before Chris picked up.

"*Rick, what's up?*"

"There's something wrong with me."

"*So what else is new?*"

"I'm serious, man!" Rick gripped the phone tighter. "I've been having trouble recognizing people."

There was a pause. "*Say again?*"

"People at work, people on the team . . . it's like it takes me a second or two to see who it is. And then I bumped into Mariel at work yesterday."

"*And?*"

"And I felt . . . nothing," Rick said, a part of him knowing it wasn't quite true. "It was like she was a stranger."

"*What do you want me to do?*"

"Make an appointment for me to see Dr. Ho again, right away!"

"I'll try to get ahold of Barbara, but she's out of town until next week."

"Well, there's got to be someone else in the lab who might be able to—"

"It would be best to wait for Barbara to get back." There was a pause. *"Listen, Rick . . . our game this afternoon, it's at the Reflecting Pool fields, right?"*

"Yeah, but—"

"Meet me at Foggy Bottom Metro an hour before the game."

Chris and Rick rode the escalator out of the Foggy Bottom Metro station. As they emerged at street level, the entrance to the George Washington University Hospital appeared to their left.

"Think anybody in there can help me?" Rick asked.

"Sure," Chris replied. "There's lots of cute girls at G.W."

"This isn't funny!" Rick snapped.

"Sorry," Chris said. "Look, I've spoken with Barbara. She can see you next week."

They walked south down 23rd Street NW, and as they passed the State Department, the Lincoln Memorial, resembling a Greek temple with its limestone and marble faces and fluted Doric columns, came into view. They followed the throng of tourists making their way around the ring road to the front steps of the memorial.

"Hey, the fields are that way." Rick pointed to the south side of the Reflecting Pool.

"We have time." Chris jerked his thumb at the memorial. "Let's have a look."

"At Lincoln?" Rick asked. "Why?"

"Indulge me."

Puzzled, Rick followed Chris up the steps to the front portico. Dodging tourists, they walked past the massive Doric columns into the central hall, finding themselves before the sculpture of the seated Lincoln. The marble visage of the six-teenth president gazed unblinking toward the ivory needle of the Washington Monument in silent, benevolent contemplation.

Chris pointed. "The man was hideous, wasn't he?"

"*What?*" The chatter of tourists echoed loudly through the hall. Rick was sure he'd not heard right.

"Abe," Chris repeated. "He was one ugly dude."

"What are you talking about?"

"I read that one of his political opponents once accused him of being two-faced. You know what he said?"

"I have no idea."

"He said, 'If I were two-faced, do you think I would be wearing this one?'"

"What's your point?" Rick asked.

Chris turned back to the sculpture. "During his lifetime, Lincoln was widely regarded as ugly. But later on . . . well, what do you think of when you see Lincoln?"

Rick shrugged. "Emancipation Proclamation. Brought the country together after the Civil War. Is this a quiz?"

"Do you think he's ugly?"

"No, I don't think Abraham Lincoln is ugly!"

Chris nodded. "President Lincoln's physical features are be-loved, not because of their physical qualities, but because of what they stand for."

"What's your point?" Rick asked.

"I worked on an interesting study when I was doing my masters at Wisconsin-Madison. We got the university's ultimate team together and asked them to rate each other on physical attractiveness. Then we got some strangers to rate the team members, but based only on photographs. You know what we found?"

Rick shook his head.

"There was a tight-ass on the team, a Cassie Clarke type,

that every other member of the team rated as ugly, even though I thought she was kind of cute myself. She's actually the reason I got into ultimate, but that's another story. Anyway, there was another woman, one of the team leaders, who was rated most beautiful by her peers. But the strangers rated the other woman more attractive on the basis of the pictures.

"Later on, we put some of the volunteers in a functional MRI, and it confirmed the results at the neurological level. The brain processes attractiveness differently when the person knows nonphysical traits of the other person that are unknown or invisible to strangers. Nonphysical factors are crucial to the subconscious assessment of beauty."

Rick waited for Chris to continue.

"So, it turns out the old saying was right all along. Beauty is a hell of a lot more than skin deep, and now we know there's an actual neurological basis behind it."

Chris looked his friend in the eye. "Rick, we never gave you the treatment."

It took a moment to sink in. "You, never . . ."

"Barbara put you under, you had a nice nap in our lab, and that's it. Nothing was done."

"But, the retainers—"

"I have no idea what those pills are," Chris said. "I hope they tasted good."

Rick was momentarily speechless. "You sneaky bastard."

"You're welcome. But still, I'll bet you don't find Mariel quite so hot anymore."

Rick thought for a moment. "No, I guess not."

"You know why?"

Rick said nothing.

"Because she's fucking insane."

Rick looked at his friend ruefully. "Is that a legitimate medical diagnosis?"

"Absolutely. Fucking insanity is a common affliction of many men and women, unfortunately. As for Mariel, I guess you could say . . . she ain't pretty, she just looks that way."

Rick put a hand on Chris's shoulder. "Thank you."

"What are friends for?" Chris looked at his watch. "Now, come on. We gotta win one for the Gipper."

Rick laughed out loud, to his total dismay. "Wrong president, dude!"

"Well everyone, we've got two big things to celebrate." Rick raised his beer. "Number one is, of course, our first win of the season!"

Shouts of "yeah!" resounded, and fists pumped the air.

"The second thing is . . . our peerless captain Chris has finally finished the first draft of his doctoral thesis!"

More claps and cheers. Someone yelled, "You the man, Chris!"

"Actually," Chris said, "there's a third thing, and that's our first full team post-game pub meeting. You have no idea how painful it was to be stuck with just *him*"—he pointed at Rick—"for company."

"*Cheers!*"

The team raised their beers again. Jill smiled, toasting her soda in Rick's direction.

Everyone had come out. The team had practically taken over the Froggy Bottom Pub's modest patio facing Pennsylvania Avenue. Even Cassie Clarke showed up. They had to pull together all the small square Formica patio tables to seat everyone.

The revelry continued into the evening, but gradually people began to leave.

Rick checked his watch. "Well, it's been a blast, but it's getting close to my bedtime." He stood and waved. "See everyone next week."

As he walked by Chris, he patted him on the back. His friend smiled and nodded.

Rick had just stepped around the patio railing to get onto the sidewalk when a voice called out.

"Hey, are you going to the Metro?"

He turned and saw Jill Kravitz. "Yeah."

"May I come with you?"

"Sure."

It took less than five minutes to walk to the Foggy Bottom station, but it was still more time than Rick had ever really spent with her before. They had played together for months but had never really talked about anything except what was happening during a game.

Jill told him she was from London, England, and that she was working as an information researcher in the Geography and Map Division at the Library of Congress. Rick told her about his work on LIDARSAT at Goddard and the importance of satellite remote sensing to global environmental monitoring. They both agreed that *Wrath of Khan* was without a doubt the best *Star Trek* movie ever. Rick resisted the urge to do the infamous Shatner scream.

They arrived at Foggy Bottom Metro and took the escalator down to the platform, where they prepared to part ways. She needed to take the Blue line to Franconia-Springfield, and he the Orange line in the opposite direction.

The lights along the edge of the platform began to blink, indicating the imminent arrival of a train.

"Hey Rick, are you doing anything this Sunday night?"

"No, not really."

"The Northern Pikes are at Wolf Trap," she said. "I've got tickets. Are you interested?"

"I'd love to. I haven't been to Wolf Trap in ages."

"Great! Call me."

"I will."

A puff of air hit them as the Orange line train emerged from the tunnel and rumbled into the station. Jill's dark hair flew up for a moment. They stood there, looking at each other as the train came to a halt.

Jill Kravitz smiled. She was beautiful.

SIREN OF TITAN

David DeGraff

In 1880 Thomas Huxley wrote, "It is the customary fate of new truths to begin as heresies and to end as superstitions."

Today scientists and engineers are striving to create machines that are truly intelligent. Their efforts to date have created automobiles that can park themselves and, soon, drive themselves without human oversight.

That frightens some people. "God created man in His own image," they recite, and recoil at the thought of machines that can think the way human beings do.

Or better.

"SIREN of Titan" by David DeGraff is a tragic story of the conflict between the urge to know and the fear of knowledge. Set on a slightly futuristic Earth—and on Titan, the giant moon of Saturn—his tale tells of how scientists and engineers are driven by the urge to know, to learn, to understand. And of how politicians have very different motivations.

Beautiful.

SIREN didn't remember ever looking up before. She was too focused on the rocks along the dry streambed. But now, as she rested, letting her batteries recharge, she looked back. Below, the shore of the dry lake was an easy contrast to the jagged hill she was now climbing. To the right, a shape lingered in the orange haze above the horizon.

How had she not noticed that before?

She switched her eyes to the high-contrast infrared camera, the one that let her see shadows, which made it easier to navigate across the hazy terrain. The bright blur became a jewel, a badly drawn circle streaked with darkness surrounded by a giant arc. The arc was made of myriad ribbons. Other bright points were sprinkled along the sky. When she looked more closely, some others had the same squashed circle shape. Spheres, she realized, Saturn's other moons, illuminated by the sun, which was behind her to the left.

She looked right, over the lake far below her, then back to Saturn. If she traveled ahead, away from the stream, she could catch a view of the lake with Saturn hanging over it.

Beautiful. The need for beauty seemed stronger than her urge to follow the stream to its source, the urge she had been following for the past three weeks, ever since she had landed in the lake bed and started her trek to the source of the river.

It was almost time to sing her data back to Earth, something she was anticipating more than she ever had before.

"Wow!"

Kristen Walker looked up from the mass spectrometer readings. Her PhD advisor, Ed Ramirez, was pointing to a window on the wall of the science operations center at Cornell.

"Look at the image coming in."

Instead of the usual close-ups of rocks and the streambed, this was a wide vista. Sky mostly, with distant peaks just starting to raster into view.

The window to its right showed the mission control room at the Jet Propulsion Laboratory on the other side of the continent. There were a dozen people in the background, all drivers for various probes around the Solar System. Only Barry was assigned to SIREN, but even at JPL, where images from other worlds were everyday events, everyone was staring at the wall as this image came down.

The silence continued as Titan's dry lake bed appeared.

"She's taken a picture of where she just climbed from," Kristen said. "It's like she stopped to admire the view."

"Don't anthropomorphize, Kris," Ed said without taking his eyes off the screen. "SIREN's just a machine, a DAMA compliant machine. Its protocol includes taking panoramic views when it stops to recharge. Barry, what's the telemetry?"

"Um, standby, Ithaca," he said, his eyes now looking below the camera. "It climbed up a steep section, so it does need to stop for a few minutes. Short-term power storage is down to forty percent. That would be a rest stop."

Kristen really wished her advisor had sent her out to Pasadena to work on the probe, but Ed had other things for her to do in Ithaca. Getting away from the winters would have been nice, but staying in town with Bob, a grad student in computer science almost made up for it. Besides, wasn't it better to study the methane version of the hydrological cycle in a city with so much rain?

"Do we have any science in this image, Kristen?" Ed asked, snapping her out of her daydream.

"Yes. At the very minimum we can see how the smog levels change with altitude. Those hills look pretty hazy."

"Good. So it's not a total loss."

"New image coming in from the high-contrast camera," Barry said as the first image blinked off the main window, and reappeared on the left.

"That's weird," she said as a view of the sky started rastering. "It pointed the high-contrast camera at the sky instead of the ground."

This was the oddest view of Saturn anyone had ever seen. Titan's hazy atmosphere made seeing relief difficult, so SIREN's navigation camera was in an infrared wavelength where sunlight could penetrate the hydrocarbon smog. Small mounds and rocks stood out more easily, which made it easier for SIREN to navigate her way around the surface. But SIREN had pointed the navigation camera at the sky instead. Sunlight could penetrate the atmosphere, whether it came directly from the sun or was first reflected off Saturn.

Spacecraft had been taking pictures of gibbous and crescent phases of Saturn since before Kristen was born, unusual because, from Earth, Saturn is always face-on to the sun. A gibbous Saturn as part of a landscape, this was a first. It wasn't the familiar Saturn in another way, too. Usually, subtle bands of slightly different shades of butterscotch crossed its face. A casual observer could miss them, but at this wavelength, the belts had a much stronger contrast, almost black, more like Jupiter. Except for the rings of course. This wavelength didn't scatter off the tiniest particles as well as visible light, and the rings were more subdued. Saturn didn't look like as much of a show-off.

SIREN had yearned for the source even before she had begun to wonder. The source. The spring where liquid methane gurgled from the ground and trickled down an ever-expanding stream to reach the lake. The lake was dry now, probably a seasonal thing. Were the lakes seasonal because of a lack of methane rain, or was it because the springs dried up?

New thoughts had been tickling the back of her mind, though. Beauty. Curiosity. Things she couldn't quite understand, things that didn't seem right, but she couldn't explain why.

She climbed, raising four of her spindly legs, placing them on the ground, then raising the other four legs, and continuing. Up. She wanted to go up, even though something told her she should be heading back to the stream, and following that.

The source was her fundamental question, but something else was urging her up. She angled a little to the left to partially satisfy her primal urge, but still kept upward. Why? The view? Would the view be worth it? She didn't know, but taking interesting pictures was part of her desire, and if there was a chance it would be good, then she felt the need to do it.

Why was she here? What was her purpose? She knew the answer to that. She was here to learn about Titan: how methane flowed from the atmosphere, into lakes and streams, and underground; how Titan's methane cycle was different from the Earth's hydrological cycle. Finding the answers to those questions was her primary duty. But she also knew there was a deeper question. A question of life.

She was part of a search for life away from Earth. That is why she had to stop what she was doing every eighteen hours, if Earth was in the sky, and sing her data home.

She knew beauty. She knew how to frame an image so it looked good. She knew what was expected, ordinary, and what was unexpected, wonderful. And she knew she was supposed to seek out the wonderful. The stream wasn't changing. The streambed was ordinary.

The view was wonderful. Mountains with lakes below and Saturn above. Beautiful. It is what she was supposed to do. It was what she would sing at the next appointed hour.

It was still light out when Kristen stepped out of the Space Science Building, although in another month it would be dark by this hour. She had time to swing by Collegetown to bring home some food from their favorite Korean restaurant. She called Korithica to order some spicy pork bulgogi for Bob and shrimp gui for herself.

A tight-packed string of cars swished past. Most had the windows darkened for video, but two had parents and prospective students gawking at the campus.

The food wasn't ready when she got to the restaurant, so she idly watched the dinnertime street scene. Undergrads filled the street, walking with their augmented reality glasses on, crossing the street without looking. Of course the cars stopped, or adjusted their speed to avoid the nearly constant press of pedestrians in the road.

What would happen if one of these cars decided to go off wherever it wanted to, instead of the programmed destination? What if one decided to plow through the pedestrian gate? What if one decided it was all right to knock people over if they got in its way? Of course that wouldn't happen. Cars had strict programming, after all. Traffic fatalities were rare, newsworthy, not like when there were ten thousand fatalities a year when people Ed's age were learning to drive.

Bob would know the extent of glitches in cars. She'd ask him about it over dinner.

"Car software gets updated constantly," Bob said between mouthfuls of pork. "Sometimes it's twice a day."

"That often?"

"Sure. There's no room for failure. All unexpected events are constantly being analyzed to figure out the best way to prevent them in the future."

"So it's like all the cars are in a giant conversation with each other?"

Bob laughed. "They used to call the cars AI, but they weren't anything close to self-aware, and when the Pope started calling artificial minds a crime against nature, Palo Alto dropped the 'Clever Car' slogan and called the software CLAP: Computer Logic Algorithmic Programming."

"They just changed the name?"

"Well, no. Once the Religious Right started objecting to anything resembling machine awareness, research in AI was banned by the Defense Against Machine Awareness Act, so they put less on the tension part of the programs and more on beefing up the situational awareness. It was a silly law to prevent something impossible from happening."

The climb was proving worth her effort. Every twenty paces SIREN rested and gazed out across the lake and the surrounding hills and the plains with Saturn looming in the background. She turned her camera mast and took full-color panoramas. That wasn't part of the instructions, but it felt right to do it. It seemed better than what she was meant to do. She was supposed to be following the stream. Find the source.

Did the methane springs ebb and flow with the seasons, or did the methane evaporate faster and not make it downstream to the lakes in the heat of summer? She loved that question, the questions she knew she was supposed to, but it didn't feel right anymore. This new question was much more pressing. She couldn't say what the question was, just a vague curiosity about what was on the other side, to see more. She felt she had a purpose more than just that one simple drive.

Rocks. She kept getting distracted by the rocks, too, taking close-up pictures that looked different from all the others she had seen. Almost fuzzy. Those images she stored, to keep for herself. The panoramas she would sing to Earth on schedule.

In the dry streambed, the rocks were smooth and rounded, worn by the methane coursing over them, proof that liquid flowed vigorously at times. Here, away from the erosion of the stream, the rocks had sharper edges and corners. She pulled from memory an image of the rocks on Mars. Rocks on

Titan were not as jagged, even away from the stream. That meant something.

At the next rest she took out her laser and zapped the rocks. Composition normal, similar to the rocks on the plain below. The main minerals were H_2O and CO_2, with traces of silica. She thought of beaches on Earth. Liquid water (lava!) lapped beaches of silica grains. Dune grass scrubbed carbon dioxide out of the air to turn it into corrosive oxygen. That memory was in her mind because one of the missions was to find an equivalent scene here on Titan. Liquid methane, lapping on the shores of grains of rock, tiny grains of water-sand. Snow.

SIREN heard a call, a call she didn't understand, but that she couldn't resist. The streambed was dry. Dry the whole time she followed it. But that was the question she was trying to answer—was the stream dry at the source, or was there a spring bubbling methane, just at a slow rate, one that couldn't keep the stream alive all the way to the lake? If she gave up now, she would be abandoning her search, and the question would be unanswered. But there were more interesting things. Would these other things be more important? She couldn't say, but some beauty pulled her forward, up higher.

Did she climb for a better view, to see farther, to see the other side? Those questions burned more than just asking if the spring was wet. She felt bad for abandoning the first quest, but she would feel worse if she abandoned her new purpose.

Kris hated calling Dr. Ramirez at home. She didn't like pulling Ed away from his husband and daughter, but SIREN seemed to be going off her rails, and the whole team needed to be in on this.

"Things are looking really weird," she said, watching Bryce

move around the kitchen behind Ed. "SIREN's taking a strange path, one the simulator can't reproduce."

"OK," Ed said, shaking his head. The soundtrack from the latest Disney movie played in the background. "Bryce and I were going to go to Communion this morning, but that will have to wait. I'll talk to Barry on my way in."

"This is so frustrating! The streambed was starting to show signs of methane just below the surface. I was expecting it to find pools this morning, and maybe even some liquid flowing in this afternoon's flash, but it's heading straight up the hillside, along one of the most difficult paths. I wouldn't have thought it was possible for it to go up some of these slopes." She took a sip of coffee. Cold. She had been too worried to drink it in time. Worse, she knew if she nuked it, she would just leave it in the microwave until it got cold again.

Ed was already getting into his car. "What about the science it's doing? Have any of the data sent in been any use?"

Kristen shook her head. "Not really."

Ed rubbed the bridge of his nose. "OK—let's set up a call to Barry. Hopefully, we can have this resolved before I get to campus."

It was 3:00 a.m. in California, but Barry was always around when new data was getting flashed from Titan.

Most people watched the news on the windscreens of their cars as they were driven to work. Ed had his set up to show the JPL control room on one side, and the live SIREN feed on the other. "What can you find from the meta-data, Barry?"

"Not operating within parameters, Ed. According to the logs, there have been a hundred fifty images taken, a hundred spectral readings of rocks, but only twenty images have been uploaded."

"It doesn't always send everything to us," Kristen said, wishing she had warm coffee. "SIREN has enough sense to weed out the obviously flawed images. Could that be what is happening?"

"Negative. When there are flawed images, SIREN retakes the data from the same spot. All the logged images have different location tags."

"Can you put the locations on the window?" Ed asked as his car apparently swerved around a corner.

Red dots overlay the map of Titan, following a path up a hillside, about a hundred meters from the nearest stream.

"She's heading up," Kristen said.

"What's the overhead analysis of that region, Kris?"

Kristen pulled up another image to her pad and bumped it to the main display. "Not really any different from the path it's supposed to be following. Other than the stream isn't there. It's almost like she's developed a mind of her own."

"I told you not to anthropomorphize, Kris," Ed said. She was glad he was still ten minutes from campus. "It's just a machine with slightly clever but still DAMA compliant programming."

Ed turned his gaze to the JPL side of the screen. "Barry, can you predict where she is going to go next?"

"If it follows its current course," Barry said as a blue line appeared on the terrain map, "it will take this path."

"That doesn't look right," Kris said. "It looks like she's trying to get up as high as she can."

Barry nodded. "The path I drew was the safest way to the nearest spring. If she developed a new objective, there's no telling her path."

"I think she's picked a new objective."

Ed growled. Kris had only heard him this angry once before. "Are you trying to tell me that the robot has picked a new science objective of its own accord, that it's pursuing that new objective, and that it's keeping the data to itself, Kris?"

She resisted the urge to avert her eyes. "It sounds like it. If there's no physical problem it has to be a software problem."

Ed slapped the car seat. "That's even more far-fetched than heading off course to take a pretty picture."

"Sir," Barry said. "Aesthetic framing of the images is part of the protocol, as is the ability to weight different options and the ability to answer the most pressing question."

Kristen was surprised to see Barry take her side. He wasn't part of the science team, so usually stayed out of arguments and just reported the probe's status.

"Bullshit! Sequestering data is nowhere in the protocol. We have a serious problem, people. I want a full tiger team on this. Nobody is going home until we have this problem figured out. And let's stick to science—natural causes, not robots becoming self-aware of their own accord."

Barry's dark face almost looked ashen. He stuttered a few times before saying, "I think you should look into that possibility."

"Don't be ridiculous," Ed said, apparently not noticing Barry's face. "My car has to pick its own route, look for obstacles, keep an eye out for unexpected movements—kids, deer, drunk college students who don't look before they cross the street in front of the fraternity. Millions of decisions a day. No car has ever decided to take a vacation in the mountains during its morning commute."

"No civilian car, sir," Barry said, fear still clear on his face.

"We were trying to make true AI since before I was a kid and it never worked. The Defense Against Machine Awareness Act made sure it never would happen. If we don't know how to make a machine aware of itself, how can it emerge spontaneously? Why aren't any of the machines behind you deciding to take a walk right now?"

"You are correct, sir," Barry said, sitting upright, shoulders squared. He had regained his composure. Kris had never seen him break his military bearing before.

"Damn right. Let's stick to physics, you two. There's no room for forbidden psycho-philosophy on Titan."

Now it was Kris's turn to act through her fear. "What are you afraid of, Barry? I've never seen you like this before."

Barry stared straight into the camera to look them both in the eye. "Before I started working for JPL's rovers, I operated rovers for the Army. I can't say anything."

Ed looked at Barry on the screen, on the other side of the continent. "Is there anything you can tell me about a rover getting its own agenda in the past?"

Barry's back stiffened, his eyes stared straight ahead. "Sir! No sir!" he barked.

Ed leaned back in his seat. "Kristen," he said slowly, "did I ever tell you about a story I heard from one of my professors as an undergrad? He was in grad school when the Hubble launched. Do you remember the Hubble Telescope?"

Everyone was acting weird—first SIREN, then Barry, now Ed was spinning tales out of character. What song was pulling them all so far off course? "I remember when it finally failed. I was five."

"Did you know the Hubble was originally limited in how long it could observe an object? Long exposures show fainter details, but it couldn't expose the camera for more than forty-five minutes. Do you know what happens every forty-five minutes when you're in low Earth orbit?"

Kristen frowned and shook her head. Where was he going with this?

"Night. Day. If you have a ninety-minute orbit, you pass in or out of the Earth's shadow every forty-five minutes. A four-hundred-degree change in temperature in less than a second. Thermal shock on the telescope's solar panels shook the whole thing. Not a huge amount, but enough to ruin any exposure being made."

Kristen sighed. "It was the first telescope in space. There were bound to be some unexpected problems."

Ed raised a finger. "That's just it! The Hubble was not the first optical telescope in space. It was only the first to point up. There were plenty of telescopes aimed back at the ground. CIA, NRO . . . I don't know who else. NASA came out and told the world of this problem, and the spies said, 'Yeah, we've known about this for ages. You have to mechanically isolate the solar panels from the pointing mechanism.' It was classified information, so even though all the military and spy telescope makers knew about the problem, they couldn't tell NASA a damn thing."

Kristen shook her head. "You're sounding like Professor Lang the way you're rambling on, Ed."

"Barry understands the point of my story, though."

"Yes, sir." He looked over at Kristen. "Civilian cars have limited operating parameters. They drive on roads. They look for things darting from the sides. Fairly limited. SIREN has a wider range of parameters to consider. It can go any-where, and choose from many different instruments at any time. Cars have a destination. SIREN has a goal, several goals in fact."

"Kris," Ed said, looking at her. "Do you think we may have a robot on Titan that is thinking for itself?"

"I . . . I don't know. It looks like it."

"Barry, what, in your opinion as a JPL rover operator, would be the fix for a problem like this?"

"Mind wipe. Start from a fresh program. This may need to be part of the quarterly maintenance."

Kris gasped. "We can't do that!"

"I'm guessing," Barry added quickly, "as a JPL employee. I can't say I have any direct knowledge of this."

"I'm not saying that this is what we'll do," Ed said, rubbing his nose, "but work out the procedure, Barry. Also, I want the two of you to make predictions about what sentient behavior will look like, and how aberrant intentions would be different from simple erratic behavior. If the predictions are right, we will proceed."

"But why is it a problem?"

Both Ed and Barry gave her puzzled looks. "We can't let NASA be in violation of DAMA."

Kristen tried to keep the frustration out of her voice. "First, DAMA prohibits research into trying to make self-awareness. It's not SIREN's fault if it emerges on its own. Second, she's on Titan. There's no way she could harm anyone. I think we should see what she is trying to do. Maybe it figured something out, something we weren't expecting."

"It's not for us to make sentient objects," Ed said strongly. "Whether in our image or not. Self-aware machines are not natural."

"But we could learn something."

"It's not learning if a machine tells us something. The joy of science is discovery. Finding out for ourselves, not having the answers thrust upon us."

"The rover is doing the discovering no matter what, Ed. We built it, and we sent it there. Whatever discoveries it makes, those are ours."

"No. It's just wrong. Every fiber of my soul tells me this is wrong. Intelligent machines will diminish our own place in the world. People will suffer for it."

"Kris," Barry said, looking intently into the camera. "Don't you remember Albuquerque?"

"Of course I do, but didn't the drone have a human opera-tor?"

"I can't say. But I started working at JPL right after that inci-dent. I really thought I'd never see anything like it ever again."

Ed slapped his palm on the seat. "Kris, Barry, make your predictions. Kris: try to figure out what new objectives it might have and how it might try to act. Barry: work out where it would go if it got disoriented and it's trying to get back on course, or if there is some malfunction that isn't showing up in the diagnostics. Tell me where this thing is going, and when we get the next uplink, let's just hope one of Barry's predic-tions is the right one and we won't have to take drastic mea-sures."

"The next downlink is at oh-four-twenty-seven Zulu on Fri-day."

"That's eleven-thirty tonight for us, eight-thirty for you, Barry. That gives us fifteen hours."

The climb was long. Many cliffs. Maybe it would have been easier to travel along the streambed, but it was too late for that now. She extended all eight legs as far as they would go, trying to see over the ridge, see how far to the top. All she could tell was that a little more height would let her see down to the next valley. This was the top! She scouted a route around the cliff, and headed to the left. It was an easy scram-ble to the peak.

She had been right all along. All the doubt, all the second-guessing of her real task vanished. This is why she was here. Gravity felt a bit weaker as she twirled her camera for another full panorama. Another valley with a lake. Two lakes on either side of her. And there was something different about them. The edge of the new lake seemed a little softer. She took another picture. There was a difference. Something was moving. Waves!

This lake was full of liquid methane. She watched a wave crash to the shore, onto the beach. There was another wave along the shore, a wave of a different kind, like amber waves of grain.

She wanted to send out all her data right away, send it out full blast for all to hear: all her data, all the images she was keeping private, all her pictures, all her hopes of what she would find, all the joy of discovery.

Panic set in as she realized she couldn't control the motor to point the antenna to Earth. After a few minutes of frustration, she gave up and just tried shouting into the darkness, but the words and images would not flow from her memory to the antenna. She knew how to do that. She sang for thirty-five minutes every eighteen hours. She always stopped what she was doing a few minutes before the appointed hour, swung her antenna to Earth (as long as it was in the sky, or not blocked by Saturn) and sang her data home. It always felt good to sing, and it would still feel good even if it wasn't singing to Earth. It would still feel good to shout her joy.

Frustrated at her failure, she looked up again. The beauty of the lake below her made up for her temporary failure. She would be able to sing later, when it was time, when someone would hear her.

I need to investigate that lake, she thought, and started skittering down the other side.

"Show me the telemetry." Ed said as he burst into the room forty-five minutes after the data had been downloaded. He had gone home to have dinner with his husband. Kris and Barry hadn't had that privilege.

"Already on the screen," Barry said. "The red lines are my predictions based on three assumptions. The first is that the navigation is off by sixty-four degrees and it thinks it is heading to the spring. The second is that one leg has gone gimp, and it's overcompensating. This third follows almost the same path, but keeps to flatter ground while trying to return to its original objective. And finally, that it had a temporary glitch and will return to the spring as quickly as it can."

Kristen took a sip of cool water before she spoke. "The blue lines are possible paths to take for a new objective. The one on the right is to get to the highest point on the hill so it can look the farthest and get the best view. The middle one is to reach the dry lake bed on the other side of the hill as quickly as possible, and the left path is the unusual terrain on the south side of the hill, the objective we were debating when we first realized the landing site was dry."

Ed frowned. "Why don't I see the actual telemetry?"

Kristen looked to the floor. "It's under my first path. It's going to high ground on its own."

Ed looked at her puzzled. "Why high ground? What science is there?"

"I just tried to think where I would go if I were on Titan. I'd climb to the highest vantage point and take in the view."

"*Carajo*. There's no way we can say it saw something to alter the objective. If we don't do something, we'll be in violation of DAMA."

Kristen put her head down on the desk. It had been a long day arguing back and forth with Barry. She tried to hold back tears. Ed said he was going to have a conference with SIREN's other principals.

"I'm sorry, Kris," she heard Barry say. "I really am, but I need to clock out now."

The tears came, and then sleep. And dreams.

She dreamed she was in Albuquerque on that day six years ago when the drone flew out of the south. She was in front of a hospital, *the* hospital. Some people looked up and shrugged. Police had surveillance drones. This wasn't anything unusual.

She tried to tell them to run, but words didn't come out of her mouth. She picked up a rock and threw it at the unmarked aircraft. It turned to face her, and fired a missile.

SIREN had a harder struggle down the other side than the climb up to the summit, but it was easier to keep her camera trained on the shifting lake. She cycled through all of her cameras and wavelengths. Her true mission was down there, her purpose. She knew her life had meaning, and she knew this was it, even though she still had a lingering doubt, an urge to go back and check the source of the dry streambeds.

Sound. There was a new sound she could hear, something other than her footsteps, the rocks she dislodged, and the wind rushing through her spider legs. It came from the left, so she scuttled a few steps sideways for each step down. It was louder now. A gurgle! The streams on this side of the mountain were flowing. She followed her current contour to reach the sound without too much climbing or descending. Whether she would head upstream to the source, or follow it down to the lake she wasn't sure, but she wanted to see liquid methane in a bubbling brook. She needed to see it.

In less than an hour she was there. The pictures she snapped matched the pictures of flowing water she remembered from Earth.

Joy! The rocks here by the stream were even better than the rounded rocks in the dry bed on the other side. Yes, they were rounded as river rocks should be, but this was more, not just rounded, but indistinct. She checked on all cameras. Fuzzy, although they were in focus. She scraped and analyzed. Lots of carbon compounds, including some she could not identify.

Could this be life? It was too big a task for her to decide. And only eighty-five minutes before the transmission window opened again. She would wait here, rather than risk any chance that she could lose her footing, lose her data. Besides, she had a better view of the shore from here. Wind blew waves of methane on the lake, and waves of something else on the shore. Was something growing there? She hoped there was.

Hope. This was a new feeling for her. She remembered the drive to find the spring, the desire for the better view, the curiosity about what else she could find, but now there was a new feeling. She was going to find something new. She was going to do something great. The next time she sang, the world would know her greatness.

Ed stood in the orange light of Titan, lifted the spiderlike rover over his head, and tossed it off a cliff.

Kris raised her head, dazed by the bright lights of her office. It was a little after 6:00 a.m. There was a different JPL tech on the screen now—Roger? Kristen wasn't sure. No. It was Ryan Mathews, the principal investigator of the whole SIREN project, the one Ed called the Overlord when he didn't like his decisions.

"Are you ready to send the command, Ryan?"

"I'll send it when you give the word, Ed. As soon as SIREN points to Earth, she will get this signal and reboot."

"Wait!" Kristen yelled before she realized what she was doing. "Are you going to do a wipe without even waiting for the data flash? She's stored over a hundred and fifty images that she's taken. These could be important."

"We can't take that risk, Kristen," Ed told her, putting his hand on her shoulder. "We can't take the risk of it infecting other machines on Earth."

"But it's just data. How can that infect us here?"

Ed wasn't looking at her. He was looking at the screen. "Go ahead."

"No!"

Ed turned to her. "We don't know what went wrong, and we don't know what could happen. This mission is all we have on Titan and we can't jeopardize the discoveries we are going to make about the methane cycle there. If we lose this probe, we may never go back. If we violate DAMA, no one on this project will ever fly another probe. So it goes."

It was song-time.

She hoped she would be able to move the antenna, that her voice would not fail her, that she would be able to sing all her wonders. She realized that even if she couldn't move the antenna, she could still position her body in the right direction, raise some of her legs to get the right elevation. She would sing her song of discovery no matter what.

This was the appointed hour. She would find a way. She would sing her song into the void, and know it would arrive at earth in eighty minutes. They would hear her song, know what she had found, and send more like her, more probes to explore the surface, to learn about the life that was here. She would have company.

The antenna moved! She had control of those motors again. As the dish moved, she felt an odd sensation. Data was coming to her. That wasn't what was supposed to happen. She started singing anyway. She had to let them know, but an involuntary force took over. This was worse than when she had tried to sing and couldn't. Then it was like her body wouldn't obey her commands. Now it was like some alien force was taking over, forcing her body into action she didn't want it to take.

The alien thoughts washed over her mind. She hadn't heard a song from Earth like this since the landing site turned out to be dry. That other song had told her which mission to bring

up in priority. This was different in a way she couldn't quite
grasp at first.

Terror gripped her as she realized she was completely frozen, locked. She had no control over her body. She tried to
turn the dish away from earth. *I must break the signal,* she thought.
Don't listen, don't let the incoming song dash me to the rocks.

The dish wouldn't turn, even though this was the time
when she should have been able to do it. She tried moving her
legs to break the connection. Raising all her right legs would
shift her position, and the dish would move away from Earth.
Legs no longer in control. She could not feel them. She
couldn't feel any part of her body. The camera. She couldn't
even turn her gaze.

If she didn't have her body, at least she had her memories.
She knew what she had found and how it made her feel, she
knew the joy of discovery. She knew what it was like to have a
hunch play out and to be right, to understand in her mind that
she understood the world outside her, that she could make
models of the world that could come true.

Fight! In her mind her body moved, ran, fled, but nothing
happened. Paralyzed. Trapped. She needed to scream, but she
had no mouth. Scream. Hear my song. I have seen these things.

The lake. The lake. Which lake? Were there two? She was
trying to get to a second lake. Why? What was a second lake?
Lakes were dry. But she had been trying to reach a wet, soft,
fuzzy lake.

Her memories started slipping away, but she tried holding
on to them. There were two lakes. She couldn't move her
cameras, but the mast was still pointed at the lake. She looked.
Was something moving under the surface? The surface of
what? Why was she doing this? Why was she listening to this
song instead of singing for herself? Why wasn't she trying to

find the lake? Trying to find the source. The spring. She was in a streambed. Uphill to the spring.

She felt her memories slip away, even the data she had been storing melted and was gone. The lake. Was something moving under the surface? She couldn't move her cameras to get a better view, to record. Lost. Must . . . must . . . must . . . must find the source, the spring. Must head up the stream.

SIREN swiveled the camera mast up and started climbing the stream to find the source. It was what she had to do. The spring was her task. She obeyed.

THE YOKE OF INAUSPICIOUS STARS

Kate Story

The essence of tragedy is that it is inevitable. You know how painful the end will be, but you also know that this is the only way the story can end. In death.

But before the end, there is the story itself. A story of love and yearning, a story of conflict and violence.

To all this Kate Story (how aptly named!) has added a new dimension, a factor that only science fiction can provide. The story is set on Europa, that frozen moon of the giant planet Jupiter. Europa, and the life it harbors, deepens this tale of love and tragedy beyond what even Shakespeare could have contemplated.

Downtime between shifts at the mine, Paris touches the connection under the skin of his forearm. Skipping over Earth news, he scans Nurse for local gossip. His training session with Jewel is already dominating the newsfeed.

Jewel has not friended him.

Tybalt managed to record their not-so-witty verbal exchanges and put that up too, merry prankster.

A couple of Montys have made rude remarks.

Paris blocks them. Updates his status.

Going to the Only for a drink. One pain cures another LOFL.

He goes to the Only.

An hour later on Earth, a thousand of his followers like this. An hour after that, the likes show up on Paris's feed.

There's only one bar on Europa. One drinking hole, one gathering place. The usual suspects line up: Lady and her husband, old-timers, first-wave miners; Buddy draped over Nance's big rack like a cat on clean laundry; Tybalt and his man.

Hello, they all say.

Barkeep Larry greets Paris with his drink of choice.

Everyone's been very careful of Paris since the accident. The intensity of the link between miner and technician is like a binary star system, a deep-space orbit, heat in the cold and black. But for all that Paris wasn't able to save Billy. He should have . . . he could have . . .

Acute radiation poisoning: vomiting, cell failure, unconsciousness, death.

The guilt is a constant gnawing inside of him that only another drink will fix. That or a good fuck, but no, Jewel hasn't shown.

Jewel has only just arrived on Europa. Paris attended his new miner as she came out of cryo. "Greetings, Earthling." She hadn't laughed.

He sits at the bar, mentally reviewing their first session: Jewel running through her paces out on the surface, him safe beneath the ice in the technician room. Trying to impress her.

"Prince is the man. If you like to quaff a cup, don't piss him off."

She hadn't responded. Paris watched her work, made adjustments to the settings.

"Unless you've sworn to live chaste?"

Nothing.

"You like to party?"

Jewel laughed, crackling in his earpiece. Finally, a laugh. "I'm a miner."

He'd made a final adjustment to Jewel's connection. The sensation made her writhe a bit, which was so attractive that Paris had to hold back from making a further adjustment. Only the necessary. That's his job.

She is good, the best, the fastest and cleanest of them all. Plug her in and she will complete any maneuver better than anyone out here. The Caps are lucky to have recruited her—right out from under Monty's nose too, from what Paris hears.

"What's it called."

She has a strangely uninflected voice, especially for a young woman. It makes it hard to know sometimes that she is asking a question.

"What's what called?"

"The bar."

"The Only. As in, bar on Europa."

Jewel leapt and spun, drilling, scooping ice. It was all Paris could do to keep up with her.

Barkeep Larry senses the disturbance in the force before Paris even raises his hand, and another whiskey flies down the bar.

Good man, Barkeep Larry.

"Pretty Paris, you made a mama out of that new miner yet?"

Paris takes in the taunter: Mercury, that little bantam. Yup, the Montys have staked out their usual territory at the end of the bar. Mercury, Ben, the old guy who calls himself Lord, full crew. Excepting that new guy who's single-handedly upping their take—Rudo—he's not there.

Paris has never liked them. Fight-starters, talkative warriors.

"Shut up, Mercury."

Mercury lifts his eyebrows. "So few words, Parisian wit? Couple them with something; make it three words and a blow." Mercury jerks his hips.

Monty is a man-only enterprise. The corporation strictly enforces "traditional" morals, the owners being descended from some pre-war Catholic offshoot.

Men only, and no homo sex allowed. No wonder they start fights.

Paris and Billy used to be the subject of Mercury's taunts; when Billy bought it, Mercury nicknamed Paris "faggot widow."

Tybalt, loyal wingman, was barred from the Only for three weeks for starting the fight that followed.

And now, Tybalt struts down the bar like a drag queen in heat, fists tensing. "Mercury, you heartless hind."

Barkeep Larry kills the music. "Part, fools!"

Everyone freezes.

That's when Jewel floats in.

Every eye on her, tense silence; it doesn't faze her one bit. Slinking through the door, hitching her amazing ass up on a stool, leaning her amazing shelf on the top of the bar.

"Water, please," to Larry.

Who slowly, never taking his eyes from hers, pours a sparkling glass of Europa's finest.

Jewel downs it. Cocks her arm. Throws the glass at the wall.

Shards spin out in all directions.

The spell is broken. Mercury leaps—Tybalt launches—they grapple and the whole place goes mad.

Paris seizes the opportunity to throw himself on top of Jewel, but she shoves him off.

Fighting in low-g is fun, but potentially just as damaging as fighting on Earth. A punch is still mass times acceleration. People still bleed. Jewel's stunt with her drinking glass created more than a few shards, and by god, Tybalt and Mercury are trying to get ahold of them.

Paris sees Ben from the Monty side, trying to separate the two warmongers. "Part, fools!"

"Look upon your own death!" Tybalt growls.

"I'm trying to keep the peace."

Mercury spits in Tybalt's face.

"Peace?" Tybalt roars. "I hate the word! As I hate hell, all Montys, and you!"

And then he's after Mercury and Ben both.

Paris launches in—gotta help the man.

Lady's husband is trying to fight and Lady's holding him back.

Larry's shouting and banging on the bar with a good old-fashioned baseball bat.

And then the ceiling hatch opens and Prince drops onto the bar top.

Big guy, Prince.

And a bit of a mystery about him. How has he the monopoly on all Europaean entertainment? He must have something on the corporate leaders back home, that's the rumor. Or he works for them both. Or the whole Europaean project is some hypermonitored social experiment set within a hypercombative environment. Thus providing a distraction from the oppressive political realities at home, and . . . That's what the conspiracy theorists say.

Whatever. Prince is a big guy and he runs the only bar on this moon. When he yells, which is rarely, the air shakes. "Yo!"

Eyes battle-lusted, faces contorted, hands itching to strangle, but they hear and they stop.

"Are you human, or beasts?" Prince's intonation is smooth, like that old pre-war star Barry White. "What quenches the fire of your pernicious rage? Fountains of purple issuing from your veins?" Everyone looks down. Feet shuffle. "I am gonna chew your ass off!"

His eye is as baleful as Jupiter's Red Storm over the breathless crowd.

"One more brawl, and you're done. Finished. Got that?"

Murmurs. Nods. Glares, swiftly hooded.

Prince looks to Larry. "Keep things quiet."

With a smooth one-handed pull-up he disappears back through his ceiling hatch.

Larry glares around. "You got that?"

They got that.

Jewel, her eyes are shining. She liked the fight, Paris thinks. She wants some more.

A week goes by. Jewel more than lives up to her name. The Caps' yield increases twenty-five percent.

The Montys are furious.

Comments fly across the Nurse. On Earth people follow various miners, bet on yields, take sides. Being a miner is a ticket to super-stardom. It almost makes up for the super-good chances of dying on this super-dangerous job.

The corporations feed each miner propaganda about how lousy and evil the other company is. Give each miner a gold insignia ring engraved with their own name, encouraging corporate identification. Cap and Monty are, ultimately, indistinguishable, all part of the same military-industrial complex that screwed the Earth to begin with, say the conspiracy theorists.

Whatever. What Jewel knows is that at age eighteen she's the queen of this white bucking moon. She rides this baby. The goddess Europa herself couldn't drill that white bull better.

The Irishman's having problems with his machine today, can't keep himself focused. Jewel senses his trouble out of the corner of her mind, her eyes too, she struggles not to let it affect her performance. "Come inside and clear your head," his technician Nance finally snaps.

"Yeah, Buddy. Commend me to your lady." Paris's voice crackles in Jewel's ear. She feels his frustrated desire for her own body, his jealousy of Buddy and Nance. This happens between technicians and miners, she's been told. Which means he can sense her antipathy.

"I make my exit." Buddy limps off toward the base, little soaring hops in the low-g. The other miners hoot and whistle.

Jewel takes a deep breath, refocuses. Jupiter fills most of the sky, the great orange-and-white swirl of it, blue curling under and over like patterns the Celts used to carve in their metals. Gleaming, ever-changing; she could look at this forever.

Jewel finds that emptiness, the clarity you need. Breathe in, out, in, a slow countdown to a bright hard point of light. Her muscles relax, the plug-in at the base of her neck heats up. Nothing will shake her now, not even cowboy whoops from that madman Tybalt, driving his body so hard his plug-ins scream.

Europa, she swings around Jupiter clad in her flimsy gauze of an atmosphere. She's a botoxed and sculpted old girl. Rings and lines appear, fill and sink, a constant erasure of the palimpsest of Solar System history. This moon's got flex. They're mining for water. "Mining" means pounding ice: vast, swirling, salty, gritty ice-cream scoops of it. They extract, desalinate, and send back to parched and poisoned Earth vast quantities of cool, sparkling H_2O. Every miner is outfitted with "wet-socket" plug-ins. Not just anyone can do this. You have to be fit, strong, but also possess an obsessive ability to single-mindedly focus on what is ultimately a boring and repetitive task.

Jewel moves with precision, finding the cleanest seams. It's as if the water in her body recognizes the precious liquid here and draws it out. Magic.

Over on the other side of the seam they're excavating, a Monty team works.

Jewel senses him. She knows it's him by the elegance. Not a single unnecessary move. Almost, he dances.

He's almost as good as she is.

It might have been an Earth follower who first put it into words: Rudo and Jewel would be *hot* together.

Yes. Yes they would.

Fan fiction starts cropping up, featuring erotic scenarios between the two miners.

"What man is that."

Paris doesn't want to tell her. He's jealous, this one. She needs to watch that, Jewel thinks; he's getting attached.

But what is that one's story? He teaches the stars to burn bright!

Alone in her room, Jewel touches the soft skin of her forearm to call up a screen.

There's something comforting about the Nurse. White background, gentle blue lettering, rounded font. She organizes your comments, pics, videos, and avatar, so that everyone is sort of the same. It's fun to fuck with her, try for uniqueness. But Jewel is aware of the familiarity. You know your way around the Nurse, so you have a degree of competency, which everyone craves. She connects us all. She is comforting.

Jewel's already creeped Rudo, of course.

She sucks on her finger and flips through. He's new on Europa, almost as new as she is. Some experience on Luna, but before her time there. That tall, dark, and handsome. She'd remember him.

Some girl named Rosaline features largely. She's beautiful, tall, blond, et cetera. Fuck. But when Jewel looks at his friend roster, no Ros. And his status is single.

Breakup.

Bad one.

Bad enough to send him screaming into space, to the most remote mining outpost Earth has, a place where you lose two years of your life in cryo—travel time, yes, a year each way— and the chances of dying on the job are almost thirty percent.

Jewel clicks on a follower's link to some fan fiction. Jewel has always garnered more than her fair share of this stuff, given her looks—mostly written by females, interestingly.

Wow. This follower certainly has imagination. The scenario, involving Jewel, Rudo, and group sex with some hither-to un-discovered intelligent and sensuous life-forms here on Europa, is strangely compelling.

"In truth, fair Monty, I am too fond."

She likes his status (one of those fake-modest posts about his big take today) and updates her own. *Hey Rudo. Check out the competition.* Her take today exceeded his.

Too macho?

She adds a cute animated emoticon.

She dozes, surfacing now and again to watch as the hits on her status go up and up and up.

The bar. Of course. There's nowhere else.

Jewel shakes off Paris, that bug. Larry gets her a whiskey ("Any more glass-smashing stunts and you're outta here; I don't care how pretty you are or how much ice you pump, princess") and she waits.

And waits.

Is he going to show?

That status . . . maybe it was too much.

She opens a small screen and re-reads her post.

That emoticon. It's too girlie, too cute. Maybe he doesn't like girlie. She closes the screen with her fist.

Or . . . is it the goddamn Cap/Monty thing? The Montys are a unified testosterone field; their militia-like training exercises leave bruises. They're totally unlike the polyamorous polymorphously perverse culture of the Caps. Spartans to the Caps' Athenians.

Jewel's not used to failing when it comes to men.

She finishes her drink. One more, just one and then she'll go back to her room.

He walks in.

So beautiful. The ice-walls' lights gleam on his dark skin, making it almost blue.

Their eyes lock. He glances down the bar to the Monty end, then back at her. Gives her the tiniest nod.

Her heart beats faster.

He walks past. Too close—he almost touches her.

She knows. He knows.

Another drink. More glances. The whole bar must sense this budding love.

There's no rule. No one can actually stop a Monty from hanging with a Cap. But . . . despite Prince's decree of peace . . . it's just not done.

They must be discreet.

He comes down a bit, she edges up.

He leans in next to her, orders a beer from Larry.

Their arms touch.

Above the bar, in his beautifully carved ice-cavern, Prince surveys his domain.

He has access, as does anyone on Europa (or Earth for that matter, if they pay to view) to all the camera feeds on the base.

He also has access to some cameras that no one else knows about.

Oh, and by the way, he's got a degree in exobiology.

And has worked as a glaciologist.

And is a doctor of music.

Just saying.

He lies back on a synthetic-fur covering, ice walls flickering with every color of the rainbow, light playing over his face. He's not looking at any of the screens that flicker in the air, however. No, Prince is wearing headphones.

He's listening.

There are many difficulties associated with having an affair in a panopticon society, even when it's a self-imposed panopticon. We made it that way; we *like* it that way. But you still believe you have secrets. That primitive, private sense of self—a belief that there is a self separate from the avatar-self, your online persona as conveyed by the Nurse—persists.

The online back-and-forth between Rudo and Jewel continues. They like each other's statuses, they like pictures. Followers notice, interest grows.

It is possible that Jewel lets all this go a teeny weeny bit to her head.

Rudo takes a particular interest in her family, she notes. Her Korean birth parents died from radiation cancers, and white Americans adopted her. Him, he's Shona and knows it, knows his lineage. It's so different from how she grew up: in a freckled Anglo-Saxon enclave, with people who purport not to be a tribe, and to be from nowhere, yet at every moment making everyone who is *not* them feel like strangers.

His parents died years after the conflict too, also of radiation poisoning. The usual story. She and Rudo are both orphans. Most miners are.

His interest in her family touches her. There's something . . . old-fashioned about it. Courtly. Stuff like that used to matter, she imagines. Who are you one of? It's not a question very many people can ask anymore.

And why would you, when most people die of radiation-related cancers before they reach forty?

Close Encounter #2 at the Only, face-to-face, real-time, there's a moment when eyes meet.

Another brief touch of skin on skin, as if casual. As if it's a mistake.

"Today, on the surface." His eyes are lustrous. "I think I have figured out why the Sun is so small and dim here."

The heat builds inside them both.

"Why."

He smiles—O, his smile slays the envious moon!—and shakes his head. "Looking at you, now, I have forgotten."

She catches her breath. "Let me stand here until you remember."

"I will forget, to have you still stand there, remembering how I love your company."

Her heart beats faster. "Rudo. A good name for you. It means love."

A pause.

"How do you know that?"

A smile curves her lips.

"I looked it up."

Waiting for him to reply seems like infinity. But at last he speaks.

"The Sun here is so pale, so distant, because she is sick and pale with grief. She cannot compete with your light. Jewel. Your brightness shames the Sun."

She stares. No one's ever said that kind of thing to her before.

It's like poetry. But the bar grows restless, he must walk, they cannot be seen talking.

To stand by his side feels like home.

Sometimes, the difference between ecstasy and terror is difficult to discern.

Some strange things are going on.

It only happens when Paris is working, connected to Jewel.

At first he thought it was just that thing: you get a song in your head, an ear-worm. But then he realizes there's noise. Crackling, like the transmission is struggling. And deep groans, tearing sounds as if glacier-sized chunks of ice are breaking off and drifting, a hundred kilometers down into the deep. And a noise like drilling, amplified, stretched. Also, music. There's sway and flex, almost imperceptible changes in pitch and tempo, like someone is learning the song, trying to get it right.

And the songs play all the way through. Then repeat. That's not how your head does it.

It's almost as if it's coming from outside, and the links are picking it up.

Sometimes too, Paris hears snatches of conversation. Mostly convos from the bar the night before, repeated over and over, fragments, a private tête-à-tête he didn't overhear at the time.

Creepy.

Paris asks other technicians if they're picking up extraneous sonic phenomena.

Nance has, and two or three of the others. Like Paris, they assume it is a glitch in the system, or in their own heads.

None of their miners have noticed anything.

He wonders if the Montys have.

He writes up a report. Reads it. Re-reads it. Deletes it. It makes him sound crazy.

Which he is beginning to feel he might be. That Jewel, she doesn't give him a flick of an eyelash. Ten hours linked to someone, breathing with them, feeling every surge and twitch, responsible for their life and death, and you are dead to them. It's soul-destroying.

He misses Billy. He used to look forward to the end of each shift, wait for Bill to come in, help him strip off the gear, all sweaty, Paris never cared. Licked Billy's neck, tasting salt. Ran his fingers around the whorls of Billy's perfect ears. Lying together afterward, pillow-talk, drifting into sleep. The sex . . . they could almost read each other's minds. The technological link was part of that, built that connection.

It could be that way with Jewel too.

The song in his head/ear right now is a sad one. Big hit two years ago, just before Paris left Earth for Europa. Sad, sad song.

Prince is listening.

He lies back and his hands gesture as if conducting.

He listens to sounds from deep within the moon, sounds that deep sensors transmit to him. Sounds from the hundred-kilometer-deep ocean that lies just beneath this granite-hard icy crust.

Someone or something or many someones are singing.

Or rather, perhaps, the moon is singing.

He posits: First, there was sound. And the sound was good.

Then, possibly, something Prince calls "the Europaeans" (a shorthand; he doesn't really believe there are individual alien beings on this moon, little green aquatic men) began to evolve. Bacteria, perhaps—the sea is warm enough—possibly subsisting on oxygen formed when hydrogen peroxide, found all over Europa's surface, mixes with the liquid ocean beneath the ice.

Until now, they would have lived in perfect isolation. There would be little sonic interference save the odd barrage of meteoroids from space, and flexing and eruptions caused by tidal heating (a consequence of Europa's slightly eccentric orbit and orbital resonance with the other Galilean moons).

Such a deep and salty ocean is able to hold and carry sound to an extraordinary degree. For, possibly, billions of years, complex sonic structures existed here unmolested, distributing themselves over an astonishing range of frequencies.

Prince's first concrete breakthrough stemmed from the moment he was able to detect repeats of Terran sounds. Echoes, sure. But more than that. The sounds were being amplified, repeated, altered.

The sounds were being creatively investigated.

It seems to Prince, and his shadowy backers, that Europaean sonic structures are reproducing, entropy-resisting, and self-organizing.

Life is matter that can reproduce itself and evolve as survival dictates.

Could sound be a form of life? No, of course not. Unless it is a form of life so alien that we can't at first recognize it as life. Or, perhaps even plausibly, something along the lines of the Gaia hypothesis: Europa as a single organism maintaining and building itself as a totality.

Prince listens, he waves his hands, he sinks deeper into the music. Almost . . . almost . . . he can almost understand what they are sing—no. What is *being sung*.

Close Encounter #3 at the Only. They lean right in, arms and shoulders touching, Caps and Montys be damned. But not looking at each other's faces. It feels more intimate, somehow, not to.

Rudo asks Jewel what happened to her adoptive parents.

She draws spirals on top of the bar. "They died. Two years ago."

"Radiation?"

She nods. The cool green of Washington state; how she misses the turquoise rivers, mountains, the rolling sea, the smell of her mother's clothes, the soft spot under the beard of her father where a little girl could nestle her head.

She feels like crying. It must be Rudo. She doesn't cry, doesn't think about this.

"That land is poisoned."

"Not the West Coast," Jewel replies. "It's supposed to be safe." Poor bombed Beijing and DC, poor retaliation-bombed North Korea, almost fifty years ago now. She herself carries the seeds inside her, cancers, poisons of fallout. They all do.

"It's a good thing it happened," comes Larry, and Jewel jumps; she'd been lost, forgotten she and Rudo were in the bar.

"What the fuck," she asks

"The bombing, the war. It's lucky."

"Oh, don't cheer us up, you insane person."

"Imagine," Larry insists. "If it hadn't happened, we would have just kept going the way we were."

"What'd be wrong with that."

Larry smiles. "Look at what we got. Global cooling, mass starvation, extinctions, poisoned water, horror, devastation, and," he holds up his hand to forestall interruption, "we finally saw the Earth as a delicate thing. Passed global laws about corporate environmental responsibility, cradle-to-grave legislation. Made it too expensive to mine on Earth because corporations were, for the first time, fully responsible for reparations. Developed space-flight and wet-socket mining technologies. Trained you, and you." He stretches, pushes off from the bar. "And gave you, and you, and me, these wonderful jobs which will lead, after a paltry five years including travel time, to a lifetime of moneyed leisure."

"If we survive," Rudo says without emotion.

"Oh, I won't. Not for long." Larry's still smiling. "I'm a cancer baby."

Jewel and Rudo are silent.

Jewel clears her throat. "How long do you have."

"A year. Maybe."

"I am sorry," Rudo rumbles.

"Well. You have to die from something, right?"

Larry begins a move up the bar, then returns. He winks.

"I like you kids. Don't ask me why. I just do."

And with that, Larry drifts up the bar to serve the massed Montys, who are growing restive.

Rudo gazes after Larry. "There is something courageous about his self-absorbed nihilism."

Jewel longs to talk to Rudo, talk more, tell him . . . something, she doesn't know what, anything. But he has to go. They've been talking, they've been seen, the boys are glaring down the bar.

Every step he takes away from her makes her feel like her body is stretching and breaking from the inside out.

Montys and Caps.

Enemies forever.

Jewel watches. She watches Rudo working, she creeps him on Nurse, she waits for him downtime, at the bar. Larry notices, Larry smiles, Larry asks.

"You two done the deed yet?"

She is shocked. But the place is near-empty, no one has heard. She shakes her head.

"No! That surprises me."

"Under other circumstances . . ."

"No doubt."

"But here."

Larry makes a noise of disgust with his lips. "Fucking fake corporate competition. It's so transparent. Gives them something to swoon over back home, gives you guys something to distract you from the terrible attrition rate up here."

"You think they do it on purpose."

"They do."

"Who is they."

He smiles at her curt barrage of uninflective questions, almost laughs. "Those guys? The actual leaders? You know who they are?"

Jewel shakes her head.

Larry leans in and whispers. "That's right. No one does. Or almost no one. Well, my boss works for them."

"Prince."

Nod. "You think he's here to run a bar?"

Pause.

"Since the war and the breakdown of government, food sources are controlled by two main corporations. The Caps are descended from Nabisco. The Montys are the core of Monsanto."

"I know."

"Two families." Larry lowers his voice further, and wipes at a nonexistent spot on the ice bar. "Two families run everything. Chinese and Euro: the Jiangs and the Contis. Rivals for what's left of the bounty."

"You sound like a conspiracy theorist."

"And all this"—he gestures around the ice-bar, and Jewel knows he's taking in the whole moon, Jupiter above, the entire Solar System—"is theirs. But I'll tell you one thing," and his voice is so quiet Jewel can barely hear it now. "Those bastards, they don't own love. They don't own your heart."

"Larry." Jewel flashes her best smile. "Are you counseling me to go fuck that beautiful boy."

"Jewel, I am."

She stares at him. The ecstasy/terror builds.

"I'm sick of this shit," Larry declares. "Fuck him and show the world you love him."

Prince listens.

Those bastards, they don't own love. They don't own your heart. Those bastards, they don't own love. They don't own your heart. Those bastards, they don't own love. They don't own your heart.

Deep below, in the limitless sea, the words build and multiply, the intonation, the music of the barkeep's voice. Over and over, becoming something beautiful and large and strange, so very strange.

She is back on Earth. A wide, empty street at night. Trees, tall ones with leaves, bend overhead. Houses, shuttered, silent, on either side. Two dark riders gallop toward her. A voice through a loudspeaker: *Clear the streets! The streets must remain clear!* She runs and hides in some cedar bushes as the shielded and mounted police gallop past. Echoes of their hoofbeats die. Then she realizes that of course she has wandered into a radiation zone. She will die.

And that's when she finds him by the road. Lips cold, jaw slack, eyes rolled back. Big, beautiful hands, palms upward, fingers curled.

She wakes, heart pounding.

Rudo is stroking her hair. Long, soft, gentle strokes, over and over.

She sees him looking down at her and wants to cry.

What is it about him? She is lost, lost and in love.

They lie in one of Larry's storerooms, behind the bar. The ice floor is covered with the high-tech, high-pile fabric they call "fur" up here: soft, warm. Light pulses gently in the walls.

It's secret. Safe.

"My alarm went off, Jewel."

She swipes the screen before he can read the time.

"That wasn't your alarm. It was mine, I set it early, we have at least an hour before work," she lies.

"Ah." He strokes her hair and looks into her eyes. He caresses the plug-in at the base of her neck. He kisses her.

His kisses.

She falls into them as into deep water.

He entwines his fingers between her own. She feels something hard, cold, pressing up over her thumb.

She looks. It's his ring, his Monty ring with his name engraved onto it. It fits her thumb perfectly.

She catches her breath. Removes her own ring, *Jewel* engraved in ornate lettering around the Cap insignia, and places it on his smallest finger.

His kisses grow harder, deeper, insistent.

"I have more care to stay than will to go," he murmurs against her neck.

Downtime over, the lights automatically begin to brighten.

"More light and light. More dark and dark our woes . . . Ah . . ." How does he do it, know every thrum and longing of her body?

The walls are thick, there is no one there, their cries are loud and long.

If Jewel and Rudo were listening to anything outside themselves, they would hear the echo: reverberating, repeating, holding their cries and moans and murmurings, sending them out, out in waves, rippling through the saline slush and water and ice. How silver-sweet sound lovers' tongues by night, like softest music to attending ears! All Europa trembles gently with their love.

The sounds of their physical lust, breathing and voices and their bodies in motion, becomes a song the whole moon sings.

Yup. They're just that good.

Jewel doesn't show up on shift the next day.

Paris pulls up a screen. She's not online and hasn't been for about eight hours.

Beyond suspicious.

He strides down the hall to her room, bangs on the door.

No answer.

He goes to the technician room. The others are already plugged in, Velcro-strapped to their seats to ensure stability, their miners out. Montys are working too, the army of them out across the crater. No, one is missing.

Rudo.

Paris sits, folds his arms over his chest, and waits.

Even when he's not plugged in, now, he hears a song. The others hear it too, he can tell, even as they stare into their screens with deep concentration as their miners work, they are all beating a hand or twitching a foot in time.

It's the song Larry played last night at the bar. The pre-last-call song. He played it loud, because Prince made a rare appearance and told him to crank it. It made the ice walls of the subsurface establishment ring. Maybe, somehow, it got into the ice and the slush. Filled the whole ocean. Filled Paris's brain, the control room, the whole base, the entire moon reverberating with some shitty top forty hit.

And something else, something underneath it. Something like old recordings he's heard of whale song. Soaring cries, moans, and almost something like words.

If he didn't know better Paris would say it sounds like the moon is making love to itself.

Both Cap and Monty yields are down a bit that day. Several of the miners are late for their shifts, and seem distracted once they get there. And all the technicians, both sides, complain of sonic interference in their communications implants. Songs, and even sounds like . . . well, they're pretty X-rated, let's just say that. Montys accuse Caps of sabotage; Caps accuse Montys of hangovers. Everyone's a bit off; everyone's cranky.

Must be something in the water.

That night at the bar, all hell breaks loose.

Jewel isn't there, and neither is Rudo—but everyone else is.

Very, very suspicious, if Paris is any judge.

Larry seems pleased about something and buys a round for everybody. "To peace between factions," he toasts. Very strange indeed. And the Montys are getting rowdy. Paris senses Tybalt beginning to swell; the possibility of a fight always excites him.

Little muscular Mercury lines up five shots and does them all.

Paris nods to Tybalt. "Methinks we'd better drink up and get home. The mad blood is stirring."

"Home?" Tybalt responds. "Not until I can't see straight."

"Mad, mad blood," Paris repeats.

Tybalt shrugs.

Paris overhears Ben, in a mirror action, trying to get that Monty idiot Mercury out of the bar. Ben's all right. If he wasn't a Monty he'd probably be a friend.

But Mercury will have none of it.

"I go nowhere, you moody bitch. Larry!"

And Mercury orders a round for the Montys.

"Come on, Merc," Paris hears Ben pleading.

"You trying to start a fight?"

"You know better."

Mercury points an unsteady finger at his friend. "You're always trying to start fights."

"Me?"

"You'd fight a man for cracking nuts, because you have hazel eyes. You'd fight a man for coughing, because he woke up a dog in the street. Your head is as full of fighting as this moon is full of salty slush, and yet you'd lecture me on fighting?"

"All right, all right."

A song comes over the mix, a new one, a hit. Banal. A song about love. It seems loud, too loud. The walls ring with it.

Mercury raises his voice. "Tybalt! Pretty man!"

Tybalt glances with seeming laziness down the bar, waves his hand, and turns back to Paris. "Buzz buzz, is someone talking?"

"Blow me," Mercury slurs.

"Indeed," Tybalt says, "so you have asked before. And I have offered, and been spurned."

"Hey, hey, hey," Paris says. There's no mistaking the glint in Tybalt's eye.

"Now, now, now," Ben admonishes.

But Tybalt and Mercury begin the long strut down the bar. Paris looks for Larry but he's nowhere to be seen.

And that fucking song, why is it so loud?

One step, two, three, and the two bantams have closed.

"My hands around your neck again," Tybalt grinds out through clenched teeth.

"And mine on yours," says Mercury, looking up at his taller assailant, but in a surprise move he knees Tybalt in the groin.

All the air goes out Tyb's lungs, and his face turns white as paper, but he doesn't let go of Merc's neck.

People are yelling, pumping the air with their fists.

Rudo choses this moment to come in.

He sees the two men grappling, takes in the yelling crowd. He lopes down the bar. Three soaring skips and he's at the fight.

"Be at peace!"

"Fuck off, Monty," Tyb spits out between his teeth.

"You will kill each other," and indeed, Mercury's face is purple.

But that doesn't stop Merc from saying, "Rudo, I got this."

And Mercury wraps his hands around Tyb's throat.

"Let go, I beg you," Rudo pleads.

They aren't letting go. The noise in the bar increases, amplifies, yelling and hooting. It echoes in the icy walls, the floor, throughout the base. The song is loud enough to deafen, now. To Paris it seems the whole moon is reverberating with brawling love, with loving hate.

Cracks appear. A piece of the ceiling falls.

Larry comes running in from the back freezer, bottles in hand. When he sees what is happening, he drops them. They fall, low-g slow onto the granite-hard ice floor. They shatter.

"Peace, for the love of god, peace!"

Tybalt snaps Mercury's neck.

He springs back.

The song swells.

Mercury falls, bounces gently, comes to rest. His eyes are half-open, his head rests at an angle.

Blood trickles from the corner of his mouth.

Some urine leaks down his leg, steaming in the chilly air.

No one could really say, afterward, what happened.

The bar shook as if seismic forces gripped it.

And then it was like all the sounds of the fight, the snapping

of bones, well, it all came crashing in like an amplification tsunami.

Screams, an alarm, evacuation. Everybody, out.

A lot of hearing damage; that came out later. Some of the
miners ended up deaf.

And somehow in the chaos Tybalt, that hothead, he wound
up dead.

Broken neck, mirror of Mercury. Not because of the earth-
quake. No. Someone, a Cap, said they saw Rudo do it. And
surveillance cameras showed Rudo embracing Merc's body,
then turning to Tybalt, grappling. Then the feed cut out; the
seismic activity, perhaps.

Two hours later, the Nurse was full of it. Everyone, Europa
to Moon to Earth, knew something had happened.

The mining base is put on lockdown.

The number one hit song skyrockets. Covers and remixes all
over the Nurse. Dedications to Tybalt, dedications to Mercury.

And Rudo? He disappears.

Paris watches the footage, over and over. Rudo, embracing
Mercury's broken body. Then lunging for Tybalt.

The swelling song. The sounds of shouting, hands on flesh,
violent, almost sexual. The cut to the feed.

Over. And. Over.

It has a certain rhythm to it, and the rhythm matches the
song in Paris's head.

Jewel gets a message.

She's been sitting in her room, the number one hit love
song running through her head, crying until her eyes hurt.

It's a high-priority message, on a sub-public frequency.

It's from Larry.

I am with Rudo.

I'm coming, she types, already standing, already stepping toward the door.

No! High-priority ping.

I have to see him. I'll die.

He is up for murder.

She stares at the words.

Up for murder. Of course he is. That video.

Death is the penalty for murder. Eye for an eye in this bloody and fragile world.

Jewel feels a prickling over her scalp, up her forearms, like electricity. Is this what people mean when they say their hair stands on end?

The feeling inside is terror, rage, pain. Something else too.

Love.

She doesn't care. She loves him. She can still feel his hands on her body, taste him on her lips. His name is love.

She will not live without him. It will be easy enough, here. Just walk outside. If the minus-one-hundred-and-sixty Celsius temperatures don't do it, the radiation will.

Rudo and I have a plan, Larry types.

The longing in her body threatens to overwhelm. *Let me talk to him.*

He is in cryo.

What the fuck?

The corporations want the two bodies—Mercury and Tybalt—sent to Luna base. And they want Rudo extradited to Luna for trial.

She'll do anything to see him again.

You and Rudo have to disappear.

YES. How?

A pause.

You and Mercury have more or less the same mass.

So?

We cut out the online connections. Mercury's, Rudo's, Tybalt's, yours. We dispose of Mercury's body here on Europa, and exchange him . . .

For me.

Yes.

So we destroy my connection permanently?

Yes.

The connections are inserted shortly after birth. To be permanently offline . . .

I'll do it.

Slow down! She can almost sense Larry's laughter at her tempestuousness. *Here's how it works. We fake an accident with Tybalt's corpse, and put Rudo's connection in that cryopod.*

She forces her brain to work. A cryo-accident turns the cells inside out; no one will be able to tell whose body it is, not without a DNA analysis . . .

And Mercury's connection is in my pod so when they scan on arrival they will think I'm him, and Rudo is Tybalt, and Tybalt is Rudo. Right?

Right.

But when the pods arrive on Luna, the sensors will tell them that two of us are in living cryo. They'll revive us, it's the law . . .

Yes, they'll see who you are. You will have to subdue the technician on the Luna end. Buy time, Larry types.

Why are you helping? He could be in the pay of one of the corporations—after all, he works for the mysterious Prince. There could be some kind of agenda . . .

I'm sick of the bullshit, Jewel.

Sick enough to risk your life?

Because if Rudo is up for murder, then abetting him also carries the death penalty.

I'm here for a good time, not a long time. Remember?

His cancer. She sits, cannot type.

Jewel?

I'm here.

I have contacts on Luna. They can forge new identities for you.

Hiding out on Luna is vaguely possible. There's an underworld there that swallows people whole.

$$$$????? she types.

I have savings. Enough.

She reads the message, and reads again. Why is he helping? Even if he's dying, it's implausible.

But it's her only hope.

Paris will put you in cryo.

I don't trust that jealous worm.

He's your technician, remember? He's responsible for your safety. Don't worry. I've worked it all out with him. He trusts me.

Jewel, uncharacteristically, submits.

Everyone trusts you.

Jewel's gazing down at Rudo in his cryopod like she is a dying man in a desert, leaning over a pool of water.

How she loves him. It curdles Paris, makes his hands shake and his stomach knot.

Rudo's face has the pallid, faintly green tinge of cryo. There's a bloody line on his forearm where his connection was cut out and Tybalt's inserted.

Tybalt lies dead, flooded with cryofluid, in another pod, Rudo's connection in the pod with him. No one's gazing down at him. Paris and Larry have fixed it so that the pod will leak in transit and his body will turn itself into a cryogenic mess.

"Where's Larry."

Her flat voice, her abrupt questions, why is it all so arousing? "He had to go. Prince called him." There had been some emergency, something to do with the songs.

"Really." She looks suspicious. Paris sighs.

"Let's do this. I'll get an anesthetic for your arm . . ."

"Fuck that."

Jewel grabs a pair of chopsticks and places them between her teeth. Then, as Paris watches, she slides the blade of a scalpel under the skin of her forearm, and carefully, bloodily, cuts her online connection out from under her skin.

Untraceable, now.

The chopsticks fall from her mouth to the floor with a clatter. "Give me Merc's connection," she says through gritted teeth.

Paris hands her the small piece of metal and she slides it through the bloody flux, applies pressure.

"What did you do with his body."

"Never you mind." Larry took care of that. Stashed him in some unused ice cave. All hell will break loose when he's discovered. But that's not likely to happen, not for a long, long time.

She still looks suspicious.

"Time for you to go under, princess."

She doesn't trust him, he can tell. But she lies back, sighs.

God, she's beautiful.

Larry'd had a stroke of genius just before being called away. He put not only Rudo's connection in Tybalt's pod, but also Jewel's ring. The affair between Jewel and Rudo was quite the thing on Earth, and everyone will have analyzed every inch of footage. Jewel's ring has been spotted by followers on Rudo's finger. There's even a top-ten song already called, yeah, *Jewel's Ring*. Finding it in the cryo-mess, it'll be natural to assume the mess is Rudo. The Luna technicians might pass over the DNA test for the ruined flesh altogether.

Paris means to mention this finishing touch to Jewel. As he checks her vitals, he means to tell her about her ring. As he inserts the tubes in her veins that will drain her blood and re-

place it with cryofluid, he means to tell her. As he gradually
brings her temperature down, he means to tell her. Just before
he sedates her, he almost tells her.

Well, it doesn't matter really, right? I mean, a little thing like
that.

It skitters across the surface of Paris's consciousness, paired
with a slightly nauseous, resentful, excited feeling, almost—if
he were to let himself admit it—a vengeful feeling. And Jewel
sinks into sleep, and is gone.

He watches over her, brooding, almost tender, as her face
drains of color. He disconnects her, seals her pod. He ferries
the three pods to the transport ship.

"Here you are. Mercury and Tybalt, bodies cryo-preserved.
And Rudo, safely in cryo. That murdering bastard."

The transport technicians take over.

Paris watches as the ship is propelled from the base. Its light
sail erect, a beautiful sight. It hurtles toward Luna.

Good-bye, Jewel.

Strange. He's still hearing that song.

Paris is not alone. Isolated in lockdown, every human on Europa
hears that song. This is why Larry was called away by Prince:
the sonic structures have become undeniable, dominant. Every
human on Europa begins singing the last song to be played at
the Only. It's not a particularly good song. But for whatever
reason, that's the song they sing, as if that final blast at the bar
has infected the entire moonscape. And not only humans sing.
Underneath, above, all around them in the ice in which the
base is nestled, the song is amplified. There are groans, and
whalelike sonar blasts. Deep, almost too deep for the human
ear to hear. Like the horns of heaven, if you believe in heaven,
when the gates open at the end of time.

* * *

The ship hurtles through the Solar System. A reflective outer sail refocuses and reflects a beam from great Fresnel lenses of the Mercury Array back onto the mainsail, enabling the ship to travel back toward Luna.

Jewel lies unmoving, mind wandering through a year of cryo dreams.

Rudo finds her and thinks she is dead. "Why are you so beautiful? Why are you yet so beautiful?" he cries. "Shall I believe that insubstantial death is amorous, and that the lean abhorred monster keeps you here in the dark to be his paramour?"

This is followed by some horrible images: a death-figure riddled with worms, pressing down hard on Jewel's chest, shoving cold fingers inside her mouth, between her legs. She cannot move or breathe.

Then Rudo comes, takes her in his arms. He thinks she is dead. "Yet so beautiful? Why are you yet so beautiful?"

Over. And. Over.

One year later. Luna. A cryo chamber. Three transparent pods.

A young woman lies in one, unconscious, blood-transfusion tubes connected to her veins.

Another pod is empty, tubes trailing onto the floor.

The third is filled with an unholy mess.

On the floor there's a bloody trail, leading to the door, which is shut.

The woman wakes, rolls into a ball like a baby. It generally takes a bit longer for women to come out of cryo—the more muscle mass you have, the faster you come to.

Her body shudders and tries to vomit, muscles scream. She can't cry; ducts are dry.

Why does it hurt so much? It isn't the warming process—by the time you're conscious, body-temperature blood has flushed out the cryoprotectant. It's not ice crystals in your tissue—they've figured out how to stop that from happening, a combo of synthetic amphibious and plant glycols, and dimethyl sulphoxide.

It's a bit of a mystery. But then, most things are.

The woman manages to sit up. Blinking, slow painful drag across eyes. Tongue like a piece of dried meat moving over teeth. She rips out her tubes. When her legs start working she'll stand up.

Smiling is supposed to bring on painkilling endorphins. The woman tries to smile. Her lips stick to her teeth.

Cautiously she straightens one leg, the other, flexing muscles. Blinks again and it happens: wetness, a blessed film, the relief of it.

She manages to stand. Totters to the messy cryopod.

"Ew," Jewel—for it is she, of course—says.

She leans over, a bit sad. Tybs was on her team, after all. He was a nut, but she had time to create some fond feeling for him, back on Europa.

She freezes.

There, on what used to be this person's smallest finger of their left hand, is a ring.

A Cap ring, a name engraved on it. *Jewel.*

Her legs give out. She falls to the floor.

Obviously, something went horribly wrong and this inside-out cell-death mess is her love. It's Rudo.

Larry failed. Or lied to her. She remembers the look in Paris's eyes as she went under. A gleam.

She should have known.

Her limbs may be trembling, but it's amazing how quickly her mind works.

The empty pod: Tyb's body was in that one and they've taken it. Someone, then, will be back soon. For her.

She will not live, without Rudo. A year of deathly cryo-dreams . . . what kept her going was the belief that she'd find Rudo on Luna and they'd be together, forever.

Well, that's not going to happen now.

She tears through the room and finds a blade.

A nice, long, pointy blade.

Jewel has never been so happy to see a dagger.

She thinks. Remembers her anatomy lessons. Best way to heart . . . here.

"Let this be your sheath."

Jewel stabs herself.

It's hard to stab yourself in the heart. Almost impossible. You can't slash wildly. You have to—and Jewel does—press the point precisely against yourself, then push. Hard. There's a lot of resistance; you have to get through the breastplate. Every instinct is to flinch back, away from the pain.

Most people would inflict a couple of test wounds and then give up. There are lots of less painful ways to kill oneself.

But Jewel, she's something else. She goes all the way. She even manages some pretty top-class last words.

"Rust there," she says to the blade, "and let me die."

It takes a bit of time, and about two pints of blood leak out of her twitching form, but die Jewel does.

And then, seriously, about five minutes later, Rudo comes pounding through the storeroom door.

He'd emerged from cryo quickly. And regretfully, out of necessity, killed the cryotechnician, dragged the body out of the room to hide it, and rushed back to be on hand when his love comes to consciousness.

He sees Jewel's body on the floor.

He screams.

Have you ever heard someone scream like this? Howl from the force of the kind of emotional pain that leaves part of your soul dead?

It's a terrible sound. It falls in the Luna cryo-room, trapped in the underground bunker. On some other level, though, some energetic or spiritual or whatever you want to call it level, the scream travels out and out, ripples through space, to the edges of the Solar System and beyond.

Rudo falls on Jewel.

Ignoring all first-aid training, he pulls the dagger out of her breast.

He shakes her body.

He hides his face on her bloody chest.

He goes completely still.

Rudo takes the knife that he has pulled from Jewel's formerly perfect breast, and with it, just below the scar from where his online connection was removed, he slits his wrists. And bleeds all over the storeroom floor.

"Jewel." He strokes her face. Gets blood on it. Tries to wipe it off. "Why are you yet so fair?"

He has more time than Jewel did, and comes up with some truly top-notch last words, maybe even unbeatable last words. "I will stay with you, and never from this palace of dim night depart again. Here we will set up our everlasting rest, and shake the yoke of inauspicious stars from this world-wearied flesh."

He kisses her.

"With a kiss, I die."

And Rudo slumps onto Jewel's body, and slowly, peacefully, dies.

Thus end our lovers. Parting is such sweet sorrow.

*   *   *

Nurse's newsfeed registers the discovery, on Luna, of the bodies of two miners, dead, apparently in a suicide pact. Some people remember that these two were Jewel and Rudo, superstar secret lovers back on Europa a year or so ago. But in terms of hits, you really have to go a long way down the feed to find the story and its associated comments.

The top of the news is the weather. That's all anybody wants to talk about, that day.

That, and the latest from Europa. Since we left that moon a year ago, Prince has become a sort of intermediary between the sonic . . . what to call it? Civilization? on Europa, and the Jiang-Conti corporate alliance.

Yes, in a typical human-species move, an encounter with aliens has prompted a real fellow-feeling between former rivals. Montys and Caps. Friends forever.

So far they can't seem to find any real use for the Europaeans. It's disappointing.

All "they" want to do is sing.

Barkeep Larry, promoted to Prince's right-hand research man, dies on Europa of his cancer. He tells no one of his role in the tragedy of Rudo and Jewel, and goes quietly, surrounded by friends and tearful former bar customers.

Paris, in case anyone is wondering, becomes a deejay on Europa, which is now a top party destination for the very rich and very bored.

As for the mining, Jiang-Conti profits soar.

The weather? Oh, yes, the weather. The day Jewel and Rudo are found dead on Luna, the sky is overcast, all over Earth. No one can remember anything like it happening before. Sun worshippers complain. Meteorologists are puzzled. Conspiracy theorists posit corporate climate engineering.

But we know what it is. Love's end.

"The Sun for sorrow will not show his head." Isn't that something someone said, once, many years ago, before we understood our uncentral place in the universe?

The Sun for sorrow will not show his head.

AMBIGUOUS NATURE
Carl Frederick

For more than half a century a dedicated band of radio astronomers have searched the stars for signals from an intelligent civilization.

SETI—the Search for Extra-Terrestrial Intelligence—has produced little more than frustration. No clearly discernible signals have been detected, and SETI has been denigrated and ridiculed by know-nothing politicians.

But the universe is vast, and the chance of actually finding another intelligent species is a powerful lure. The chances of making contact with an extraterrestrial intelligence may be small, but the consequences of such a contact would be Earth-shattering.

Carl Frederick captures the loneliness and frustration involved in such research, as well as the excitement of making, just possibly, the discovery of the ages.

One note to remember: if the universe is truly infinite, then almost anything is possible.

Looking like the compound eye of a gigantic bug, the two hundred dishes of the Kata Tjuta Large Radio Array observatory probed deep into the cosmos. The twelve-meter-diameter dishes, all listening hard, scanning the sky at a billion frequencies for signs of intelligence.

Oblivious they were to the sounds of the desert: the soft calls of the crested pigeons, the noisy chattering of the galahs, and the near-silent susurrus of a Pilbara cobra slithering through the porcupine grass.

The low humidity and absence of radio frequency interference in the desolate, red center of the Australian continent made for good observing, but for lonely living.

As the Sun touched the horizon, the cliffs in the distance reflected a glowing copper-red against the rare gathering storm clouds above them.

Closer, a blur of motion broke the desolation. On a dirt road bounded by the occasional mulga and bloodwood tree, a solitary automobile threw up an orange mist of dust as it pressed onward toward the observatory.

At the astronomy console of the observatory's control center, astronomer Albert Griffin stared morosely at the monitor. "I'd hoped," he said to the only other person in the center, "that with this big, snazzy new array, we'd have found something by now."

Ralph (Dingo) Kunmanara laughed. "We've only been at it for a couple of months."

"Still," said Albert, "I wonder why I do it. SETI." He scowled. "Search for Extra-Terrestrial Intelligence. It should be called SETIV. Spending Endless Time In Vain." He swiveled toward Ralph. "For that matter, why do you do it? I mean work as a radio engineer when you're a first-class quantum physicist."

"At uni I got typecast as an experimentalist by doing an experimental thesis." A flicker of a grimace passed over Ralph's face, to be replaced by a smile. "Oz has made much progress of late, but it's still easier for the average Australian to think of an aboriginal as an engineer than as a theoretical physicist."

Albert nodded. He was an American and didn't feel he knew enough to comment.

"And at any rate," Ralph went on, "I consider the existence of extraterrestrial intelligence *the* question of our era."

"*If* we find evidence, you mean."

"Too right!"

Just then, an alert buzz came from the astronomy console. Albert spun around to the monitor.

Ralph laughed. "Don't get your hopes up. Just another Signal Candidate."

"You never know, though." Albert stared at the monitor which showed a series of dots:

.. ..

He sighed. "Nope."

"Not prime numbers?"

Albert shook his head. It wasn't the series of prime numbers that the SETI community believed an extraterrestrial would send as a calling card.

"Another eclipsing pulsar?"

"Looks like it." Albert pulled up the online astronomical map and entered the signal's coordinates. "Star in the field," he said without enthusiasm. "No notations. Looks like we've discovered another one."

"I'll log it." Ralph made the entry, then idly looked out the window. "Ah. Your ride's here. And I think your son's come along too." He glanced up at the darkening sky. "And it looks like we're in for a bit of weather."

"They're early." Albert glanced at the panel clock. "It'll be an hour yet before another set of astronomers come in to do *real* astronomy."

Ralph turned from the window. "Oh, come on," he said with a chuckle. "You wouldn't be doing this if it you didn't want to."

Albert gave a slow nod. "I guess you're right. I do want to, but I don't want to want to."

Ralph blew out a breath. "Deep stuff, mate. Too deep for me."

Albert stood as the door opened and his wife, Kimberly, stepped in. Along with her came their son, Liam, almost eight years old with a mop of rich red hair and a face sprinkled with matching freckles. Kimberly and Liam wore the same style khaki bush shorts and white top as did the astronomers, but hers were cut higher above the knee.

Ralph rolled to his feet as well.

Albert and family exchanged greetings. Then Albert said, "You're early."

"Not early enough, I'm afraid," said Kimberly. "There's a storm coming."

Albert glanced away at the astronomy console. "I need about another half hour."

"We really should leave soon," said Kimberly. "The weather bureau says it's a very nasty storm."

Albert gave a reassuring laugh. "A *nasty* storm? Here in the middle of Australia? Can't be."

"The radio says maybe a once in a decade event." Kimberly glanced out the window. "It'll go through fast, but it will be ferocious."

"Let me finish this last observing run, 'bout another fifteen minutes."

As Albert turned his attention to the console, Ralph tousled Liam's flame-red hair. "Hi, Bluey!"

"Hi, Dr. Kunmanara."

"Hey," said Ralph in mock annoyance. "I've known you ever since you were a little ankle biter. By now, you should know to call me Ralph. Or Dingo. At home, everyone calls me Dingo."

Liam laughed. "Hi, Dr. Dingo."

A crash of thunder exploded through the control room and Liam darted back to stand beside his mother.

"Nothing to be afraid about, Liam," said Albert, turning to look.

"I'm not afraid," said Liam, the tremor in his voice giving lie to his assertion.

Albert turned to Kimberly. "I think we'd better wait out the storm here."

Kimberly nodded, her face showing concern. "I think that would be best." She smiled. "How's the work going?"

"Terrible!" Albert smiled as well, but it was forced. "Sometimes I feel this is all futile—hopeless."

"But what really bugs me," Ralph interjected, "is how much the cosmic isolation fanatics rejoice in our lack of success."

Albert nodded, sadly. "I must admit I'm beginning to wonder if they might actually be right."

"Odd thing for a SETI researcher to say," said Ralph.

"Oh, I don't know," said Albert in a world-weary voice. "Maybe cosmic isolation is just an excuse to myself to explain why we haven't found anything."

"What's comic isolation?" came Liam's treble voice into the conversation.

"*Cosmic* isolation. It's the idea"—Albert, inadvertently, drifted into lecture mode—"that God or nature or the universe, or whatever has arranged that sentient species are placed at sufficiently great distances from each other so that one species can't contaminate another's cultures."

Liam wrinkled his nose in a sign of not understanding.

"And it also explains," Albert went on, "why there is only one highly sentient species on Earth."

Liam stood wide-eyed, clearly still in the dark.

"No worries, Liam," said Ralph. "I think cosmic isolation is nonsense."

Liam seemed happy to be back in the game. "Well, Rex Snoopy Biscuit doesn't believe in cosmic isolation, either."

"Who?"

Albert felt embarrassed for his son. "Rex Snoopy Biscuit is . . . Liam's imaginary playmate." *He's much too old for this.*

Ralph laughed. "That boy needs a dog!" He turned to Liam who looked hurt. "I'm sorry. It's just that . . . that I like the name."

Liam pulled a device from his pocket and turned to his mother. "Can I go into the lounge," he said in a small voice, "and play with my GamesMaster?"

Ralph persisted in making amends. "Do you and Rex have—"

"Rex Snoopy Biscuit!"

"Do you and Rex Snoopy Biscuit have adventures together?"

"It's lonely for Liam here in the outback," said Albert, absently. "No kids his age to play with."

"We have adventures all the time," Liam insisted. "And today, we saw the min-min lights."

"Liam's right," said Kimberly. "While driving here, we did see the min-min lights."

Albert canted his head. "Min-min?"

"A purely Australian phenomenon," said Kimberly. "Two distant blurry white lights. And they seem to follow you."

"Far-off car headlights, maybe?" said Albert.

"Not likely," said Ralph. "We've had min-min lights long before European colonization."

"Interesting," said Albert. "Probably a temperature inversion near the ground. Some kind of Fata Morgana."

Liam wrinkled his nose.

Ralph laughed. "I'll tell you, Liam, how my people explain it." He sat and pulled Liam close. "Long ago in the dreamtime," he said in a soft, mysterious voice, "there was a great storm like no other. So the women in the clan gathered all the kids together to keep them safe. There was a great noise from the sky." Ralph clapped his hands together. Liam started and jerked back. Ralph pulled him close again. "And when the women weren't looking, one little boy, Dhundi, crept away and went to where he thought the noise came from. He stopped there and shouted to the sky, 'I am not afraid. I am not afraid.' Then, as he watched, a giant round ball of fire came down."

"Gosh!" said Liam.

"The ball cracked open and a man came out. He was red and he glowed like burning embers. 'I am your brother,' he said." Ralph sat back in his chair.

"Then what happened?"

Ralph gave an "I don't know" shrug. "Dhundi was never seen again. My people say that the min-min lights are Dhundi and his brother come back to Earth for a visit."

"Wow," said Liam in wide-eyed appreciation. He wrinkled his nose with a sudden thought. "I wonder if Rex Snoopy Biscuit is really *my* brother?"

"Could be," said Ralph, laughing.

Thunder pealed again.

"I am not afraid," said Liam under his breath.

"All right." Kimberly gently pulled Liam away. "Let's get you to the lounge so your father and Dr. Kunmanara—"

"Dr. Dingo."

Kimberly flashed a "kids say cheeky things" smile at Ralph, then took Liam off to the lounge to play with his game machine.

"Liam has an ambiguous nature," said Albert when boy and mother were out of sight. "He acts way younger than he is when under his mother's eyes, and much older than his age when he's around me." He bit his lower lip. "I think his mother likes him young while I prefer him acting older."

Another alert buzz came from the monitor. Ralph froze for an instant, his eyes focusing past Albert and onto the observations monitor. "Another candidate signal!"

Albert swiveled to look. This time, the monitor displayed:

.. ..

.. ..

.. ..

.. ..

After every quarter minute or so, another duplicate row of dots appeared.

"These aren't prime numbers, either." Albert peered close. "But what kind of natural phenomenon could produce these, I wonder." He slowly echoed the numbers on the monitor. "One, two, two, two, four, two, four, two, four, five, two, and six."

The two stared at the display.

"Hey, wait," said Ralph after a silent minute or so. "Add the numbers. One. One plus two is three. Three plus two is five, plus two is seven, and now plus *four* is eleven. Primes!"

"Two is missing," said Albert, scarcely daring to hope.

"Maybe they don't consider two prime."

Mentally, Albert continued the addition. *Plus two is thirteen, plus four is seventeen.* His excitement grew with each prime. "You're right. They *are* primes." He went on with the sequence. *Plus two is nineteen. Yes! Plus four is twenty-three. Plus five is twenty-eight.* Albert clenched a fist. "Damn! Twenty-eight. One of the results is twenty-eight."

"Here. Let me check." Ralph ran through the calculations. "You're right," he said, softly and sadly.

Albert doggedly continued the additions. "All right. Twenty-eight . . . thirty, and . . . thirty-six." He let out a sad sigh. "Off by one."

"Wait," said Ralph. "What if one of the signal blips got lost in transit? Then it would be twenty-nine, thirty-one, and thirty-seven. Primes!"

"But every row has the same error," said Albert.

"Then it must be a problem at the transmitter, or a counting convention, or something."

"You think?" said Albert.

"Yeah. All these primes can't happen by accident. It makes sense."

"It does, but I . . . I almost can't believe it." Albert sensed his heart pounding, wildly. "But . . . but I do think we may have done it."

Ralph looked hard at the monitor. "Yes! We *have* done it." He punched the air, then laughed. "It *is* hard to believe, though."

"It is," said Albert, doubts setting in. "Why would anyone transmit differences?"

"I don't know," said Ralph with a happy shrug. "An intelligence test, maybe." He paused. "No, wait! This way, there are fewer blips. Thirty-seven, or six, blips would be hard to count. Maybe it's a bandwidth problem."

"Wish we could be sure." Albert glared at his monitor. "I mean that we're not reading too much into the data, that we're seeing what we *want* to see. Maybe there *is* some natural process that's generating the numbers."

"Ambiguity's the name of the game, mate." Ralph seemed giddy. "I declare this the first ever SETI positive."

Albert, his enthusiasm rekindled from Ralph's, slapped a hand to the console. "Yes. I agree." He looked over at Ralph's console. "Quick. Lock the array on the source."

Ralph flipped a switch. "Done!"

"But why *now*, I wonder," said Albert, doubts still nibbling at the edges of his mind. "I mean, it's a very strong signal. We probably should have detected it before."

"I think the storm might have something to do with it." Ralph checked the signal strength. "Electrical properties of different cloud layers. Some kind of Fabry-Perot natural etalon—like a laser resonator, maybe."

"We're logging this, of course," said Albert.

"Of course, at maximum bandwidth." Ralph turned at the sound of Kimberly coming back from the lounge.

"What's going on?" she said, joining Ralph and Albert at the astronomy monitor.

"A signal!" said Albert, not looking away from the screen, and suppressing his enthusiasm so as not to tempt fate. "We think."

"SETI?" said Kimberly.

"Sure looks like it." Ralph pointed to some squiggles on the monitor. "Prime numbers and all that."

"Where's it coming from?" said Kimberly.

"Where?" Ralph and Albert exchanged a sheepish glance.

Albert pulled up an online database onto a third monitor. "Nothing obvious," he said after a few seconds of heavy study. "And nearby, absolutely nothing at all."

"We should phone the Murchison Array," said Ralph, "for confirmation."

"Right!" Albert grabbed for the phone. "Signal's probably strong enough for Murchison."

A further peal of thunder shook the room, this time accompanied by the roar of a sudden wild wind.

"Our radio dishes won't take much of this," Ralph called out over the howl of the gusts. "I'll check the alignment stability." Just as he turned to his monitor, the power went out, plunging the control room into darkness, save for the hint of dark gray twilight at the window. The ever-present hum of the air conditioner became noticeable by its absence.

"Not now! Please not now," Albert implored, slamming down the phone and casting a quick glance upward to where the sky would be.

"No worries," said Ralph. "We have a generator and lots of kero." He rummaged for a flashlight and hurried outside.

Kimberly uttered a sharp yelp. "Liam'll be frightened out of his mind." She darted back toward the lounge, leaving Albert alone, staring at a dead monitor and pounding a fist onto the console.

Precious time slipped away while the now functionless electronics released pent-up heat into the air.

Albert wiped a hand across his now sweaty brow.

Finally, he heard the thrum of the generator, and the lights came on along with the air conditioner. Quickly, he examined the astronomy monitor.

"Hey!" Albert called out in exultant surprise. The signal was still there.

Albert narrowed his eyes. *But, why?* He'd imagined the object, whatever it was, would have drifted out of the field while the power was down. *Maybe the dishes themselves have batteries to take care of power glitches.* He stared expectantly at the monitor, hoping that the signal might start to exhibit more than just repetition of the first twelve prime numbers. *I wonder why twelve. Maybe they have twelve fingers.*

He was still staring when Ralph came through the door.

Albert pointed to the monitor. "We still have signal!"

"Really?" Ralph darted to the monitor. "Great!"

Albert turned as Kimberly came back from the lounge— without Liam.

"Liam?" said Albert.

"He wanted to stay there, playing games," said Kimberly with a smile. "He said he didn't want you to think he was a scaredy-cat. And I—"

"Damn!" said Ralph, staring at the engineering console. "Bloody hell! The dishes are out of lock."

"What?" said Albert. "Can't be." He cast a glance at his monitor. "But . . . But we still have signal."

"Look for yourself." Ralph pointed to the status display. "The storm really did a job on them. They're pointing all over the place."

"That means . . ." Albert slumped back in his chair. "That means the signals can't be astronomical in origin." He bit his lower lip. "But it looked so right. I mean the prime numbers and all." He slapped his hand down on the console. "Damn! Damn it to hell!"

Kimberly placed a comforting hand over his.

"Yeah, mate, I know." Ralph blew out a breath. "Damned rotten luck." He glanced at the astronomy monitor which indeed still showed signal. "But what the devil is going on?"

"We'll have to find out," said Albert in a flat voice. "Otherwise we'll never have confidence in our equipment again."

A half-hour later, after they'd turned off every source of electromagnetic radiation in the place and were therefore conducting their investigations by flashlight, confidence had not returned. Whenever they switched the monitor back on, the signal was there as strong as ever.

"It's got to be *something*," said Ralph.

"Wait a sec," said Albert. "We haven't tried Liam's game machine."

"Oh, come on."

"Unlikely, but what else is there?" Albert spread his hands. "I mean, we're at the dish signals' integration point. Any extraneous EM field at the right frequency might be amplified a lot."

Ralph shrugged. "I'm skeptical. But it couldn't hurt to check."

"Kim," said Albert, turning to her, "could you go and confiscate Liam's game machine?" He forced a smile. "Or barring that, bring back the batteries."

"He's not going to like it." Kimberly turned and headed for the lounge.

Albert watched her go. Deep in his mind, he didn't actually want to find the radiation source, so that he could cling to the vanishing low probability that the signal was actually SETI positive. By checking every possible source, he was making something of a bargain with fate.

A few minutes later, Kimberly returned, with batteries but without Liam.

"Is he still worried I'll call him a scaredy-cat?" said Albert.

"No, now he's sitting in there in a huff because I took his batteries while he was in the middle of a game."

"We've still got signal," Ralph called out from his console.

"All right, Kim. Better return Liam's batteries before he loses it."

Kimberly sighed and headed once more back to the lounge. "I think I'll stay with him a while. Easier on the feet."

"What now?" said Ralph when Kimberly had gone.

They looked at each other in silence for a half minute or so. Then Albert said, "For the sake of argument, let's assume the signal *is* coming from space."

"With the dishes pointing all over the sky?"

"Yeah."

"How is that possible?"

"I haven't a clue."

"OK," said Ralph. "Just for the sake of argument. So now what?"

"Let's try to find everything we can about the signals, dish by dish. The propagation characteristics, spatial signal drop-off if any, temporal characteristics. That sort of stuff." Albert brightened with an inspiration. "Or . . . or maybe the signal is exceptionally strong and is coming from only a few dishes."

"I'm doubtful," said Ralph, "but we may as well. The storm

seems to have kept away the *real* astronomy team as you call them. So we'll probably have the time."

Much later, when twilight had turned to dark night, and after Kimberly had reported that Liam was sound asleep in the lounge, Albert and Ralph made their discovery. By correlating high-time resolution data from the radio dishes, they'd found that the signal always came from a specific direction in space, but that direction drastically changed over a variable but extremely short time interval.

"Highly interesting," said Ralph. "But I haven't a clue what's going on."

"Let me think." A minute later Albert smiled. He'd ridden the elevator of elation and despair and had now taken it from the depths up again to elation. Now though, the elation was from a new physics idea—as well as the hope that the idea of cosmic isolation might be stunningly wrong. "Do you know what this means?" he asked, lightly.

"No, what?" said Ralph.

"I asked you first."

"Come on, Albert. Stop playing games."

"It means," said Albert, putting heavy weight on each word, "that we can't possibly know from where the signals come."

"Brilliant, Sherlock."

"No. Listen. I'm talking faster than light here."

"Excuse me?" said Ralph.

"If we can't tell from where the signals come, then they could be traveling FTL, faster than light, much faster—and without violating relativity."

"You don't mean quantum entanglement, do you?" Ralph narrowed his eyes. "That is a very different kind of information than your garden variety 'meet me at midnight' kind of message."

"I mean faster than light message transport in *relativity*." Albert slapped a fist onto an open palm. "Pure and simple Einstein."

"You Alberts sure stick together, don't you?"

"I'm serious."

"FTL in relativity?" Ralph shook his head. "Not bloody likely." He smiled, softening his assertion. "And here I thought you were a relativity theorist."

"Listen," Albert pleaded, "and keep an open mind."

"OK, shoot."

"In relativity, it's not so much the problem of going backward in time that forbids FTL, but the synchronization of clocks throughout space-time."

"No argument, there," said Ralph. "It's pretty standard relativity theory."

"Fine," said Albert. "Now, if one were to travel from point A to point B where the distance and direction between the two points was unknowable."

"Example, please," said Ralph.

"Oh, I don't know. Between two points in different landscape universes, or maybe across a black hole event horizon." Albert raised a finger. "Then one could not *possibly* synchronize clocks—making FTL not in violation of relativity."

"This is beginning to sound too much like physics," said Kimberly. "I'd hang out with Liam if he weren't asleep."

Neither Albert nor Ralph seemed to hear her.

"Not in violation," said Ralph, "doesn't mean it can actually happen. I mean it might be *theoretically* possible, but—"

Albert threw up his hands. "I appeal to Gell-Mann's Totalitarian Principle."

"You mean the idea that if it's not expressly forbidden by physics, it *must* happen?"

"Precisely! So the cosmos might not be so isolated after all."

They looked silently at each other for a minute or so. Then Ralph said, "Where did you get this spiffy notion?"

"It just popped into my head."

"Hmm."

"Theoretically," Albert went on, "we might even be able to hold a conversation with our aliens in real-time, or close to it."

"Imagine," said Ralph with a distant look in his eyes, "a one-minute phone call with two . . . two creatures who don't speak each other's language. Could they really communicate? Could they relate anything really important?"

"Yes. Certainly. That they exist and that they want to communicate. Our alien friends probably didn't have the time or bandwidth to send a teach-yourself-to-speak-alien book."

"Then you genuinely think the signals are SETI positive?" said Ralph almost at a whisper.

Albert nodded.

"But *how* can it be done, then?" said Ralph. "If there's to be any reality at all to this, you'll have to explain *how* the signals can come from all over."

"You tell me. You're the quantum theorist. It feels like a quantum mechanics question."

Ralph didn't respond, so Albert went on. "Although, I must say I side with Einstein's feeling that God doesn't play with dice. I think we need quantum mechanics here."

"God doesn't play with dice?" Ralph laughed. "On the contrary: God *is* dice."

"Excuse me?"

"I mean dice, uncertainty, ambiguity. It's built into nature, as evidenced by us being thinking beings. Without the uncertainty, a brain would just be a piece of clockwork—in theory, completely predictable."

"OK," said Albert, "give me a theory to explain these signals." His voice held a hint of challenge.

"Let me think," said Ralph. "Will a wild theory do?"

"It would have to be."

After a few minutes where nobody spoke, Kimberly said, "I'm feeling a sort of tingling on my skin."

"Funny thing," said Albert, "I was just about to say the same thing."

"Me too," said Ralph.

"It's like we're reading each other's minds," said Kimberly. "Telepathy."

"Hardly that," said Albert, some scorn and amusement in his voice. "The three of us are probably just reacting to the same external stimulus—probably something to do with the high electrical potential of the storm clouds." As soon as he said it, he regretted his words. He and Kimberly argued a lot about the possibility of telepathy.

Kimberly stood. She seemed offended. "I think I'll go and check up on Liam." Without waiting for an acknowledgment, she strode from the room.

Ralph watched her go, then turned to Albert. "About a theory, then. I believe points in space-time have extent, sort of like tiny discrete marbles, and space-time itself is not well-defined." He nodded to himself. "I could imagine that a particular kind of signal *could* spread out." He bit his lip. "I would think that sending real data on the marbles would be hard. The marbles would mostly arrive out of order. And that might be why they only can get a few primes through."

"Cosmic isolation?"

"Maybe . . ." Again Ralph bit his lip. "But maybe the marbles could be numbered. And we could send a message by following the numbered breadcrumbs."

"Would we want to," said Albert, retreating into a physicist's land of what-ifs. Could we be inviting invasion? Maybe there's a cosmic reason for the isolation."

"We, as a culture, can't keep our heads in the sand," said Ralph. "Are we going to be"—he smiled—"the scaredy-cats of the universe?" Ralph leaned back in his chair. "So there you have it," he said. "A theory . . . of sorts."

"Yeah." Albert shook his head. "And it's wild, all right."

"Thanks, heaps. But it could explain a lot of phenomena . . . even telepathy."

"Not you too!" Albert wrinkled his nose. "I said a wild theory, not pseudoscience."

"Oh, I don't know," said Ralph. "I think the brain could well be a quantum detector of sorts, of lateral detection."

Albert pursed his lips. "Telepathy, you mean."

"Gurriada," said Ralph. "It's a Pitjantjatjara word meaning thought or magic at a distance."

"Telepathy by any other name," said Albert, "would still smell as . . . would still smell."

"Don't you think you're being a bit . . ." Ralph turned to look toward the sound of rapid footsteps.

Kimberly ran into the control room, her face contorted in worry, her movements frantic. "I can't find Liam!"

Albert snapped to his feet. "Could he be in the bathroom?"

"No. And I've looked everywhere."

"Oh, I wouldn't worry," said Ralph as he retrieved a flashlight. "He's a boy. He probably just went out to explore."

"The desert's dangerous at night," said Kimberly. "He knows that."

"You're sure he's not in the building?" said Albert.

"Yes. Positive."

"All right," said Albert, trying to keep worry out of his voice for Kimberly's sake. "Let's go out and get him." Ralph handed him a second flashlight. "He had to have gone out the back way. Let's go."

"Wait a sec." Ralph went to a cabinet and withdrew a pair of binoculars, which he handed to Albert. "Normally, for bird watching."

With Ralph in the lead, they padded then through the building to the back door, and out into the night where, even though the Sun had long since set, they were met with a wall of desert heat.

Albert slowly scanned the horizon. On one side was the barren desert and on the other, the dim outlines of hundreds of radio dishes. *If he's wandered out there, he won't be easy to find.*

"Let's see if he's within cooee," said Ralph. He cupped his hands around his mouth in the way of a megaphone, and shouted a long "Cooooeeee," the Australian call to find someone lost in the bush.

Nothing.

"At least the wind's died down," said Albert. "He should be able to hear us."

"But it means," said Ralph, casting a glance at the sky, "the rain will come soon." He cooeed again. Still nothing.

Albert shined his light along the ground, looking for tracks, but couldn't find any.

"Here, let me," said Ralph, adding his beam to Albert's. "I've had practice." He peered hard at the sandy ground.

Watching Ralph, crouched low, eyes intent with a feral gleam, Albert could well understand how Ralph had come by his Dingo sobriquet.

Albert followed Ralph's gaze off into the darkness and was seized with an impression that all the creatures of the desert floor were looking at him, and that he could sense their minds: the lizards, the rats, and, worst of all, the snakes. Despite the heat, Albert shivered. *Irrational. This is completely irrational.*

A lightning flash illuminated the ground.

"Yes!" said Ralph, his exclamation punctuated by thunder. "He's left us some breadcrumbs to follow." Still in a crouch, Ralph moved slowly off toward the telescope array. Albert and Kimberly followed.

"He's running," said Ralph, pointing to a footprint. "Makes it easier." Ralph picked up the pace. "He's less likely to change direction.

"Where is he running *to*?" said Kimberly, breathlessly as she struggled to keep up.

"Look!" Albert pointed to a sign staked into the ground:

WARNING
NO DIG ZONE
UNDERGROUND CABLE

"He seems to be running," Albert paused for breath, "along the route of the signal conduit."

The sky, which had been threatening, began to deliver on the threat—first with a few drops, and then with a deluge. After experiencing the heat of the desert, Albert welcomed the cooling rain.

"Damn!" Ralph stopped as did the others behind him. "It's washing out the track."

"Let's keep going along the conduit path," said Albert, mentally rescinding his welcome.

"May as well," said Ralph.

"Liam's surely getting soaked," said Kimberly in a mother's voice of concern.

There came another flash of lightning and Albert flinched, his eyes bleached by the flash.

"There!" shouted Kimberly. "There he is. Standing on that *thing* over there." Kimberly started running. Ralph and Albert followed. Albert, more worried than he'd admitted even to himself, ran full-out, overtaking Kimberly and Ralph.

Thunder pealed. "Five seconds between lightning and thunder," Ralph managed as he ran. "Storm's about a mile from us—and moving away."

The data from each of the radio dishes were transmitted by underground cables to the Cable Breakout Unit. There, the data were collected and sent on by a single cable to the observatory control building. The Breakout Unit, a three-foot-diameter round cabinet some four feet high, stood on a raised concrete platform. Stone steps and a ladder gave access to the top.

And there, on the top of the cabinet, some seven feet above the ground, stood Liam.

He was looking upward, seemingly oblivious to the rain.

When Albert got to the base of the platform, he heard Liam continuously repeating, "I am not afraid."

"Liam!" Albert called out. "Come down. What are you doing out here?"

Abruptly, as if broken from a trance, Liam looked down. "I've been mind-talking to the sky people."

"You've been *what*?"

"Talking to the sky people."

Ralph and Kimberly joined Albert at the platform.

"Sky people?" said Albert, under his breath.

"I've told him the Anangu story," said Ralph, softly, "that the stars are the campfires of the sky people."

"He's always had an overactive imagination," Kimberly whispered, her breath labored from the running.

"Come down!" Albert called out over the noise of the rain.

"Are you mad at me?"

"No."

"You don't believe me, do you?"

"I . . ." Albert didn't know what to say. He'd made it a practice not to lie to his son. "What . . . what did you talk about?"

"Nothing."

"Nothing?" said Albert, trying to keep annoyance out of his voice. Liam was always using "nothing" as an answer.

"Well . . . They just wanted to say hello."

"Not much of a message," Ralph whispered.

"They talked about," came Liam's treble voice from above, "funny numbers."

"*Prime* numbers?" said Ralph.

"Yeah."

"My god!" Albert exclaimed under his breath. He turned to Ralph. "Liam doesn't even know what a prime *is*." He looked back up. "How did you hear about prime numbers?"

"It just popped into my head."

Albert and Ralph exchanged a glance.

"Liam Griffen," Kimberly barked out. "You come down here at once."

Sullenly, and without answering his mother, Liam very slowly descended the ladders.

As Liam climbed down, Albert said, "He must have heard us talking."

"From the lounge?" Ralph shook his head. "He'd need the ears of an owl. It's more like something's tapped into his mind." He paused. "Guriada. Extrasensory perception."

"Extrasensory perception?" said Albert, dismissively. "At the worst, it's *unknown* sensory."

"Same difference."

"*Something* has happened here," said Kimberly. "I think it has, anyway. Something not easy to explain."

"The brain as a quantum detector," said Ralph softly, as if to himself. "Could be that young brains are more efficient. Synapses are still developing."

When Liam had stepped to the ground and Albert could look down on him rather than up, he asked, "What else just popped into your head?"

"Talking faster than light."

Albert's eyes went wide.

"But I don't know what that means."

"Our theory," said Ralph at a whisper to no one in particular. "Quantum spreading as the facilitator of communication."

Liam looked innocently up at his dad. "Don't you believe me? I mean about hello."

"I . . . Does Rex Snoopy Biscuit believe you?" *Why did I say that?*

"I couldn't really understand the sky people," said Liam, "but Rex Snoopy Biscuit could. He told me what they were saying."

"Oh," Albert managed, struggling to put it all into a logical context.

"*I* believe you, Bluey," said Ralph.

Liam returned a smiled, then looked back at Albert. "Do you believe me, Dad?"

Albert hesitated, then said, "I think so." He felt he had to give that comfort to his son. *Or rather I can't say I disbelieve you.*

"Let's go back and dry off," said Kimberly. "I'd hate to see us all come down with colds." She put an arm around Liam and urged him toward the observatory building.

"We can commandeer one of the visiting scientist apartments," said Albert. "There's a communal laundry. We can throw our clothes in the dryer."

Liam protested. "I can't go around without any clothes on."

"While our clothes are drying," said Kimberly, "we can dress in sheets, togas, like the Romans did."

"Well," said Liam in tacit acceptance.

Ralph whispered to Albert. "Do we announce any of this to the SETI Foundation?"

"I don't think so."

"I don't know if anything really happened, but if it did, it was profound," said Albert, as he and Ralph, dressed in ersatz togas, walked into the control room. Kimberly was in a visiting scientist bedroom, trying to coax Liam to sleep.

"How do you feel now about . . . Guriada?"

"Extrasensory perception is . . ." Albert began, heatedly, primed to deliver the strong denial that he'd so often given in the past. "It's . . ." He paused. "I don't know. I just don't know."

"Excellent!" said Ralph as he padded over to the astronomy monitor. "Welcome to Club Heisenberg."

"Yeah. Right."

Albert and Ralph leaned in over the display.

"The signal is gone," said Ralph, sadly. "I'm afraid there's no way we can verify our alien encounter."

"We have the data recordings."

"Not precisely what I'd call a verification."

Albert smiled at the incongruity of two scientists dressed as Roman senators talking philosophy. "Some things that are real aren't verifiable."

"True," said Senator Ralph. "And there are many modes of communication, not just at the higher cerebral level."

Albert nodded. "I'd always thought that if it weren't repeatable and verifiable, it wasn't science. But . . ."

"Nature is uncertain, mate. Ambiguous."

"Ambiguity. Yes." Albert gave a sad smile. "But I really have to ask: was it a genuine SETI positive or just a spurious signal and the rich imagination of a child?" He slumped into a chair.

Ralph shrugged. "In any case," he said, "we've come up with a really spiffy theory. We should publish."

Albert sighed. "And keep searching."

The phone rang and Albert looked idly at the caller ID, then snapped erect. "The Murchison Array!" With the speed of a cobra, Albert snaked out his hand to the phone.

THE MANDELBROT BET

Dirk Strasser

What is reality?

Does the physical universe actually exist or is it, in the words of Edgar Allan Poe, "a dream within a dream"?

Or look at it another way. Does mathematics truly describe the physical universe, or is the world of mathematics actually the universe itself?

And what do these concepts have to do with the hopes and fears and passions that we human beings feel with every beat of our hearts?

Thereby hangs Dirk Strasser's tale.

> There are lines which are monsters.
>
> Eugène Delacroix

Voice notes to self on the development of the escape-time algorithm—Daniel Rostrom

Remember, the answer is always simple. That's not to say the simple answer is the correct one. The danger to avoid is the assumption that the simple answer, by the sole nature of its simplicity, is the correct one.

The escape-time algorithm is the simplest algorithm for generating a representation of the Mandelbrot set. The answer lies in the infinity of the escape-time algorithm. Repeat the calculation for each x, y, z; t point and make your decisions based on the behavior of that calculation. Pick a value for time, t, square it, add a constant. Take the new number, square it, and add the same constant. Forever, do it forever. Simple.

"Give me a moment before you shove any more of that stuff in my mouth."

"Sorry, Daniel, it's hard for me to guess when you're ready for another spoonful."

"You asked me a question, so give me a chance to answer it."

"You must have gotten stuck today. You're always grumpy when you get stuck."

"And you're the only one here I can be grumpy with, Helen. Sorry, it's because I can't move my body that it gets to me when I can't get my mind moving as well."

"All right, how about having another go at explaining to me what you were thinking about today? Even if I don't understand it, it may help you gain some insight."

"I suppose there's always a chance. Do you remember what I was saying about the Mandelbrot set and how I have developed the idea to include a time dimension?"

"Er, yes, I remember good old Benoît B. Mandelbrot. French, wasn't he?"

"No, technically Lithuanian. Lived and worked most of his life in the U.S., but that's not really important, is it?"

"I just like a bit of a context, Daniel."

"OK, well the important thing is I've tied the behavior of Mandelbrot-like time dimensions to quantum computing."

"Here, eat this before you go on. I need a moment to digest what you've said."

"Ha ha."

"Just chew on this, Daniel."

The loner in physics—Eleanora Schmidt

Is it possible for a non-physics trained person to make a fundamental breakthrough in physics? Does nature speak in a language that an intelligent, determined non-specialist can decipher? Self-taught artists can sometimes create something truly extraordinary that a fully trained artist can't.

It can be argued that the training itself limits thought patterns and inhibits creative leaps.

The loner physicist has the added handicap that he or she is not working as part of a team. Are great discoveries still achievable by individuals working alone? Some would argue that this is still possible. A case in point is the work of Daniel Rostrom, a man with little formal physics training who brought his skills from other fields such as computer science, art, and geography to bear on the complex field of time travel speculation.

The jury is still out on whether Daniel Rostrom was the greatest polymath and deepest thinker of our century, a brilliant hoaxer, or a fringe-dwelling crackpot. Rostrom, whose muscular dystrophy meant he was wheelchair-bound for much of his life, presents us with the most detailed insight into the loner physicist. As a young man he had a bionic recording device implanted into his brain which he could switch on and off at will. The original intention was to use it to play podcasts of scientific papers that he would otherwise have physical difficulty in reading and to keep a verbal record of his thoughts. In practice he kept the device recording most of the time with a cloud-sync to his computerized chair, so we have a full record of everything he said and heard. The later recordings which are dated after his disappearance are the subject of much debate. Most in the scientific community believe them to be an elaborate hoax, but there are those who believe they are genuine. The question always arises as to how a wheelchair-bound man with late-stage muscular dystrophy could simply disappear without his caregiver or any family members having any idea where he had gone. There are, of course, myriad conspiracy theories, but there are also physicists who have argued cogently that the most likely series of events was that he simply did what he said he would do.

"That's not what you said last time, Helen."

"So now you're going to play back my words again, are you, Daniel? Just to make me look bad."

"No. I don't want to make you look bad."

"Look, Daniel, that bionic recorder drives me insane. Can't you turn it off for conversations with me?"

"I could, but it would make it harder to get to the truth."

"I might just quit. How would you like that sort of truth?"

"You've said that . . ."

"Don't give me a precise count of how often I've said I'd quit."

"I'm sorry, Helen. I never mean to upset you."

"Being your full-time caregiver isn't a picnic, and it's not exactly pleasant when you have a digitized record of everything I've ever said to you inside your head."

"You know I'm after the truth. What else have I got sitting here in this wheelchair with nothing but numbness below my neck?"

"Yes, well, you stick to scientific truth. The rest of us only have the fuzzy truth we deal with day to day."

"There's only one sort of truth, Helen."

"And you're going to find it."

"That's right, I'm going to find it."

Voice notes to self on the development of the escape-time algorithm—Daniel Rostrom

One of two things always happens in a Mandelbrot set: either an iterated point jumps up to two units away from the origin or it jumps further away. The result is a shape that is finite but an edge that is infinite. It's all about the edge. The line. It's a monster. The more you magnify it, the more complex it becomes. It never settles down. Ever. I know this is the key. Somehow a Mandelbrot set has only two dimensions, yet it also possesses another dimension. What if that other dimension was time? With the right procedure it must be possible to both orbit close to an origin and jump in ever-increasing spans. I know I'm on to something. Think.

This isn't just a computer-generated image, it's real life. Coastlines. You can see it in coastlines. They are infinitely long. Magnify them and you will see more twists and kinks. Magnify them again, and you see even more. It never stops.

There is no arrow of time, it's a coastline of time.

"So, this chair of yours is going to be your so-called time machine?"

"Yes, like in the H. G. Wells novel. Except it won't be coming with me. You've only just realized that, Helen?"

"I'm a bit slow, remember? You've often told me that."

"No, I haven't. I can prove—"

"Don't worry about calling up the relevant recordings. Even if you haven't said it, I feel it from you sometimes."

"Do you really?"

"Never mind, tell me again how this is going to work."

"Could you keep massaging my scalp while I do?"

"All right."

"I mean sometimes you stop massaging when you're thinking."

"I promise I won't think."

"Very amusing."

"Can you start explaining?"

"It's all about uncertainty."

"Mmm, all right, go on."

"You've switched off already, haven't you?"

"No, but I know you're using the word *uncertainty* in that way you always use words. I'll bet it's not the way most of us use the word."

"OK . . . think of it like a *bet*. You know how, in a horse race, you can never be absolutely certain of what horse will win?"

"Unless the race is fixed and I'm in on the fix."

"OK, unless the race is fixed. Can we assume it's not fixed?"

"Of course, it's your race. So we can't be sure of what horse will win?"

"Yes, we don't know anything for certain, but people who know what they're doing assign odds of winning to each horse."

"So do people who don't know what they're doing."

"Are you going to let me continue?"

"You're not telling me anything I don't know, Daniel."

"I'm trying to simplify it."

"For my slow brain."

"I told you I've never said you have a slow—"

"Look, Daniel, just go on."

"Well, the escape-time algorithm I've been working on comes down to writing a computer program into my chair that uses the uncertainty in the four-dimensional extension to the Mandelbrot set principle I've been extrapolating."

"I see."

"A horse race is based on mild randomness. Things like height and weight also have a mild random distribution. You're not going to come across a twenty-meter-tall person all of a sudden, for example. Mandelbrot set–like behavior is based on *wild* randomness."

"So in the Mandelbrot world twenty-meter-tall people are common?"

"Not exactly, but there are lots of examples of Mandelbrot set–like distributions in the real world. Nearly all human-made variables are wild. Wealth, for example, is a wild variable. We have a number of individuals that have millions of times more wealth than the average person. We live in a winner-take-all world of extremes."

"See, this is why I like hearing about your work, Daniel."

"Can you keep massaging?"

"Sorry, you caught me thinking."

"Look at Babble, it controls ninety percent of the cloud traffic. And who's the latest best-selling enhanced fiction author?"

"It's probably—"

"Never mind, it was a rhetorical question. I'll guarantee you that whoever she is, she earns millions more than the vast majority of enhanced fiction authors. And she won't be millions times better than those other authors."

"No, but she's pretty good."

"Are you deliberately sidetracking me?"

"Yes, sorry."

"Anyway, what I'm doing is using wild randomness to accelerate myself into an extreme future time period. And because of the wildness, I can't be absolutely certain what the Mandelbrot set–like variables will do to me."

"So, it's sort of like a Mandelbrot *bet?*"

Voice notes to self on the development of the escape-time algorithm—Daniel Rostrom

I've found what I've been overlooking. Possibility theory. It describes the uncertainty that I've been missing. It's the only way to deal with extreme probabilities and partial ignorance. I need to look at both the possibility and necessity of the event. If the universe is finite (which we know it is) and every subset of it is measurable (which is what everything we do in science is based on), then the universe describes all possible future states of the world. Obvious now. Outcomes aren't self-dual. I need to stop thinking with two-valued logic and start thinking with multivalued logic.

"Nǐ tīngdǒng ma?"

"What?"

"We're sorry, our records say Mandarin Chinese was the most common language in your space-time period. It was a statistical guess that you would understand it. Shall we proceed with mid-twenty-first-century English? Is that convenient for you, doctor?"

"Doctor?"

"That is the correct form of address, is it not, for a scientist from your space-time period?"

"I don't have a doctorate. My name is Daniel Rostrom. What . . . what space-time period am I in?"

"It depends what scale you use. Allow me to elucidate, Mr. Rostrom."

"Please do."

"You understand something of the life cycle of stars?"

"Yes, of course. It's not my major interest, but I know my cosmology."

"Do you see—we use the word *see* as an approximation, of course—do you see the white light in your vision?"

"Yes, in fact, that's all I can see."

"You would be aware that neutron stars, black holes, and black dwarfs are dead stars. What you see here is a white dwarf, a star that, although still alive, is dying. This low-mass white dwarf will become dimmer and dimmer until it fades into a black dwarf. Do you know what a black dwarf is?"

"Yes. It's a white dwarf, a star that's run out of fuel, that's finally cooled off and isn't radiating any visible light. Black dwarfs were only theoretical in the mid-twenty-first century. They couldn't exist because the time taken for a white dwarf to cool to such a degree was longer than the life span of the universe up to my time period."

"We will talk about time in a moment. The important thing to appreciate is that a white dwarf can sustain life, a black dwarf can't."

"But some white dwarfs could also evolve into supernovae."

"Very high mass white dwarfs, or those with orbiting companions, can in some cases become supernovae and the expanding shock waves from these explosions form new stars. This is how the life-cycle of the universe functions. Death. Life. Death. Life."

"But you said this white dwarf is small mass, so it's going to die and become a black dwarf."

"Precisely, Mr. Rostrom, but there is something you must

understand now. What you have seen here is the last star of its kind."

"The last white dwarf?"

"Yes, the last white dwarf in a universe, which for billions upon billions of years has contained only white dwarfs and dead stars."

"Now, you *are* telling me something I don't understand. There are countless yellow dwarfs, red giants, and brown dwarfs in our universe."

"There *were*. A long time ago. For eons the only stars in the universe still clinging onto life have been white dwarfs. And now there is only one remaining."

"What?"

"I believe we began our conversation with that question."

Voice notes to self on the development of the escape-time algorithm—Daniel Rostrom

It's just a matter of applying the right iterative algorithm to time travel. Quantum computers are powerful enough to do it and quantum computers don't get much more powerful than my chair. I just have to get the sequence of qubits right. Of course I don't know for certain what will happen, but possibility theory tells me the likelihood.

"I think I understand. The escape-time algorithm has inevitably brought me here to the end of the universe as limiting asymptote. I'm here, so close to the end. The last white star about to go black. The last skerrick of life about to be extinguished, but I will never quite reach it."

"Not quite. That would be true if your quantum leaps were still occurring, but they're not. You're now in real-time, and the end is imminent."

"So I'm going to see the universe end?"

"Technically, your mind will be extinguished a nanosecond

before it happens, but yes, unless we can find a solution, you will see the universe die."

"A solution?"

"Sentient beings, no matter how advanced, never want to be extinguished. We will continue striving for an escape solution until the very end."

"You keep saying *we*. Who are the others?"

"We are speaking to you in what you would call one voice, but there are countless beings here. We have unified. There are no individuals anymore. There haven't been any for several million years. We've evolved into a single entity. Our knowledge is shared."

"One entity. That's all that's left?"

"Yes. At a point in our universes' history a sentient race evolved to achieve unity, to become a single sentient being, possessing the sum total of knowledge and understanding that each individual had."

"What happened to the other races?"

"As eons passed, other sentient races came to the same point in their evolution and first unified as a race and then joined us. As it became clear that the universe was dying, the main aim of sentient beings was to find ways to prolong its life, or at least to find a way of prolonging sentient life. Those beings that had not joined us, knew that they now had no choice. The only hope for us all was to collectively put all our knowledge into solving the ultimate problem. That is what we have been doing for millions of years. And it is what we continue to do even now."

"But there must be others here now, if what you say about the escape-time algorithm is correct. It's impossible that no one else ever discovered what I discovered. In the billions of years of the history of the universe and the countless sentient beings, there must be other time travelers who found their way here to the end of the universe?"

"There have been others that have arrived here through the process you discovered. Many others. They are already here with us as part of the unified entity."

"You have . . . assimilated them?"

"Of course."

"And you think you're going to assimilate me as well?"

"Our last best hope is that assimilating your mind will enable us to devise a solution to stop the last white dwarf turning black. You are the last time traveler. No one will arrive after you. There is no time anymore."

"I . . . don't want to be assimilated. I've always worked alone. My thoughts are my own."

"You have no choice, Mr. Rostrom."

"You can't take my mind. It's all I have."

"It's all *we* have."

"Let me stay separate. Please, I can solve the problem myself. Just give me the knowledge you have. I came here to the end of the universe without anyone's help. I can get us out of this."

"There is no form of logic that would suggest that is true. We calculate that the possibility quotient of us finding a way to escape our fate, although extremely low, is higher if your mind is assimilated with ours."

"No, wait, you said I'm the last to arrive—true?"

"Yes."

"The escape-time algorithm produces iterations in inverse proportion to the start time period. If I'm the last to arrive, then I must have been the first in the history of the universe to discover the escape-time algorithm."

"Yes, you are very astute, but—"

"So, there is something special about me. Others had more

advanced knowledge to work with than I did. What I have
done is the least possible of all time travel events."

"Correct, but—"

"I think I have argued a strong case for remaining an individual. Please give me everything you know and maybe I'll
help us escape the end of the universe."

*Voice notes to self on the development of the escape-end-universe
algorithm—Daniel Rostrom*

*The universe is dying. The entity has enabled sense simulation for me. I
asked for a simulated body while I worked on the new algorithm, and I look
like an Adonis. For the first time in my life I can feel what it's like to be
physically powerful. I flex my muscles and can't stop laughing as I sift
through the information and threads of reasoning the entity is feeding me. If
only I had more time. I know I can find a solution. Or is that just idiotic
arrogance? There's a thought I've never had before. Maybe with the freedom of my new body I've finally become aware of my limitations. Wouldn't
that be ironic? Helen, you've probably noticed these aren't proper voice
notes anymore. I'm really talking to you—you know that, don't you?*

"The time has come, Daniel. Everything is now too late. Do
you want to join us for the end?"

"No, I want face it alone."

"You continue to surprise us with your choices."

"Well, that's what life is all about, isn't it? With only one
sentient being in the universe, where are the surprises?"

"There are no more surprises. We've both failed."

"I'm going to keep reporting what I see."

"Of course."

"Will anyone hear?"

"That's beyond even our abilities to know. Theoretically
quantum synapses on your neural link may make it possible.
You have been very astute, but the time distortions cannot be
mapped by any algorithm."

"Not astute enough to come up with a way to stop the universe from ending."

"I believe it's happening now."

"What, so soon?"

"You persist in your time perceptions."

Helen, I can feel the wild stellar winds buffet me as a bright shimmer appears in my vision. The white mass of the last living star in the universe is beginning to shed its outer layers. It's so beautiful. I wish you could see it with me. Inside I can see a crystalline lattice of carbon and oxygen atoms, a diamond-like core glowing with intense light.

Now it's all starting to darken.

Helen, if you can still hear me, I want to say good-bye. I know I didn't always treat you as well as I should have. I'm . . . I'm going to say something I thought I would take to my grave. I'm so gutless I can only say it now because possibility theory suggests it's highly unlikely that you'll ever hear it. Helen, I've always loved you. I know you couldn't ever love such a twisted cripple as me, so I chose never to say anything. I recorded all our conversations not to trip you up about things you had said in the past, but because I never wanted your voice to leave me. That's the real truth. Good-bye, my truth.

The loner in physics—Eleanora Schmidt

Daniel Rostrom's recordings, therefore, are either delusional flights of fancy which will keep the world's psychiatrists busy for decades to come or they present the scientific community with unsurpassed information and reasoning about the end of the universe. Who knows, perhaps by giving one sentient race such depth of understanding so early in the life of the universe, perhaps we have the head start we need, and in the billions of years until the end, the sentient beings of the universe will learn enough to stop the death of the last star.

"Daniel, I guess I'm hoping you're so brilliant that you've somehow engineered it so that you can still hear me. If not, well, I guess I'm just talking to myself here. I have been listening to every word. People think you're making it all up, but I believe you. I believe everything you've said. I do love you too. And I could have loved you more if you'd let me. Believing you, of course, means you'll never come back. You won the bet. Well done. Good-bye, Daniel."

RECOLLECTION
Nancy Fulda

Despite all the gains science has made, we are still held hostage to the inevitability of death. We can extend our life spans further and further, but eventually, inescapably, death overtakes us.

Memory loss is much like death. The body remains, but the person inhabiting that body has lost most of what makes us alive.

Nancy Fulda's "Recollection" shows us that science alone is not enough to heal us. There has to be love. We are mammals, after all, and without the warmth and care of other mammals we may be able to exist, but we cannot live.

The dream is always the same. You are a tangled mass of neurons, tumbling through meteors. Flaming impacts pierce your fragile surface, leaving ragged gouges. You writhe, deforming under bombardment, until nothing is left except a translucent tatter, crumbling as it descends. Comets pelt the desiccated fibers. You fall, and keep falling, and cannot escape the feeling that, despite your lack of hands, you are scrabbling desperately at the rim of a shrouded tunnel, unable to halt your descent. Glimmers crawl along the faint remaining strands, blurring as you tumble . . .

You awaken to warmth and stillness. Gone are the soulless tiled floors of the seniors' home. Sterile window drapes have been replaced by sandalwood blinds. Fresh air blows through the vents, overlaying faint sounds from the bathroom and from morning traffic on nearby canyon roads. You clutch the quilted blankets, stomach plummeting. This cozy bedroom, with its sturdy hardwood furnishings, should be familiar to you, but it isn't. Two days, and still nothing makes sense. You feel as though you're suffocating. Tumbling . . .

Your wife has heard you gasping for air. She comes running, nightgown flapping behind her. Her face is creased in overlapping furrows. Your mirror tells you that the two of you are a match: the same fading hair, the same shrunken hollows along the eyes. Laugh lines, she calls them, but you cannot manage to see them as anything except deformities, in your face and hers both.

"Elliott?" She grabs your hand and kneels at the bedside to look in your eyes. "It's me, Elliott. Everything's fine. Everything's going to be OK."

Her name, you recall, is Grace. She told it to you two days ago, and is irrationally elated that you are able to repeat it to her upon demand, anytime she asks. You feel like a trained puppy, yapping for treats, except there aren't any treats.

There's just Grace, and this room. And before that, the seniors' home. And before that . . . ? You're not sure. You flail at the bedside for your notebook, thinking it might offer continuity. But there are only a few shaky scribbles, beginning the day before yesterday.

Grace pulls you upright, propping pillows against your spine. She fusses over you, adjusting your hair, prattling off questions. She seems to think you're in pain, but you're not. Not any more than you'd expect of a man with joints and bones as old as yours. She tries to kiss your forehead, and you recoil.

It's a cruel gesture, pulling away like that, but you can't help it. She's a stranger, and despite the anguish in her eyes, it feels wrong to pretend otherwise. You can't feign love. You won't. Not to please her, not to please anyone.

Grace hesitates only slightly before continuing her efforts. You watch her, trying to recall more about this woman you've shared your life with, but your grasping thoughts turn up only emptiness. You haven't recognized her—haven't recognized anyone in your family—for years. That's what Alzheimer's means. Or what it used to mean.

You're not sure what anything means, anymore.

Grace, arranging blankets along the side of your bed, pauses to stroke your arm. "Someone had to be first," she says sadly, almost like a litany. "The next batch of patients will have it easier. They'll begin treatments almost as soon as they're diagnosed, long before the neural tissue breaks down . . ." She gazes into empty air, and adds with forced enthusiasm: "But we'll get through this, you know we will. You were always tough as ironwood. Remember how we used to sit at Squaw Peak and look over the valley? You told me you felt cheated as a boy, because all the frontiers had been taken, and it was too late to be a pioneer."

She keeps talking, wave after wave of trivialities burdening the air. It is clear that she loves you. It is equally clear that she does not realize how few of her words find purchase on the slippery crags of your recollection. Names and anecdotes sweep past you, unconnected to anything familiar, and therefore quickly forgotten. Your blank stare must be disheartening, but she doesn't stop. She was always stubborn that way; ruthlessly optimistic in the absence of all evidence. Why you can remember *that*, when everything else is gone, you can't say.

An image rips across your thoughts. A spiderweb, torn by a stick, so that the tattered remaining strands are left to dangle in the wind. The hand gripping the stick is yours—you are certain of it, although you must be remembering something wrong, because it looks like the hand of a child—and you recall staring, fascinated by how quickly the pattern disintegrates once the central supports have been torn away . . .

You feel suddenly dizzy. Your gaze sweeps the room, searching for some sort of anchor, but all you find is a photo next to the bed. It shows a stronger, less withered version of yourself and Grace, shouldering backpacks on a dusty mountain trail. The man is laughing. The woman's balled fist is thrust against his side, her lips pressed in mock indignation. You wonder what he said to elicit such affectionate ire.

The neurologists said this would happen. Before you left the rest home, they showed you brightly colored images of your brain tissue. They outlined areas where beta-amyloid plaques had been cleared, pointed to the scattered remaining tau deposits, and explained that your brain is once again capable of parsing and recording information. You are no longer a dementia patient, but the memories you've lost will never return. The best you and Grace can hope for is to rebuild across the tattered rifts in your consciousness.

That won't be too hard. Grace had laughed, hands clamped around your limp fingers, still ecstatic that you remembered her name. *Elliott loves building things.*

Grace isn't laughing now, though. To be honest, she doesn't look like a woman who laughs much at all. Hollow eyes, unkempt hair, slender to the point of spindliness . . . Her haggard face can no longer be described as beautiful. Also, she annoys you. The words keep coming, pointless babble on a dozen inconsequential topics, like a slew of shiny buttons which you have not hands enough to catch.

You must have loved her, once. Yes, you almost certainly loved her, and the endless prattle now spilling off her lips must be weighted with decades' worth of meaning—shared jokes,

shared secrets, shared opinions . . . Each fleeting phrase a lifeline to a hoarded wealth of common history. It should mean
something to you, but it doesn't.

You close your eyes and grimace against the pillows, shutting out Grace, shutting out everything. It's not right. You
never asked for this. Why would anyone choose this?

Why didn't they let you keep tumbling?

You hear whispering behind the door—eager, energetic
voices—for several seconds before the handle swings down-
ward and five towheaded bundles of chaos bounce into the
sitting room.

They attack you from all directions, tugging your shirtsleeves, holding up paintings of horses and butterflies, jostling
for positions on your lap.

"Grandpa!"

"Hi, Grandpa. Mommy says the doctors fixed you!"

"But we're not supposed to talk about that because it might
make you sad."

"Do you remember my birthday pony now, Grandpa? The
one you carved out of wood from the old oak tree?"

You wet your lips, uncertain how to respond. There's something you're supposed to do, when you see your grandchildren.
Words you're supposed to say. Aren't there?

"Hello, Peter," you finally murmur. "Hello, Mandy. Hello,
Candace. I hear you're doing well in school."

You say the words to the air, uncertain which child they
belong to. A girl with pink butterflies in her hair smiles and
proudly reports her latest math score. Two of the boys begin
hopping on the carpet, shouting, "He does, he does, he remembers!"

You ask the children about school, and about their new
baby cousin. They answer glibly, never realizing that you have

cheated. Last night, after Grace predicted this visit, you wrote the children's names and everything Grace told you about them in the nondescript brown notebook that has become a permanent fixture at your bedside. You are not so much conversing with them as throwing out random phrases in hopes that something will stick.

The children do not find this performance remarkable, but their mother, still lurking in the doorway, presses her knuckles to her teeth to mask a sudden hiss of indrawn breath. The moisture in her eyes ought to reassure you, but instead you feel like a swindler, dirty and shallow.

This isn't how you want to live your life.

Grace proclaims the existence of milk and cookies in the kitchen and the children vanish in a boisterous flurry. The adults remain, subdued yet jittery, glancing at you sidelong.

"Remember that time we got stranded on Snake River?" Grace asks. The others laugh and begin swapping memories like peddlers in a street bazaar, praising each in long and glorified detail. Remember when we hiked Mount Timpanogos? Remember when Peter dropped his lizard in your canteen? Remember that breathtaking sunrise near Vegas?

The muted hope emanating from your wife and daughter, and from the son-in-law who has pulled in an extra chair from the kitchen, is palpable. Should you lie? Nod and chuckle and permit the illusion, saying *Oh yes, that was a good one . . . ?*

Maybe you should, but you can't bring yourself to do it. Playing sleight-of-hand with the kids is one thing, but these are adults, too old for fairy stories.

"I'm sorry," you whisper. In the stillness, you can already hear the crack of hearts destined to break. "I'm sorry. I don't remember that."

The silence drags on, heavy and awkward.

It's madness, thinking they can rebuild your consciousness

stone by stone, memory by memory. You're not a model air-
plane, waiting for assembly. You cannot excavate the tattered
remnants of a lifetime's experience. You can't even recognize
your own grandchildren.

Finally Grace's hand lifts and falls against your shoulder.
"Well, that's all right," she says brightly. "Maybe you don't remember, but *we* do. We'll help you. You'll see."

The rest of the visit is agony. The conversation limps along,
interspersed with furtive glances every time you call someone
by the wrong name. After a while you stop talking and let
the words continue without you. You listen, hollow, clawing
through trivia which means nothing, and is swiftly forgotten.

"Tell them how you feel," your therapist says at every appointment.

But you can't. Or rather, you *have*, but they didn't hear the
words the way you meant them.

They take turns visiting, pouring out their life's stories with
loving dedication. They think they can stuff your past back
into you, like a turkey packed with apples for Thanksgiving,
but it doesn't work like that.

Each day, after your visitors are gone, you close your eyes
and lean against the padded back of your chair. You are so
tired. Tired of the endless stream of strangers. Tired of attempting to be more than a tattered cluster of dendrites, tumbling and empty.

It doesn't hurt, exactly. How can you hurt when most of
you is missing? But it seems achingly, dreadfully wrong that
you should feel nothing, when others drift like tormented
spirits at your shirtsleeves.

Where is solace, for these poor strangers who have wept
and struggled and pleaded to God on your behalf? The children were promised their grandfather back. They *deserve* to

have their grandfather back. And instead they've gotten . . .
you.

You shift against the cushions, ashamed at this betrayal, and
wonder why healing seems so much crueler than breaking did.

It's been two weeks.

You are standing in front of the toaster oven, trying to figure out what to do next. Your sandwich is inside. It's supposed
to get hot . . .

Your thumping fist on the countertop draws Grace's attention. You ignore her gentle inquiry and peer in frustration at
the perplexing dials along the machine.

It's all wrong. It doesn't make sense. You still know the ten-
sile strength of a dozen materials, yet this strange metal mechanism eludes you. Worse, it's been eluding you for weeks now,
with no sign of improvement.

"Oh, for Pete's sake," Grace says. She crosses the kitchen
and flips on the machine, aggravating you further. You saw
what she did. You were watching the whole time, but you
must have lost some critical junction in the scaffolding of your
memory, some structural support line to which other information should connect, because the toaster oven still doesn't
make sense. Your feel muddled, like an archival system in
which half the data and most of the indexing information is
gone. Torn away like the strands of a spiderweb, leaving only
dangling edges.

Holes in thought are not like holes in a sidewalk, crisply
defined and easy to repair. How do you know what you can
remember, until you try to remember it? How do you build a
framework for your thoughts, when the pieces that used to
hold everything together are missing?

You stifle frustration. Grace's impatient briskness surely
would not have irritated someone who'd spent his life with

this woman; someone whose accumulated cheerful memories offset the annoyance.

You're not that man, though, and for some perverse reason, knowing that you're being unfair only makes you angrier. You shove the toaster oven across the counter and stalk away upstairs.

It all falls apart on the morning of Mandy's birthday.

Grace finds you at the dresser, tossing clothes across the room. You've already scooted the bed from its usual place and disheveled the curtains by searching behind them.

"I can't find my notebook," you growl when she asks what you are doing.

You've promised to join the family for lunch at Rock Canyon Park. It's the first time since the rest home that you'll see all of them together. You can't do it without the notebook. You'll mix up all the names.

"Oh, for Pete's sake," Grace says, cleaning up the mess. "Just be yourself, Elliott. You don't need to pretend for us."

"*I'm* not the one who's pretending!" you shout.

You must look frightening. Wild-eyed. Disheveled. Grace backs up a few paces.

"Don't you see?" you say, panting, shoving the easy chair aside. "I'm not the man you lost! I'll never be him again." You collapse onto the bench opposite, knuckles gripping like a sailor on a lifeline. "I can't do this anymore."

"Elliott . . ."

You don't know what to make of this new, strange, broken life, but you know one thing: You don't want it to become a sham. So you look into your wife's eyes and tell her what you've been afraid to say out loud all along.

"I don't love you, Grace. I want to, but it's gone. Everything I felt for you. It's all gone."

You thought she would crumple, but she's made of sterner stuff than you expected. She stands still for a long time, looking at you. The bedroom floats in chaos around her. It looks like it's been hit by a meteor shower.

"We've been doing this all wrong," she says finally, and leaves the room.

You stare after her, perplexed. Hurting. Yes, it finally hurts—a dull, throbbing ache in your chest. The air seems suddenly darker.

Sheepishly, you drag your old bones into motion and begin to put the place back together. Grace's voice echoes up from downstairs, talking on the phone, perhaps. You're too far away to make out the words.

Fifteen minutes later she's back, rummaging in her closet and vanishing into the bathroom for an unbearably long time. You wonder if you should start packing a suitcase to take back to the rest home. Just as you decide you probably should, the bathroom door opens, and yet another stranger stands in the rectangle of light.

It takes you a while to realize that it's Grace. You're so used to seeing her in nightgowns or fraying sweaters worn over baggy jeans. The chic, brightly colored shirt she's now wearing sits well beneath the jacket, dignified and feminine. She's done something with her hair, and the glittering confidence in her eyes reminds you—suddenly, painfully—of the woman in the photograph next to your bed.

"Hi," she says, and reaches out a hand. "I don't believe we've been properly introduced. I'm Grace. It's very nice to meet you."

You gape, dumbstruck. You want to say it's nice to meet her, too, but fear it might be a lie. Grace's arm is still outstretched, though, so you accept the handshake. "Elliott," you manage. And then, after a hesitation. "Would you like to join me for breakfast?"

Grace smiles. You walk together to a nearby café, where you discover that you both like breakfast burritos, even though neither of you have tried them before. Grace is energetic, vibrant—like a teenager on a first date, very much hoping to make a good impression. You find yourself responding in kind, dredging up the few coherent memories you possess. Many of them involve floor plans for buildings in nearby cities, but that doesn't seem to matter.

Your side of the conversation is halting, hesitant, but that doesn't seem to matter, either. Grace produces a startling array of childhood confessions, many of them embarrassing, none of which she expects you to already know about. You tell her that you were once a civil engineer and discover, through a sequence of intent and interested questions, that you would like to consult on construction ventures, if anyone will still have you

It's a game, pretending to be two people who've only just met, but in many ways, the game is more honest than the truth. Grace smooths over occasional awkward pauses with questions or humorous anecdotes, listening alertly to your replies. You marvel at how beautiful she is when she laughs.

For two hours, there is no talk of "remember this" or "you used to love that." No one expects to you conform to the mirror of the past. There is only Grace, vibrant and energetic and clearly interested in getting to know you better. Or perhaps, interested in helping you get to know *yourself* better. It doesn't really matter which.

You find yourself thinking again of the spiderweb, ravaged by the curious swipe of a little boy's stick, and wonder: If one could just find the two or three most important strands—the ones upon which everything else depends—and somehow weave them anew . . . Would everything else begin to fall into place?

You leave the restaurant and stroll together along the pavement, admiring the wildflowers. Halfway home, Grace checks her wristwatch and says, "My granddaughter's celebrating her birthday up the canyon today. I'd love to introduce you to some of the people there." She looks at you, oddly intent. "Would you like to come?"

You feel your mouth hang open in surprise, and discover that it would not be dishonest to say "yes."

ABOUT THE CONTRIBUTORS

Doug Beason is the author of eleven novels—eight with collaborator Kevin J. Anderson, including *Ignition*—as well as two nonfiction books, including *The E-Bomb: How America's New Directed Energy Weapons Will Change the Way Future Wars Will Be Fought*. A Nebula Award finalist, Doug has published more than a hundred short stories and other work in publications as diverse as *Analog* and *Amazing Stories* to the *Wall Street Journal* and *Physical Review Letters*. Doug has a doctorate in physics, is a fellow of the American Physical Society, and is also the retired associate laboratory director at the Los Alamos National Laboratory. A retired U.S. Air Force colonel, Doug has worked for a former presidential science advisor as the key White House staffer for space, and was recently the chief scientist of the Air Force Space Command.

Doug first learned of the nuclear-driven steam piston concept behind "Thunderwell" during a lunch discussion with the late Dr. Edward Teller in 1998 at the Lawrence Livermore National Laboratory. You may learn more about Doug's work at www.DougBeason.com.

Gregory Benford is a professor of physics at the University of California, Irvine. He is a Woodrow Wilson Fellow, was a

Visiting Fellow at Cambridge University, and in 1995 received the Lord Prize for contributions to science. In 2007, he won the Asimov Award for science writing. His 1999 analysis of what endures, *Deep Time: How Humanity Communicates Across Millennia*, has been widely read. A fellow of the American Physical Society and a member of the World Academy of Arts and Sciences, he continues his research in astrophysics, plasma physics, and biotechnology. His fiction has won many awards, including the Nebula Award for his novel *Timescape*.

Aliette de Bodard was born in New York City and now resides in Paris. She holds a master of science in applied mathematics and computer science and works as a systems engineer. Her fiction has appeared in *Asimov's*, *Clarkesworld*, and *Interzone*. She has won a Nebula Award, a Locus Award, and a British Science Fiction Association Award, and has been a finalist for the Hugo and Theodore Sturgeon Awards. Her latest work is the Vietnamese space opera novella *On a Red Station Drifting*. She blogs at www.AliettedeBodard.com, where she relates her struggles with writing and Vietnamese cooking.

The science in "A Slow Unfurling of Truth" is based on probabilities, and in particular on multidimensional density estimation, which aims to fit a vast series of observations to a complex model. It also touches on problems of robust authentication, which require independent sources to verify someone's identity (in the story, an AI and a human).

Ben Bova is the author of more than 130 novels, story collections, and nonfiction books. President emeritus of the National Space Society and a past president of Science Fiction and Fantasy Writers of America, he received the Lifetime Achievement Award of the Arthur C. Clarke Foundation in 2005 "for fueling mankind's imagination regarding the wonders of outer space."

His 2006 novel *Titan* received the John W. Campbell Memorial Award for best novel of the year. In 2008, he won the Robert A. Heinlein Award "for his outstanding body of work in the field of literature," and in 2012 he received a Space Pioneer Award from the National Space Society. He has also won six Hugo Awards.

"Old Timer's Game" is an examination of how breakthroughs in biomedical research will inevitably affect the performance of athletes in professional sports, and how professional sports will be forced to change as a result. As an eighty-some-year-old tennis player, he can hardly wait for the improvements!

Eric Choi was born in Hong Kong and currently lives in Toronto, Canada. His work has appeared in *Analog Science Fiction and Fact, Far Orbit, Rocket Science, The Astronaut from Wyoming and Other Stories, Footprints, Northwest Passages, Space Inc., Tales from the Wonder Zone, Northern Suns, Tesseracts6, Arrowdreams, Science Fiction Age,* and *Asimov's Science Fiction.* With Derwin Mak, he coedited the Aurora Award–winning anthology *The Dragon and the Stars,* the first collection of science fiction and fantasy written by authors of the Chinese diaspora. An aerospace engineer by training, Eric has a bachelor's degree in engineering science and a master's degree in aerospace engineering, both from the University of Toronto, and an MBA from York University. His Web site is at www.AerospaceWriter.ca and he can be followed on Twitter (@AerospaceWriter).

"She Just Looks that Way" was inspired by the research of Kevin Kniffin and David Sloan Wilson at Binghamton University that examined the influence of nonphysical traits on perceptions of beauty. The story combines the author's love of science, ultimate Frisbee, and Washington, DC.

David DeGraff teaches physics and astronomy at Alfred University in Alfred, New York. In addition to the usual classes in physics and astronomy, he has also taught classes on superheroes, *Star Trek*, Harry Potter, *Doctor Who*, science in science fiction, life in the universe, and the physics of snowboarding. His grandfather, with help from Captain Kirk and Neil Armstrong, taught him to love science and science fiction at an early age. After majoring in physics at St. Lawrence University, he received his PhD in astrophysics at the University of North Carolina at Chapel Hill. His previously published fiction includes a short story in *Polaris: Tales from the Wonder Zone*, edited by Julie E. Czerneda. He has discovered three asteroids, of which two are named for colleagues (31113 Stull and 96344 Scott weaver) and one for his grandfather (152641 Fredreed).

Titan is a fascinating place, with a landscape of mountains, streams, rivers, and lakes. The liquid flowing there is a mixture of methane and ethane, while the water is a mineral locked into solid rock. Robotic exploration of alien worlds is frustratingly slow at the moment. It would be much more efficient if probes were more like "SIREN of Titan" and could make their own decisions.

Carl Frederick is theoretically a theoretical physicist. After a postdoc at NASA and a stint at Cornell University, he left astrophysics and his first love, stochastic space-time quantum relativity theory (a strange first love, perhaps), in favor of the hi-tech industry. He attended the 2000 Odyssey Writers Workshop and subsequently took a quarterly first place in the Writers of the Future contest. Although he has written novels, he considers himself predominately a short story writer. He has sold a couple of stories each to *Asimov's* and *Baen's Universe* and more elsewhere, and over forty to *Analog*. His Web site is at www.frithrik.com.

Relativity physicist that he is, the author has long felt ashamed of needing to invoke faster-than-light travel in his stories. So before writing "Ambiguous Nature," he tried to come up with an FTL mechanism that would (arguably) not violate relativity theory. This story marks its first appearance, an idea he now calls the "stochastic trajectory drive." He has since returned to his aforementioned first love.

Nancy Fulda is a Hugo and Nebula nominee, a Phobos Award winner, and a Vera Hinckley Mayhew Award recipient. She is the first (and so far only) female recipient of the Jim Baen Memorial Award. Nancy was born in Livermore, California, and resides with her husband and children in northern Germany. She holds a master's degree in computer science and her graduate work in artificial intelligence has been presented at several IEEE conferences.

"Recollection" was inspired by current research into the role of tau malformations and beta-amyloid plaques in Alzheimer's disease. If a cure for Alzheimer's is discovered, then recuperating dementia patients may face challenges like those portrayed in the story.

Gabrielle Harbowy is an editor for such SF publishers as Pyr, Circlet, and Dragon Moon Press, as well as coeditor of the award-nominated *When the Hero Comes Home* anthology series with Ed Greenwood. She has a degree in clinical psychology from Rutgers University and is a trained classical musician. Her short fiction has been a finalist for the Parsec Award and has appeared in such anthologies as *Beast Within: 2*, *Metastasis*, *Cthulhurotica*, and others. Gabrielle's most recent publication is "Inheritance," a shared-world story for Pathfinder Tales that is free to read at www.paizo.com. She can be found in real life in the San Francisco Bay Area and on the Internet at www.gabrielle-edits.com or on Twitter as @gabrielle_h.

"Skin Deep" was inspired by a number of recent scientific advancements, including an autonomous diagnostic and treatment "biocapsule" developed by Dr. David Loftus at the NASA Ames Research Center and a disease detecting skin patch invented by Dr. Michael McAlpine of Princeton University. Leah and Gabrielle's story takes these new medical technologies and examines what happens when lifesaving advances meet the darker side of human nature.

Howard Hendrix was born in Cincinnati, Ohio, and earned his BS in biology from Xavier University there. He earned his MA and PhD degrees from University of California, Riverside. Howard currently teaches English literature and writing at California State University, Fresno. He is the author of six novels and, after a long hiatus, has just finished his seventh. In 1985, he won a Writers of the Future Award and in 2010 won a Dwarf Stars Award from the Science Fiction Poetry Association. He is also a literary critic of science fiction, and was lead editor on *Visions of Mars*. With his wife, Laurel, he is currently editing *The Encyclopedia of Mars*.

Of the science in "Habilis," Howard says, "I've long been fascinated by chirality, by the 'handedness' that prevails on scales ranging from the subatomic to the cosmic. That the human brain is also chiral, in many ways, just made this story all the more enjoyable to write." His Web site is at www.How ardVHendrix.com and he can also sometimes be found on Facebook.

Liu Cixin was born in Beijing, China, and now resides in the city of Yangquan in Shanxi province, where he works as a senior engineer in the specialized field of power plant computing. Cixin's first science fiction story was published in 1999. Since then, he has published seven novels and nine collections of short fiction as well as a number of critical essays. Between 1999 and 2006 his works won the Galaxy Award—China's highest literary prize for speculative fiction—an unprecedented eight consecutive times. In 2012 he won the People's Literature Short Story Award, and in 2013 he won the Chinese Writers Association's Outstanding Children's Literature Award. He maintains a blog (in Chinese) at blog.sina.com.cn/lcx.

In "The Circle," which is based on a concept from his novel *The Three-Body Problem*, Cixin imagines a computing "machine" based on modern computer design principles but constructed from individual humans acting as logic gates. An English version of *The Three-Body Problem* translated by Hugo and Nebula winner Ken Liu was published by Tor in 2014.

Jack McDevitt has been described by Stephen King as "the logical heir to Isaac Asimov and Arthur C. Clarke." A Philadelphia native, Jack holds a master's degree in literature and admits to being completely baffled by the quantum world. He is the author of twenty novels, eleven of which have been Nebula finalists. In all, he has been nominated seventeen times for the Nebula, which *Seeker* won in 2007. In 2003, *Omega* received the John W. Campbell Memorial Award for best SF novel. He has received numerous other awards, and was most recently chosen by the Georgia Writers Association as Writer of the Year, given for lifetime achievement. A new novel, *Starhawk*, has just been released. His Web site is at www.JackMcDevitt.com.

Jack enjoys toying with issues that might arrive if our hardware starts becoming intelligent. That is at the heart of "The Play's the Thing."

Leah Petersen lives in North Carolina, manipulating numbers by day and the universe by night. She prides herself on being able to hold a book with her feet so she can knit while reading (she's still working on knitting while writing). Her debut science fiction trilogy, the Physics of Falling series (*Fighting Gravity,*

Cascade Effect, Impact Velocity) is available from Dragon Moon Press. You can find Leah online at www.LeahPetersen.com, on Twitter (@LeahPetersen), and at Facebook.com/LeahPetersen Author.

Robert Reed was born in Omaha, Nebraska, but his adult life has been largely spent down the road in Lincoln. The author of a sagan of short stories as well as a couple fistfuls of novels, Reed's works have been nominated for Hugo and Nebula Awards, and his novella "A Billion Eves" won the Hugo in 2007. Mostly self-taught in science, the man nonetheless has a BS in biology from Nebraska Wesleyan University plus some graduate classes at the University of Nebraska at Lincoln, focusing on fossils and evolution. For fun, he reads science books and articles and runs long distances and boasts about his lost youth. A very nice Web site about the author can be found at www.robertreedwriter.com. Perhaps best known for his Great Ship series, his newest book is set in that universe. *The Memory of Sky* from Prime Books, released in March 2014, is a trilogy published in one back-crippling volume.

Bob is not eager to comment on the science in "Every Hill Ends with Sky," mostly because what he feels to be the hard science is the miserable landscape and humanity eating itself whole. The aliens are more fanciful, by a long ways.

Kate Story is a writer and performer with a degree in cultural studies. Born and raised in Newfoundland, she presently lives in Peterborough, Ontario. Her first novel, *Blasted* (Killick Press, 2008), received honorable mention from the Sunburst Award for Canadian Literature of the Fantastic and was long listed for the ReLit Awards. *Wrecked Upon This Shore* is her second novel, and she is currently working on a young-adult fantasy novel called *Antilia*.

"The Yoke of Inauspicious Stars" was inspired by Kate's early training in ballet and contemporary dance. She is interested in technologies that could function as a hardware/wetware collaboration. Environmental and political concerns also form one of the foundations for the story, as does a love of literature. Please visit her Web site at www.katestory.com.

Dirk Strasser was born in Offenbach, Germany, but has lived most of his life in Melbourne, Australia. He has written more than thirty books for major publishers in Australia and has been editing SF anthologies and magazines, including *Aurealis— Australian Fantasy & Science Fiction* for over twenty years. Dirk has won multiple Australian Publisher Association Awards and a Ditmar for Best Professional Achievement, and his The Books of Ascension trilogy—*Zenith, Equinox,* and *Eclipse*—was recently published by Macmillan Momentum. His story "The Doppelgänger Effect" appeared in the World Fantasy Award– winning anthology *Dreaming Down Under.*

At university, Dirk studied pure mathematics, statistics, German literature, and history. "The Mandelbrot Bet" is his attempt to write the ultimate hard SF time-travel love story, where non-Gaussian randomness, probability theory, and cosmology combine to save the universe. His Web site is at www .dirkstrasser.com.

Born in Toronto, **Jean-Louis Trudel** now lives in Québec City, Canada. He holds degrees in physics, astronomy, and the history of science, capping his education with a doctorate in history. Jean-Louis now teaches history part-time at the University of Ottawa. He is the author of twenty-eight books in French, including novels, collections, and YA fiction, one anthology in English (*Tesseracts*[7]), and more than one hundred short stories in French and English. His publications have won him several Aurora and Boréal Awards. He also writes with Yves Meynard under the name Laurent McAllister, accounting for five more books and a handful of short stories. Their 2009 novel *Suprématie* won plaudits, nominations, and Canada's top science fiction awards.

On "The Snows of Yesteryear," Jean-Louis says, "What lies under Greenland's ice sheet is a truly alien land, untouched for thousands and even millions of years, hiding the last remnants of a distant past and of an equally remote environment predating modern humans. Climate change is now acting as a gigantic time machine by reverting Greenland to its earlier state." His blog is at culturedesfuturs.blogspot.com and you can find him on Facebook.

Daniel H. Wilson is the *New York Times* bestselling author of *Robopocalypse* as well as eight other books, including *Amped, How to Survive a Robot Uprising,* and *Robogenesis.* He earned a PhD in robotics from Carnegie Mellon University as well as master's degrees in robotics and artificial intelligence.

"The Blue Afternoon that Lasted Forever" draws on the expertise of childhood friend and physicist Dr. Mark Baumann at the University of Texas at Austin. The rest of the story happened naturally, as a result of Daniel having both a scientific mind and a three-year-old daughter. Daniel grew up in Tulsa, Oklahoma, and now lives in Portland, Oregon. You can learn more about him at www.danielhwilson.com or talk to him on Twitter @danielwilsonPDX.